NATIONALISM &

RABINDRANATH TAGORE ... was one of the key figures of the Bengal Renaissance. He started writing at an early age, and by the turn of the century had become a household name in Bengal as a poet, a songwriter, a playwright, an essayist, a short story writer and a novelist. In 1913 he was awarded the Nobel Prize for Literature for his verse collection *Gitanjali*. Around the same time, he founded Visva-Bharati, a university located in Santiniketan near Kolkata. Called the 'Great Sentinel' of modern India by Mahatma Gandhi, Tagore steered clear of active politics, but is famous for returning the knighthood conferred on him as a gesture of protest against the Jallianwala Bagh massacre in 1919.

Tagore was a pioneering literary figure, renowned for his ceaseless innovations in poetry, prose, drama, music and painting, which he took up late in life. His works include some sixty collections of verse, novels like *Gora*, *Chokher Bali* and *Ghare Baire*, plays like *Raktakarabi* and *Dakghar*, dance dramas like *Shyama*, *Chandalika* and *Chitrangada*, over a hundred short stories, essays on religious, social and literary topics, and over 2500 songs, including the national anthems of India and Bangladesh.

SUGATA BOSE is the Gardiner Professor of history at Harvard University. He was educated at Presidency College, Kolkata, and the University of Cambridge where he obtained his PhD and was later a fellow of St Catharine's College. Before taking up the Gardiner Chair at Harvard in 2001, he was professor of history and diplomacy at Tufts University. Bose was a recipient of the Guggenheim Fellowship in 1997 and gave the G.M. Trevelyan Lecture at the University of Cambridge.

Bose's many books include *The Nation as Mother and Other Visions of Nationhood*, the much-acclaimed *A Hundred Horizons: The Indian Ocean in the Age of Global Empire* and *His Majesty's Opponent: Subhas Chandra Bose and India's Struggle against Empire*. He has also made documentary films on South Asian history and politics and published recordings of his translations of Tagore.

SREEJATA GUHA has an MA in comparative literature from State University of New York at Stony Brook. She has previously translated *Picture Imperfect*, a collection of Saradindu Bandyopadhyay's Byomkesh Bakshi stories, Taslima Nasrin's novel *French Lover*, Saratchandra Chattopadhyay's *Devdas*, Bankim Chandra Chattopadhyay's *Rajani* and Tagore's *A Grain of Sand: Chokher Bali* and *The Prince and Other Modern Fables* for Penguin.

STUDENTS' EDITION

RABINDRANATH
TAGORE

NATIONALISM
&
HOME AND
THE WORLD

Introduction by
SUGATA BOSE

Ghare Baire translated from the Bengali by Sreejata Guha

PENGUIN BOOKS
An imprint of Penguin Random House

PENGUIN BOOKS

USA | Canada | UK | Ireland | Australia
New Zealand | India | South Africa | China

Penguin Books is part of the Penguin Random House group of companies
whose addresses can be found at global.penguinrandomhouse.com

Published by Penguin Random House India Pvt. Ltd
4th Floor, Capital Tower 1, MG Road,
Gurugram 122 002, Haryana, India

Penguin
Random House
India

This translation of *Ghare Baire* first published by Penguin Books India 2005
Nationalism published by Penguin Books India 2009
This compendium first published in Penguin Books by Penguin Random
House India 2021

ISBN 9780143450368

Typeset in Minion Pro by Manipal Technologies Limited, Manipal
Printed at Replika Press Pvt. Ltd, India

www.penguin.co.in

Contents

Introduction

Sugata Bose

'Even though from childhood I had been taught that idolatry of the Nation is almost better than reverence for God and humanity,' Rabindranath Tagore writes in 'Nationalism in India', 'I believe I have outgrown that teaching, and it is my conviction that my countrymen will truly gain their India by fighting against the education which teaches them that a country is greater than the ideals of humanity.'(p. 66 of this volume) It is this ethical stance that provides the connecting thread between Tagore's lectures on nationalism and his novel *Home and the World*. Entranced by Sandip's wizardry with words, Bimala's cardinal error of placing adoration of the nation above solicitude for humanity could only end in tragedy. This students' edition bringing together fiction with non-fiction should serve as an invitation to continue the fight against a false education that Tagore began more than a hundred years ago.

The Bengali novel *Ghare Baire* was serialized in the journal *Sabuj Patra* from April 1915 until February 1916. In the spring of 1916, Tagore edited out what he thought were superfluous passages before sending it for publication as a book. By the time the novel appeared in book form, Tagore had already embarked on his voyage to Japan. During his summer sojourn in Japan Tagore drafted his lectures on nationalism that he would deliver in the United States of America. The novel had none of the hallmarks of instruction with which the essays were infused. A female reader had inquired of Tagore his *uddeshya*, or intent, behind writing *Ghare Baire*. Tagore had responded with an analogy. A deer's spots were designed as camouflage in its forest habitat, but the deer was unaware of that intent. Much the same could be said about an author. The temporal environment casts its influence on the author in ways conscious as well as unconscious and perhaps expresses its own intent through the medium of the writer.[1] The subtlety of the novel should not be violated by efforts to draw lessons from it.

Tagore was quite sensitive about the complexity of the key characters he had created in *Home and the World* and resisted their easy categorization in terms of traditional or modern. The easier accessibility of Satyajit Ray's film version of the novel makes it even more imperative for students to read it in the original or in translation. The privileging of the visual over the textual has led to superficial commentaries on the novel's take on the nation.[2] Ray's Sandip is so one-dimensional in his villainy that it is hard for the viewer to figure out why Bimala should feel in the least bit attracted to him. The unnecessary diminution of one of the two principal male characters results in doing some injustice to the female protagonist in the triangle. Even though Nikhilesh embodied some of Tagore's own deeply held values and sensibilities, Tagore had drawn the character of Sandip with a deft touch. Sandip's manipulative guile did not mean he was entirely devoid of the charisma that buttressed the seductive power of nationalism.

Bimala witnessed 'the compelling aura of the man!'. The words of his speech 'seemed to carry the gust of a storm' and 'his boldness knew no limits'. His eyes, 'bright as Orion in the sky', settled on her face. (pp. 105–06) Sandip was as intensely argumentative as Tagore's other immortal character Gora. 'He must have known,' Bimala mused, 'that in an argument his razor-sharp mind shone in all its brilliance . . . I noticed that in my presence he never let slip the slightest opportunity for a debate.' (p. 111) She also described how by getting her to give him Nikhilesh's money Sandip 'lost his powers' over her: 'You can't shoot arrows at something that is already within your fist. So, today Sandip lacked his brave warrior charm. His words held the despicable, harsh echoes of squabbling.' (p. 259)

Nikhilesh took his moral stand against coercion in political mobilization in favour of Swadeshi. Forced boycott of foreign goods was an expensive indulgence for the poor. More important, Nikhilesh was resolute in his respect for difference, especially religious diversity. He was 'loath to offer any assistance in building up this tavern of illusion over my motherland'. This enlightened zamindar tried to reason with his co-religionists: 'We are free to practice our own religion but others' religion is out of bounds. Just because I am a Vaishnav doesn't mean the Kali worshipper should give up bloodshed. There is no choice. The Muslims should be allowed to practice their religion in their way. Don't create a problem over this.' (p. 266) As he reflected on his relationship with Bimala, he also came to the conclusion that it was better to avoid a benign form of coercion. He would not wish to bind his fellow traveller 'in the chains of idealism'. (p. 305)

Nikhilesh would say to Bimala: 'Those who sacrificed for the country, are the great souls. But those who troubled others in the name of the nation, are the enemies. They want to hack

away at the roots of freedom and nourish its trunk and leaves.'
(p. 191) Ashis Nandy is correct in noting that 'Bimala,
symbolizing Bengal' confronts 'the choice between two forms
of patriotism', represented by Nikhilesh and Sandip. Georg
Lukacs in a 1922 review had committed the grotesque blunder
of believing Tagore had modelled Sandip on a caricature of
Gandhi. Not only did Lukacs get the chronology of the writing
of the novel and the emergence of Gandhi in Indian politics
hopelessly wrong, he also failed to notice Tagore's old-world
patriotism that was distinct from modern nationalism. *Ghare
Baire*'s 'critique of nationalism' was balanced, as Nandy points
out, by 'a perspective on the form anti-imperialism should take
in a multi-ethnic, multi-religious society'.[3]

In Tagore's novel, the home and the world were never
hermetically sealed separate domains as some latter-day theorists
of nationalism like Partha Chatterjee have made them out to be.[4]
The drawing room in Nikhilesh's home was 'an ambiguous space,
neither indoors nor outdoors'. (p. 134) Also, Tagore was not
then and never became, as claimed by Nandy, 'almost a counter-
modernist critic of the imperial West'.[5] His profound scepticism
about one of the signs of modernity—nationalism—did not
lead him towards an all-encompassing rejection of modernity.
The ambiguity at the end of *Home and the World* might be
interpreted as Tagore's faith in modernity and a glimmer of hope
for a generous conception of patriotism under assault by the
hubris of narrow and arrogant nationalism. Unlike Ray's film, in
which Nikhilesh dies, leaving Bimala in widow's garb, his fate is
uncertain in Tagore's telling: 'The doctor said, "Can't say for sure.
Serious head injury."' (p. 311)

The wound inflicted on a capacious conception of
patriotism by overzealous Swadeshi agitators permeated the
plot of *Home and the World*. The carnage of the First World

War unleashed by clashing European nationalisms provided the context for Tagore's critical lectures delivered in Japan and the United States. 'The Nation,' Tagore wrote in his resounding rebuke in 'Nationalism in the West', 'has thriven long upon mutilated humanity. Men, the fairest creations of God, came out of the National manufactory in huge numbers as war-making and money-making puppets, ludicrously vain of their pitiful perfection of mechanism.' (p. 58)

With war raging in Europe and the Middle East, Tagore had set off on a global oceanic voyage from Calcutta on 3 May 1916, on an easterly route for the first time in his life.[6] In the midst of a terrific storm in the South China Sea on 21 May 1916, Tagore composed his only song on a journey that was going to see him concentrate on his prose writings in Bengali and English. In 'Bhuban Jora Ashankhani' he asked the Almighty to spread his seat of universality in the individual's heart:

> Your universe-encompassing prayer mat
> Spread it out in the core of my heart.
> The night's stars, the day's sun, all the shades of darkness
>   and light,
> All your messages that fill the sky –
> Let them find their abode in my heart.
> May the lute of the universe
> Fill the depths of my soul with all its tunes.
> All the intensity of grief and joy, the flower's touch, the
>   storm's touch –
> Let your compassionate, auspicious, generous hands
> Bring into the core of my heart.[7]

Tagore was warmly received when he arrived in Kobe by the *Tosa Maru* on 29 May 1916. He had long been an admirer of

Japan. He had met scholar and art critic Okakura Tenshin in both Calcutta and Boston and shared his ideal of an Asian renaissance. He was familiar with the artistic excellence of Yokoyama Taikan, who had taught the Japanese wash technique to his nephew Abanindranath. During his 1916 visit he was very impressed by the perfection that Japan had reached in the field of the visual arts. What he saw of Japan's expedition on the path of nationalistic imperialism worried and repulsed him. 'What is dangerous for Japan,' Tagore declared, 'is not the imitation of the outer features of the West, but the acceptance of the motive force of western nationalism as her own.' (p. 21)

After he had delivered his rebukes on nationalism, few showed up to see him off as he began the long Pacific crossing on the *Canada Maru* on 7 September 1916. Once he reached Seattle, Tagore travelled down the US west coast and then from the west to the east coast across middle America on a hectic speaking tour. It was a Presidential election season. Woodrow Wilson was campaigning for re-election on the slogan that he had kept America out of the war. He won by a narrow margin. Tagore's stern warnings against nationalism had a mixed but on the whole positive reception in a country that had not yet entered the First World War. 'The Nation, with all its paraphernalia of power and prosperity, its flags and pious hymns, its blasphemous prayers in the churches, and the literary mock thunders of its patriotic bragging,' Tagore argued passionately, 'cannot hide the fact that the Nation is the greatest evil for the Nation, that all its precautions are against it, and any new birth of its fellow in the world is always followed in its mind by the dread of a new peril.' (p. 49)

Tagore had composed his own beautiful hymns to the motherland during the Swadeshi movement of 1905. His strictures on nationalism must not be read as a rejection of the love for one's country. 'Neither the colourless vagueness of cosmopolitanism, nor the fierce self-idolatry of nation-worship,' he explained, 'is the goal of human history.' (p. 33) He saw no contradiction between a colourful cosmopolitanism rooted in local languages, literatures and cultures and a broad-minded patriotism respectful of difference.[8] He scolded the United States for its deep-seated prejudice against Asians and African Americans. 'Either you shut your doors against the aliens,' he said, 'or reduce them into slavery.' (p. 73)

In 'Nationalism in India', Tagore had no qualms about describing nationalism as 'a great menace'. (p. 69) Yet he did not abandon an anti-colonial stance. He seemed to have imbibed the basic tenets of economic nationalism as propounded by Dadabhai Naoroji and Romesh Chunder Dutt. 'It must be remembered,' he wrote, 'that at the beginning of the British rule in India our industries were suppressed, and since then we have not met with any real help or encouragement to enable us to make a stand against the monster commercial organizations of the world. The nations have decreed that we must remain purely an agricultural people, even forgetting the use of arms for all time to come.' (p. 78) At the same time, Tagore was unsparing in his denunciation of the narrow-mindedness of his compatriots. 'The social habit of mind,' he contended, 'which impels us to make the life of your fellow-beings a burden to them where they differ from us even in such a thing as their choice of food is sure to persist in our political organization and result in creating engines of coercion to crush every rational difference which is the sign of life.' 'And,' he warned with remarkable foresight, 'tyranny will only add to the inevitable lies and hypocrisy in our political life.' (p. 77)

E.P. Thompson rightly regarded Tagore's book *Nationalism* as 'prescient', even 'prophetic'.[9] While recognizing the book's profound insights and lofty ethical commitments, students need not read it uncritically. When Tagore had read out a draft of his lecture 'The Cult of Nationalism' to C.F. Andrews in Japan, Andrews had suggested that Tagore was confusing the distinct concepts of nation and state.[10] Tagore did not accept that criticism. Yet it is worth considering whether Andrews to whom Tagore dedicated his book *Nationalism* (and also *Personality*) had a point. The First World War, which Tagore saw as 'the war of retribution' (p. 57), was in origin a conflict between European nation states. On reading reports of Tagore's lectures in the *Modern Review*, Deshbandhu Chittaranjan Das had felt the 'whole of this anti-nation idea' to be 'insubstantial – based upon a vague and nebulous conception of universal humanity'. For Das, the First World War was 'the consequence of nationalism pushed to its excess'; but Indian nationalism could be very different from European nationalisms. 'Distinctiveness', in his view, could 'never be abolished' even while accepting 'the deeper harmony which underlies all outer differences between different nationalities'.[11] Tagore's extolling of the 'no-nation' status of Indian society in 'Nationalism in India' also constrained his critique of caste. His comment that 'in her caste regulations India recognized differences, but not the mutability which is the law of life' (p. 72) would appear today as a rather muted comment on a pernicious social system.

This book presents to students Tagore the essayist and Tagore the novelist. But, of course, this multifaceted genius was at his core a poet. The phase of his creativity which produced *Home and the World* and *Nationalism* also witnessed the publication of the scintillating poems of *Balaka* (1916).[12] In searching for a poetic conclusion to *Nationalism*, Tagore reached back to a few poems of *Noibedya* composed towards the very end of the nineteenth century and presented them in an English rendering as 'Sunset of the Century'. Tagore appended a note to the English poem that said 'Written in the Bengali on the last day of the last century'. Poem number 64 of *Noibedya* on which he drew most heavily was most likely composed in Shelidah on 31 December 1900, and first published in *Bangadarshan* on 15 May 1901. However, the English version took elements from poems 65, 66, 67 and 68 of *Noibedya* as well.[13] The lines inspired by the spirit of *Noibedya* provided a ringing finale in verse to the cautionary lesson on nationalism that he had sought to convey in prose:

> The last sun of the century sets amidst the blood-red
>   clouds of the West and the whirlwind of hatred.
> The naked passion of self-love of Nations, in its drunken
>   delirium of greed, is dancing to the clash of steel
>   and the howling verses of vengeance. . . .
>
> Keep watch, India. . . .
>
> Let your crown be of humility, your freedom the
>   freedom of the soul.
> Build God's throne daily upon the ample bareness of
>   your poverty
> And know that what is huge is not great and pride is not
>   everlasting.[14]

Notes

1.   Prabhat Kumar Mukhopadhyay, *Rabindrajiboni o Rabindrasahitya-prabeshak* Volume 2 (Calcutta: Visva-Bharati, fourth edition 1976), p. 546.

2.   The limitations of relying on the film rather than the novel are
      evident in Nicholas Dirks, 'Home and the World: The Invention
      of Modernity in Colonial India', *Visual Anthropology Review*, 9, 2
      (Fall 1993).

3.   Ashis Nandy, *The Illegitimacy of Nationalism* (Delhi: Oxford
      University Press, 1994), pp. 12, 19. Georg Lukacs's review 'Tagore's
      Gandhi Novel' first appeared in *Die Rote Fahne* (Berlin, 1922) and
      reprinted in Georg Lukacs, *Essays and Reviews* (London: Merlin
      Press, 1983).

4.   Partha Chatterjee, *The Nation and Its Fragments* (Princeton:
      Princeton University Press, 1994).

5.   Nandy, *Illegitimacy of Nationalism*, p. 4.

6.   On more on this voyage, see Sugata Bose, *A Hundred Horizons:
      the Indian Ocean in the Age of Global Empire* (Cambridge, MA:
      Harvard University Press, 2006), pp. 108–09 and Sugata Bose,
      The Nation as Mother and Other Visions of Nationhood (Gurgaon:
      Penguin Viking, 2017), pp. 116–17.

7.   Rabindranath Tagore, *Tagore: The World Voyager*, translated by
      Sugata Bose (Noida: Random House India, 2013), pp. 15–16.

8.   Sugata Bose, 'Different Universalisms, Colorful Cosmopolitanisms:
      the Global Imagination of the Colonized' in *The Nation as Mother*,
      pp. 107–26.

9.   E.P. Thompson, 'Introduction' to Rabindranath Tagore,
      Nationalism (Calcutta: Rupa, 1992).

10.   Mukhopadhyay, *Rabindrajiboni*, Volume 2, p. 569.

11.   Deshbandhu Chittaranjan Das, 'Bengal and the Bengalees' in
      *Brief Survey of Life and Work, Provincial Conference Speeches,
      Congress Speeches* (Calcutta: Rajen Sen and B.K. Sen, n.d.),
      pp. 19–24, 31–32.

12.   Krishna Bose and Sugata Bose, 'The East in Its Feminine Gender:
      A Historical and Literary Introduction' in Rabindranath Tagore,
      Purabi: The East in Its Feminine Gender (translated by Charu C.

Chowdhuri, edited and introduced by Krishna Bose and Sugata
Bose, Calcutta: Seagull, 2007), pp. 10–12.

13. See '*Anubadaker Nibedan*' in Sugata Bose, *Bharatmata* (Bengali
translation of Sugata Bose, *The Nation as Mother*, by Ashis Lahiri,
Kolkata: Ananda, 2017), pp. 185–90. Beautiful recordings of
Tagore's *Noibedya* poems can be heard in Krishna Bose, *Bharat
Bhabna* (Kolkata: Bhavna Records and Cassettes, 2019).

14. Rabindranath Tagore, 'The Sunset of the Century' in *Nationalism*
(Westport, Connecticut: Greenwood Press, 1973, originally
published New York: Macmillan, 1917), pp. 157–59.

Nationalism

Nationalism in Japan

I

The worst form of bondage is the bondage of dejection, which keeps men hopelessly chained in loss of faith in themselves. We have been repeatedly told, with some justification, that Asia lives in the past—it is like a rich mausoleum which displays all its magnificence in trying to immortalise the dead. It was said of Asia that it could never move in the path of progress, its face was so inevitably turned backwards. We accepted this accusation, and came to believe it. In India, I know, a large section of our educated community, grown tired of feeling the humiliation of this charge against us, is trying with all its resources of self-deception to turn it into a matter of boasting. But boasting is only a masked shame, it does not truly believe in itself.

When things stood still like this, and we in Asia hypnotised ourselves into the belief that it could never by any possibility be otherwise, Japan rose from her dreams, and in giant strides left centuries of inaction behind, overtaking the present time in its foremost achievement. This has broken the spell under which we lay in torpor for ages, taking it to be the normal condition of certain races living in certain geographical limits. We forgot that in Asia great kingdoms were founded, philosophy, science, arts and literatures flourished, and all the great religions of the world had their cradles. Therefore it cannot be said that there is anything inherent in the soil and climate of Asia to produce mental inactivity and to atrophy the faculties which impel men to go forward. For centuries we did hold torches of civilisation in the East when the West slumbered in darkness, and that could never be the sign of sluggish minds or narrowness of vision.

Then fell the darkness of night upon all the lands of the East. The current of time seemed to stop at once, and Asia ceased to take any new food, feeding upon its own past, which is really feeding upon itself. The stillness seemed like death, and the great voice was silenced which sent forth messages of eternal truth that have saved man's life from pollution for generations, like the ocean of air that keeps the earth sweet, ever cleansing its impurities.

But life has its sleep, its periods of inactivity, when it loses its movements, takes no new food, living upon its past storage. Then it grows helpless, its muscles relaxed, and it easily lends itself to be jeered at for its stupor. In the rhythm of life, pauses there must be for the renewal of life. Life in its activity is ever spending itself, burning all its fuel. This extravagance cannot go on indefinitely, but is always followed by a passive stage, when all expenditure is stopped and all adventures abandoned in favour of rest and slow recuperation.

The tendency of the mind is economical: it loves to form habits and move in grooves which save it the trouble of thinking anew at each of its steps. Ideals once formed make the mind lazy. It becomes afraid to risk its acquisitions in fresh endeavours. It tries to enjoy complete security by shutting up its belongings behind fortifications of habits. But this is really shutting oneself up from the fullest enjoyment of one's own possessions. It is miserliness. The living ideals must not lose their touch with the growing and changing life. Their real freedom is not within the boundaries of security, but on the high-road of adventures, full of the risk of new experiences.

One morning the whole world looked up in surprise when Japan broke through her walls of old habits in a night and came out triumphant. It was done in such an incredibly short time that it seemed like a change of dress and not like the building up of a new structure. She showed the confident strength of maturity, and the freshness and infinite potentiality of new life at the same moment. The fear was entertained that it was a mere freak of history, a child's game of Time, the blowing up of a soap-bubble, perfect in its rondure and colouring, hollow in its heart and without substance. But Japan has proved conclusively that this sudden revealment of her power is not a short-lived wonder, a chance product of time and tide, thrown up from the depth of obscurity to be swept away the next moment into a sea of oblivion.

The truth is that Japan is old and new at the same time. She has her legacy of ancient culture from the East—the culture that enjoins man to look for his true wealth and power in his inner soul, the culture that gives self-possession in the face of loss and danger, self-sacrifice without counting the cost or hoping for gain, defiance of death, acceptance of countless social obligations that we owe to men as social beings. In a word, modern Japan has come out of the immemorial East like a lotus blossoming in easy grace, all the while keeping its firm hold upon the profound depth from which it has sprung.

And Japan, the child of the Ancient East, has also fearlessly claimed all the gifts of the modern age for herself. She has shown her bold spirit in breaking through the confinements of habits, useless accumulations of the lazy mind, which seeks safety in its thrift and its locks and keys. Thus she has come in contact with the living time and has accepted with eagerness and aptitude the responsibilities of modern civilisation.

This it is which has given heart to the rest of Asia. We have seen that the life and the strength are there in us; only the dead crust has to be removed. We have seen that taking shelter in the dead is death itself, and only taking all the risk of life to the fullest extent is living.

I, for myself, cannot believe that Japan has become what she is by imitating the West. We cannot imitate life, we cannot simulate strength for long, nay, what is more, a mere imitation is a source of weakness. For it hampers our true nature; it is always in our way. It is like dressing our skeleton with another man's skin, giving rise to eternal feuds between the skin and the bones at every movement.

The real truth is that science is not man's nature, it is mere knowledge and training. By knowing the laws of the material universe you do not change your deeper humanity. You can borrow knowledge from others, but you cannot borrow temperament.

But at the imitative stage of our schooling we cannot distinguish between the essential and the non-essential, between what is transferable and what is not. It is something like the faith of the primitive mind in the magical properties of the accidents of outward forms which accompany some real truth. We are afraid of leaving out something valuable and efficacious by not swallowing the husk with the kernel. But while our greed delights in wholesale appropriation, it is the function of our vital nature to assimilate, which is the only true appropriation for a living organism. Where there is life it is sure to assert itself by its choice of acceptance and refusal according to its constitutional necessity. The living organism does not allow itself to grow into its food; it changes its food into its own body. And only thus can it grow strong and not by mere accumulation, or by giving up its personal identity.

Japan has imported her food from the West, but not her vital nature. Japan cannot altogether lose and merge herself in the scientific paraphernalia she has acquired from the West and be turned into a mere borrowed machine. She has her own soul, which must assert itself over all her requirements. That she is capable of doing so, and that the process of assimilation is going on, have been amply proved by the signs of vigorous health that she exhibits. And I earnestly hope that Japan may never lose her faith in her own soul, in the mere pride of her foreign acquisition. For that pride itself is a humiliation, ultimately leading to poverty and weakness. It is the pride of the fop who sets more store on his new head-dress than on his head itself.

The whole world waits to see what this great eastern nation is going to do with the opportunities and responsibilities she has accepted from the hands of the modern time. If it be a mere reproduction of the West, then the great expectation she has raised will remain unfulfilled. For there are grave questions that western civilisation has presented before the world but not completely answered. The conflict between the individual and the state, labour and capital, the man and the woman; the conflict between the greed of material gain and the spiritual life of man, the organised selfishness of nations and the higher ideals of humanity; the conflict between all the ugly complexities inseparable from giant organisations of commerce and state and the natural instincts of man crying for simplicity and beauty and fulness of leisure—all these have to be brought to a harmony in a manner not yet dreamt of.

We have seen this great stream of civilisation choking itself from debris carried by its innumerable channels. We have seen that with all its vaunted love of humanity it has proved itself the greatest menace to Man, far worse than the sudden outbursts of nomadic barbarism from which men suffered in the early ages of history. We have seen that, in spite of its boasted love of freedom, it has produced worse forms of slavery than ever were current in earlier societies—slavery whose chains are unbreakable, either because they are unseen, or because they assume the names and appearance of freedom. We have seen, under the spell of its gigantic sordidness, man losing faith in all the heroic ideals of life which have made him great.

Therefore you cannot with a light heart accept the modern civilisation with all its tendencies, methods and structures, and dream that they are inevitable. You must apply your eastern mind, your spiritual strength, your love of simplicity, your recognition of social obligation, in order to cut out a new path for this great unwieldy car of progress, shrieking out its loud discords as it runs. You must minimise the immense sacrifice of man's life and freedom that it claims in its every movement. For generations you have felt and thought and worked, have enjoyed and worshipped in your own special manner; and this cannot be cast off like old clothes. It is in your blood, in the marrow of your bones, in the texture of your flesh, in the tissue of your brains; and it must modify everything you lay your hands upon, without your knowing, even against your wishes. Once you did solve the problems of man to your own satisfaction, you had your philosophy of life and evolved your own art of living. All this you must apply to the present situation, and out of it will arise a new creation and not a mere repetition, a creation which the soul of your people will own for itself and proudly offer to the world as its tribute to the welfare of man. Of all countries in

Asia, here in Japan you have the freedom to use the materials you have gathered from the West according to your genius and your need. Therefore your responsibility is all the greater, for in your voice Asia shall answer the questions that Europe has submitted to the conference of Man. In your land the experiments will be carried on by which the East will change the aspects of modern civilisation, infusing life in it where it is a machine, substituting the human heart for cold expediency, not caring so much for power and success as for harmonious and living growth, for truth and beauty.

I cannot but bring to your mind those days when the whole of eastern Asia from Burma to Japan was united with India in the closest tie of friendship, the only natural tie which can exist between nations. There was a living communication of hearts, a nervous system evolved through which messages ran between us about the deepest needs of humanity. We did not stand in fear of each other; we had not to arm ourselves to keep each other in check; our relation was not that of self-interest, of exploration and spoliation of each other's pocket; ideas and ideals were exchanged, gifts of the highest love were offered and taken; no difference of languages and customs hindered us in approaching each other heart to heart; no pride of race or insolent consciousness of superiority, physical or mental, marred our relation; our arts and literatures put forth new leaves and flowers under the influence of this sunlight of united hearts, and races belonging to different lands and languages and histories acknowledged the highest unity of man and the deepest bond of love. May we not also remember that in those days of peace and goodwill, of men uniting for those supreme ends of life, your nature laid by for itself the balm of immortality which has helped your people to be born again in a new age, to be able to survive its old outworn structures and take on a new young body, to come out unscathed from the shock of the most wonderful revolution that the world has ever seen?

The political civilisation which has sprung up from the soil of Europe and is overrunning the whole world, like some prolific weed, is based upon exclusiveness. It is always watchful to keep the aliens at bay or to exterminate them. It is carnivorous and cannibalistic in its tendencies, it feeds upon the resources of other peoples and tries to swallow their whole future. It is always afraid of other races achieving eminence, naming it as a peril, and tries to thwart all symptoms of greatness outside its own boundaries, forcing down races of men who are weaker, to be eternally fixed in their weakness. Before this political civilisation came to its power and opened its hungry jaws wide enough to gulp down great continents of the earth, we had wars, pillages, changes of monarchy and consequent miseries, but never such a sight of fearful and hopeless voracity, such wholesale feeding of nation upon nation, such huge machines for turning great portions of the earth into mince-meat, never such terrible jealousies with all their ugly teeth and claws ready for tearing open each other's vitals. This political civilisation is scientific, not human. It is powerful because it concentrates all its forces upon one purpose, like a millionaire acquiring money at the cost of his soul. It betrays its trust, it weaves its meshes of lies without shame, it enshrines gigantic idols of greed in its temples, taking great pride in the costly ceremonials of its worship, calling this patriotism. And it can be safely prophesied that this cannot go on, for there is a moral law in this world which has its application both to individuals and to organised bodies of men. You cannot go on violating these laws in the name of your nation, yet enjoy their advantage as individuals. This public sapping of ethical ideals slowly reacts upon each member of society, gradually breeding weakness where it is not seen, and causing that cynical distrust of all things sacred in human nature, which is the true symptom of senility. You must keep in mind that this political civilisation, this creed of national patriotism, has not been given a long trial. The lamp of ancient Greece is extinct in the land where it was first lighted; the power of Rome lies dead and buried under the ruins of its vast empire. But the civilisation, whose basis is society and the spiritual ideal of man, is still a living thing in China and in India. Though it may look feeble and small, judged by the standard of the mechanical power of modern days, yet like small seeds it still contains life and will sprout and grow, and spread its beneficent branches, producing flowers and fruits when its time comes and showers of grace descend upon it from heaven. But ruins of skyscrapers of power, and broken machinery of greed, even God's rain is powerless to raise up again; for they were not of life, but went against life as a whole—they are relics of the rebellion that shattered itself to pieces against the eternal.

But the charge is brought against us that the ideals we cherish in the East are static, that they have not the impetus in them to move, to open out new vistas of knowledge and power, that the systems of philosophy which are the mainstays of the time-worn civilisations of the East despise all outward proofs, remaining stolidly satisfied in their subjective certainty. This proves that when our knowledge is vague we are apt to accuse of vagueness our object of knowledge itself. To a western observer our civilisation appears as all metaphysics, as to a deaf man piano-playing appears to be mere movements of fingers and no music. He cannot think that we have found some deep basis of reality upon which we have built our institutions.

Unfortunately all proofs of reality are in realisation. The reality of the scene before you depends only upon the fact that you can see, and it is difficult for us to prove to an unbeliever that our civilisation is not a nebulous system of abstract speculations, that it has achieved something which is a positive truth—a truth that can give man's heart its shelter and sustenance. It has evolved an inner sense—a sense of vision, the vision of the infinite reality in all finite things.

But he says, 'You do not make any progress; there is no movement in you.' I ask him, 'How do you know it? You have to judge progress according to its aim. A railway train makes its progress towards the terminus station—it is movement. But a full-grown tree has no definite movement of that kind; its progress is the inward progress of life. It lives, with its aspiration towards light tingling in its leaves and creeping in its silent sap.'

We also have lived for centuries; we still live, and we have our aspiration for a reality that has no end to its realisation—a reality that goes beyond death, giving it a meaning, that rises above all evils of life, bringing its peace and purity, its cheerful renunciation of self. The product of this inner life is a living product. It will be needed when the youth returns home weary and dust-laden, when the soldier is wounded, when the wealth is squandered away and pride is humbled, when man's heart cries for truth in the immensity of facts, and harmony in the contradiction of tendencies. Its value is not in its multiplication of materials, but in its spiritual fulfilment.

There are things that cannot wait. You have to rush and run and march if you must fight or take the best place in the market. You strain your nerves and are on the alert when you chase opportunities that are always on the wing. But there are ideals which do not play hide-and-seek with our life; they slowly grow from seed to flower, from flower to fruit; they require infinite space and heaven's light to mature, and the fruits that they produce can survive years of insult and neglect. The East with her ideals, in whose bosom are stored the ages of sunlight and silence of stars, can patiently wait till the West, hurrying after the expedient, loses breath and stops. Europe, while busily speeding to her engagements, disdainfully casts her glance from her carriage window at the reaper reaping his harvest in the field, and in her intoxication of speed cannot but think of him as slow and ever receding backwards. But the speed comes to its end; the engagement loses its meaning and the hungry heart clamours for food, till at last she comes to the lowly reaper reaping his harvest in the sun. For if the office cannot wait, or the buying and selling, or the craving for excitement, love waits, and beauty, and the wisdom of suffering and the fruits of patient devotion and reverent meekness of simple faith. And thus shall wait the East till her time comes.

I must not hesitate to acknowledge where Europe is great, for great she is without doubt. We cannot help loving her with all our heart and paying her the best homage of our admiration— the Europe who, in her literature and art, pours out an inexhaustible cascade of beauty and truth fertilising all countries and all time; the Europe who, with a mind which is titanic in its untiring power, is sweeping the height and the depth of the universe, winning her homage of knowledge from the infinitely great and the infinitely small, applying all the resources of her great intellect and heart in healing the sick and alleviating those miseries of man which up till now we were contented to accept in a spirit of hopeless resignation; the Europe who is making the earth yield more fruit than seemed possible, coaxing and compelling the great forces of nature into man's service. Such true greatness must have its motive power in spiritual strength. For only the spirit of man can defy all limitations, have faith in its ultimate success, throw its searchlight beyond the immediate and the apparent, gladly suffer martyrdom for ends which cannot be achieved in its lifetime and accept failure without acknowledging defeat. In the heart of Europe runs the purest stream of human love, of love of justice, of spirit of self-sacrifice for higher ideals. The Christian culture of centuries has sunk deep in her life's core. In Europe we have seen noble minds who have ever stood up for the rights of man irrespective of colour and creed; who have braved calumny and insult from their own people in fighting for humanity's cause and raising their voices against the mad orgies of militarism, against the rage for brutal retaliation or rapacity that sometimes takes possession of a whole people; who are always ready to make reparation for wrongs done in the past by their own nations and vainly attempt to stem the tide of cowardly injustice that flows unchecked because the resistance is weak and innocuous on the part of the injured. There are these knight-errants of modern Europe who have not lost their faith in the disinterested love of freedom, in the ideals which own no geographical boundaries or national self-seeking. These are there to prove that the fountainhead of the water of everlasting life has not run dry in Europe, and from thence she will have her rebirth time after time. Only there, where Europe is too consciously busy in building up her power, defying her deeper nature and mocking it, she is heaping up her iniquities to the sky, crying for God's vengeance and spreading the infection of ugliness, physical and moral, over the face of the earth with her heartless commerce heedlessly outraging man's sense of the beautiful and the good. Europe is supremely good in her beneficence where her face is turned to all humanity; and Europe is supremely evil in her maleficent aspect where her face is turned only upon her own interest, using all her power of greatness for ends which are against the infinite and eternal in Man.

Eastern Asia has been pursuing its own path, evolving its own civilisation, which was not political but social, not predatory and mechanically efficient but spiritual and based upon all the varied and deeper relations of humanity. The solutions of the life problems of peoples were thought out in seclusion and carried out behind the security of aloofness, where all the dynastic changes and foreign invasions hardly touched them. But now we are overtaken by the outside world, our seclusion is lost for ever. Yet this we must not regret, as a plant should never regret when the obscurity of its seed-time is broken. Now the time has come when we must make the world problem our own problem; we must bring the spirit of civilisation into harmony with the history of all nations of the earth; we must not, in foolish pride, still keep ourselves fast within the shell of the seed and the crust of the earth which protected and nourished our ideals; for these, the shell and the crust, were meant to be broken, so that life may spring up in all its vigour and beauty, bringing its offerings to the world in open light.

In this task of breaking the barrier and facing the world Japan has come out the first in the East. She has infused hope in the heart of all Asia. This hope provides the hidden fire which is needed for all works of creation. Asia now feels that she must prove her life by producing living work; she must not lie passively dormant, or feebly imitate the West, in the infatuation of fear and flattery. For this we offer our thanks to this Land of the Rising Sun and solemnly ask her to remember that she has the mission of the East to fulfil. She must infuse the sap of a fuller humanity into the heart of modern civilisation. She must never allow it to get choked with noxious undergrowth, but lead it up towards light and freedom, towards the pure air and broad space where it can receive, in the dawn of its day and the darkness of its night, heaven's inspiration. Let the greatness of her ideals become visible to all men like her snow-crowned Fuji rising from the heart of the country into the region of the infinite, supremely distinct from its surroundings, beautiful like

a maiden in its magnificent sweep of curve, yet firm and strong
and serenely majestic.

II

I have travelled in many countries and have met with men of
all classes, but never in my travels did I feel the presence of the
human so distinctly as in this land. In other great countries
signs of man's power loomed large, and I saw vast organisations
which showed efficiency in all their features. There, display and
extravagance, in dress, in furniture, in costly entertainments,
are startling. They seem to push you back into a corner, like a
poor intruder at a feast; they are apt to make you envious, or take
your breath away with amazement. There, you do not feel man
as supreme; you are hurled against a stupendousness of things
that alienate. But in Japan it is not the display of power or wealth
that is the predominating element. You see everywhere emblems
of love and admiration, and not mostly of ambition and greed.
You see a people whose heart has come out and scattered itself in
profusion in its commonest utensils of everyday life, in its social
institutions, in its manners, which are carefully perfect, and in
its dealings with things which are not only deft but graceful in
every movement.

What has impressed me most in this country is the
conviction that you have realised nature's secrets, not by methods
of analytical knowledge, but by sympathy. You have known her
language of lines, and music of colours, the symmetry in her
irregularities, and the cadence in her freedom of movements;
you have seen how she leads her immense crowds of things yet
avoids all frictions, how the very conflicts in her creations break
out in dance and music, how her exuberance has the aspect of
the fulness of self-abandonment, and not a mere dissipation of

display. You have discovered that nature reserves her power in forms of beauty; and it is this beauty which, like a mother, nourishes all the giant forces at her breast, keeping them in active vigour, yet in repose. You have known that energies of nature save themselves from wearing out by the rhythm of a perfect grace, and that she, with the tenderness of her curved lines, takes away fatigue from the world's muscles. I have felt that you have been able to assimilate these secrets into your life, and the truth which lies in the beauty of all things has passed into your souls. A mere knowledge of things can be had in a short enough time, but their spirit can only be acquired by centuries of training and self-control. Dominating nature from outside is a much simpler thing than making her your own in love's delight, which is a work of true genius. Your race has shown that genius, not by acquirement but by creation, not by display of things but by manifestation of its own inner being. This creative power there is in all nations, and it is ever active in getting hold of men's natures and giving them a form according to its ideals. But here, in Japan, it seems to have achieved its success, and deeply sunk into the minds of all men, and permeated their muscles and nerves. Your instincts have become true, your senses keen, and your hands have acquired natural skill. The genius of Europe has given her people the power of organisation, which has specially made itself manifest in politics and commerce and in co-ordinating scientific knowledge. The genius of Japan has given you the vision of beauty in nature and the power of realising it in your life.

All particular civilisation is the interpretation of particular human experience. Europe seems to have felt emphatically the conflict of things in the universe, which can only be brought under control by conquest. Therefore she is ever ready for fight, and the best portion of her attention is occupied in organising forces.

But Japan has felt, in her world, the touch of some presence, which has evoked in her soul a feeling of reverent adoration. She does not boast of her mastery of nature, but to her she brings, with infinite care and joy, her offerings of love. Her relationship with the world is the deeper relationship of heart. This spiritual bond of love she has established with the hills of her country, with the sea and the streams, with the forests in all their flowery moods and varied physiognomy of branches; she has taken into her heart all the rustling whispers and sighing of the woodlands and sobbing of the waves; the sun and the moon she has studied in all the modulations of their lights and shades, and she is glad to close her shops to greet the seasons in her orchards and gardens and cornfields. This opening of the heart to the soul of the world is not confined to a section of your privileged classes; it is not the forced product of exotic culture, but it belongs to all your men and women of all conditions. This experience of your soul, in meeting a personality in the heart of the world, has been embodied in your civilisation. It is a civilisation of human relationship. Your duty towards your state has naturally assumed the character of filial duty, your nation becoming one family with your Emperor as its head. Your national unity has not been evolved from the comradeship of arms for defensive and offensive purpose, or from partnership in raiding adventures, dividing among each member the danger and spoils of robbery. It is not an outcome of the necessity of organisation for some ulterior purpose, but it is an extension of the family and obligations of the heart in a wide field of space and time. The ideal of *maitri* is at the bottom of your culture—*maitri* with men and *maitri* with Nature. And the true expression of this love is in the language of beauty, which is so abundantly universal in this land. This is the reason why a stranger like myself, instead of feeling envy or humiliation before these manifestations of beauty, these creations of love, feels a readiness to participate in the joy and glory of such revealment of the human heart.

And this had made me all the more apprehensive of the change which threatens Japanese civilisation, as something like a menace to one's own person. For the huge heterogeneity of the modern age, whose only common bond is usefulness, is nowhere so pitifully exposed against the dignity and hidden power of reticent beauty as in Japan.

But the danger lies in this, that organised ugliness storms the mind and carries the day by its mass, by its aggressive persistence, but its power of mockery is directed against the deeper sentiments of the heart. Its harsh obtrusiveness makes it forcibly visible to us, overcoming our senses—and we bring sacrifices to its altar, as does a savage to the fetish which appears powerful because of its hideousness. Therefore its rivalry with things that are modest and profound and have the subtle delicacy of life is to be dreaded.

I am quite sure that there are men in your country who are not in sympathy with your inherited ideals, whose object is to gain and not to grow. They are loud in their boast that they have modernised Japan. While I agree with them so far as to say that the spirit of the race should harmonise with the spirit of the time, I must warn them that modernising is a mere affectation of modernism, just as an affectation of poesy is poetising. It is nothing but mimicry, only affectation is louder than the original, and it is too literal. One must bear in mind that those who have the true modern spirit need not modernise, just as those who are truly brave are not braggarts. Modernism is not in the dress of the Europeans, or in the hideous structures where their children are interned when they take their lessons, or in the square houses with flat, straight wall-surfaces, pierced with parallel lines of windows, where these people are caged in their lifetime; certainly modernism is not in their ladies' bonnets, carrying on them loads of incongruities. These are not modern, but merely European. True modernism is freedom of mind, not slavery of taste. It is independence of thought and action, not tutelage under European schoolmasters. It is science, but not its wrong application in life—a mere imitation of our science teachers who reduce it into a superstition, absurdly invoking its aid for all impossible purposes.

Life based upon mere science is attractive to some men, because it has all the characteristics of sport; it feigns seriousness, but is not profound. When you go a-hunting, the less pity you have the better; for your one object is to chase the game and kill it, to feel that you are the greater animal, that your method of destruction is thorough and scientific. And the life of science is that superficial life. It pursues success with skill and thoroughness, and takes no account of the higher nature of man. But those whose minds are crude enough to plan their lives upon the supposition that man is merely a hunter and his paradise the paradise of sportsmen will be rudely awakened in the midst of their trophies of skeletons and skulls.

I do not for a moment suggest that Japan should be unmindful of acquiring modern weapons of self-protection. But this should never be allowed to go beyond her instinct of self-preservation. She must know that the real power is not in the weapons themselves, but in the man who wields those weapons; and when he, in his eagerness for power, multiplies his weapons at the cost of his own soul, then it is he who is in even greater danger than his enemies.

Things that are living are so easily hurt; therefore they require protection. In nature, life protects itself within its coverings, which are built with life's own material. Therefore they are in harmony with life's growth, or else when the time comes they easily give way and are forgotten. The living man has his true protection in his spiritual ideals which have their vital connection with his life, and grow with his growth. But, unfortunately, all his armour is not living—some of it is made of steel, inert and mechanical. Therefore, while making use of it, man has to be careful to protect himself from its tyranny. If he is weak enough to grow smaller to fit himself to his covering, then it becomes a process of gradual suicide by shrinkage of the soul. And Japan must have a firm faith in the moral law of existence to be able to assert to herself that the western nations are following that path of suicide, where they are smothering their humanity under the immense weight of organisations in order to keep themselves in power and hold others in subjection.

What is dangerous for Japan is not the imitation of the outer features of the West, but the acceptance of the motive force of western nationalism as her own. Her social ideals are already showing signs of defeat at the hands of politics. I can see her motto, taken from science, 'Survival of the fittest', writ large at the entrance of her present-day history—the motto whose meaning is, 'Help yourself, and never heed what it costs to others', the motto of the blind man who only believes in what he can touch, because he cannot see. But those who can see know that men are so closely knit that when you strike others the blow comes back to yourself. The moral law, which is the greatest discovery of man, is the discovery of this wonderful truth, that man becomes all the truer the more he realises himself in others. This truth has not only a subjective value, but is manifested in every department of our life. And nations who sedulously cultivate moral blindness as the cult of patriotism will end their existence in a sudden and violent death. In past ages we had foreign invasions, but they never touched the soul of the people deeply. They were merely the outcome of individual ambitions. The people themselves, being free from the responsibilities of the baser and more heinous side of those adventures, had all the advantage of the heroic and the human disciplines derived from them. This developed their unflinching loyalty, their single-minded devotion to the obligations of honour, their power of complete self-surrender and fearless acceptance of death and danger. Therefore the ideals, whose seats were in the hearts of the people, would not undergo any serious change owing to the policies adopted by the kings or generals. But now, where the spirit of western nationalism prevails, the whole people is being taught from boyhood to foster hatreds and ambitions by all kinds of means—by the manufacture of half-truths and untruths in history, by persistent misrepresentation of other races and the culture of unfavourable sentiments towards them, by setting up memorials of events, very often false, which for the sake of humanity should be speedily forgotten, thus continually brewing evil menace towards neighbours and nations other than their own. This is poisoning the very fountainhead of humanity. It is discrediting the ideals which were born of the lives of men who were our greatest and best. It is holding up gigantic selfishness as the one universal religion for all nations of the world. We can take anything else from the hands of science, but not this elixir of moral death. Never think for a moment that the hurts you inflict upon other races will not infect you, or that the enmities you sow around your homes will be a wall of protection to you for all time to come. To imbue the minds of the whole people with an abnormal vanity of its own superiority, to teach it to take pride in its moral callousness and ill-begotten wealth, to perpetuate the humiliation of defeated nations by exhibiting trophies won from war, and using these in schools in order to breed in children's minds contempt for others, is imitating the West where she has a festering sore, whose swelling is a swelling of disease eating into its vitality.

Our food crops, which are necessary for our sustenance, are products of centuries of selection and care. But the vegetation, which we have not to transform into our lives, does not require the patient thoughts of generations. It is not easy to get rid of weeds; but it is easy, by process of neglect, to ruin your food crops and let them revert to their primitive state of wildness. Likewise the culture, which has so kindly adapted itself to your soil—so intimate with life, so human—not only needed tilling and weeding in past ages, but still needs anxious work and watching. What is merely modern—as science and methods of organisation—can be transplanted; but what is vitally human has fibres so delicate, and roots so numerous and far-reaching, that it dies when moved from the soil. Therefore I am afraid of the rude pressure of the political ideals of the West upon your own. In political civilisation, the state is an abstraction and the relationship of men utilitarian. Because it has no root in sentiments, it is so dangerously easy to handle. Half a century has been enough for you to master this machine; and there are men among you whose fondness for it exceeds their love for the living ideals, which were born with the birth of your nation and nursed in your centuries. It is like a child who, in the excitement of his play, imagines he likes his play-things better than his mother.

Where man is at his greatest, he is unconscious. Your civilisation, whose mainspring is the bond of human relationship, has been nourished in the depth of a healthy life beyond reach of prying self-analysis. But a mere political relationship is all-conscious; it is an eruptive inflammation of aggressiveness. It has forcibly burst upon your notice. And the time has come when you have to be roused into full consciousness of the truth by which you live, so that you may not be taken unawares. The past has been God's gift to you; about the present, you must make your own choice.

So the questions you have to put to yourselves are these: 'Have we read the world wrong, and based our relation to it upon an ignorance of human nature? Is the instinct of the West right, where she builds her national welfare behind the barricade of a universal distrust of humanity?'

You must have detected a strong accent of fear whenever the West has discussed the possibility of the rise of an eastern race. The reason of it is this, that the power by whose help she thrives is an evil power; so long as it is held on her own side she can be safe, while the rest of the world trembles. The vital ambition of the present civilisation of Europe is to have the exclusive possession of the devil. All her armaments and diplomacy are directed upon this one object. But these costly rituals for invocation of the evil spirit lead through a path of prosperity to the brink of cataclysm. The furies of terror, which the West has let loose upon God's world, come back to threaten herself and goad her into preparations of more and more frightfulness; this gives her no rest, and makes her forget all else but the perils that she causes to others and incurs herself. To the worship of this devil of politics she sacrifices other countries as victims. She feeds upon their dead flesh and grows fat upon it, so long as the carcasses remain fresh—but they are sure to rot at last, and the dead will take their revenge by spreading pollution far and wide and poisoning the vitality of the feeder. Japan had all her wealth of humanity, her harmony of heroism and beauty, her depth of self-control and richness of self-expression; yet the western nations felt no respect for her till she proved that the bloodhounds of Satan are not only bred in the kennels of Europe but can also be domesticated in Japan and fed with man's miseries. They admit Japan's equality with themselves, only when they know that Japan also possesses the key to open the floodgate of hell-fire upon the fair earth whenever she chooses, and can dance in their own measure the devil dance of pillage, murder and ravishment of innocent women, while the world goes to ruin. We know that, in the early state of man's moral immaturity, he only feels reverence for the god whose malevolence he dreads. But is this the ideal of man which we can look up to with pride: after centuries of civilisation nations fearing each other like the prowling wild beasts of the night-time; shutting their doors of hospitality; combining only for purpose of aggression or defence; hiding in their holes their trade secrets, state secrets, secrets of their armaments; making peace-offerings to each other's barking dogs with the meat which does not belong to them; holding down fallen races which struggle to stand upon their feet; with their right hands dispensing religion to weaker peoples, while robbing them with their left—is there anything in this to make us envious? Are we to bend our knees to the spirit of this nationalism, which is sowing broadcast over all the world seeds of fear, greed, suspicion, unashamed lies of its diplomacy, and unctuous lies of its profession of peace and goodwill and universal brotherhood of Man? Can our minds be free from doubt when we rush to the western market to buy this foreign product in exchange for our own inheritance? I am aware how difficult it is to know one's self; and the man who is intoxicated furiously denies his drunkenness; yet the West herself is anxiously thinking of her problems and trying experiments. But she is like a glutton, who has not the heart to give up his intemperance in eating, and fondly clings to the hope he can cure his nightmares of indigestion by medicine. Europe is not ready to give up her political inhumanity, with all the baser passions of man attendant upon it; she believes only in modification of systems, and not in change of heart.

We are willing to buy their machine-made systems, not with our hearts, but with our brains. We shall try them and build sheds for them, but not enshrine them in our homes or temples.

There are races who worship the animals they kill; we can buy meat from them when we are hungry, but not the worship which goes with the killing. We must not vitiate our children's minds with the superstition that business is business, war is war, politics is politics. We must know that man's business has to be more than mere business, and so should be his war and politics. You had your own industry in Japan; how scrupulously honest and true it was, you can see by its products—by their grace and strength, their conscientiousness in details, where they can hardly be observed. But the tidal wave of falsehood has swept over your land from that part of the world where business is business, and honesty is followed merely as a best policy. Have you never felt shame when you see the trade advertisements, not only plastering the whole town with lies and exaggerations, but invading the green fields, where the peasants do their honest labour, and the hill-tops, which greet the first pure light of the morning? It is so easy to dull our sense of honour and delicacy of mind with constant abrasion, while falsehoods stalk abroad with proud steps in the name of trade, politics and patriotism, that any protest against their perpetual intrusion into our lives is considered to be sentimentalism, unworthy of true manliness.

And it has come to pass that the children of those who would keep their word at the point of death, who would disdain to cheat men for vulgar profit, who even in their fight would much rather court defeat than be dishonourable, have become energetic in dealing with falsehoods and do not feel humiliated by gaining advantage from them. And this has been effected by the charm of the word 'modern'. But if undiluted utility be modern, beauty is of all ages; if mean selfishness be modern, the human ideals are no new inventions. And we must know for certain that however modern may be the proficiency which cripples man for the sake of methods and machines, it will never live to be old.

But while trying to free our minds from the arrogant claims of Europe and to help ourselves out of the quicksands of our infatuation, we may go to the other extreme and bind ourselves with a wholesale suspicion of the West. The reaction of disillusionment is just as unreal as the first shock of illusion. We must try to come to that normal state of mind by which we can clearly discern our own danger and avoid it without being unjust towards the source of that danger. There is always the natural temptation in us of wishing to pay back Europe in her own coin, and return contempt for contempt and evil for evil. But that again would be to imitate Europe in one of her worst features, which comes out in her behaviour to people whom she describes as yellow or red, brown or black. And this is a point on which we in the East have to acknowledge our guilt and own that our sin has been as great, if not greater, when we insulted humanity by treating with utter disdain and cruelty men who belonged to a particular creed, colour or caste. It is really because we are afraid of our own weakness, which allows itself to be overcome by the sight of power, that we try to substitute for it another weakness which makes itself blind to the glories of the West. When we truly know that Europe which is great and good, we can effectively save ourselves from the Europe which is mean and grasping. It is easy to be unfair in one's judgement when one is faced with human miseries—and pessimism is the result of building theories while the mind is suffering. To despair of humanity is only possible if we lose faith in truth which brings to it strength, when its defeat is greatest, and calls out new life from the depth of its destruction. We must admit that there is a living soul in the West which is struggling unobserved against the hugeness of the organisations under which men, women and children are being crushed, and whose mechanical necessities are ignoring laws that are spiritual and human—the soul whose sensibilities refuse to be dulled completely by dangerous habits of heedlessness in dealings with races for whom it lacks natural sympathy. The West could never have risen to the eminence she has reached if her strength were merely the strength of the brute or of the machine. The divine in her heart is suffering from the injuries inflicted by her hands upon the world—and from this pain of her higher nature flows the secret balm which will bring healing to these injuries. Time after time she has fought against herself and has undone the chains which with her own hands she fastened round helpless limbs; and though she forced poison down the throat of a great nation at the point of the sword for gain of money, she herself woke up to withdraw from it, to wash her hands clean again. This shows hidden springs of humanity in spots which look dead and barren. It proves that the deeper truth in her nature, which can survive such a career of cruel cowardliness, is not greed, but reverence for unselfish ideals. It would be altogether unjust, both to us and to Europe, to say that she has fascinated the modern eastern mind by the mere exhibition of her power. Through the smoke of cannons and dust of markets the light of her moral nature has shone bright, and she has brought to us the ideal of ethical freedom, whose foundation lies deeper than social conventions and whose province of activity is worldwide.

The East has instinctively felt, even through her aversion, that she has a great deal to learn from Europe, not merely about the materials of power, but about its inner source, which is of the mind and of the moral nature of man. Europe has been teaching us the higher obligations of public good above those of the family and the clan, and the sacredness of law, which makes society independent of individual caprice, secures for it continuity of progress, and guarantees justice to all men of all positions in life. Above all things Europe has held high before our minds the banner of liberty, through centuries of martyrdom and achievement—liberty of conscience, liberty of thought and action, liberty in the ideals of art and literature. And because Europe has won our deep respect, she has become so dangerous for us where she is turbulently weak and false—dangerous like poison when it is served along with our best food. There is one safety for us upon which we hope we may count, and that is that we can claim Europe herself as our ally in our resistance to her temptations and to her violent encroachments; for she has ever carried her own standard of perfection, by which we can measure her falls and gauge her degrees of failure, by which we can call her before her own tribunal and put her to shame—the shame which is the sign of the true pride of nobleness.

But our fear is that the poison may be more powerful than the food, and what is strength in her today may not be a sign of health, but the contrary; for it may be temporarily caused by the upsetting of the balance of life. Our fear is that evil has a fateful fascination when it assumes dimensions which are colossal—and though at last it is sure to lose its centre of gravity by its abnormal disproportion, the mischief which it creates before its fall may be beyond reparation.

Therefore I ask you to have the strength of faith and clarity of mind to know for certain that the lumbering structure of modern progress, riveted by the iron bolts of efficiency, which runs upon the wheels of ambition, cannot hold together for long. Collisions are certain to occur, for it has to travel upon organised lines; it is too heavy to choose its own course freely, and once it is off the rails its endless train of vehicles is dislocated. A day will come when it will fall in a heap of ruin and cause serious obstruction to the traffic of the world. Do we not see signs of this even now? Does not the voice come to us through the din of war, the shrieks of hatred, the wailings of despair, through the churning of the unspeakable filth which has been accumulating for ages in the bottom of this nationalism—the voice which cries to our soul that the tower of national selfishness, which goes by the name of patriotism, which has raised its banner of treason against heaven, must totter and fall with a crash, weighed down by its own bulk, its flag kissing the dust, its light extinguished? My brothers, when the red light of conflagration sends up its crackle of laughter to the stars, keep your faith upon those stars and not upon the fire of destruction. For when the conflagration consumes itself and dies down, leaving its memorial in ashes, the eternal light will again shine in the East—the East which has been the birthplace of the morning sun of man's history. And who knows if that day has not already dawned, and the sun not risen, in the easternmost horizon of Asia? And I offer, as did my ancestor *rishis*, my salutation to that sunrise of the East, which is destined once again to illumine the whole world.

I know my voice is too feeble to raise itself above the uproar of this bustling time, and it is easy for any street urchin to fling against me the epithet of 'unpractical'. It will stick to my coat-tail, never to be washed away, effectively excluding me from the consideration of all respectable persons. I know what a risk one runs from the vigorously athletic crowds in being styled an idealist in these days, when thrones have lost their dignity and prophets have become an anachronism, when the sound that drowns all voices is the noise of the market-place. Yet when, one day, standing on the outskirts of Yokohama town bristling with its display of modern miscellanies, I watched the sunset in your southern sea, and saw its peace and majesty among your pine-clad hills—with the great Fujiyama growing faint against the golden horizon, like a god overcome with his own radiance—the music of eternity welled up through the evening silence, and I felt that the sky and the earth and the lyrics of the dawn and the dayfall are with the poets and idealists, and not with the marketmen robustly contemptuous of all sentiment—that, after all the forgetfulness of his divinity, man will remember again that heaven is always in touch with his world, which can never be abandoned for good to the hounding wolves of the modern era, scenting human blood and howling to the skies.

Nationalism in the West

Man's history is being shaped according to the difficulties it encounters. These have offered us problems and claimed their solutions from us, the penalty of non-fulfilment being death or degradation.

These difficulties have been different in different peoples of the earth, and in the manner of our overcoming them lies our distinction.

The Scythians of the earlier period of Asiatic history had to struggle with the scarcity of their natural resources. The easiest solution that they could think of was to organise their whole population, men, women, and children, into bands of robbers. And they were irresistible to those who were chiefly engaged in the constructive work of social co-operation.

But fortunately for man the easiest path is not his truest path. If his nature were not as complex as it is, if it were as simple as that of a pack of hungry wolves, then, by this time, those hordes of marauders would have overrun the whole earth. But man, when confronted with difficulties, has to acknowledge that he is man, that he has his responsibilities to the higher faculties of his nature, by ignoring which he may achieve success that is immediate, perhaps, but that will become a death-trap to him. For what are obstacles to the lower creatures are opportunities to the higher life of man.

To India has been given her problem from the beginning of history—it is the race problem. Races ethnologically different have in this country come into close contact. This fact has been and still continues to be the most important one in our history. It is our mission to face it and prove our humanity by dealing with it in the fullest truth. Until we fulfil our mission all other benefits will be denied us.

There are other peoples in the world who have to overcome obstacles in their physical surroundings, or the menace of their powerful neighbours. They have organised their power till they are not only reasonably free from the tyranny of Nature and human neighbours, but have a surplus of it left in their hands to employ against others. But in India, our difficulties being internal, our history has been the history of continual social adjustment and not that of organised power for defence and aggression.

Neither the colourless vagueness of cosmopolitanism, nor the fierce self-idolatry of nation-worship, is the goal of human history. And India has been trying to accomplish her task through social regulation of differences on the one hand, and the spiritual recognition of unity on the other. She has made grave errors in setting up the boundary walls too rigidly between races, in perpetuating in her classifications the results of inferiority; often she has crippled her children's minds and narrowed their lives in order to fit them into her social forms, but for centuries new experiments have been made and adjustments carried out.

Her mission has been like that of a hostess who has to provide proper accommodation for numerous guests, whose habits and requirements are different from one another. This gives rise to infinite complexities whose solution depends not merely upon tactfulness but upon sympathy and true realisation of the unity of man. Towards this realisation have worked, from the early time of the *Upanishads** up to the present moment, a series of great spiritual teachers, whose one object has been to set at naught all differences of man by the overflow of our consciousness of God. In fact, our history has not been of the rise and fall of kingdoms, of fights for political supremacy. In our country records of these days have been despised and forgotten, for they in no way represent the true history of our people. Our history is that of our social life and attainment of spiritual ideals.

But we feel that our task is not yet done. The world-flood has swept over our country, new elements have been introduced, and wider adjustments are waiting to be made.

We feel this all the more because the teaching and example of the West have entirely run counter to what we think was given to India to accomplish. In the West the national machinery of commerce and politics turns out neatly compressed bales of humanity which have their use and high market value; but they are bound in iron hoops, labelled and separated off with scientific care and precision. Obviously God made man to be human, but this modern product has such marvellous square-cut finish, savouring of gigantic manufacture, that the Creator will find it difficult to recognise it as a thing of spirit and a creature made in His own divine image.

But I am anticipating. What I was about to say is this. Take it in whatever spirit you like, here is India, of about fifty centuries at least, who tried to live peacefully and think deeply, the India devoid of all politics, the India of no nations, whose

---

* About 200 prose and verse treatises on metaphysical philosophy, dating from around 400 BC.

one ambition has been to know this world as of soul, to live here every moment of her life in the meek spirit of adoration, in the glad consciousness of an eternal and personal relationship with it. It was upon this remote portion of humanity, childlike in its manner, with the wisdom of the old, that the Nation of the West burst in.

Through all the fights and intrigues and deceptions of her earlier history India had remained aloof. Because her homes, her fields, her temples of worship, her schools, where her teachers and students lived together in the atmosphere of simplicity and devotion and learning, her village self-government with its simple laws and peaceful administration—all these truly belonged to her. But her thrones were not her concern. They passed over her head like clouds, now tinged with purple gorgeousness, now black with the threat of thunder. Often they brought devastations in their wake, but they were like catastrophes of nature whose traces are soon forgotten.

But this time it was different. It was not a mere drift over her surface of life—drift of cavalry and foot soldiers, richly caparisoned elephants, white tents and canopies, strings of patient camels bearing the loads of royalty, bands of kettle-drums and flutes, marble domes of mosques, palaces and tombs, like the bubbles of the foaming wine of extravagance; stories of treachery and loyal devotion, of changes of fortune, of dramatic surprises of fate. This time it was the Nation of the West driving its tentacles of machinery deep down into the soil.

Therefore I say to you, it is we who are called as witnesses to give evidence as to what our Nation has been to humanity. We had known the hordes of Mughals and Pathans who invaded India, but we had known them as human races, with their own religions and customs, likes and dislikes—we had never known them as a nation. We loved and hated them as the occasions arose; we fought for them and against them, talked with them in a language which was theirs as well as our own, and guided the destiny of the Empire in which we had our active share. But this time we had to deal, not with kings, not with human races, but with a nation—we, who are no nation ourselves.

Now let us, from our own experience, answer the question: what is this Nation?

A nation, in the sense of the political and economic union of a people, is that aspect which a whole population assumes when organised for a mechanical purpose. Society as such has no ulterior purpose. It is an end in itself. It is a spontaneous self-expression of man as a social being. It is a natural regulation of human relationships, so that men can develop ideals of life in co-operation with one another. It has also a political side, but this is only for a special purpose. It is for self-preservation. It is merely the side of power, not of human ideals. And in the early days it had its separate place in society, restricted to the professionals. But when with the help of science and the perfecting of organisation this power begins to grow and brings in harvests of wealth, then it crosses its boundaries with amazing rapidity. For then it goads all its neighbouring societies with greed of material prosperity, and consequent mutual jealousy, and by the fear of each other's growth into powerfulness. The time comes when it can stop no longer, for the competition grows keener, organisation grows vaster, and selfishness attains supremacy. Trading upon the greed and fear of man, it occupies more and more space in society, and at last becomes its ruling force.

It is just possible that you have lost through habit the consciousness that the living bonds of society are breaking up, and giving place to merely mechanical organisation. But one sees signs of it everywhere. It is owing to this that war has been declared between man and woman, because the natural thread is snapping which holds them together in harmony; because man is driven to professionalism, producing wealth for himself and others, continually turning the wheel of power for his own sake or for the sake of the universal officialdom, leaving woman alone to wither and to die or to fight her own battle unaided. And thus there, where co-operation is natural, has intruded competition. The very psychology of men and women about their mutual relation is changing and becoming the psychology of the primitive fighting elements, rather than of humanity seeking its completeness through the union based upon mutual self-surrender. For the elements which have lost their living bond of reality have lost the meaning of their existence. Like gaseous particles forced into a too narrow space, they come in continual conflict with each other till they burst the very arrangement which holds them in bondage.

Then look at those who call themselves anarchists, who resent the imposition of power, in any form whatever, upon the individual. The only reason for this is that power has become too abstract—it is a scientific product made in the political laboratory of the Nation, through the dissolution of personal humanity.

And what is the meaning of these strikes in the economic world, which like the prickly shrubs in a barren soil shoot up with renewed vigour each time they are cut down? What but that the wealth-producing mechanism is incessantly growing into vast stature, out of proportion to all other needs of society, and the full reality of man is more and more crushed under its weight? This state of things inevitably gives rise to eternal feuds among the elements freed from the wholeness and wholesomeness of human ideals, and interminable economic war is waged between capital and labour. For greed of wealth and power can never have a limit, and compromise of self-interest can never attain the final spirit of reconciliation. They must go on breeding jealousy and suspicion to the end—the end which only comes through some sudden catastrophe or a spiritual rebirth.

When this organisation of politics and commerce, whose other name is the Nation, becomes all-powerful at the cost of the harmony of the higher social life, then it is an evil day for humanity. When a father becomes a gambler and his obligations to his family take the secondary place in his mind, then he is no longer a man, but an automaton led by the power of greed. Then he can do things which, in his normal state of mind, he would be ashamed to do. It is the same thing with society. When it allows itself to be turned into a perfect organisation of power, then there are few crimes it is unable to perpetrate, because success is the object and justification of a machine, while goodness only is the end and purpose of man. When this engine of organisation begins to attain a vast size, and those who are mechanics are made into parts of the machine, then the personal man is eliminated to a phantom, everything becomes a revolution of policy carried out by the human parts of the machines, with no twinge of pity or moral responsibility. It may happen that even through this apparatus the moral nature of man tries to assert itself, but the whole series of ropes and pulleys creak and cry, the forces of the human heart become entangled among the forces of the human automaton, and only with difficulty can the moral purpose transmit itself into some tortured shape of result.

This abstract being, the Nation, is ruling India. We have seen in our country some brand of tinned food advertised as entirely made and packed without being touched by hand. This description applies to the governing of India, which is as little touched by the human hand as possible. The governors need not know our language, need not come into personal touch with us except as officials; they can aid or hinder our aspirations from a disdainful distance, they can lead us on a certain path of policy and then pull us back again with the manipulation of office red tape. The newspapers of England, in whose columns London street accidents are recorded with some decency of pathos, need take but the scantiest notice of calamities which happen in India over areas of land sometimes larger than the British Isles.

But we, who are governed, are not a mere abstraction. We, on our side, are individuals with living sensibilities. What comes to us in the shape of a mere bloodless policy may pierce into the very core of our life, may threaten the whole future of our people with a perpetual helplessness of emasculation, and yet may never touch the chord of humanity on the other side, or touch it in the most inadequately feeble manner. Such wholesale and universal acts of fearful responsibility man can never perform, with such a degree of systematic unawareness, where he is an individual human being. These only become possible where the man is represented by an octopus of abstractions, sending out its wriggling arms in all directions of space, and fixing its innumerable suckers even into the far-away future. In this reign of the nation, the governed are pursued by suspicions; and these are the suspicions of a tremendous mass of organised brain and muscle. Punishments are meted out which leave a trail of miseries across a large bleeding tract of the human heart, but these punishments are dealt by a mere abstract force in which a whole population of a distant country has lost its human personality.

I have not come here, however, to discuss the question as it affects my own country, but as it affects the future of all humanity. It is not a question of the British government, but of government by the Nation—the Nation which is the organised self-interest of a whole people, where it is least human and least spiritual. Our only intimate experience of the Nation is with the British Nation, and as far as the government by the Nation goes there are reasons to believe that it is one of the best. Then, again, we have to consider that the West is necessary to the East. We are complementary to each other because of our different outlooks upon life which have given us different aspects of truth. Therefore if it be true that the spirit of the West has come upon our fields in the guise of a storm it is nevertheless scattering living seeds that are immortal. And when in India we become able to assimilate in our life what is permanent in western civilisation we shall be in a position to bring about a reconciliation of these two great worlds. Then will come to an end the one-sided dominance which is galling. What is more, we have to recognise that the history of India does not belong to one particular race but to a process of creation to which various races of the world contributed—the Dravidians and the Aryans, the ancient Greeks and the Persians, the Mohammedans of the West and those of central Asia. Now at last has come the turn of the English to become true to this history and bring to it the tribute of their life, and we neither have the right nor the power to exclude this people from the building of the destiny of India. Therefore what I say about the Nation has more to do with the history of Man than specially with that of India.

This history has come to a stage when the moral man, the complete man, is more and more giving way, almost without knowing it, to make room for the political and the commercial man, the man of the limited purpose. This process, aided by the wonderful progress in science, is assuming gigantic proportion and power, causing the upset of man's moral balance, obscuring his human side under the shadow of soulless organisation. We have felt its iron grip at the root of our life, and for the sake of humanity we must stand up and give warning to all, that this nationalism is a cruel epidemic of evil that is sweeping over the human world of the present age and eating into its moral vitality.

I have a deep love and a great respect for the British race as human beings. It has produced great-hearted men, thinkers of great thoughts, doers of great deeds. It has given rise to a great literature. I know that these people love justice and freedom, and hate lies. They are clean in their minds, frank in their manners, true in their friendships; in their behaviour they are honest and reliable. The personal experience which I have had of their literary men has roused my admiration not merely for their power of thought or expression but for their chivalrous humanity. We have felt the greatness of this people as we feel the sun; but as for the Nation, it is for us a thick mist of a stifling nature covering the sun itself.

This government by the Nation is neither British nor anything else; it is an applied science and therefore more or less similar in its principles wherever it is used. It is like a hydraulic press, whose pressure is impersonal, and on that account completely effective. The amount of its power may vary in different engines. Some may even be driven by hand, thus leaving a margin of comfortable looseness in their tension, but in spirit and in method their differences are small. Our government might have been Dutch, or French, or Portuguese, and its essential features would have remained much the same as they are now. Only perhaps, in some cases, the organisation might not have been so densely perfect, and therefore some shreds of the human might still have been clinging to the wreck, allowing us to deal with something which resembles our own throbbing heart.

Before the Nation came to rule over us we had other governments which were foreign, and these, like all governments, had some element of the machine in them. But the difference between them and the government by the Nation is like the difference between the hand-loom and the power-loom. In the products of the hand-loom the magic of man's living fingers finds its expression, and its hum harmonises with the music of life. But the power-loom is relentlessly lifeless and accurate and monotonous in its production.

We must admit that during the personal government of former days there have been instances of tyranny, injustice, and extortion. They caused sufferings and unrest from which we are glad to be rescued. The protection of law is not only a boon, but it is a valuable lesson to us. It is teaching us the discipline which is necessary for the stability of civilisation and for continuity of progress. We are realising through it that there is a universal standard of justice to which all men, irrespective of their caste and colour, have their equal claim.

This reign of law in our present government in India has established order in this vast land inhabited by peoples different in their races and customs. It has made it possible for these peoples to come in closer touch with one another and cultivate a communion of aspiration.

But this desire for a common bond of comradeship among the different races of India has been the work of the spirit of the West, not that of the Nation of the West. Wherever in Asia the people have received the true lesson of the West it is in spite of the western Nation. Only because Japan had been able to resist the dominance of this western Nation could she acquire the benefit of western civilisation in fullest measure. Though China has been poisoned at the very spring of her moral and physical life by this Nation, her struggle to receive the best lessons of the West may yet be successful if not hindered by the Nation. It was only the other day that Persia woke up from her age-long sleep at the call of the West to be instantly trampled into stillness by the Nation. The same phenomenon prevails in this country also, where the people are hospitable, but the Nation has proved itself to be otherwise, making an Eastern guest feel humiliated to stand before you as a member of the humanity of his own motherland.

In India we are suffering from this conflict between the spirit of the West and the Nation of the West. The benefit of western civilisation is doled out to us in a miserly measure by the Nation, which tries to regulate the degree of nutrition as near the zero-point of vitality as possible. The portion of education allotted to us is so raggedly insufficient that it ought to outrage the sense of decency of western humanity. We have seen in these countries how the people are encouraged and trained and given every facility to fit themselves for the great movements of commerce and industry spreading over the world, while in India the only assistance we get is merely to be jeered at by the Nation for lagging behind. While depriving us of our opportunities and reducing our education to the minimum required for conducting a foreign government, this Nation pacifies its conscience by calling us names, by sedulously giving currency to the arrogant cynicism that the East is east and the West is west and never the twain shall meet. If we must believe our schoolmaster in his taunt that, after nearly two centuries of his tutelage, India not only remains unfit for self-government but unable to display originality in her intellectual attainments, must we ascribe it to something in the nature of western culture and our inherent incapacity to receive it or to the judicious niggardliness of the Nation that has taken upon itself the white man's burden of civilising the East? That Japanese people have some qualities which we lack we may admit, but that our intellect is naturally unproductive compared to theirs we cannot accept even from them whom it is dangerous for us to contradict.

The truth is that the spirit of conflict and conquest is at the origin and in the centre of western nationalism; its basis is not social co-operation. It has evolved a perfect organisation of power, but not spiritual idealism. It is like the pack of predatory creatures that must have its victims. With all its heart it cannot bear to see its hunting-grounds converted into cultivated fields. In fact, these nations are fighting among themselves for the extension of their victims and their reserve forests. Therefore the western Nation acts like a dam to check the free flow of western civilisation into the country of the No-Nation. Because this civilisation is the civilisation of power, therefore it is exclusive; it is naturally unwilling to open its sources of power to those whom it has selected for its purposes of exploitation.

But all the same, moral law is the law of humanity, and the exclusive civilisation which thrives upon others who are barred from its benefit carries its own death-sentence in its moral limitations. The slavery that it gives rise to unconsciously drains its own love of freedom dry. The helplessness with which it weighs down its world of victims exerts its force of gravitation every moment upon the power that creates it. And the greater part of the world which is being denuded of its self-sustaining life by the Nation will one day become the most terrible of all its burdens, ready to drag it down into the bottom of destruction. Whenever the Power removes all checks from its path to make its career easy, it triumphantly rides into its ultimate crash of death. Its moral brake becomes slacker every day without its knowing it, and its slippery path of ease becomes its path of doom.

Of all things in western civilisation, those which this western Nation has given us in a most generous measure are law and order. While the small feeding-bottle of our education is nearly dry, and sanitation sucks its own thumb in despair, the military organisation, the magisterial offices, the police, the Criminal Investigation Department, the secret spy system, attain to an abnormal girth in their waists, occupying every inch of our country. This is to maintain order. But is not this order merely a negative good? Is it not for giving people's life greater opportunities for the freedom of development? Its perfection is the perfection of an egg-shell, whose true value lies in the security it affords to the chick and its nourishment and not in the convenience it offers to the person at the breakfast table. Mere administration is unproductive; it is not creative, not being a living thing. It is a steam-roller, formidable in its weight and power, having its uses, but it does not help the soil to become fertile. When after its enormous toil it comes to offer us its boon of peace we can but murmur under our breath that 'peace is good, but not more so than life, which is God's own great boon'.

On the other hand, our former governments were woefully lacking in many of the advantages of the modern government. But because those were not the governments by the Nation, their texture was loosely woven, leaving big gaps through which our own life sent its threads and imposed its designs. I am quite sure in those days we had things that were extremely distasteful to us. But we know that when we walk barefooted upon ground strewn with gravel, our feet come gradually to adjust themselves to the caprices of the inhospitable earth; while if the tiniest particle of gravel finds its lodgement inside our shoes we can never forget and forgive its intrusion. And these shoes are the government by the Nation—it is tight, it regulates our steps with a closed-up system, within which our feet have only the slightest liberty to make their own adjustments. Therefore, when you produce your statistics to compare the number of gravels which our feet had to encounter in former days with the paucity in the present regime, they hardly touch the real point. It is not a question of the number of outside obstacles but the comparative powerlessness of the individual to cope with them. This narrowness of freedom is an evil which is more radical, not because of its quantity but because of its nature. And we cannot but acknowledge this paradox: that while the spirit of the West marches under its banner of freedom, the Nation of the West forges its iron chains of organisation which are the most relentless and unbreakable that have ever been manufactured in the whole history of man.

When the humanity of India was not under the government of the Organisation, the elasticity of change was great enough to encourage men of power and spirit to feel that they had their destinies in their own hands. The hope of the unexpected was never absent, and a freer play of imagination, on the part of both the governor and the governed, had its effect in the making of history. We were not confronted with a future, which was a dead white wall of granite blocks eternally guarding against the expression and extension of our own powers, the hopelessness of which lies in the reason that these powers are becoming atrophied at their very roots by the scientific process of paralysis. For every single individual in the country of the No-Nation is completely in the grip of a whole nation, whose tireless vigilance, being the vigilance of a machine, has not the human power to overlook or to discriminate. At the least pressing of its button the monster organisation becomes all eyes, whose ugly stare of inquisitiveness cannot be avoided by a single person amongst the immense multitude of the ruled. At the least turn of its screw, by the fraction of an inch, the grip is tightened to the point of suffocation around every man, woman and child of a vast population, for whom no escape is imaginable in their own country or even in any country outside their own.

It is the continual and stupendous dead pressure of the inhuman upon the living human under which the modern world is groaning. Not merely the subject races, but you who live under the delusion that you are free, are every day sacrificing your freedom and humanity to this fetish of nationalism, living in the dense poisonous atmosphere of world-wide suspicion and greed and panic.

I have seen in Japan the voluntary submission of the whole people to the trimming of their minds and clipping of their freedom by their government, which through various educational agencies regulates their thoughts, manufactures their feelings, becomes suspiciously watchful when they show signs of inclining towards the spiritual, leading them through a narrow path not towards what is true but what is necessary for the complete welding of them into one uniform mass according to its own recipe. The people accept this all-pervading mental slavery with cheerfulness and pride because of their nervous desire to turn themselves into a machine of power, called the Nation, and emulate other machines in their collective worldliness.

When questioned as to the wisdom of its course, the newly converted fanatic of nationalism answers that 'so long as nations are rampant in this world we have not the option freely to develop our higher humanity. We must utilise every faculty that we possess to resist the evil by assuming it ourselves in the fullest degree. For the only brotherhood possible in the modern world is the brotherhood of hooliganism.' The recognition of the fraternal bond of love between Japan and Russia, which has lately been celebrated with an immense display of rejoicing in Japan, was not owing to any sudden recrudescence of the spirit of Christianity or of Buddhism, but it was a bond established according to the modern faith in a surer relationship of mutual menace of bloodshedding. Yes, one cannot but acknowledge that these facts are the facts of the world of the Nation, and the only moral of it is that all the peoples of the earth should strain their physical, moral and intellectual resources to the utmost to defeat one another in the wrestling match of powerfulness. In ancient days Sparta paid all her attention to becoming powerful;

she did become so by crippling her humanity, and died of the amputation.

But it is no consolation to us to know that the weakening of humanity from which the present age is suffering is not limited to the subject races, and that its ravages are even more radical because insidious and voluntary in peoples who are hypnotised into believing that they are free. This bartering of your higher aspirations of life for profit and power has been your own free choice, and I leave you there, at the wreckage of your soul, contemplating your protuberant prosperity. But will you never be called to answer for organising the instincts of self-aggrandisement of whole peoples into perfection and calling it good? I ask you: what disaster has there ever been in the history of man, in its darkest period, like this terrible disaster of the Nation fixing its fangs deep into the naked flesh of the world, taking permanent precautions against its natural relaxation?

You, the people of the West, who have manufactured this abnormality, can you imagine the desolating despair of this haunted world of suffering man possessed by the ghastly abstraction of the organising man? Can you put yourself into the position of the peoples, who seem to have been doomed to an eternal damnation of their own humanity, who not only must suffer continual curtailment of their manhood, but even raise their voices in paeans of praise for the benignity of a mechanical apparatus in its interminable parody of providence?

Have you not seen, since the commencement of the existence of the Nation, that the dread of it has been the one goblin-dread with which the whole world has been trembling? Wherever there is a dark corner, there is the suspicion of its secret malevolence; and people live in a perpetual distrust of their back where they have no eyes. Every sound of a footstep, every rustle of movement in the neighbourhood, sends a thrill of terror all around. And this terror is the parent of all that is base in man's nature. It makes one almost openly unashamed of inhumanity. Clever lies become matters of self-congratulation. Solemn pledges become a farce—laughable for their very solemnity. The Nation, with all its paraphernalia of power and prosperity, its flags and pious hymns, its blasphemous prayers in the churches, and the literary mock thunders of its patriotic bragging, cannot hide the fact that the Nation is the greatest evil for the Nation, that all its precautions are against it, and any new birth of its fellow in the world is always followed in its mind by the dread of a new peril. Its one wish is to trade on the feebleness of the rest of the world, like some insects that are bred in the paralysed flesh of victims kept just enough alive to make them toothsome and nutritious. Therefore it is ready to send its poisonous fluid into the vitals of the other living peoples who, not being nations, are harmless. For this the Nation has had and still has its richest pasture in Asia. Great China, rich with her ancient wisdom and social ethics, her discipline of industry and self-control, is like a whale awakening the lust of spoil in the heart of the Nation. She is already carrying in her quivering flesh harpoons sent by the unerring aim of the Nation, the creature of science and selfishness. Her pitiful attempt to shake off her traditions of humanity, her social ideals, and spend her last exhausted resources in drilling herself into modern efficiency, is thwarted at every step by the Nation. It is tightening its financial ropes round her, trying to drag her up on the shore and cut her into pieces, and then go and offer public thanksgiving to God for supporting the one existing evil and shattering the possibility of a new one. And for all this the Nation has been claiming the gratitude of history and all eternity for its exploitation, ordering its band of praise to be struck up from end to end of the world, declaring itself to be the salt of the earth, the flower of humanity, the blessing of God hurled with all His force upon the naked skulls of the world of No-Nations.

I know what your advice will be. You will say: form yourselves into a nation, and resist this encroachment of the Nation. But is this the true advice, that of a man to a man? Why should this be a necessity? I could well believe you if you had said: be more good, more just, more true in your relation to man; control your greed, make your life wholesome in its simplicity and let your consciousness of the divine in humanity be more perfect in its expression. But must you say that it is not the soul, but the machine, which is of the utmost value to ourselves, and that man's salvation depends upon his disciplining himself into a perfection of the dead rhythm of wheels and counterwheels, that machine must be pitted against machine, and nation against nation, in an endless bullfight of politics?

You say: these machines will come into an agreement for their mutual protection, based upon a conspiracy of fear. But will this federation of steam-boilers supply you with a soul, a soul which has her conscience and her God? What is to happen to that larger part of the world where fear will have no hand in restraining you? Whatever safety they now enjoy, those countries of No-Nation, from the unbridled licence of forge and hammer and turn-screw, results from the mutual jealousy of the powers. But when, instead of being numerous separate machines they become riveted into one organised gregariousness of gluttony, commercial and political, what remotest chance of hope will remain for those others, who have lived and suffered, have loved and worshipped, have thought deeply and worked with meekness, but whose only crime has been that they have not organised?

But, you say, 'That does not matter, the unfit must go to the wall—they shall die, and this is science.'

No, for the sake of your own salvation, I say, they shall *live*, and this is truth. It is extremely bold of me to say so, but I assert that man's world is a moral world, not because we blindly agree to believe it, but because it is so in truth which would be dangerous for us to ignore. And this moral nature of man cannot be divided into convenient compartments for its preservation. You cannot secure it for your home consumption with protective tariff walls, while in foreign parts making it enormously accommodating in its free trade of licence.

Has not this truth already come home to you now, when this cruel war has driven its claws into the vitals of Europe, when her hoard of wealth is bursting into smoke and her humanity is shattered into bits on her battlefields? You ask in amazement: what has she done to deserve this? The answer is that the West has been systematically petrifying her moral nature in order to lay a solid foundation for her gigantic abstractions of efficiency. She has all along been starving the life of the personal man into that of the professional.

In your mediaeval age in Europe, the simple and the natural man, with all his violent passions and desires, was engaged in trying to find out a reconciliation in the conflict between the flesh and the spirit. All through the turbulent career of her vigorous youth the temporal and the spiritual forces both acted strongly upon her nature, and were moulding it into completeness of moral personality. Europe owes all her greatness in humanity to that period of discipline—the discipline of the man in his human integrity.

Then came the age of intellect, of science. We all know that intellect is impersonal. Our life and our heart are one with us, but our mind can be detached from the personal man and then only can it freely move in its world of thoughts. Our intellect is an ascetic who wears no clothes, takes no food, knows no sleep, has no wishes, feels no love or hatred or pity for human limitations, who only reasons unmoved through the vicissitudes of life. It burrows to the roots of things, because it has no personal concern with the thing itself. The grammarian walks straight through all poetry and goes to the root of words without obstruction, because he is seeking not reality, but law. When he finds the law, he is able to teach people how to master words. This is a power—the power which fulfils some special usefulness, some particular need of man.

Reality is the harmony which gives to the component parts of a thing the equilibrium of the whole. You break it, and have in your hands the nomadic atoms fighting against one another, therefore unmeaning. Those who covet power try to get mastery of these aboriginal fighting elements, and through some narrow channels force them into some violent service for some particular needs of man.

This satisfaction of man's needs is a great thing. It gives him freedom in the material world. It confers on him the benefit of a greater range of time and space. He can do things in a shorter time and occupies a larger space with more thoroughness of advantage. Therefore he can easily outstrip those who live in a world of a slower time and of space less fully occupied.

This progress of power attains more and more rapidity of pace. And, for the reason that it is a detached part of man, it soon outruns the complete humanity. The moral man remains behind, because it has to deal with the whole reality, not merely with the law of things, which is impersonal and therefore abstract.

Thus man, with his mental and material power far outgrowing his moral strength, is like an exaggerated giraffe whose head has suddenly shot up miles away from the rest of him, making normal communication difficult to establish. This greedy head, with its huge dental organisation, has been munching all the topmost foliage of the world, but the nourishment is too late in reaching his digestive organs, and his heart is suffering from want of blood. Of this present disharmony in man's nature the West seems to have been blissfully unconscious. The enormity of its material success has diverted all its attention towards self-congratulation on its bulk. The optimism of its logic goes on basing the calculations of its good fortune upon the indefinite prolongation of its railway lines towards eternity. It is superficial enough to think that all tomorrows are merely todays, with the repeated additions of twenty-four hours. It has no fear of the chasm, which is opening wider every day, between man's ever-growing storehouses and the emptiness of his hungry humanity. Logic does not know that, under the lowest bed of endless strata of wealth and comforts, earthquakes are being hatched to restore the balance of the moral world; and one day the gaping gulf of spiritual vacuity will draw into its bottom the store of things that have their eternal love for the dust.

Man in his fulness is not powerful, but perfect. Therefore, to turn him into mere power, you have to curtail his soul as much as possible. When we are fully human, we cannot fly at one another's throats; our instincts of social life, our traditions of moral ideals stand in the way. If you want me to take to butchering human beings, you must break up that wholeness of my humanity through some discipline which makes my will dead, my thoughts numb, my movements automatic, and then from the dissolution of the complex personal man will come out that abstraction, that destructive force, which has no relation to human truth, and therefore can be easily brutal or mechanical. Take away man from his natural surroundings, from the fulness of his communal life, with all its living associations of beauty and love and social obligations, and you will be able to turn him into so many fragments of a machine for the production of wealth on a gigantic scale. Turn a tree into a log and it will burn for you, but it will never bear living flowers and fruit.

This process of dehumanising has been going on in commerce and politics. And out of the long birth-throes of mechanical energy has been born this fully developed apparatus of magnificent power and surprising appetite which has been christened in the West as the Nation. As I have hinted before, because of its quality of abstraction it has, with the greatest ease, gone far ahead of the complete moral man. And having the conscience of a ghost and the callous perfection of an automaton, it is causing disasters with which the volcanic dissipations of the youthful moon would be ashamed to be brought into comparison. As a result, the suspicion of man for man stings all the limbs of this civilisation like the hairs of the nettle. Each country is casting its net of espionage into the slimy bottom of the others, fishing for their secrets, the treacherous secrets which brew in the oozy depths of diplomacy. And what is their secret service but the nation's underground trade in kidnapping, murder and treachery and all the ugly crimes bred in the depth of rottenness? Because each nation has its own history of thieving and lies and broken faith, therefore there can only flourish international suspicion and jealousy, and international moral shame becomes anaemic to a degree of ludicrousness. The nation's bagpipe of righteous indignation has so changed its tune according to the variation of time and to the altered groupings of the alliances of diplomacy, that it can be enjoyed with amusement as the variety performance of the political music hall.

I am just coming from my visit to Japan, where I exhorted this young nation to take its stand upon the higher ideals of humanity and never to follow the West in its acceptance of the organised selfishness of Nationalism as its religion, never to gloat upon the feebleness of its neighbours, never to be unscrupulous in its behaviour to the weak, where it can be gloriously mean with impunity, while turning its right cheek of brighter humanity for the kiss of admiration to those who have the power to deal it a blow. Some of the newspapers praised my utterances for their poetical qualities, while adding with a leer that it was the poetry of a defeated people. I felt they were right. Japan had been taught in a modern school the lesson how to become powerful. The schooling is done and she must enjoy the fruits of her lessons. The West in the voice of her thundering cannon had said at the door of Japan: let there be a nation—and there was a Nation. And now that it has come into existence, why do you not feel in your heart of hearts a pure feeling of gladness and say that it is good? Why is it that I saw in an English paper an expression of bitterness at Japan's boasting of her superiority of civilisation—the thing that the British, along with other nations, have been carrying on for ages without blushing? Because the idealism of selfishness must keep itself drunk with a continual dose of self-laudation. But the same vices which seem so natural and innocuous in its own life make it surprised and angry at their unpleasantness when seen in other nations. Therefore, when you see the Japanese nation, created in your own image, launched in its career of national boastfulness, you shake your head and say, it is not good. Has it not been one of the causes that raise the cry on these shores for preparedness to meet one more power of evil with a greater power of injury? Japan protests that she has her *bushido*, that she can never be treacherous to America to whom she owes her gratitude. But you find it difficult to believe her—for the wisdom of the Nation is not in its faith in humanity but in its complete distrust. You say to yourself that it is not with Japan of the *bushido*, the Japan of the moral ideals, that you have to deal—it is with the abstraction of the popular selfishness, it is with the Nation; and

Nation can only trust Nation where their interests coalesce, or at least do not conflict. In fact your instinct tells you that the advent of another people into the arena of nationality makes another addition to the evil which contradicts all that is highest in Man and proves by its success that unscrupulousness is the way to prosperity—and goodness is good for the weak and God is the only remaining consolation of the defeated.

Yes, this is the logic of the Nation. And it will never heed the voice of truth and goodness. It will go on its ring-dance of moral corruption, linking steel unto steel, and machine unto machine, trampling under its tread all the sweet flowers of simple faith and the living ideals of man.

But we delude ourselves into thinking that humanity in these modern days is more to the front than ever before. The reason for this self-delusion is because man is served with the necessaries of life in greater profusion and his physical ills are being alleviated with more efficacy. But the chief part of this is done, not by moral sacrifice, but by intellectual power. In quantity it is great, but it springs from the surface and spreads over the surface. Knowledge and efficiency are powerful in their outward effect, but they are the servants of man, not the man himself. Their service is like the service in a hotel, where it is elaborate, but the host is absent; it is more convenient than hospitable.

Therefore we must not forget that the scientific organisations vastly spreading in all directions are strengthening our power, but not our humanity. With the growth of power the cult of the self-worship of the Nation grows in ascendancy, and the individual willingly allows the Nation to take donkey-rides upon his back; and there happens the anomaly which must have such disastrous effects, that the individual worships with all sacrifices a god which is morally much inferior to himself. This could never have been possible if the god had been as real as the individual.

Let me give an illustration of this point. In some parts of India it has been enjoined as an act of great piety for a widow to go without food and water on a particular day every fortnight. This often leads to cruelty, unmeaning and inhuman. And yet men are not by nature cruel to such a degree. But this piety being a mere unreal abstraction completely deadens the moral sense of the individual, just as the man who would not hurt an animal unnecessarily would cause horrible suffering to a large number of innocent creatures when he drugs his feelings with the abstract idea of 'sport'! Because these ideas are creations of our intellect, because they are logical classifications, therefore they can so easily hide in their mist the personal man.

And the idea of the Nation is one of the most powerful anaesthetics that man has invented. Under the influence of its fumes the whole people can carry out its systematic programme of the most virulent self-seeking without being in the least aware of its moral perversion—in fact can feel dangerously resentful if it is pointed out.

But can this go on indefinitely, continually producing barrenness of moral insensibility upon a large tract of our living nature? Can it escape its nemesis for ever? Has this giant power of mechanical organisation no limit in this world against which it may shatter itself all the more completely because of its terrible strength and velocity? Do you believe that evil can be permanently kept in check by competition with evil, and that conference of prudence can keep the devil chained in its makeshift cage of mutual agreement?

This European war of Nations is the war of retribution. Man, the person, must protest for his very life against the heaping up of things where there should be the heart, and systems and policies where there should flow living human relationship. The time has come when, for the sake of the whole outraged world, Europe should fully know in her own person the terrible absurdity of the thing called the Nation.

The Nation has thriven long upon mutilated humanity. Men, the fairest creations of God, came out of the National manufactory in huge numbers as war-making and money-making puppets, ludicrously vain of their pitiful perfection of mechanism. Human society grew more and more into a marionette show of politicians, soldiers, manufacturers and bureaucrats, pulled by wire arrangements of wonderful efficiency.

But the apotheosis of selfishness can never make its interminable breed of hatred and greed, fear and hypocrisy, suspicion and tyranny, an end in themselves. These monsters grow into huge shapes but never into harmony. And this Nation may grow on to an unimaginable corpulence, not of a living body, but of steel and steam and office buildings, till its deformity can contain no longer its ugly voluminousness—till it begins to crack and gape, breathe gas and fire in gasps, and its death-rattles sound in cannon roars. In this war the death-throes of the Nation have commenced. Suddenly, all its mechanism going mad, it has begun the dance of the Furies, shattering its own limbs, scattering them into the dust. It is the fifth act of the tragedy of the unreal.

Those who have any faith in Man cannot but fervently hope that the tyranny of the Nation will not be restored to all its former teeth and claws, to its far-reaching iron arms and its immense inner cavity, all stomach and no heart; that man will have his new birth, in the freedom of his individuality, from the enveloping vagueness of abstraction.

The veil has been raised, and in this frightful war the West has stood face to face with her own creation, to which she had offered her soul. She must know what it truly is.

She had never let herself suspect what slow decay and decomposition were secretly going on in her moral nature, which often broke out in doctrines of scepticism, but still oftener and in still more dangerously subtle manner showed itself in her unconsciousness of the mutilation and insult that she had been inflicting upon a vast part of the world. Now she must know the truth nearer home.

And then there will come from her own children those who will break themselves free from the slavery of this illusion, this perversion of brotherhood founded upon self-seeking, those who will own themselves as God's children and as no bond-slaves of machinery, which turns souls into commodities and life into compartments, which, with its iron claws, scratches out the heart of the world and knows not what it has done.

And we of the No-Nations of the world, whose heads have been bowed to the dust, will know that this dust is more sacred than the bricks which build the pride of power. For this dust is fertile of life, and of beauty and worship. We shall thank God that we were made to wait in silence through the night of despair, had to bear the insult of the proud and the strong man's burden, yet all through it, though our hearts quaked with doubt and fear, never could we blindly believe in the salvation which machinery offered to man, but we held fast to our trust in God and the truth of the human soul. And we can still cherish the hope that, when power becomes ashamed to occupy its throne and is ready to make way for love, when the morning comes for cleansing the blood-stained steps of the Nation along the high-road of humanity, we shall be called upon to bring our own vessel of sacred water—the water of worship—to sweeten the history of man into purity, and with its sprinkling make the trampled dust of the centuries blessed with fruitfulness.

Nationalism in India

Our real problem in India is not political. It is social. This is a condition not only prevailing in India, but among all nations. I do not believe in an exclusive political interest. Politics in the West have dominated western ideals, and we in India are trying to imitate you. We have to remember that in Europe, where peoples had their racial unity from the beginning, and where natural resources were insufficient for the inhabitants, the civilisation has naturally taken on the character of political and commercial aggressiveness. For on the one hand they had no internal complications, and on the other they had to deal with neighbours who were strong and rapacious. To have perfect combination among themselves and a watchful attitude of animosity against others was taken as the solution of their problems. In former days they organised and plundered; in the present age the same spirit continues—and they organise and exploit the whole world.

But from the earliest beginnings of history India has had her own problem constantly before her—it is the race problem. Each nation must be conscious of its mission, and we in India must realise that we cut a poor figure when we try to be political, simply because we have not yet been finally able to accomplish what was set before us by our providence.

This problem of race unity which we have been trying to solve for so many years has likewise to be faced by you here in America. Many people in this country ask me what is happening to the caste distinctions in India. But when this question is asked me, it is usually done with a superior air. And I feel tempted to put the same question to our American critics with a slight modification: 'What have you done with the Red Indian and the Negro?' For you have not got over your attitude of caste towards them. You have used violent methods to keep aloof from other races, but until you have solved the question, here in America, you have no right to question India.

In spite of our great difficulty, however, India has done something. She has tried to make an adjustment of races, to acknowledge the real differences between them where these exist, and yet seek for some basis of unity. This basis has come through our saints, like Nanak, Kabir, Chaitanya* and others, preaching one God to all races of India.

In finding the solution of our problem we shall have helped to solve the world problem as well. What India has been, the whole world is now. The whole world is becoming one country through scientific facility. And the moment is arriving when you must also find a basis of unity which is not political. If India can offer to the world her solution, it will be a contribution to humanity. There is only one history—the history of man. All national histories are merely chapters in the larger one. And we are content in India to suffer for such a great cause.

Each individual has his self-love. Therefore his brute instinct leads him to fight with others in the sole pursuit of his self-

---

* Nanak (1469–1533), Kabir (1440–1518), Chaitanya (1485–1533).

interest. But man has also his higher instincts of sympathy and mutual help. The people who are lacking in this higher moral power and who therefore cannot combine in fellowship with one another must perish or live in a state of degradation. Only those peoples have survived and achieved civilisation who have this spirit of co-operation strong in them. So we find that from the beginning of history men had to choose between fighting with one another and combining, between serving their own interest or the common interest of all.

In our early history, when the geographical limits of each country and also the facilities of communication were small, this problem was comparatively small in dimension. It was sufficient for men to develop their sense of unity within their area of segregation. In those days they combined among themselves and fought against others. But it was this moral spirit of combination which was the true basis of their greatness, and this fostered their art, science and religion. At that early time the most important fact that man had to take count of was the fact of the members of one particular race of men coming in close contact with one another. Those who truly grasped this fact through their higher nature made their mark in history.

The most important fact of the present age is that all the different races of men have come close together. And again we are confronted with two alternatives. The problem is whether the different groups of peoples shall go on fighting with one another or find out some true basis of reconciliation and mutual help; whether it will be interminable competition or co-operation.

I have no hesitation in saying that those who are gifted with the moral power of love and vision of spiritual unity, who have the least feeling of enmity against aliens, and the sympathetic insight to place themselves in the position of others, will be the fittest to take their permanent place in the age that is lying before us, and those who are constantly developing their instincts for fight and intolerance of aliens will be eliminated. For this is the problem before us, and we have to prove our humanity by solving it through the help of our higher nature. The gigantic organisations for hurting others and warding off their blows, for making money by dragging others back, will not help us. On the contrary, by their crushing weight, their enormous cost and their deadening effect upon living humanity, they will seriously impede our freedom in the larger life of a higher civilisation.

During the evolution of the Nation the moral culture of brotherhood was limited by geographical boundaries, because at that time those boundaries were true. Now they have become imaginary lines of tradition divested of the qualities of real obstacles. So the time has come when man's moral nature must deal with this great fact with all seriousness or perish. The first impulse of this change of circumstance has been the churning up of man's baser passions of greed and cruel hatred. If this persists indefinitely, and armaments go on exaggerating themselves to unimaginable absurdities, and machines and storehouses envelop this fair earth with their dirt and smoke and ugliness, then it will end in a conflagration of suicide. Therefore man will have to exert all his power of love and clarity of vision to make another great moral adjustment which will comprehend the whole world of men and not merely the fractional groups of nationality. The call has come to every individual in the present age to prepare himself and his surroundings for this dawn of a new era, when man shall discover his soul in the spiritual unity of all human beings.

If it is given at all to the West to struggle out of these tangles of the lower slopes to the spiritual summit of humanity then I cannot but think that it is the special mission of America to fulfil this hope of God and man. You are the country of expectation, desiring something else than what is. Europe has her subtle habits of mind and her conventions. But America, as yet, has come to no conclusions. I realise how much America is untrammelled by the traditions of the past, and I can appreciate that experimentalism is a sign of America's youth. The foundation of her glory is in the future, rather than in the past, and if one is gifted with the power of clairvoyance, one will be able to love the America that is to be.

America is destined to justify western civilisation to the East. Europe has lost faith in humanity, and has become distrustful and sickly. America, on the other hand, is not pessimistic or blasé. You know, as a people, that there is such a thing as a better and a best, and that knowledge drives you on. There are habits that are not merely passive but aggressively arrogant. They are not like mere walls, but are like hedges of stinging nettles. Europe has been cultivating these hedges of habits for long years, till they have grown round her dense and strong and high. The pride of her traditions has sent its roots deep into her heart. I do not wish to contend that it is unreasonable. But pride in every form breeds blindness at the end. Like all artificial stimulants its first effect is a heightening of consciousness, and then with the increasing dosage it muddles it and brings an exultation that is misleading. Europe has gradually grown hardened in her pride in all her outer and inner habits. She not only cannot forget that she is western, but she takes every opportunity to hurl this fact against others to humiliate them. This is why she is growing incapable of imparting to the East what is best in herself, and of accepting in a right spirit the wisdom that the East has stored for centuries.

In America national habits and traditions have not had time to spread their clutching roots round your hearts. You have constantly felt and complained of your disadvantages when you compared your nomadic restlessness with the settled traditions of Europe—the Europe which can show her picture of greatness to the best advantage because she can fix it against the background of the past. But in this present age of transition, when a new era of civilisation is sending its trumpet-call to all peoples of the world across an unlimited future, this very freedom of detachment will enable you to accept its invitation and to achieve the goal for which Europe began her journey but lost herself mid-way. For she was tempted out of her path by her pride of power and greed of possession.

Not merely your freedom from habits of mind in individuals, but also the freedom of your history from all unclean entanglements, fits you in your career of holding the banner of civilisation of the future. All the great nations of Europe have their victims in other parts of the world. This not only deadens their moral sympathy but also their intellectual sympathy, which is so necessary for the understanding of races which are different from one's own. Englishmen can never truly understand India, because their minds are not disinterested with regard to that country. If you compare England with Germany or France you will find she has produced the smallest number of scholars who have studied Indian literature and philosophy with any amount of sympathetic insight or thoroughness. This attitude of apathy and contempt is natural where the relationship is abnormal and founded upon national selfishness and pride. But your history has been disinterested, and that is why you have been able to help Japan in her lessons in western civilisation, and that is why China can look upon you with the best confidence in this, her darkest period of danger. In fact you are carrying all the responsibility of a great future because you are untrammelled by the grasping miserliness of a past. Therefore, of all countries of the earth, America has to be fully conscious of this future; her vision must not be obscured and her faith in humanity must be strong with the strength of youth.

A parallelism exists between America and India—the parallelism of welding together into one body various races.

In my country we have been seeking to find out something common to all races, which will prove their real unity. No nation looking for a mere political or commercial basis of unity will find such a solution sufficient. Men of thought and power will discover the spiritual unity, will realise it, and preach it.

India has never had a real sense of nationalism. Even though from childhood I had been taught that idolatry of the Nation is almost better than reverence for God and humanity, I believe I have outgrown that teaching, and it is my conviction that my countrymen will truly gain their India by fighting against the education which teaches them that a country is greater than the ideals of humanity.

The educated Indian at present is trying to absorb some lessons from history contrary to the lessons of our ancestors. The East, in fact, is attempting to take unto itself a history, which is not the outcome of its own living. Japan, for example, thinks she is getting powerful through adopting western methods but, after she has exhausted her inheritance, only the borrowed weapons of civilisation will remain to her. She will not have developed herself from within.

Europe has her past. Europe's strength therefore lies in her history. We in India must make up our minds that we cannot borrow other people's history, and that if we stifle our own we are committing suicide. When you borrow things that do not belong to your life, they only serve to crush your life.

And therefore I believe that it does India no good to compete with western civilisation in its own field. But we shall be more than compensated if, in spite of the insults heaped upon us, we follow our own destiny.

There are lessons which impart information or train our minds for intellectual pursuits. These are simple and can be acquired and used with advantage. But there are others which affect our deeper nature and change our direction of life. Before we accept them and pay their value by selling our own inheritance, we must pause and think deeply. In man's history there come ages of fireworks which dazzle us by their force and movement. They laugh not only at our modest household lamps but also at the eternal stars. But let us not for that provocation be precipitate in our desire to dismiss our lamps. Let us patiently bear our present insult and realise that these fireworks have splendour but not permanence, because of the extreme explosiveness which is the cause of their power, and also of their exhaustion. They are spending a fatal quantity of energy and substance compared to their gain and production.

Anyhow, our ideals have been evolved through our own history, and even if we wished we could only make poor fireworks of them because their materials are different from yours, as is also their moral purpose. If we cherish the desire of paying our all to buy a political nationality it will be as absurd as if Switzerland had staked her existence on her ambition to build up a navy powerful enough to compete with that of England. The mistake that we make is in thinking that man's channel of greatness is only one—the one which has made itself painfully evident for the time being by its depth of insolence.

We must know for certain that there is a future before us and that future is waiting for those who are rich in moral ideals and not in mere things. And it is the privilege of man to work for fruits that are beyond his immediate reach, and to adjust his life not in slavish conformity to the examples of some present success or even to his own prudent past, limited in its aspiration, but to an infinite future bearing in its heart the ideals of our highest expectations.

We must recognise that it is providential that the West has come to India. And yet someone must show the East to the West, and convince the West that the East has her contribution to make to the history of civilisation. India is no beggar of the West. And yet even though the West may think she is, I am not for thrusting off western civilisation and becoming segregated in our independence. Let us have a deep association. If Providence wants England to be the channel of that communication, of that deeper association, I am willing to accept it with all humility. I have great faith in human nature, and I think the West will find its true mission. I speak bitterly of western civilisation when I am conscious that it is betraying its trust and thwarting its own purpose. The West must not make herself a curse to the world by using her power for her own selfish needs but, by teaching the ignorant and helping the weak, she should save herself from the worst danger that the strong is liable to incur by making the feeble acquire power enough to resist her intrusion. And also she must not make her materialism to be the final thing, but must realise that she is doing a service in freeing the spiritual being from the tyranny of matter.

I am not against one nation in particular, but against the general idea of all nations. What is the Nation?

It is the aspect of a whole people as an organised power. This organisation incessantly keeps up the insistence of the population on becoming strong and efficient. But this strenuous effort after strength and efficiency drains man's energy from his higher nature where he is self-sacrificing and creative. For thereby man's power of sacrifice is diverted from his ultimate object, which is moral, to the maintenance of this organisation, which is mechanical. Yet in this he feels all the satisfaction of moral exaltation and therefore becomes supremely dangerous to humanity. He feels relieved of the urging of his conscience when he can transfer his responsibility to this machine which is the creation of his intellect and not of his complete moral personality. By this device the people which loves freedom perpetuates slavery in a large portion of the world with the comfortable feeling of pride in having done its duty; men who are naturally just can be cruelly unjust both in their act and their thought, accompanied by a feeling that they are helping the world to receive its deserts; men who are honest can blindly go on robbing others of their human rights for self-aggrandisement, all the while abusing the deprived for not deserving better treatment. We have seen in our everyday life even small organisations of business and profession produce callousness of feeling in men who are not naturally bad, and we can well imagine what a moral havoc it is causing in a world where whole peoples are furiously organising themselves for gaining wealth and power.

Nationalism is a great menace. It is the particular thing which for years has been at the bottom of India's troubles. And inasmuch as we have been ruled and dominated by a nation that is strictly political in its attitude, we have tried to develop within ourselves, despite our inheritance from the past, a belief in our eventual political destiny.

There are different parties in India, with different ideals. Some are struggling for political independence. Others think that the time has not arrived for that, and yet believe that India should have the rights that the English colonies have. They wish to gain autonomy as far as possible.

In the beginning of the history of political agitation in India there was not the conflict between parties which there is today. At that time there was a party known as the Indian Congress;* they

---

* The Indian National Congress was founded in 1885.

had no real programme. They had a few grievances for redress by the authorities. They wanted larger representation in the Council House, and more freedom in Municipal Government. They wanted scraps of things, but they had no constructive ideal. Therefore I was lacking in enthusiasm for their methods. It was my conviction that what India most needed was constructive work coming from within herself. In this work we must take all risks and go on doing the duties which by right are ours, though in the teeth of persecution, winning moral victory at every step, by our failure and suffering. We must show those who are over us that we have in ourselves the strength of moral power, the power to suffer for truth. Where we have nothing to show, we have only to beg. It would be mischievous if the gifts we wish for were granted to us at once, and I have told my countrymen, time and again, to combine for the work of creating opportunities to give vent to our spirit of self-sacrifice, and not for the purpose of begging.

The party, however, lost power because the people soon came to realise how futile was the half policy adopted by them. The party split,* and there arrived the Extremists, who advocated independence of action, and discarded the begging method—the easiest method of relieving one's mind from his responsibility towards his country. Their ideals were based on western history. They had no sympathy with the special problems of India. They did not recognise the patent fact that there were causes in our social organisation which made the Indian incapable of coping with the alien. What should we do if, for any reason, England was driven away? We should simply be victims for other nations. The same social weaknesses would prevail. The thing we in

---

* In 1907, at the annual session of the Indian National Congress, held at Surat.

India have to think of is this: to remove those social customs and ideals which have generated a want of self-respect and a complete dependence on those above us—a state of affairs which has been brought about entirely by the domination in India of the caste system, and the blind and lazy habit of relying upon the authority of traditions that are incongruous anachronisms in the present age.

Once again I draw your attention to the difficulties India has had to encounter and her struggle to overcome them. Her problem was the problem of the world in miniature. India is too vast in its area and too diverse in its races. It is many countries packed in one geographical receptacle. It is just the opposite of what Europe truly is; namely, one country made into many. Thus Europe in its culture and growth has had the advantage of the strength of the many as well as the strength of the one. India, on the contrary, being naturally many, yet adventitiously one, has all along suffered from the looseness of its diversity and the feebleness of its unity. A true unity is like a round globe; it rolls on, carrying its burden easily. But diversity is a many-cornered thing which has to be dragged and pushed with all force. Be it said to the credit of India that this diversity was not her own creation; she has had to accept it as a fact from the beginning of her history. In America and Australia, Europe has simplified her problem by almost exterminating the original population. Even in the present age this spirit of extermination is making itself manifest, in the inhospitable shutting out of aliens, by those who themselves were aliens in the lands they now occupy. But India tolerated difference of races from the first, and that spirit of toleration has acted all through her history.

Her caste system is the outcome of this spirit of toleration. For India has all along been trying experiments in evolving a social unity within which all the different peoples could be held together, while fully enjoying the freedom of maintaining their own differences. The tie has been as loose as possible, yet as close as the circumstances permitted. This has produced something like a United States of a social federation, whose common name is Hinduism.

India had felt that diversity of races there must be and should be, whatever may be its drawbacks, and you can never coerce nature into your narrow limits of convenience without paying one day very dearly for it. In this India was right; but what she failed to realise was that in human beings differences are not like the physical barriers of mountains, fixed for ever—they are fluid with life's flow, they are changing their courses and their shapes and volumes.

Therefore in her caste regulations India recognised differences, but not the mutability which is the law of life. In trying to avoid collisions she set up boundaries of immovable walls, thus giving to her numerous races the negative benefit of peace and order but not the positive opportunity of expansion and movement. She accepted nature where it produces diversity, but ignored it where it uses that diversity for its world-game of infinite permutations and combinations. She treated life in all truth where it is manifold, but insulted it where it is ever moving. Therefore Life departed from her social system and in its place she is worshipping with all ceremony the magnificent cage of countless compartments that she has manufactured.

The same thing happened where she tried to ward off the collisions of trade interests. She associated different trades and professions with different castes. This had the effect of allaying for good the interminable jealousy and hatred of competition— the competition which breeds cruelty and makes the atmosphere thick with lies and deception. In this also India laid all her emphasis upon the law of heredity, ignoring the law of mutation, and thus gradually reduced arts into crafts and genius into skill.

However, what western observers fail to discern is that in her caste system India in all seriousness accepted her responsibility to solve the race problem in such a manner as to avoid all friction, and yet to afford each race freedom within its boundaries. Let us admit India has not in this achieved a full measure of success. But this you must also concede: that the West, being more favourably situated as to homogeneity of races, has never given her attention to this problem, and whenever confronted with it she has tried to make it easy by ignoring it altogether. And this is the source of her anti-Asiatic agitations for depriving aliens of their right to earn their honest living on these shores. In most of your colonies you only admit them on condition of their accepting the menial positions of hewers of wood and drawers of water. Either you shut your doors against the aliens or reduce them into slavery. And this is your solution to the problem of race-conflict. Whatever may be its merits you will have to admit that it does not spring from the higher impulses of civilisation, but from the lower passions of greed and hatred. You say this is human nature—and India also thought she knew human nature when she strongly barricaded her race distinctions by the fixed barriers of social gradations. But we have found out to our cost that human nature is not what it seems, but what it is in truth, which is in its infinite possibilities. And when we in our blindness insult humanity for its ragged appearance it sheds its disguise to disclose to us that we have insulted our God. The degradation which we cast upon others in our pride or self-interest degrades our own humanity—and this is the punishment which is most terrible, because we do not detect it till it is too late.

Not only in your relation with aliens but with the different sections of your own society you have not achieved harmony of reconciliation. The spirit of conflict and competition is allowed the full freedom of its reckless career. And because its genesis is the greed of wealth and power it can never come to any other end but to a violent death. In India the production of commodities was brought under the law of social adjustments. Its basis was co-operation, having for its object the perfect satisfaction of social needs. But in the West it is guided by the impulse of competition, whose end is the gain of wealth for individuals. But the individual is like the geometrical line; it is length without breadth. It has not got the depth to be able to hold anything permanently. Therefore its greed or gain can never come to finality. In its lengthening process of growth it can cross other lines and cause entanglements, but will ever go on missing the ideal of completeness in its thinness of isolation.

In all our physical appetites we recognise a limit. We know that to exceed that limit is to exceed the limit of health. But has this lust for wealth and power no bounds beyond which is death's dominion? In these national carnivals of materialism are not the western peoples spending most of their vital energy in merely producing things and neglecting the creation of ideals? And can a civilisation ignore the law of moral health and go on in its endless process of inflation by gorging upon material things? Man in his social ideals naturally tries to regulate his appetites, subordinating them to the higher purpose of his nature. But in the economic world our appetites follow no other restrictions but those of supply and demand which can be artificially fostered, affording individuals opportunities for indulgence in an endless feast of grossness. In India our social instincts imposed restrictions upon our appetites—maybe it went to the extreme of repression—but in the West the spirit of economic organisation with no moral purpose goads the people into the perpetual pursuit of wealth; but has this no wholesome limit?

The ideals that strive to take form in social institutions have two objects. One is to regulate our passions and appetites for the harmonious development of man, and the other is to help him to cultivate disinterested love for his fellow-creatures. Therefore society is the expression of those moral and spiritual aspirations of man which belong to his higher nature.

Our food is creative, it builds our body; but not so wine, which stimulates. Our social ideals create the human world, but when our mind is diverted from them to greed of power then in that state of intoxication we live in a world of abnormality where our strength is not health and our liberty is not freedom. Therefore political freedom does not give us freedom when our mind is not free. An automobile does not create freedom of movement, because it is a mere machine. When I myself am free I can use the automobile for the purpose of my freedom.

We must never forget in the present day that those people who have got their political freedom are not necessarily free; they are merely powerful. The passions which are unbridled in them are creating huge organisations of slavery in the disguise of freedom. Those who have made the gain of money their highest end are unconsciously selling their life and soul to rich persons or to the combinations that represent money. Those who are enamoured of their political power and gloat over their extension of dominion over foreign races gradually surrender their own freedom and humanity to the organisations necessary for holding other peoples in slavery. In the so-called free countries the majority of the people are not free; they are driven by the minority to a goal which is not even known to them. This becomes possible only because people do not acknowledge moral and spiritual freedom as their object. They create huge eddies with their passions, and they feel dizzily inebriated with the mere velocity of their whirling movement, taking that to be freedom.

But the doom which is waiting to overtake them is as certain as death—for man's truth is moral truth and his emancipation is in the spiritual life.

The general opinion of the majority of the present-day nationalists in India is that we have come to a final completeness in our social and spiritual ideals, the task of the constructive work of society having been done several thousand years before we were born, and that now we are free to employ all our activities in the political direction. We never dream of blaming our social inadequacy as the origin of our present helplessness, for we have accepted as the creed of our nationalism that this social system has been perfected for all time to come by our ancestors, who had the superhuman vision of all eternity and supernatural power for making infinite provision for future ages. Therefore, for all our miseries and shortcomings, we hold responsible the historical surprises that burst upon us from outside. This is the reason why we think that our one task is to build a political miracle of freedom upon the quicksand of social slavery. In fact we want to dam up the true course of our own historical stream, and only borrow power from the sources of other peoples' history.

Those of us in India who have come under the delusion that mere political freedom will make us free have accepted their lessons from the West as the gospel truth and lost their faith in humanity. We must remember that whatever weakness we cherish in our society will become the source of danger in politics. The same inertia which leads us to our idolatry of dead forms in social institutions will create in our politics prison-houses with immovable walls. The narrowness of sympathy which makes it possible for us to impose upon a considerable portion of humanity the galling yoke of inferiority will assert itself in our politics in creating the tyranny of injustice.

When our nationalists talk about ideals they forget that the basis of nationalism is wanting. The very people who are upholding these ideals are themselves the most conservative in their social practice. Nationalists say, for example: look at Switzerland where, in spite of race differences, the people have solidified into a nation. Yet, remember that in Switzerland the races can mingle, they can intermarry, because they are of the same blood. In India there is no common birthright. And when we talk of western nationality we forget that the nations there do not have that physical repulsion, one for the other, that we have between different castes. Have we an instance in the whole world where a people who are not allowed to mingle their blood shed their blood for one another except by coercion or for mercenary purposes? And can we ever hope that these moral barriers against our race amalgamation will not stand in the way of our political unity?

Then again we must give full recognition to this fact that our social restrictions are still tyrannical, so much so as to make men cowards. If a man tells me that he has heterodox ideas, but that he cannot follow them because he would be socially ostracised, I excuse him for having to live a life of untruth, in order to live at all. The social habit of mind which impels us to make the life of our fellow-beings a burden to them where they differ from us even in such a thing as their choice of food, is sure to persist in our political organisation and result in creating engines of coercion to crush every rational difference which is the sign of life. And tyranny will only add to the inevitable lies and hypocrisy in our political life. Is the mere name of freedom so valuable that we should be willing to sacrifice for its sake our moral freedom?

The intemperance of our habits does not immediately show its effects when we are in the vigour of our youth. But it gradually consumes that vigour, and when the period of decline sets in then we have to settle accounts and pay off our debts, which leads us to insolvency. In the West you are still able to carry your head high, though your humanity is suffering every moment from its dipsomania of organising power. India also in the heyday of her youth could carry in her vital organs the dead weight of her social organisations stiffened to rigid perfection, but it has been fatal to her, and has produced a gradual paralysis of her living nature. And this is the reason why the educated community of India has become insensible of her social needs. They are taking the very immobility of our social structures as the sign of their perfection—and because the healthy feeling of pain is dead in the limbs of our social organism they delude themselves into thinking that it needs no ministration. Therefore they think that all their energies need their only scope in the political field. It is like a man whose legs have become shrivelled and useless, trying to delude himself that these limbs have grown still because they have attained their ultimate salvation, and all that is wrong about him is the shortness of his sticks.

So much for the social and the political regeneration of India. Now we come to her industries, and I am very often asked whether there is in India any industrial regeneration since the advent of the British government. It must be remembered that at the beginning of the British rule in India our industries were suppressed, and since then we have not met with any real help or encouragement to enable us to make a stand against the monster commercial organisations of the world. The nations have decreed that we must remain purely an agricultural people, even forgetting the use of arms for all time to come. Thus India is being turned into so many predigested morsels of food ready to be swallowed at any moment by any nation which has even the most rudimentary set of teeth in its head.

India therefore has very little outlet for her industrial originality. I personally do not believe in the unwieldy organisations of the present day. The very fact that they are ugly shows that they are in discordance with the whole creation. The vast powers of nature do not reveal their truth in hideousness, but in beauty. Beauty is the signature which the Creator stamps upon His works when He is satisfied with them. All our products that insolently ignore the laws of perfection and are unashamed in their display of ungainliness bear the perpetual weight of God's displeasure. So far as your commerce lacks the dignity of grace it is untrue. Beauty and her twin brother Truth require leisure and self-control for their growth. But the greed of gain has no time or limit to its capaciousness. Its one object is to produce and consume. It has pity neither for beautiful nature nor for living human beings. It is ruthlessly ready without a moment's hesitation to crush beauty and life out of them, moulding them into money. It is this ugly vulgarity of commerce which brought upon it the censure of contempt in our earlier days, when men had leisure to have an unclouded vision of perfection in humanity. Men in those times were rightly ashamed of the instinct of mere money-making. But in this scientific age money, by its very abnormal bulk, has won its throne. And when from its eminence of piled-up things it insults the higher instincts of man, banishing beauty and noble sentiments from its surroundings, we submit. For we in our meanness have accepted bribes from its hands and our imagination has grovelled in the dust before its immensity of flesh.

But its very unwieldiness and its endless complexities are its true signs of failure. The swimmer who is an expert does not exhibit his muscular force by violent movements, but exhibits some power which is invisible and which shows itself in perfect grace and reposefulness. The true distinction of man from animals is in his power and worth which are inner and invisible. But the present-day commercial civilisation of man is not only taking too much time and space but killing time and space. Its movements are violent; its noise is discordantly loud. It is carrying its own damnation because it is trampling into distortion the humanity upon which it stands. It is strenuously turning out money at the cost of happiness. Man is reducing himself to his minimum in order to be able to make amplest room for his organisations. He is deriding his human sentiments into shame because they are apt to stand in the way of his machines.

In our mythology we have the legend that the man who performs penances for attaining immortality has to meet with temptations sent by Indra, the Lord of the Immortals. If he is lured by them he is lost. The West has been striving for centuries after its goal of immortality. Indra has sent her the temptation to try her. It is the gorgeous temptation of wealth. She has accepted it, and her civilisation of humanity has lost its path in the wilderness of machinery.

This commercialism with its barbarity of ugly decorations is a terrible menace to all humanity, because it is setting up the ideal of power over that of perfection. It is making the cult of self-seeking exult in its naked shamelessness. Our nerves are more delicate than our muscles. Things that are the most precious in us are helpless as babes when we take away from them the careful protection which they claim from us for their very preciousness. Therefore, when the callous rudeness of power runs amuck in the broadway of humanity it scares away by its grossness the ideals which we have cherished with the martyrdom of centuries.

The temptation which is fatal for the strong is still more so for the weak. And I do not welcome it in our Indian life, even though it be sent by the Lord of the Immortals. Let our life be simple in its outer aspect and rich in its inner gain. Let our civilisation take its firm stand upon its basis of social co-operation and not upon that of economic exploitation and conflict. How to do it in the teeth of the drainage of our lifeblood by the economic dragons is the task set before the thinkers of all oriental nations who have faith in the human soul. It is a sign of laziness and impotency to accept conditions imposed upon us by others who have other ideals than ours. We should actively try to adapt the world powers to guide our history to its own perfect end.

From the above you will know that I am not an economist. I am willing to acknowledge that there is a law of demand and supply and an infatuation of man for more things than are good for him. And yet I will persist in believing that there is such a thing as the harmony of completeness in humanity, where poverty does not take away his riches, where defeat may lead him to victory, death to immortality, and where in the compensation of Eternal Justice those who are the last may yet have their insult transmuted into a golden triumph.

Home and the World

Bimala

Oh Mother, today I remember the sindoor on your forehead, the red-bordered sari you used to wear, and your eyes—calm, serene and deep. They touched my heart like the first rays of the sun. My life started out with that golden gift. What happened after that? Did the dark clouds come charging like brigands? Did they destroy the gift of light? And yet, that touch of the chaste dawn at the most important moment of one's life may perhaps be clouded by disaster, but it can never be erased completely.

In our land, only the fair-skinned are considered beautiful. But the sky that radiates light is dark. My mother was dark-skinned; her glow came from her inner goodness. Her virtue could put the vanity of beauty to shame. They all said I looked like my mother. As a child, this was my quibble with the mirror. I felt my entire being had been wronged—the colour of my skin was not my own, it was someone else's, a mistake from start to finish.

I was not beautiful. But I prayed to God with all my heart that, like my mother, I would be blessed with the gift of chastity. At the time of my marriage, the astrologer from my in-laws' came to read my palm and said, 'This girl has all the signs of good fortune and she will make a virtuous wife.' All the women said, 'Well, naturally. After all, isn't Bimala the spitting image of her mother?'

I married into an aristocratic family. Their title could be traced back to the days of the Mughals. I had heard fairy tales as a child and created the image of a prince in my mind. An aristocratic prince: his body would be like chameli petals; his face would be shaped as a result of the long and fervent prayers that a young maiden offered to Lord Shiva. Those eyes, that nose! His slim, newly emerged moustache would be as dark and delicate as the wings of a bumblebee.

When I saw my husband, he didn't exactly match this description. Even his skin, I noticed, was just as dark as mine. It did take away some of my regret about my own lack of beauty, but a sigh escaped my lips as well. I could have lived with remorse for my own looks, if only I could have one glimpse of the prince of my dreams!

But perhaps it is best when beauty slips past the sentry of the eyes and secretly shows up in the heart. There, on the banks that are lapped with the swelling waves of reverence, beauty can come unadorned. In my childhood, I have seen how the glow of bhakti turns everything beautiful. Even as a child I felt the caress in my mother's gracious, nurturing hands and the love from my mother's heart that poured out and plunged into a sublime ocean of beauty when she carefully peeled the fruits for my father and arranged his meal on a white marble plate, when she kept aside the paan for him, wrapped in fine cloth sprinkled with keora water, and as she gently fanned him and kept the flies off his plate when he sat down to eat.

Didn't the same strain of reverence run in me? It did. No debate, no deliberations over good or bad—it was just an inexorable strain! An entire lifetime spent playing it like a hymn in praise of the Lord Almighty in a corner of His temple—if that made sense, then that strain of melody heard in the early hours of my life had begun its work.

I remember, when I woke up at dawn and, very cautiously, touched my husband's feet, the sindoor on my forehead seemed to shine brighter than ever. One day he woke up, laughed and asked, 'What's this, Bimal, what are you doing!' I was so embarrassed. Perhaps he felt that I sought his blessings furtively. But no, oh no, it wasn't for the blessings—it was the woman's heart, where love itself seeks to worship.

The family I married into was very orthodox. Here, some rules were as old as the Mughals and some were even older, set by Manu and Parashar. But my husband was very modern in his outlook. He was the first in his family to be highly educated; he had earned an MA. Both his elder brothers died young from intemperance, they had no children. My husband did not drink and he was solemn by nature; this was unusual in this family and not everyone appreciated it. They thought such purity only suited those who were not blessed by the goddess of wealth. Only the expanses of the moon could contain blemishes with ease.

My husband's parents had died a while ago. The household was run by his grandmother. My husband was the jewel in her crown, the apple of her eye. This was the reason he dared to transgress the bounds of conformity. So, when he appointed Miss Gilby as my companion and tutor, tongues started wagging at home and outside, and yet, my husband's will won in the end.

At that time he had completed his BA and was studying for his MA. He had to stay in Calcutta for his classes in college. He wrote me a letter nearly every day. They were short and simple. That rounded, distinct writing from his hand stared back at me serenely.

I stored his letters in a sandalwood box. Every morning I picked some flowers from the garden and covered the box with them. By then my prince of the fairy tales had vanished like the moon on a sunny morning. The true prince of my heart had gained his rightful place. I was his princess and my place was beside him; but it was a greater joy to take my place at his feet.

I am educated. I am acquainted with this day and age in today's language. The words I speak now sound inordinately poetic even to my own ears. If I had never known today's world, I would have found my thoughts and feelings of those bygone days quite commonplace—I'd have thought, just as my being a woman was a fact, it's equally natural that a woman would turn her love into devotion. I wouldn't waste a moment's thought on whether there was any extraordinary kind of poetic beauty in this sentiment or not.

But from those days of my childhood to this day of my youth, I seem to have traversed an entire age. Thoughts, once as natural as breath, have to be constructed as poetic craft. The impassioned poets of today sing loud praises about the incredible beauty in a wife's chastity and a widow's celibacy. It is evident that truth and beauty have parted ways at this juncture of life. So then, can Truth be salvaged only under the guise of beauty?

All women don't think the same way. But this I know for certain—I have that element of my mother in me, the urge to revere. Today, when it is no longer considered natural by society, it is clear to me that it is an innate quality in me.

But woe for my Fate, my husband didn't wish to give me an opportunity to revere him. That was his generosity of spirit: at the holy place, the greedy priest grapples to get worshipped because he doesn't deserve it rightfully. In this world, only the weak demand reverence from their wives as their due. It shames both the worshipper and the worshipped.

But why this abundance of luxury for my benefit? It was as if his affection overflowed and flooded my banks, with maids and material things and creature comforts. How was I to push through all this and find a gap to offer myself up to him? I needed ways to offer more than to take. Love is, after all, reclusive by nature. It will blossom profusely and carelessly on the dust by the roadside. But it can't bloom in all its glory, trapped in a ceramic pot in a sitting room.

My husband couldn't violate all the orthodox rules and customary regulations of the inner chambers of the house. It wasn't possible for me to meet him freely in the mornings or at any odd hour of the day. I knew exactly when he would come in; so we would never meet casually, for no rhyme or reason. Our meeting was like a poem: it came with its own meter and its own rhythm. After the day's work, I freshened up, tied my hair carefully, dotted my forehead with sindoor, wore a freshly creased sari, collected my scattered mind and body from all its domestic concerns and offered myself on a golden tray at a special time to a special person. The time was little, but in itself it was boundless.

My husband always claimed that men and women have equal rights over one another and hence their love is also on an equal footing. I have never argued with him on this. But my heart says that devotion doesn't stop people from being equals. It tries to equalize people by elevating them. Hence, the pleasure of becoming equal is ever-present in it and it never turns into a thing of indifference. On the tray of love, devotion is like the light of the lamp in the ritual of worship—it falls the same way upon the worshipper and the worshipped. Today I know for sure that a woman's love is sanctified only through her own veneration—or else it's worth nothing. When the lamp of our love glows, the flame rises upwards and only the burnt-up oil remains at the bottom.

Dearest, it is your greatness that you refused my invocation, but it would have been best if you'd accepted it. You have loved me by adorning me, by educating me, by granting me what my heart desired and even what it did not desire, your love did not take time out to blink and I have seen the stolen sighs you have spent over your love for me. You have loved my body as if it was a parijata flower from the heavens, my soul you have loved as if it was your good fortune. This makes me proud; I feel that it is the wealth of *my* attributes that have thus drawn you to me. It makes me feel like the rightful occupant of the queen's throne—I sit here and demand homage. The demands increase constantly and can never be met. 'I have the power to conquer a man'—does this thought alone bring joy to a woman or for that matter, is it even good for her? Her salvation lies in the act of setting adrift such thoughts on the currents of reverence. Shiva came to Annapurna in a beggar's guise; but if she hadn't done penance for him, would she have succeeded in thus enduring his empyrean powers?

I can remember how many people used to burn in the slow fire of envy at my good fortune. It was something that warranted envy all right—I came by it as a bonus, without deserving it. But luck doesn't last long. One has to pay the price or Fate does not put up with it. The price of good fortune has to be paid over years, every day and only then can ownership claims be staked. God is quite capable of granting it to us, but we have to receive it on our own merit. Sometimes we are not blessed enough to live with what has been bestowed upon us.

Many a girl's father sighed at my good fortune. It was the talk of many households all over town: how I didn't deserve to be married into this family, since I have no great beauty or qualities to boast of. My grandmother-in-law and mother-in-law were known for their extraordinary beauty. My sisters-in-law were also confirmed beauties. Gradually, when misfortune befell both of them, my grandmother-in-law vowed that she wouldn't look for a beautiful girl for her youngest and favourite grandson. I was able to enter this house solely on the merits of the 'good omens' in my charts.

In this house, amidst such profusion of wealth, very few wives had received the true status and respect that was due to them. But apparently that was the rule; hence, even when all the tears of their life sank beneath the froth of liquor and the tinkle of the courtesans' anklets, they still clung to the pride of being a daughter-in-law of this aristocratic household and managed to keep their heads afloat. Yet, my husband never touched liquor and did not go around depleting his humane qualities seeking female flesh at the doorsteps of the houses of sin; was this, in any way, to my credit? Did Fate gift me with any special charms to control the restless, wild spirits of a man? No, it was pure good fortune and nothing else. In the case of my sisters-in-law, was Fate suddenly so ruthless that every word in store for them turned into warped expressions? Long before nightfall, all the lamps of their joyous lives were extinguished and the flames of their youth continued to burn in vain, through the night in empty ballrooms. No music—just pain.

Both my sisters-in-law pretended that they didn't think much of my husband's masculinity. To think that he steered this great vessel of life solely with the help of the lone sail of his wife's anchal! I have had to bear so many jibes from them, off and on, as if I had stolen my husband's affections, as if I was full of artifice and pretence—the insolent, modern, fashionable woman. My husband dressed me up in contemporary fashions and they would burn in envy when they saw those colourful jackets, saris, blouses, petticoats and all the other accessories. 'Such elaborate adorning when there isn't even any beauty to speak of! It is shameful how you have gone and decked your body up like it's a novelty shop!'

My husband was well aware of all this. But his heart brimmed over with sympathy for women. He would always advise me, 'Don't be upset.' I remember, once I had said to him, 'Women's minds are very crooked, very narrow.' He had replied, 'Just like the feet of Chinese women which are crooked and narrow. The entire society has squashed our women's minds from all sides and made them narrow and crooked. Fate gambles with their lives—their lives depend on the turn of the dice; do they have any powers of their own?'

My sisters-in-law always got whatever they demanded from their brother-in-law. He never stopped to think whether their demands were valid. I fumed silently when I noticed that they didn't feel a shred of gratitude. So much so, that my eldest sister-in-law—who spouted piety so freely with her holier-than-thou chants, pujas, vows and fasts, that there wasn't even an ounce left for her soul—would often quote her brother, a lawyer, that if she were to take her case to the court then my husband . . . oh, it was a lot of rubbish that she'd say! I promised my husband that under no circumstances would I ever retort to anything that either of them said. Hence my misery lay heavier on my shoulders. I felt there was a limit to forbearance and if that limit was crossed it almost made one less of a man. But he said, 'The law or society has not supported my sisters-in-law; it was a great humiliation for them to have to beg and ask for what they once knew to be rightfully theirs, by virtue of their husbands' legacy. To add to that one shouldn't ask for gratitude—how can one get kicked around and also have to shell out a tip for it?' Shall I be honest with you? I often felt that my husband ought to have been more audacious, enough for him to be a little less compassionate.

My second sister-in-law was of a different kind. She was younger and didn't have any saintly pretences. On the contrary, her comments and gestures often carried lewd suggestions. The comings and goings of the young maids she'd hired were questionable to say the least. Nobody, however, raised eyebrows as these things were supposedly customary in this house. I knew that my sister-in-law hated the fact that I was fortunate enough to have a husband who didn't have a vice. Hence, she would find several ways to waylay her brother-in-law. I am ashamed to admit that, even with a husband such as mine, I sometimes felt the slightest twinge of fear. The very air in this place was murky and even the clearest objects appeared distorted. On some days, my second sister-in-law would cook and invite her brother-in-law affectionately. I often wished desperately that he would make some excuse and refuse the invitation. She was wrong to try to trap him, and why should this wrong go unpunished? But instead, when he smiled and accepted the invitation each and every time, a niggling doubt troubled me—it was entirely my fault, but feelings wouldn't heed reason—I felt this indicated the inherent flightiness in men. At these times, however busy I was otherwise, I would find an excuse to go and sit in my sister-in-law's room. She would laugh and exclaim to my husband, 'My goodness, Chhotorani won't let you out of her sight at all—she's the strictest of guards. I must say, even in our heyday, we had never learnt how to guard so carefully.'

My husband could only see their misery and never the flaws. Once I said, 'Fine, let's assume that the fault lies entirely with society; but why do they deserve so much pity? It's all right for people to deal with a little misfortune sometimes.' But he was impossible. Instead of arguing, he just smiled a little. Perhaps he knew about the occasional pangs of doubt I suffered. The main object of my anger was neither society nor anyone else, it was just that—oh well, I won't go into that.

One day he sat me down and explained, 'All these criticisms that they direct at you—if they really thought that you were so blameworthy, would it upset them so much?'

'Then why this unfair resentment?'

'I don't know if you can call it unfair. There is a grain of truth embedded in envy; it is this: whatever brings happiness should ideally be received by every individual.'

'Then one should quarrel with one's Fate, not take it out on me.'

'But Fate isn't close at hand.'

'So then they can just go ahead and take whatever they want—you would never deprive them. Let them wear sari-jacket-jewellery-socks and shoes; if they want a memsahib to tutor them, she comes here already, and even if they want to remarry, you have the resources to be able to cross every barrier just like Vidyasagar did.'

'That is precisely the problem—it isn't always possible to hand them whatever their heart desires.'

'Is that any reason to go on playing such coy games, as if whatever one hasn't got is actually a bad thing so that when someone else gets it, one burns up in envy?'

'When someone is deprived, this is the only way they know to conquer their deprivation—it is their only consolation.'

'I don't care what you say—women are very coy. They never admit the truth and resort to many pretences.'

'That only proves how very deprived they are.'

When he brushed aside every little spiteful barb from the women of this household, I used to get very angry. There was no point discussing what society could have or may have been; but it was impossible to feel sorry for these thorns strewn on the way, the cruel jibes and the artifice.

When he heard this, he said, 'So you have enough sympathy for yourself when your own feelings are bruised, and you have none to spare for those whose lives have been ripped to shreds by the cruel arrows of society? Should the loser be made to pay a fine for losing?'

Oh well! I was narrow-minded. Except me, everyone of course was good. A little miffed, I said, 'You don't even know half of it, since you don't stay indoors—' I tried to divulge some specific information about the other part of the house, but he abruptly got up saying, 'Chandranathbabu has been waiting for me for a while now.'

I sat and wept. How could I bear to look so wretched in my husband's eyes? There was no way I could prove to him that if I had been faced with misfortune, I would never have behaved in this manner.

Sometimes I feel that if God grants women a chance to be vain about beauty, they are spared from vanity of other kinds. One could be vain about jewels and baubles, of course; but in a rich household that would be meaningless. I placed my conceit in my chastity. I knew that even my husband would have to bow before it. But every time I spoke to him about some domestic matters, I ended up looking so petty that it tore me up inside. Hence, I wanted to make him look small in turn. I said to myself, 'I'll not let your words make you look good; it is mere naivety. It's not altruism, you are being taken advantage of by others.'

My husband had a great wish that I'd step outside the inner chambers. One day I said to him, 'I don't need the world outside.'

He said, 'The world outside may be in need of you.'

'If it has survived for so long without me, it can continue to do so; it won't die of sorrow.'

'Let it die, I am not bothered. My concerns are for myself.'

'Really? And what are you worried about?'

My husband smiled and didn't reply. I knew his ways and so I said, 'No, you can't fool me by keeping quiet. You must finish your sentence.'

He said, 'Can one sentence be enough to finish the thought? There are so many thoughts that take a lifetime to finish.'

'Please stop your word-games and tell me.'

'I would like you to be mine in the world out there. We need to settle our accounts in that space.'

'Why, what's wrong with our perceptions here, in this room?'

'Over here, your eyes, ears and mouth have been wrapped in me; you don't know who you want and who you've got.'

'I know very well, dearest, I really do.'

'You think you know, but you don't even know if you really do.'

'I just hate it when you talk like this.'

'Which is why I didn't want to bring it up.'

'Your silence is even more unbearable.'

'That is why I wish that I won't have to speak or keep quiet; you should just come out there and comprehend everything by yourself. Neither you nor I were made to play the game of life within this domestic chicanery. Our love will be true only if we really know each other in the midst of truth.'

'Maybe you are yet to know me wholly, but my understanding of you is complete.'

'Fair enough. Then why don't you do it just to complete my understanding?'

We had many different versions of this conversation. He'd say, the glutton who loves the fish curry would cut up the fish, stew it and cook it to his taste, but the man who truly appreciated the fish wouldn't really want to capture it in a bowl—he'd rather try to master it in the water itself, or he'd wait on land. When he returned home, he'd be happy that although he didn't get what he wanted, at least he didn't cut it up and destroy it for his own pleasure. It's best to get all of something and if that is not possible, then it's best to lose it in its entirety.

I never really liked these discussions, but that wasn't the reason why I stayed indoors at the time. My grandmother-in-law was alive then. My husband had gone against her wishes and recast nearly four-fifths of the household by twentieth-century standards, and she had accepted it. If a daughter-in-law of this aristocratic household renounced her purdah and chose to come out, she'd have accepted that too. She knew for a fact that this was bound to happen one day. But I felt, it wasn't so important that she should have to undergo the pain of it. I have read in books that we are all birds in a cage; I could not speak for others, but my cage was so full that I wouldn't find such fullness out there amidst the world. At least that is how I felt at the time.

The primary reason my grandmother-in-law loved me so much was because she thought that I had been able to hold my husband's love solely by the powers of my own qualities or the strengths of my astrological stars. She felt it was the inherent nature of a man to sink into decadence. None of her other granddaughters-in-law, with all their beauty and youth, had been able to lure her grandsons; they were destroyed by the flames of sin and no one could save them. She firmly believed that I was the one who had finally doused those flames singeing the men in this family. So she was very protective of me; my slightest ailment made her tremble with fear. She didn't really like the clothes which my husband bought from foreign stores and dressed me in. But she felt that men were bound to have some such idiosyncrasies that were quite silly and a mere waste. There was no way of restraining them, but it was important to see that it didn't lead them to total destruction. If my Nikhilesh didn't deck up his wife, he'd have done the same to another woman. So, every time a new dress arrived for me, she called my husband and riled and teased him merrily. Gradually her taste changed too. Thanks to this unholy age of modernism, a day came when her evenings would be incomplete unless her granddaughter-in-law read her stories from English books.

After her death, my husband wanted us to go and settle in Calcutta. But I just didn't feel right about it. The family roots were here—our grandmother-in-law had borne so much misery and yet held on to this home for so many years and if I just dropped everything and left, her sighs wouldn't let me rest. This thought haunted me continually—her empty seat stared me in the face. That pious woman came into this house at the age of eight and she died when she was seventy-nine. She didn't have a happy life. Fate had repeatedly shot arrows at her, but each misfortune had only made her stronger. This large household was a memento built on the piety of her tears. How could I leave this and go into the muck of Calcutta?

My husband felt that this was a chance to hand over the charges of this house to my sisters-in-law; that would make them happy and our life would be able to take its own course, in its own space, in Calcutta. But that is what I didn't want to accept. Were they to be rewarded for torturing me all these years and for envying my husband's good fortune and character? Besides, the 'royal' house was right here. All our subjects, our employees, the luckless relatives, the guests, were all strewn around, clinging to this homestead. I did not know who we were in Calcutta where no one knew us. The complete image of our status, power and wealth lay right here. Should I just hand over all this to them and go into exile, like Sita? Only to have them mock me in my absence? Did they know the value of this magnanimity that my husband wanted to show or did they even deserve it? Later when I'd have to return here someday, would I get back my rightful seat? My husband said, 'Why do you need that seat? Life has other things to offer.'

I said to myself, 'Men really don't understand these things very well. They don't know how significant the positions in the inner-chambers are since they live and breathe the air outside. Here they should abide by the advice of women.'

I thought it was most important for one to have some firmness in one's character. It would be a defeat if we went away, handing over everything to those who have only wished us ill. Although my husband was ready to do that, I wasn't. In my heart of hearts, I felt I was speaking from the righteousness of my chastity.

Why didn't my husband force me to leave? I know why. It was because he had the power to do so, that he didn't use it. He has always said to me, 'I wouldn't accept it if you were to always agree with whatever I said and had to put up with every whim of mine. I'd rather wait—if you and I come to a consensus, it'll be great. If not, there's nothing to be done.'

But there is something called firmness of character and that day I'd felt that perhaps on that score I was—no, I can't even utter those words today.

It would be impossible to close the gap between night and day if one were to start doing it slowly, over a period of time. But when the sun rises, night disappears—the lengthy reckoning is resolved in a moment. All at once, the age of swadeshi came upon Bengal; but no one knew how it arrived suddenly. It was as if the passage of time between the age of swadeshi and the one before it just didn't exist. Perhaps that was the reason why the new age swept away all our fears and worries in the blink of an eye, like a deluge. There was no time to consider what had happened and what the future had in store.

When the groom and his party are at the door, with the music playing and the lights glowing, the women of the village stream up to the terrace, scarcely caring to cover their face. Just so, when the music played, signalling the arrival of the groom of the entire country, how could the women stay busy with their household chores? Ululating and blowing on the conch, they peeped out from the door or window nearest to them.

In that moment my sight and mind, hopes and wishes, were coloured by the tempestuous new age. On that day, although the mind didn't break free of the bonds of wishes, desires and pious thoughts within which it had settled itself happily, the world that it had known till then, it did peer over it all and it heard the clarion call from far away; the meaning of that call wasn't clear, but the heart lurched dangerously.

During his college days, my husband was interested in manufacturing all that the land needed within the land itself. There were many date trees in the area and he spent several days trying to figure out how to collect the extract from all the trees at the same spot with the help of a single pipe and boil it to produce sugar. I have heard that a very effective way was indeed discovered, but it required so much more money to be spent than what could be earned, that the business soon folded up. The kinds of crops he reaped from the farmlands, through various experiments, were quite remarkable, but the money that he spent in the process was even more astonishing. He felt that the reason no large-scale industries can be sustained in our country was because there were no banks. At that time he began to teach me political economy. There was no harm in that. But he felt it was imperative to inculcate the habit and the desire to save money in banks among our people. So he started a small bank. The urge to save money in the bank was strong among the villagers because the rate of interest was very high. But for the precise reason for which the people's interest grew, the bank slipped through the high interest chasm and disappeared. His old clerks grew very upset over these eccentricities and his enemies made fun of him. One day my elder sister-in-law saw to it that I was within earshot when she exclaimed that her cousin brother, a renowned lawyer, had told her that if one pleaded the case before a judge, it may still be possible to salvage some of the reputation and wealth of this distinguished family from the hands of a lunatic.

Of all the people in this family, only my grandmother-in-law was unperturbed by all this. She called me and chided me often, saying, 'Why do you all plague him like this? Are you concerned about the fortune? In my days, I have seen this estate go into the hands of the receiver all of three times. Men are not like women. They are restless and they only know how to squander. Granddaughter-in-law, you are lucky that he isn't frittering himself away along with it. Since you have never been hurt that way, you seldom remember that.'

The list of my husband's charities was endless. If someone tried to install a loom or a rice-husking machine or something along those lines he helped him till the project was obviously a failure. He floated a swadeshi company to compete with the British ships that journeyed to Puri. Not a single ship sailed from that, but several company documents were drowned in the process.

I used to be most upset when Sandipbabu extracted money from him, giving some excuse about the country's work. Sandipbabu wanted to run a newspaper, or spread the word about swadeshi, or said that the doctor has advised him to spend a few days in Ootacamund on health grounds—and my husband casually shouldered the cost. Besides, he received a certain amount every month to meet his regular expenses. But the strangest thing was that my husband didn't even agree with him on most principles or ideologies. My husband felt that it was a kind of destitution if one failed to mine the existing resources in one's land properly and in the same way, if we couldn't discover and realize the essential richness in the heart of our land, it was the greatest shame of all. One day I was a little irked and said to him, 'You are being cheated by all these people.' He laughed and said, 'I have no qualities to speak of and yet, just by throwing away some money, I am acquiring some greatness—I am the one who's gaining something treacherously.' The moment the air of the new age brushed past me, I told my husband to burn all the foreign clothes I owned.

He said, 'Why should you burn it? Instead, stop using them for as long as you wish.'

'How can you say "as long as I wish"; never in my entire life—'

'Fine, don't wear them ever again. Why should you make a display of burning them?'

'Why are you stopping me from doing this?'

'I feel you should devote all your energy to building something instead of wasting even a quarter of it in the excitement of destroying something.'

'But this excitement helps you build something.'

'So you would claim the only way to light up one's home is by setting it on fire? I am ready to go to great lengths to light a lamp, but I don't want to set my house on fire just to get the job done quickly. That only *looks* like exuberance, but in reality it is a weak compromise.' He went on, 'Listen, I can see that my words seem futile to you today, but I suggest you consider them. Just as a mother decks each of her daughters with her own jewels, the

day has come when the earth is adorning each of its countries
with her own jewellery. Today all our needs are linked to those
of the whole world. I believe that this connection is a sign of good
fortune for every nation and there is no greatness in rebutting
that.'

Then there was another problem. When Miss Gilby first
came into the house, there was a furore for some days. Gradually
everyone became accustomed to her and there was no further
talk about it. But now all those debates surfaced again. I had quite
forgotten whether she was a Bengali or British, but the thought
crossed my mind again at this time. I said to my husband that
she'd have to go. He was silent. That day I spoke to him harshly
and he walked away, despondent. I cried my heart out. At night
when I was a little more collected after my crying bout, he said,
'I can't look at Miss Gilby in a bad light simply because she is
British. So many years of familiarity should be able to break
through the barriers of names. She happens to care for you.'

I was a little ashamed and yet, with a shade of my earlier
tantrum I said, 'Fine then, let her be. Who wants her to leave?'

Miss Gilby continued to come. One day as she walked to
church, a young boy who was a distant relation of ours, hurled a
stone at her and insulted her. Until then the boy had lived in my
husband's care; after this incident he was promptly thrown out.
This caused quite a commotion. People believed whatever that
boy went out and said to them. They began to say it was Miss
Gilby who had insulted the boy and made up the tale. I too felt
that wasn't entirely improbable. The boy didn't have a mother
and his uncle pleaded with me. I tried very hard on his behalf,
but it was of no avail.

That day, no one could pardon my husband's decision, not
even I. In my heart of hearts I criticized him. This time Miss
Gilby herself quit. She had tears in her eyes when she left, but

I didn't feel a thing. I felt for the boy: poor child, how she had ruined his life. And what a splendid boy! His enthusiasm for swadeshi had robbed him of hunger and sleep.

My husband personally escorted Miss Gilby to the station in his own car. I thought this was taking things a bit too far. I felt he deserved the censure when this incident was blown up and recounted in the local newspaper, which called him all sorts of names.

Until that day, I had suffered many anxieties on account of my husband, but never did I feel ashamed of him. That day I did. I didn't know what crime Naren had committed against Miss Gilby, but in this day and age it was shameful that one could be righteously just and be punished for it. I had no desire to smother those feelings, which made Naren act so rudely towards a British woman. When my husband refused to agree with me on this, I took it as a lack of boldness in his nature. And that made me feel shame. Moreover, what hurt me most was the fact that I had to concede defeat. My resolute nature only served to make me miserable and it couldn't raise my husband from ignominy—it was a humiliation of the power of my chastity.

Yet, it was not that my husband had no interest in matters of swadeshi or that he was opposed to it. But he could never wholly accept the absolute superiority of the 'Vande Mataram' mantra. He said, 'I am willing to serve my country; but the One whom I'll invoke is far above it. If I pray to my country, it will be disastrous for her.'

At this juncture, Sandipbabu arrived at our place with his entourage, to spread the swadeshi message. A meeting was to be held in our temple courtyard that evening. We women waited on one side of the hall, behind the woven screen. As the roars of 'Vande Mataram' drew closer, my heart began to tremble.

Suddenly a stream of young men and boys, barefoot, dressed in saffron with turbans on their heads, burst into our immense front yard like the tawny flood of the first monsoon rains along a dry river bed. The place was thronged with people. Cutting through the throng a group of ten or twelve boys held aloft a large stool, on which Sandipbabu was seated, and bore him into the yard on their shoulders. 'Vande Mataram!' 'Vande Mataram!' 'Vande Mataram!' It felt as though the sky would shatter and fall around us in tiny bits.

I had once seen a photograph of Sandipbabu. I can't say I'd really liked his looks then. He wasn't unattractive, in fact quite the opposite. Yet I had somehow felt that although his appearance was bright, it was compounded with much dross: there was something about his eyes and mouth that were not quite genuine. So, when my husband met every one of his demands without so much as a question, I wasn't pleased. I could've put up with the monetary loss, but I felt that as a friend this man was cheating my husband. He scarcely had the air of a hermit or a poor man—he looked quite the babu. Obviously, he liked his creature comforts, and yet—many such thoughts had clamoured in my mind. Today they are stirring again: but let them be.

Yet, on that day when Sandipbabu was making his speech and the heart of that huge gathering swayed and swelled, overflowing its banks, threatening to sweep everything away, I witnessed the compelling aura of the man! At a certain point, when the declining sun peeped below the rooftops and brushed his brow with its golden fingers, it felt as though a god had declared him, before all the men and women present there, to be one of the immortals. Every word of his speech, from beginning to end, seemed to carry the gust of a storm. His boldness knew no limits. The slight obstruction of the screen seemed unbearable to me. I don't remember when, quite unaware of my action, I parted the screen a little, thrust out my face and gazed steadily at him. Not a single person in that assembly had the time to spare me a glance. But at one point, I noticed that Sandipbabu's eyes, bright as Orion in the sky, settled on my face. I was past caring. At that moment I was no longer the daughter-in-law of this aristocratic household: I was the sole representative of all the women in Bengal and he was its hero. The sunbeams from the sky poured down upon his brow: it was no less needful to anoint him from the nation's womanly heart. How else could his expedition be truly propitious?

I sensed very clearly that after he looked at my face, his words took on a new fire. It was as if the divine chariot could no longer be reined in—it was like thunderbolt upon thunderbolt, lightning flash upon lightning flash. My heart said it was the flames in my heart that lit this fire; we aren't merely Lakshmi, we are also Bharati, the goddess of speech.

I returned to my room that day, full of joy and self-exaltation. A storm raging deep inside me dragged me from one state of mind to another in an instant. Like the brave women of Greece, I felt an urge to cut off my knee-length hair and hand it to that gallant warrior for his bowstring. If the ornaments on my body had any link with my heart, my necklace, torque and armlets would have dropped upon that meeting like shooting stars. I needed to do something self-destructive to be able to bear the ecstasy I felt.

When my husband returned that evening, I dreaded that he might say something about the day's speech to strike a false note amidst the blazing symphony or disagree in the slightest over something that offended his sense of integrity. Had he done so, I was quite capable of treating him with open contempt that day.

But he didn't say a word to me. That didn't please me either. He should have said, 'Sandip's words have opened my eyes today:

they have cleared my old misconceptions on these matters.' I felt that he was keeping quiet obstinately and expressing disinterest deliberately. I asked him, 'How long will Sandipbabu stay here?'

'He's leaving for Rangpur tomorrow morning.'

'Tomorrow morning?'

'Yes—he's supposed to give a speech there.'

I was silent for a while. Then I asked again, 'Can he manage to stay a day longer?'

'That won't be possible. But why do you ask?'

'I'd like to ask him to lunch and serve him myself.'

My husband was surprised. He had asked me to come out before his friends many times. I had never agreed. He looked at me fixedly, in a strange way; I couldn't really interpret that look. But I suddenly felt embarrassed and said, 'No, never mind.'

'I don't see why,' he said. 'Let me speak to Sandip. He'll stay back another day if he possibly can.'

It turned out that it was indeed possible.

I will be very honest: that day I wished God had made me beautiful. It was not to steal anyone's heart but because beauty was glory in itself. On this momentous day, the men of this land need to behold the Earth-mother (Jagatdhatri) in its women. But would male eyes be able to perceive the goddess unless there was surface beauty? Would Sandipbabu be able to glimpse in me the life force of the nation? Or would he think of me as an ordinary woman, his friend's wife and the mistress of the house?

Early in the morning I washed my long hair, left it loose and tied it neatly with a red silk ribbon. Sandipbabu was coming to lunch; so there was no time to dry my hair and tie it up. I wore a white Madras sari with a zari border, a matching blouse with short sleeves and zari piping.

I decided that this was a very modest outfit: nothing could be simpler. But suddenly my second sister-in-law came in and subjected me to a head to toe inspection. She gave a sardonic smile and laughed a little. I asked, 'Didi, why are you laughing?'

She said, 'How you have dressed up.'

I felt a little irritated. 'What's so special about my dress?' I asked.

She smiled sarcastically again and simply said, 'Nothing at all, my lady: in fact it's pretty good. But I can't help wondering if that revealing jacket of yours from that foreign shop wouldn't have completed the effort.' She finished the sentence and left, her whole body shaking with suppressed laughter. I was very angry and even considered taking everything off and wearing a simple, coarse, everyday sari instead. I still don't know why I didn't carry out that impulse in the end. I thought, 'If I don't appear decently dressed before Sandipbabu, my husband will be upset—after all, women are supposed to uphold the social prestige of the household.'

I thought I would make my appearance as Sandipbabu sat down to eat. By tending to his meal, I could dispel the embarrassment of our first meeting. But lunch was late today—it was almost one o'clock. So my husband sent for me in order to introduce us. When I first entered the room, I felt too shy to look Sandipbabu in the face. Somehow I managed to brush aside my shyness and said, a little awkwardly, 'Your lunch is a bit late today.'

He walked over quite spontaneously to the seat next to me and said, 'We get our daily rice after a fashion, but the goddess who provides it stays out of sight. Today when Annapurna has deigned to appear, the meal actually becomes insignificant.'

His conduct was as confident as his speeches. There was no hesitation about him: he seemed used to securing his rightful place within minutes in any situation. If he upset someone or even seemed offensive that did not bother him. He assumed the right to come and sit very close to one; if people looked askance, it seemed more their fault than his.

I was afraid Sandipbabu might decide that I am an old-fashioned dullard. The very thought embarrassed me. I had hoped that my speech would turn brilliant and flow smoothly so that each of my responses would fill him with wonder. But that did not happen. I agonized inwardly. Why did I suddenly decide to appear before him?

I was about to make my escape after he finished his meal. But as before, he walked up to the door casually and blocked my way, saying, 'Please don't take me for a glutton. I didn't come here to eat. I was eager to come only because you have invited me. If you run away like this after the meal, you'll be cheating your guest.'

If these remarks hadn't been uttered very frankly and persuasively they could have struck a false chord. But after all, my husband was his dearest friend and I was like a sister-in-law to him. As I was battling my own feelings and trying hard to attain the same level of informal familiarity, my husband sensed my discomfiture and said, 'Why don't you finish your lunch and then join us here again?'

Sandipbabu said, 'But promise me that you will keep your word.'

I smiled a little, 'I'll be back soon.'

'Let me explain why I don't trust you. It's nine years since Nikhilesh married. But you've cheated me of your presence all these nine years. If you disappear now for another nine years, I'll never see you again.'

I reciprocated the familiar tone and replied softly, 'Why will you *never* see me again?'

'My horoscope says I'll die young. Neither my father nor his father lived to be thirty years, and I've just completed twenty-seven.'

He knew this would distress me and so it did. Now my softly spoken words were laced with compassion as I said, 'The blessings of the entire nation will ward off the curse.'

'The nation's blessings are best received from the lips of its goddesses. That's why I'm begging you to return so that the warding off of the curse can begin from this very day.'

Flowing water, however muddy, is still good for a wash. Everything about Sandipbabu was so swift and vigorous that the same words, which may have seemed distasteful from someone else, seemed innocuous coming from him. He laughed as he said, 'Look here, I'm holding your husband hostage. If you don't return, he shan't be released.'

As I was leaving the room he spoke again, 'I have another small request.'

I stopped in my tracks and turned around. 'Don't worry, all I want is a glass of water. You must have noticed that I don't drink water during the meal. I have it some time later.'

At this, I couldn't but ask anxiously, 'Why is that so?'

Then came the history of how he was once afflicted by severe dyspepsia. I also heard how he had suffered for nearly seven months. He described the drudgery of homeopathic and allopathic treatment before being miraculously cured at last by Ayurveda. He laughed and said, 'God has fashioned even my illnesses in such a way that they refuse to be cured without Indian-made pills.'

My husband now spoke up after a long time, 'And what about the fact that bottles of allopathic medicine also refuse to leave your side? They take up nearly three shelves in your sitting room—'

'Do you know why? They're like the punitive police. They are not there because they serve a purpose; but the modern dispensation has brought them in and thrust them on us. I keep paying for them as punishment and I get my share of jabs as well.'

My husband abhors exaggeration. But rhetoric, by definition, exaggerates: it was, after all, invented by humans and not by God. Once while trying to justify a fib I had said to my husband, 'It's only trees, animals and birds that are always truthful; the poor things lack the capacity to lie. That's where humans are superior to animals, and women again are superior to men. Women are best embellished with ornaments and fabrications.'

When I came out of the room my second sister-in-law was in the corridor, prising apart one of the window blinds. 'What are you doing here?' I asked.

'I was eavesdropping,' she whispered.

Later, when I returned to the room again, Sandipbabu said sympathetically, 'You couldn't have had much to eat today.'

I was flustered. I was obviously back a little too soon. I hadn't allowed the length of time needed to finish one's meal decently. If one were to calculate, it'd be clear that I couldn't have eaten much that day. But it had hardly occurred to me that anyone might notice.

Perhaps Sandipbabu sensed my discomfiture, which was more disconcerting still. He said, 'You were all set to run away like the wild deer. I'm honoured that you did go to the trouble of keeping your word.'

I couldn't make a suitable reply. Blushing and fretting, I sat on the edge of a sofa. It had been my resolve to present myself before Sandipbabu honourably and confidently as the image of the nation's Shakti and to adorn his brow with victory garlands simply by appearing before him. So far, I had utterly failed.

At this point, Sandipbabu got into an argument with my husband quite deliberately. He must have known that in an argument his razor-sharp mind shone in all its brilliance. Many times later as well, I noticed that in my presence he never let slip the slightest opportunity for a debate.

He was aware of my husband's opinions on the Vande Mataram mantra. Referring to that he said, 'Nikhil, don't you agree that there is a space for the imagination in the act of serving the country?'

'I agree there is a space, but it isn't all of it. I intend to know that thing called "my country" in a more heartfelt, genuine fashion and that's how I'd like to have others know it. I feel quite nervous and ashamed to use some kind of entertaining hocus-pocus mantra in relation to such a profound concept.'

'That thing which you call an entertaining mantra is precisely what I call the Truth. I truly believe my country is my God. I believe God resides in man—He truly reveals Himself through men and their land.'

'If you truly believe this, then you wouldn't discriminate between two men or between two countries.'

'That's true. But I am a man of limited strengths and so I fulfil my duties towards God through the worship of my *own* land.'

'I'd never stop you from worshipping, but if you disregard the presence of God in another land and feel hatred towards it, how will your worship be complete?'

'Hatred is an aspect of puja. Arjuna got his boon only when he fought with Shiva dressed as a *kirata*. If we are ready to battle God, He will be pleased with us eventually.'

'If that were the case, then those who are ruining the country and those who are serving it are both worshipping it in the same way. So what is the point of going out of your way to spread the message of patriotism?'

'When it comes to one's own country, it's a different matter. On that the heart has clear orders to venerate.'

'In that case, why just one's own country, there are even clearer instructions about one's self. The mantra that dwells in our heart to worship God through man, is the same one that resonates throughout all the lands.'

'Nikhil, all your arguments are based on dry logic. Will you deny the fact that there is something called a heart?'

'Sandip, I'll be honest with you: when you try to pass off misdeeds as duty and irreverence as piety in the name of the nation-god, it pains my heart and I can't keep still. If I steal to satisfy my own needs, isn't it a blow to the true love that I bear for myself? That's why I can't steal. Is it because I am intelligent or because I respect my self?'

I was seething inwardly. I couldn't hold back; I said, 'English, French, German, Russian—is there a civilization that doesn't have a history of stealing for the sake of the country?'

'They will be answerable for those crimes; they're still paying for them. History hasn't yet come to an end.'

Sandipbabu said, 'Fine then, we'll pay up too. First let us stock up our home with the stolen loot and then we'll pay for them slowly over many centuries. But let me ask you, where do you see them paying the price for it as you just mentioned?'

'When Rome paid the price for her sins, there were no witnesses. There's no telling when the day of reckoning will come upon renowned brigand civilizations and when they'll have to pay for their misdeeds and at that time, no outsider will witness it. But aren't you missing something—their bag of politics is full of lies, deception, betrayals, espionage, forfeiting right and Truth for the sake of saving their face; the weight of all these sins can't be a light one. Isn't this draining the blood, drop by drop, from the heart of their civilization every day? I believe that those who don't accept the place of Truth over their land don't respect their land either.'

Never before had I seen my husband argue with an outsider. He argued with me but his tenderness for me made him feel sorry to corner me in an argument. Today I got to see his fencing skills in a debate.

Somewhere my heart refused to agree with my husband's words. I felt that there must be some appropriate rejoinders to his arguments but they wouldn't come to mind just then. The problem was that if you bring up virtue/dharma, one has to keep silent. It's difficult to claim that I don't take dharma to those extremes. I decided to write a fitting retort to this debate and hand it over to Sandipbabu one day. So I quickly noted down today's conversation once I returned to my room.

All of a sudden Sandipbabu turned to me and asked, 'What do you feel about this?'

I said, 'I won't go into subtleties; I'll state my case bluntly—I am human, I am avaricious and I'll be greedy for the sake of my country. When I want something, I'm prepared to snatch it. I feel anger and I'll use it for my land. I need someone to tear into bits, on whom I'll avenge the humiliation I have lived with for so long. I have illusions and I shall be bewitched by my country; I need a tangible form for her—which will be Mother, a goddess or Durga to me—for whom I'll sacrifice an animal and let loose a bloodbath. I am human, I am not a god.'

Sandipbabu jumped up from his seat, raised his right hand high in the air and shouted, 'Hurrah! Hurrah!' The next moment he corrected himself and exclaimed, 'Vande Mataram! Vande Mataram!'

A shadow of pain crossed my husband's face. He spoke very softly, 'Neither am I a god; I too am human and that's why I will not, at any cost, thrust all my imperfections upon the country.'

Sandipbabu replied, 'Look here Nikhil, Truth is something that is innate to womankind, at one with their heart and soul. For us men, Truth is all logic and no shades, emotions or life.

The woman's heart is the lotus on which Truth resides and it
is not insubstantial like our Reason. That is precisely why it is
only the women who can be truly heartless and not men, since
rationality weakens them. Women can destroy someone with
ease; so can men, but the threads of reason trip them up. Like
a thunderstorm, women can wreak havoc—they have a terrible
beauty—when men commit the same crimes, they look ugly
since it is tainted by the pangs of Reason. One thing, Nikhil, is
for sure—in these times, it is women who will salvage our nation.
This is not the time for us to differentiate between good and evil,
right and wrong; today unscrupulously and indifferently we have
to be ruthless and unfettered; we have to anoint sin with holy
markers and let the women of the nation receive it cordially.
Don't you remember what the poet has said?—

> Welcome sin, welcome oh beauty!
> Let the flaming tonic of your kiss Inflame my blood.
> Sound the trumpet of malevolence,
> Anoint my brow with infamy,
> Fill my heart with tumultuous,
> Dark, sinful murk, shameless.

Shame on that piety which is incapable of being callously
ruthless.'

Having said this, he stamped his foot twice very loudly.
Startled, a lot of drowsy dust rose off the carpet and into the air.
He stood straight with such pride after having scorned in an
instant the very values, which are treasured across lands over the
ages, that a shiver went down my spine as I looked at him.

Suddenly he roared again, 'I can clearly see that you are
the beautiful goddess of that fire which reduces the home to
ashes and burns down the world; today you must give us that

unconquerable strength to destroy ourselves, and you must adorn our transgression.'

It wasn't clear to whom these last words were addressed. One could assume it was to the presence that he venerated with 'Vande Mataram' or to the woman who was present there as a representative of that goddess-motherland. One could assume that just as the poet Valmiki had articulated his first meter when his impious nature was struck by compassion, Sandipbabu also uttered these words suddenly when brutality struck against righteousness—or it was perhaps a habitual display of excellent histrionics, common to the business of impressing an audience.

Perhaps he would have spoken some more. But just then my husband rose and patted him, speaking softly, 'Sandip, Chandranathbabu is here.'

The spell broke and I looked up to find the austere, serene old gentleman hesitating by the door, wondering whether to come in or not. Like the setting sun, his face glowed with the soft light of humility. My husband came up to me and said, 'He is my teacher. I have spoken to you about him many a times; touch his feet.'

I touched his feet reverently. He blessed me, 'Ma, may the lord protect you always.'

Just at that moment I was in great need of that blessing.

Nikhilesh

All my life I have believed that I have the strength to accept whatever God grants. Till date my faith has never been put to test. But now I believe the time has come.

To test the strength of my belief, I have visualized many kinds of misery—including poverty, imprisonment, humiliation and even death—to the extent that I have even tried to imagine Bimal's death. When I felt I'd be able to deal with all this and still not lose faith in Him, perhaps I wasn't very wrong. But there's just one thing that I had never ever foreseen and today I have mulled over it all day long—can I possibly go through this?

Deep down within me there is a pain. I go about my usual duties, but the hurt lingers. Even as I sleep, the pain gnaws at my ribs. When I wake up at dawn, the light seems to have gone from the day. What is it? What has happened? What is this darkness? From where has it come upon my full moon and cast its dark shadow?

My mind has suddenly become too sensitive and the lie of the past sorrows which masqueraded as joy tears me apart. The more my shame tries to hide its face as the sorrow creeps up on me, the more it lays itself bare before my heart. My heart has gained a new vision—it sits and watches what is not to be seen, what I don't even want to see.

That day has arrived when I am being made to feel every day, every moment, with every word and every glance that I was cheated and for too long; I was a mere beggar amidst all my so-called wealth. In these nine years of my youth the interest that I have paid to 'illusion' will now be exacted to the last penny by 'Truth' for the rest of my life. The weight of the heaviest debt has landed on the shoulders of the man who has lost all means of paying his debts. And yet, I pray that I can say with all my strength, 'Oh Truth, may you win, always.'

Yesterday my cousin Munu's husband came to ask for some help for his daughter's wedding. He must have looked around my house and felt that I was the happiest man in the world. I said, 'Gopal, please tell Munu that I shall come to lunch tomorrow.' Munu has turned her needy home into a haven with the goodness of her heart. On this day my heart cried out for a morsel from the hands of that pious woman. In her home, the hardships have turned into her ornaments. Today I want to go and see her once. Oh Piety, your holy grace has not yet vanished entirely off the face of this earth.

Is there any point in holding on to one's pride? Is it not better to hang my head and admit that I am not good enough? It is possible that I lack that power which women value most in men. But is power only about boasting, about whimsicality and thoughtlessly crushing underfoot—but why all these arguments? Quibbling will not make me a worthier man. Worthless, worthless, worthless. Well, perhaps I am—but love doesn't come with a price-tag and it can turn worthless into worthwhile. For the deserving, there are many prizes in this world; it is for the unworthy that Fate has reserved love alone.

Once I had asked Bimal to come out into the world. Bimal was in my home, she was a mere doll, confined to a small space, caught up in trivial duties. The love that I got from her habitually—did it stem from the deep well of her heart or was it driven by social pressures like the fixed ration of municipal water that one receives daily?

Am I greedy? Rather than being happy with my lot, did I aspire for a lot more? No, I am not greedy, I am a lover. That's why I didn't want something being kept under lock and key in an iron chest; I desired her who can only be had when she wanted to give herself to me. I do not wish to decorate my home with flowers cut out from the pages of the *Smrutisamhita* text. I had a great desire to see Bimal in all her glory, blooming with knowledge, strength and love amidst the world.

At the time I hadn't thought of one thing: that if you really must see a person in her true, free self, then you cannot expect to lay any definite claims on her. Why didn't I think of it then? Was it due to the natural arrogance of possessing one's wife? No, it was not that. It was because I had complete faith in love.

I was conceited enough to believe that I have the strength to bear the complete, stark face of Truth. Today that belief is being tested. I am still vain enough to believe that I will pass the test, even if it kills me.

Till this day, Bimal has failed to understand me in one area. I have always considered coercion to be a form of weakness. The weak man doesn't dare to judge fairly. He will avoid the responsibility of following justice and arrive at his goal quickly through unfair means. Bimal is very impatient about patience. She'd rather see in men the dynamic, the wrathful and even the unjust. In her mind, respect and fear are closely connected.

I had thought that when she came into a larger world and looked at life from a wider perspective she'd outgrow this craze for recklessness. But now I'm beginning to feel that this is a part of Bimal's nature. She has an innate passion for the grotesque. She takes the small and simple pleasures of life, rubs salt and spices into them, burning her tongue and innards all the way; any other kind of taste does not appeal to her.

In the same way, it is my firm resolution that I will not use an excitement like Dutch-courage to do my duty for the country. I'd rather tolerate inefficiency than raise my hand against a servant. My very being baulks at the thought of doing or saying something to someone in anger. I know that Bimal considers my restraint to be a form of feebleness and disrespects it. Today, for that same reason she is angry with me because I am not yelling 'Vande Mataram' and going around kicking up a ruckus.

Today I have earned everyone's displeasure since I have not sat down with a glass of liquor in my country's honour. People think I'm either scared of the police or I'm angling for a title. The police think I am masquerading as a good soul because I have other hidden agendas. Even so, I continue on this road strewn with scepticism and humiliation.

I believe that when you can't summon up the enthusiasm to serve the country by thinking of her merely as the country and its people as mere human beings, when you need to scream and shout out mantras and call her a goddess and go into a trance, then you love the craze more than you love your motherland. The need to place an obsession above Truth is an indication of our innate servility. When we set our mind free, we are no longer as strong. Unless we place an illusion, or an image or some framework of the establishment upon our listless consciousness as a rider, we cannot function. As long as we don't acquire a taste for the plain Truth, as long as we need such an obsession, it is obvious that we haven't acquired the strength to receive our country in all the glory of its freedom. Until then, whatever state we are in, either an imaginary spectre or a genuine presence will continue to trouble us.

The other day Sandip said to me, 'You may have many qualities, but you lack an imagination and that's why you can't perceive the divine form of the country as the Truth.' I noticed Bimal agreed with him. I didn't care to retaliate. There was no joy in winning this argument. This wasn't about a difference of opinion—it was about the difference in nature between Bimal and me. Within the limits of domestic trivia this disparity appears rather small; so it doesn't strike a discord in a harmonious union. In a larger space such differences resonate louder. There, the waves of discord don't just ricochet, they mutilate.

Lacking an imagination? So I guess the lamp within me holds the oil but the flame is missing. I'd say the lack is in you. Like a flint, you are the ones who lack the light. Hence, you need to be struck and make a lot of noise and then a few sparks fly—those disruptive sparks merely enhance the conceit and don't add to the vision.

Lately, I have noticed that there's a palpable sense of greed in Sandip's nature. It's this arrant addiction that made him weave myths around religion and go into a frenzy over serving the country. Since his mind is sharp, he calls his inclinations grandiose names although he is coarse by nature. He needs an expression of his hatred as badly as he needs the fulfilment of his desires. Bimal has often cautioned me that Sandip has an appetite for money. I wasn't unaware of it myself, but when it came to Sandip, I couldn't be tight-fisted. I'd be reluctant to even consider that he was cheating me. I refrained from ever taking up the issue with him, in the fear that the fact of my helping him financially could turn nasty and ugly. But today, it would be difficult to convince Bimal that a large part of Sandip's feelings for the country are a variation of this covetousness. Bimal has begun to worship Sandip in her heart. So, I hate to say anything about Sandip to her, in case it is influenced by my own insecurities and I say something that is not entirely true. Perhaps the image of Sandip that comes to my mind now is warped by the searing heat of anguish. And yet, it's better to put my thoughts down on paper than to bottle them up inside.

I have known Chandranathbabu, my mentor, for all of the thirty years of my life. He fears neither criticism, nor injury and not even death. No amount of advice could have saved my life in the house where I was born. But this person, with his calm, sincere and unsullied presence, placed his life squarely in the service of mine—in him I have perceived benevolence in its truest and most tangible form.

The same Chandranathbabu came to me the other day and asked, 'Does Sandip have to stay here much longer?'

The slightest whiff of misfortune goes straight to his heart; he senses it immediately. He is not one to be disturbed easily, but on that day he could foresee the dark shadow of some great danger. I know just how much he loves me.

Over tea I said to Sandip, 'Won't you go to Rangpur? They have written to me; they think I am the one who's holding you back.'

Bimal was pouring tea. Instantly her face paled. She simply glanced at Sandip's face once.

Sandip said, 'I have thought it over and come to the conclusion that the way we go around spreading the word about swadeshi only leads to a waste of our resources. I believe that if we work from one central base, the results would be much more long-lasting.'

He looked at Bimal and said, 'Don't you think so?'

At first Bimal didn't know what to say. A little later she said, 'One can serve the country in both ways. Whether one should roam about or stay in one place is a choice that depends on one's wish or nature. Of the two, the one that you feel like doing is the best way for you.'

Sandip said, 'Then let me be frank. All these days I thought that my duty was to go from place to place and stir up enough fervour. But I was wrong. The reason for this misunderstanding was that so far I have never found a source of energy or power that can keep me fulfilled at all times. Hence, I needed to gather the vital force for my life by travelling and whipping up excitement in others and then drawing from it to sustain myself. Today you are the motherland's message to me. Till this day I have not seen such a fire in anyone. Shame on me, that I was proud of my own strength. But now, I don't aim to be a hero for this country any more. I am audacious enough to claim that I'll be a mere instrument and stay put here, setting the country ablaze with the help of your burning fervour; no, no, please don't feel embarrassed. Your place is far above such sham coyness, qualms and humility. You are the Queen Bee of our beehive. We will stay around you and do our work, but the strength for that has to come from you and hence, if we leave your side our work will suffer. Please accept our homage unhesitatingly.'

Bimal blushed with awkwardness and pride and her hands shook as she poured the tea.

Another day Chandranathbabu came and said, 'Why don't the two of you take a trip to Darjeeling; you don't look too well these days. Are you getting enough sleep?'

The same evening I asked Bimal, 'Shall we go to Darjeeling?'

I knew she was very keen to go to Darjeeling and see the Himalayas. But that day she replied, 'No, not now.'

I guess she feared that the country's work would suffer.

I shall not lose faith; I will wait. The road that leads from narrow confines to vaster plains is a stormy one. When Bimal has left the home behind, the rules binding her to those boundaries no longer operate. Once she reconciles with the unfamiliar world and comes to an agreement with it, I shall see where my place lies. If I find that amidst the workings of this vast life, there is no room for me, then I'll know that everything I lived with for all these years was a lie. I have no use for that falsehood. If that day comes, I will not protest; slowly and silently I'll move away. Force and coercion? Whatever for! Can Truth ever be defied?

Sandip

Only the powerless claim that whatever has been given to them is all that truly belongs to them, and the feeble ones assent. This world teaches you that only whatever I can snatch and grab is rightfully mine.

Just because I was born in this country doesn't make it mine. The day I'll be able to seize the land and make it mine forcefully, is the day it'll truly be mine.

Since we have the natural right to acquire, the inclination to aspire is also natural. Nowhere does Nature claim that one has to be deprived of anything on any account. Whatever the heart desires, the body has to acquire—this is the only decree that Nature accepts. The rules that do not let you accept this Truth is what we call morality and that's why, till date, man hasn't been able to come to terms with morality.

There are a handful of weak souls in the world who do not know how to seize, cannot hold on to what they have, their fists come loose at the drop of a hat—morality is the consolation prize for these souls. But those who can desire with all their heart, savour with all their soul, those who don't suffer from hesitation and reluctance, they are the favourite sons of Nature. It is for

them that Nature has set forth all that's beautiful, all that's
valuable. They're the ones who'll swim across the rivers, scale
the walls, kick the doors open and seize all that is worth taking.
This is true pleasure, and the true measure of a valuable thing
dwells in this. Nature will surrender, but only to the brigand,
because she values the power to desire, to snatch and to receive.
Hence, she wouldn't like to grace the bony neck of the half-dead
mendicant with the garland of her favourite spring flowers. The
band is playing in the ballroom—the hours drift away and the
heart grows sad. Who is the groom? I am. The one who can grab
the groom's seat, blazing torch in hand, is the rightful owner of
that seat. Nature's groom comes without an invitation.

Shame? No, I am not ashamed. I ask for whatever I need
and sometimes I take without asking. Those who feel shy and
don't take the things that are worth taking, give great names to
that misery that stems from their denial. This world that we have
come into, is a world of reality—why has man come into this
hard world only to deceive himself with a few noble thoughts
and to go away from this materialistic market, empty-handed
and starved? Did he come here on the request of a bunch of
'pious' babus who spend their time playing sweet, set tunes on
their flutes in the fool's paradise up there in the sky? I don't
need the tunes of that flute and that fool's paradise won't fill my
stomach. When I want something, I want it with all my heart.
I'd like to mash it with my hands, crush it under my feet, wear
it all over my body and devour it. I am not ashamed to ask and I
do not falter in receiving. The feeble criticism of those who have
chewed on the famine of morality for too long and have grown
thin and pale like the bed-bugs in a long-forsaken cot, won't even
reach my ears.

I don't like to deceive because that's a sign of cowardice. But
if I'm unable to deceive even when required, that is also a form

of cowardice. If you raise walls around that which you want, I'll have to break in to get what I want. You raise walls because you covet and I break in because I crave. If you play tricks I resort to capers. This is the whole truth of Nature. All the states and kingdoms on this earth and all things that happen here, work on this same principle. And when some godly creature comes from the heavens and speaks in the language of that kingdom, it is unreal. Hence, after much shouting and screaming, those words find a place only in the corner of the weak man's home. The ones who are resilient and have taken to ruling the world cannot accept those words because that leads to loss of power and strength. That's because the words are not true in themselves. Those who don't hesitate to admit this, don't feel ashamed to accept this, are the ones who are successful; and those hapless ones who straddle both the boats of the real and the unreal, torn between Nature and the godly creature, can neither move ahead nor live.

A bunch of people are born in this world having vowed that they will not live life. There is a beauty in the sky when the sun is setting and those people are floored by that faint beauty. Our Nikhilesh belongs to that category; he seems almost lifeless. Almost four years ago, he and I had a great verbal battle on this issue. He said to me, 'I accept that you can't achieve something without power. But the debate is about what is called power and achievement. My power is more inclined towards sacrifice.'

'Meaning, you are addicted to the passion for loss.'

'Yes, just as the bird within the egg gets restless to lose the shell. The shell is very real indeed but in its stead it achieves air and light. In your opinion perhaps the bird is cheated.'

Nikhilesh talks like this, in metaphors. Thereafter it is difficult to get him to understand that those metaphors are still mere words and not the truth. Well, if he is happy with these metaphors, let him be—we are the carnivores of this earth.

We have teeth and nails, we can run, catch and rip things apart—we cannot spend the entire day romanticizing about the grass we chewed in the morning. Hence, we are not ready to accept it if you, the group of metaphor-people, stand guard at the door to the feast that's laid out for us on this earth. We will either steal or rob or we will die. We are not ready to lie around on lotus leaves, in love with death, and draw our last breath in the tenth chapter, however much it offends my Vaishnava friends!

People dismiss my thoughts with, 'Oh, it's just something you say.' That's because those people live by the same rules as I do in this world, but they spout something else. Hence, they do not know that these rules are what constitute morality. I know. It has been tested through my life that my words are not mere opinions. The rules I live by make it easy for me to win the hearts of women. They are the ones who are beings of this real world and they don't wander the clouds on balloons of vacant 'Ideas' like men. In my eyes and face, my body and soul, they can sense a tremendous desire—that desire isn't dried up by some penance, turned the other way by some logic, it is just pure and full desire—which growls away like a juggernaut: 'I want, I want, I'll have, I'll have.' From deep within, women know that this desire is the life force of this world. That life force wins out everywhere only because it refuses to acknowledge anyone other than itself. Many a time I have seen that women just let themselves go on the face of my desire, irrespective of whether they'll live or die. The power that lets you win these women is the power of the true brave, the power to win the real world. The ones who imagine they'll achieve some other world are most welcome to elevate their desire from its place on the earth and lift it skywards. Let me see how high their fountain rises and how long it lasts. Women haven't been created for these subtle beings, who rove the world of 'Ideas'.

Affinity! God has paired men and women as couples in a special way and sent them into this world; their union is truer than the harmony of the chants—I have said this several times when required, on different occasions. The problem is that people want to accept Nature, but they need to hide behind the veil of words. That's why the world is now full of lies. Why should there be one affinity? There should be thousands. No one has given it to Nature in writing that we'll have to dismiss all other affinities for the sake of just one of them. I have enjoyed several affinities in my life and that wouldn't stop me from pursuing one more. I can see her quite clearly and she has felt my affinity as well. Then? Then if I fail to win her over, I am not a man.

Bimala

Where had my sense of shame disappeared, I now wonder. I had no time to look at myself—my days and nights were swirling me around like a tornado. Hence, shame found no way to enter my soul.

One day in my presence, my second sister-in-law laughingly remarked to my husband, 'Dear brother-in-law, until today in this household only the women have cried their heart out; now it's the men's turn. From now on, we'll make you cry. Isn't that so, little princess? You've already donned the armour and now you need to just assail the hearts of men.' She looked me over from head to toe. The shades of hue that radiated from me, through my dress and manner, my every gesture, did not escape her eyes in the least. Today I feel ashamed to write this, but that day I felt no shame whatsoever. That day my very Nature was working from within, I was not thinking or understanding any of this.

Those days I know I used to dress up specially. But it was unconscious to an extent. I could clearly sense which outfit of mine pleased Sandipbabu the most. Besides, there was no need for any guesswork. Sandipbabu discussed it openly in front of everybody. In my presence, one day he said to my husband, 'Nikhil, the day I saw our Queen Bee for the first time—sitting silently, dressed in a zari-bordered sari, her eyes looking through eternity like stars that have lost their way, as if for thousands of years she has waited thus, on the banks of darkness, in search of something, waiting for someone—my heart trembled. I felt the fire in her heart was wrapped around her in the borders of her sari. This fire is what we need, these palpable flames. Queen Bee, I request you—once more, could you appear before us dressed like the fiery flame?'

Up until then I had been a nameless river in a village—I had a certain rhythm, a language. But suddenly, with no warning, the ocean flooded me and my breast swelled and heaved, my banks overflowed and on their own, my waves pulsated to the rhythm of the ocean's drumbeat. I could never really fathom the true meaning of the throbbing in my veins. Where was the old me? Suddenly, from where did these waves of beauty come lapping at my shores? Sandipbabu's famished eyes lit up like a pair of lamps to worship my beauty. Through his glances and words, he declared it like the cymbals and bells of the temple: I was awe-inspiring in my beauty and power. At that moment that sound drowned out all other sounds on this earth.

Did God create me anew today? Did He make up for his neglect of so many years? The one who was plain suddenly blossomed into a beauty. The one who was ordinary suddenly perceived the glory of the entire land within herself. Sandipbabu wasn't just one man. He alone symbolized the overflowing hearts of millions in the nation. Hence when he designated me as the Queen Bee of the beehive, I was crowned that very day amidst the whispered hymns of praise by all those who served the country. After that, in one corner of our home, my elder sister-in-law's silent disregard and my second sister-in-law's strident mockery didn't affect me at all. My relationship with the whole world changed.

Sandipbabu had successfully convinced me that the entire nation needed me badly. That day I had no trouble believing those words. I have the ability—the ability to do anything as I am now blessed by a divine strength. It was something that I'd never experienced before. There was no time for me to stop and try to comprehend the nature of this colossal wave of emotions that rose in my heart; it was as if it was mine always and yet not quite my own; as if it were somewhere beyond me, belonging to the entire nation. It was like a deluge and no backyard pond was answerable for it.

Sandipbabu consulted me about every little matter pertaining to the country. At first I was very hesitant, but that soon disappeared. Whatever I said, Sandipbabu's reaction was amazement. He'd always say, 'We, men, can only think but you can plumb the depths of Truth and so you don't need to think any more. God created women from inspiration but the men, He beat into shape with a hammer in hand.' Listening to him, I'd begun to feel that both natural intellect and power were innate parts of me in a way that I myself hadn't realized before.

Many letters came to Sandipbabu from different parts of the country regarding various matters. I read each and every one of them and none was answered without a consultation with me. On some days, Sandipbabu and I would disagree over something. I never argued with him. But a couple of days later, he'd have a realization as it were and calling me out from the inner chambers he'd say, 'Look, what you said the other day was absolutely right and all my arguments were wrong.' Sometimes he'd say, 'I'm really sorry I didn't take your advice then. Really, can you explain to me the mystery behind this?'

Gradually I began to feel more and more that at the time all that was happening in the country had Sandipbabu at its root and behind him lay the common sense of an ordinary woman. My heart was filled to the brim with the sense of a glorious duty.

My husband had no place in all these discussions that we had. Sandipbabu's manner towards my husband was like that of an older brother who loved his younger brother very much but didn't really trust his judgement on important matters. He'd often laugh patronizingly and imply that in these matters my husband was quite childish and his opinions were really quite contrary. He made it clear that he loved my husband all the more because there was a quaint humour in these strange opinions and erroneous beliefs that he held. Hence, out of this exceptional fondness for my husband, Sandipbabu kept him out of doing any work for the country.

Nature, the physician, has several ways of dulling one's pain. When a profound relationship gradually starts slipping away, one doesn't even know when those antidotes start working within oneself. Suddenly one day we wake up and realize a great chasm has opened up. When the scalpel was cutting away at the most important relationship of my life, my mind was thus shrouded by the vapours of emotion and I didn't even know about the cruel turn of events. Perhaps this is a woman's nature. When our heart is involved in one arena, we lose all our senses of other spaces. This is why we are devastating; we cause havoc through our innate nature and not through logic. We are like flowing water—when we flow between two shores, we nurture with all our might and when we overflow the banks, we destroy with equal vehemence.

Sandip

I could feel that something was amiss. The other day I got a whiff of it.

Since my arrival, the drawing room in Nikhilesh's home had turned into an ambiguous space, neither indoors nor outdoors. From the outside I had access to it and from within, the Queen Bee did. If we had used this privilege in some moderation, perhaps people would soon have got used to it. But when the dam bursts, the flow of the water is at its highest. Our meetings in the drawing room continued with such gusto that neither of us was aware of anything else.

Whenever the Bee came into the drawing room, I could somehow sense it from my room. There'd be some sounds of tinkling bangles and some other noises. She opened the door perhaps a little too loudly, needlessly. Then the door of the bookshelf, which was a little stiff, made a lot of noise when it was opened. As I came into the room, I'd find the Bee intently picking a book from the shelf, her back to the doorway. When I'd offer to help her in this arduous task, she'd be startled and protest, and then some other topic would come up.

The other day, on a Thursday afternoon, I started from my room after hearing some of the usual noises. On the way, in the corridor I found a guard standing duty. I proceeded without glancing at him. But he stood in my way and said, 'Babu, please don't go that way.'

'Don't go! But why!'

'The mistress is in the drawing room.'

'Fine. Tell the mistress that Sandipbabu would like to see her.'

'No, that's not possible. Those are the orders.'

I was very angry. I raised my voice a little and said, 'I am ordering you to go and ask her.'

The guard was a little daunted by all this. So I pushed him aside and proceeded towards the room. When I was almost at the door, he ran up to me and grabbed me by the hands, 'Babu, please don't go.'

What was this! How dare he touch me! I snatched my hand away and slapped him hard on the cheek. At this point, the Bee came out of the room and found the guard on the verge of retaliating.

I'll never forget the look on her face. It was I who discovered the beauty of the Bee. In our country most people wouldn't look at her twice. She was tall and lissome, a quality which connoisseurs of beauty would mock as 'lanky'. It was this litheness of hers that I admired the most, as if in making her a fountain of life had emanated from the cavernous heart of the maker and shot upwards animatedly. Her colour was dark, but it was the dark of a sword of steel—powerful and razor-sharp. That power blazed in her eyes and face that day. Standing on the threshold, she raised her index finger and said, 'Nanku, go away.'

I said, 'Please don't be angry. Since there are orders, I'd better leave.'

In a trembling voice, the Bee said, 'No, please don't leave. Come inside.'

This wasn't a request, it was an order. I came into the room, sat down and began to fan myself with a hand-held fan. The Bee wrote something on a piece of paper with a pencil and handed it to the bearer saying, 'Give this to the master.'

I said, 'Please forgive me, I was impatient and I hit the guard.'

The Bee said, 'Serves him right.'

'But that poor man did nothing wrong. He was following orders.'

At this point Nikhil came into the room. Hastily I got up, turned my back to him and went and stood by the window.

The Bee said to Nikhil, 'Today Nanku, the guard, has insulted Sandipbabu.'

Nikhil pretended to be such a simpleton as he said, 'Why?' that I could no longer control myself. I turned around and looked at his face steadily and thought, 'So the truthful person does lie to his wife, if she is the right sort.'

The Bee said, 'Sandipbabu was coming this way and he stopped him saying that he has orders.'

Nikhil asked, 'Whose orders?'

The Bee retorted, 'How should I know that?'

Anger and frustration almost brought tears to her eyes.

Nikhil sent for the guard. He said, 'Sire, I am not at fault. I was following orders.'

'Whose orders?'

'The elder and second mistresses called me and gave me instructions.'

For a few moments all of us were silent.

After he left, the Bee said, 'Nanku has to be sacked.'

Nikhil was silent. I knew his moral and ethical senses were strained. He was under great stress. But the problem was a difficult one. The Bee was no simple woman. On the pretext of sacking Nanku, she wanted to take revenge on her sisters-in-law.

Nikhil continued to be silent. The Bee's eyes were showering sparks of fire. Her hatred towards Nikhil's good-heartedness knew no bounds.

Without saying another word, Nikhil left the room.

From the next day, that guard was not to be seen anywhere. Upon inquiry I learnt that Nikhil had transferred him to a position in some village—the guard's losses were compensated amply.

Over this small matter, I could tell, that a few storms had blown over the house. At every point I couldn't help feeling one thing—Nikhil is strange, an absolutely insane person.

The upshot of this incident was that for the next few days the Bee started coming into the drawing room daily and sending the bearer for me to spend some time chatting with me; she didn't even bother to use any excuse of coincidence or necessity.

In this fashion the friendship, through words and gestures, spoken and unspoken, progressed. This was the lady of a household who is usually like a star in a sky, beyond an outsider's reach. There were no trodden paths here. Through this nameless vacuum we navigated our way: the gradual tension, knowing and awareness, each veil of inhibition ripping away into a formless sky and suddenly exposing nature in its naked form—this was a strange, victorious journey of Truth!

Of course this is Truth! The force of attraction between a man and a woman is a very tangible one. From the dust particle on the ground to the stars in the sky, all material things support it. And man would like to keep it shrouded by a few words, to make it his domestic property by some rules and regulations! As if it's a demand to fashion a watch-chain for one's son-in-law out of the solar system. Then, when reality awakens to the call of matter, and in an instant, brushes aside all pretense of man's words and takes its own place, neither faith nor morality can stop its progress. So many charges, regrets and commands come forth! But you need more than mere words to grapple with a storm. It doesn't answer to you, it only shakes you up—it is reality.

Hence, I am really enjoying this palpable revelation of Truth before my eyes. So much shame and fear, so many dilemmas! But without that what's the charm of Truth? This tremble in one's step, this turning away every now and then—it's all very sweet. And the deception is more against oneself than others. When reality wages war on the artificial, deception is its primary weapon because the enemies of matter mock it by calling it coarse. Hence, it needs to either keep itself hidden or use a masquerade. The way things are, it can't say boldly, 'Yes I am coarse, because I am Truth, I am corporeal, I am instinct, I am hunger, shameless and heartless—just as shameless and heartless as the gigantic boulder that's dislodged from the mountainside by the rains and comes rolling on to the heads of human habitation, irrespective of lives lost or saved.'

I can clearly see everything. There, the curtain is drifting in the wind and preparations are being made to set off on a journey of destruction. That tiny flash of red ribbon peeping from the masses of dark hair, washed and cleaned: it's the greedy tongue of the nor'wester, scarlet with the secret zeal of lust! I can clearly perceive the heat off that slight gesture of the sari-border, the little hint of the blouse. Yet, all this groundwork is taking place in a clandestine matter, unknown even to the one who is doing it.

Why doesn't she know? Because, man has destroyed with his own hands the capacity to know and understand reality fully, by always covering it up. Man is ashamed of reality. Hence, it has to work surreptitiously, from beneath the piles and swathes of wrapping that man has constructed; that's why we never come to know of its workings and then when it comes upon us suddenly, there is no way of denying it. Man wanted to evict it and called it

Satan, which is why it entered Eden masquerading as a snake and made woman rebel by just whispering into her ears and opening her eyes to the Truth. Since then, there has been no time to rest, there has been only death and nothing else!

I am materialistic. The naked reality has broken free of the prison of sentimentality today and come into the open. My joy stalks every footstep. Whatever I desire should come very close to me, I'll receive it fully, I'll hold it tight and not let it go at all; all that comes in between will shatter into little pieces, roll in the dust, flutter in the wind—this is joy, this is pleasure, this is the destructive dance of reality; after this life and death, good and bad, joy and sorrow, all is vain—mere trifles! Trifles!

My Queen Bee is walking in a trance and she doesn't know which way she's headed. It wouldn't be safe to let her know and wake her suddenly, before the time is right. It's better to let her feel that I haven't noticed anything at all. The other day as I was eating, Queen Bee stared at my face fixedly, totally unaware of what that look can possibly imply. When I looked up suddenly and met her eyes, she blushed and looked away. I said, 'You must be really surprised by the way I eat. I can conceal many traits, this greed isn't one of them. But look here, since I am not ashamed of myself, please don't feel embarrassed for my sake.'

She turned her head, blushed some more and began to say, 'No, oh no, you—'

I said, 'I know women adore greedy people because that's the way they win their hearts. I am a glutton and that's why, I've always received so much care from women that today I am in this state, where I don't feel the least bit of shame. So, please feel free to stare your eyes out as I am eating; it doesn't bother me one bit. I will chew up every one of these drumsticks and leave nothing to them—that's my nature.'

A few days ago I was reading a contemporary English book, which contained explicit details of the union between a man and a woman. I'd left it behind in the drawing room. One afternoon I walked into the room for some reason and found Queen Bee reading the book; as she heard footsteps she covered it with another book and stood up. The book she used to cover the first one was a collection of Longfellow's poems.

I said, 'Look here, it beats me why you feel embarrassed about reading poetry. It should be the men who feel shy because some of us are lawyers and some engineers. If we must read poetry, it has to be late at night behind closed doors. You, women, are the closest to poetry. The God who created you is the poet of all poets and it is at His feet that Jaidev has composed his *Lalitalabangalata*.'

The Queen Bee didn't reply; she just laughed and blushed and made as if to leave. I said, 'No, no, that won't do. Please sit and read. I'd left behind a book; I'll just take that and clear out.'

I picked up my book off the table and said, 'Thank goodness this book didn't fall into your hands, or you might have beaten me up.'

The Bee asked, 'Why?'

I replied, 'Because, this isn't poetry. What this contains is the most basic facts about human beings, spoken quite bluntly too, without any artifice. I really wanted Nikhil to read this book.'

With a slight frown, the Bee asked, 'And why is that?'

I said, 'Since he is a man and he's one of us. He loves to see this raw world through a blur and that's why he and I argue so often. You can see, that's the reason why he has taken our swadeshi issue to be like Longfellow's poetry—he'd rather we tread gently on the rhythm for every little topic. We are more prosaic than prose, we're the destroyers of rhythm.'

The Bee asked, 'How is this linked to swadeshi?'

I said, 'You'll know if you read it. Whether it's swadeshi or any other matter, Nikhil would rather go with illusory views; hence, at every step he collides with human nature and then he resorts to calling nature all sorts of names. He refuses to accept that long before views and opinions, our natures were created and they will continue to be, long after all beliefs die.'

The Bee was silent for a while; then she asked solemnly, 'Isn't it in our nature to want to rise above our innate nature?'

I laughed to myself and thought, 'Oh princess, dear one, this isn't you speaking. You've learnt this from Nikhilesh. You are a hale and hearty person, bursting with the juices of Nature; the moment you've heard the clarion call of Nature, your flesh and blood has responded to it—why would the illusory web of all that they've preached to you be enough to hold you back? Don't I know that your veins are alive with the powers of life's fire? How much longer can the wet towel of moral lectures keep you cold?'

I said, 'In this world, there are more weak people than strong; in order to save their lives, they chant those refrains into the ears of the world and drive the strong ones crazy. Only those who have been deprived by Nature and weakened, tend towards enervating other people's nature.'

The Bee said, 'We, the women, are weak too. So we should join the conspiracy of the weak.'

I laughed and said, 'Who says you're weak? Men have cajoled you into thinking that you are helpless and weakened you with shame. I believe that you are the strongest. I can give it to you in writing that women will break free of the fort of chants, take on a devastating form and gain their freedom. Men only show off their strength, but deep down they are caged beings. Until today they have bound themselves by writing their own commandments. They've huffed and puffed and turned womankind into golden chains and wrapped themselves within and without. If man didn't have this amazing capacity to trap himself with his own snares, he'd be far ahead today. The traps built by his own hands are the biggest deities for him. Man has adorned them variously, painted them in different hues and worshipped them with varied names. But women? You have desired reality in this world with your heart, soul and body, given birth to reality and nurtured it.'

The Bee was an educated woman and she didn't give up easily. She said, 'If that were the truth, would it be possible for man to love woman?'

I said, 'Women are well aware of that; they know that men, by nature, appreciate deceit. Hence they borrow words from men, mask themselves and try to entice men. They know that the naturally inebriated menfolk are more inclined towards drink than food; hence, through devious means and tricks and gestures, they try to pass themselves off as liquor and desperately hide the fact that they are actually victuals. Women are materialists and they do not need any accessory illusions; those are set out only for the benefit of men. Women have become enchantresses under duress.'

The Bee said, 'Then why do you wish to shatter the illusion?'

I said, 'Because, I want freedom. I want freedom for my country as well as for relationships between human beings. My nation is very real to me and hence I simply cannot look at her through the misty veils of moral ethics. I am very real to me, you are very real to me and hence I do not condone the business of making two people mysterious and enigmatic to one another simply by scattering a few words between us.'

I had to keep in mind that startling a sleepwalker suddenly wasn't desirable. But my nature is so aggressive that it was impossible to tread softly. I know that my words that day were a little too strong; I know that the first impact of those words could be a little harsh. But women welcome the brave. Men love the ethereal; women adore the tangible. That's why men rush to worship the avatars of their own Idea and women gather their heart's prayers at the feet of the powerful.

Just as our conversation showed signs of warming up, Nikhil's childhood teacher Chandranathbabu came into the room. On the whole, the world was a fairly nice place but the havoc caused by these teachers made one want to quit it. People like Nikhilesh would rather his world remained a school till the end of his life. We were old enough, and yet the school has to tag along; even when we've started living adult lives, the school won't let us go. It'd be quite right to drag the teacher to the pyre with us when we die. That day, the symbol of school interrupted our conversation at an ill-timed juncture. I suppose there's a student-mentality embedded deep inside all of us. Bold as I am, even I was a little taken aback. And our Bee—from her face it was apparent that in an instant she'd turned into the best student in the class and solemnly taken her place in the front bench. It's as if she had remembered suddenly that she had a responsibility to do well in her exams. Some people sit by the roadside like the points-men of the railways; they switch the train of thoughts from one track to another for no good reason whatsoever.

As soon as he entered the room, Chandranathbabu was embarrassed and was about to leave, 'I'm sorry, I—.' Even before he finished the sentence, the Bee knelt down and touched his feet and said, 'Sir, please don't leave; do have a seat.' She spoke like she was drowning in mid-sea and needed his help. Coward! Or perhaps I am wrong. Maybe there was a ploy here—a way of increasing her worth. Perhaps the Bee wanted to let me know in an elaborate fashion that, 'You may think you've overwhelmed me, but I have far greater respect for Chandranathbabu.' So, go ahead. After all, one has to respect one's teachers. I am not a teacher and so I do not want empty respect. I've already made it clear that unsubstantial things do not satiate me—I need matter.

Chandranathbabu brought up swadeshi. I decided I'd let him babble non-stop and not reply to a single comment. It's good to let old people talk; it makes them feel that they're running the world and the poor souls never find out how distanced they are from the actual running of the world. At first, I held my tongue; but even his worst enemies wouldn't accuse Sandipbabu of being a patient man. When Chandranathbabu said, 'Look, we have never done any farming and if we expect we'll reap a harvest so soon after sowing the seeds, we—' I couldn't help it; I said, 'We don't want a harvest; we say, *Ma phaleshu kadachana*—work without expectation of the result.'

Chandranathbabu was stunned, 'Then, what do you all want?'

I said, 'Poisoned weeds—it costs nothing to grow them.'

The teacher said, 'Poisoned weeds don't just hinder others, it's an encumbrance to itself too.'

I said, 'That's the moral value meant for schools. We're not writing out maxims on a board. Chalk in hand, our hearts are burning and for now that's the most important thing. Right now we'll scatter thorns on the path, keeping the soles of other people in mind. Later, when it'll hurt our own feet, there's enough time to repent at leisure. Is that too much? When we're old enough to die, the fires will have died down and now that we're young they're burning furiously, as they should.'

Chandranathbabu laughed a little and said, 'If you want to rave and rant, I guess you will. But please don't pat yourself on the back saying that it's the brave thing or the best thing to do. On this earth, only those civilizations have saved themselves that have worked hard—not the ones that have raved and ranted. Those who have always feared hard work like the devil are the only ones who wake up suddenly and believe that they'll get somewhere through the blind alley of wrongdoings.'

I was just getting ready to furnish a severe reply when Nikhil entered. Chandranathbabu rose, looked at the Bee and said, 'I'll take leave today, Ma. I have work to do.'

After he left, I showed my English novel to Nikhil and said, 'I was telling Queen Bee about this book.'

Ninety-nine per cent of the people on this earth have to be fooled by lies, but this perpetual student of the schoolteacher is most easily fooled by the truth. He is best deceived when you do it openly, telling all. It's better to play the game of truth with him.

Nikhil looked at the name of the book and kept quiet. I said, 'Man has cluttered up this earth, where he lives, with many unwieldy words and thoughts. So, writers such as this one have set forth, broom in hand, to remove the cobwebs and clearly expose the substance beneath it all. So, I was telling the Bee that you should read this book.'

Nikhil said, 'I have read it.'

I asked, 'What do you think of it?'

Nikhil said, 'For those who learn a lesson from such books, it's good; for those who want to use it for escape, it's like poison.'

I asked, 'What does that mean?'

Nikhil said, 'Look, in this day and age if someone says nobody has any right over his own property, it makes sense only if the speaker is a totally selfless man; but if he's a greedy thief, the words are a lie on his lips. If one's appetites are strong, he wouldn't really be able to make sense of this book.'

I said, 'But appetite is that gas-lamp of Nature which guides us on these roads. Those who deny the appetite wish to achieve a third eye by plucking out both their eyes.'

Nikhil said, 'I accept appetite or proclivity only when I accept renunciation at the same time. If I try to see something by stuffing it right into my eyes, I hurt my eyes and also fail to see it. When people try to realize everything through their appetite, they distort their desires without realizing the truth.'

I said, 'Look Nikhil, it is self-indulgence to see the world through glasses framed by moral ethics; that's why in a crisis you cannot see reality clearly and you cannot complete any task with vigour.'

Nikhil said, 'I don't think a job is successful only if it's done vigorously.'

'Then?'

'What's the use of arguing in vain? These matters lose their charm if they're discussed to no avail.'

I really wanted the Bee to join our discussion. Till this point she sat there without saying a word. Perhaps today I'd really shaken her mind quite deeply and so she was unsure, wanting to revalidate her lessons from the schoolteacher.

Was the dose too strong today? But the jolt was important. At the outset one must realize that something which the mind always accepted as fixed can be shaken.

I said to Nikhil, 'It's a good thing I spoke to you. I was about to let Queen Bee read this book.'

Nikhil said, 'What's the harm in that? Bimal should read any book that I've read. I'd just like to clarify one matter though; nowadays Europe is intent on analysing all things human in terms of science and all discussions rest upon premises like man is merely physiology or biology or psychology or at best, sociology. But, please, I beg you to remember that man is not just a logos, he's made up of all sciences and he goes beyond them all, stretching himself towards eternity. You accuse me that I am the schoolteacher's student; I'm not, but you are. You wish to find man through your science teachers and not through your inner beings.'

I said, 'Nikhil, why are you so excitable these days?'

He said, 'It's because I can see quite clearly that you are denigrating man, humiliating him.'

'Why do you say that?'

'I see it in the environment, through my own pain. You are intent on tortuously killing Him who is the noblest in man, the Beautiful, the Ascetic.'

'This is some mad rambling of yours!'

Abruptly Nikhil stood up and said, 'Look Sandip, I firmly believe that man can suffer endless agony and he'll still be alive; hence I'm prepared to tolerate everything knowingly.'

He finished speaking and walked out of the room.

I watched this display in amazement. Then I heard a sudden sound and turned to see that some books had dropped noisily to the floor, and Queen Bee was walking away hurriedly, keeping a distance from me.

Strange man, that Nikhilesh! He can feel distinctly that dark clouds have gathered over his home. Yet, why doesn't he just throw me out? I know he is waiting to see what Bimala does. If Bimala tells him, 'You are not the right partner for me,' only then will he lower his head and say, 'I see that there's been a mistake.' He doesn't have the strength to realize that the biggest mistake is in calling a mistake by that name. Nikhil is a perfect example of just how Idea enervates a man. I have never seen another man like him. He is an eccentric product of Nature. It'll be difficult to even construct a story or a play around him, let alone a family.

Then of course the Bee—it was obvious that the spell has broken today. She has understood the force of the tide which had her in its thrall. Now, fully aware, she has to either move forward or turn back. Not really; from now on, she'll go forward and turn back alternately. I'm not worried about that. When your clothes are on fire, you may run around as much as you please and it'll only serve to stoke the flames some more. The jolts of fear will make her emotions stronger. I have seen so many of them by now. That widow, Kusum, finally came and surrendered to me, trembling with fear. And the foreign girl who lived near our hostel—on some days when she was upset with me I felt she'd tear me to pieces. I remember that day very well, when she screamed, 'Go, go' and threw me out of her room; the moment I stepped over the threshold, she came running back, fell at my feet, cried and banged her head on the floor and fainted. I know these ones very well—call it anger, fear, shame or hatred, these only act as firewood within their heart and burn to cinder after stoking the fire in it. The only thing that can contain this fire is Idea. But women don't possess an ounce of it. They do their good deeds, go to pilgrimages, bow piously before the holy man, just as we men go to office—but they stay far away from Idea.

I won't say much to her myself; but I'll offer her some contemporary English books. Let her gradually realize that it's 'modern' to admire and accept desire as a reality. It's not 'modern' to revere control as the greater and desire as the lesser virtue. If she only takes refuge in the word 'modern' she'd gain a lot of courage, because women need a pilgrimage, a holy man, some set traditions; mere Idea alone is unappealing.

Anyway, let's see this play through till the fifth act. I cannot proclaim that I am a mere spectator sitting on a royal seat in the balcony and clapping occasionally. My heartstrings feel stretched and the veins throb from time to time. At night when I switch off the lights and retire to bed, the slightest touch, the smallest look and the tiniest word resounds in the dark. When I wake up in the morning, my heart sparkles with joy and I feel as if a pleasant refrain is flowing in my veins.

In the photo-frames on this table, there was a photograph of Nikhil and one of the Bee. I'd taken her picture out of it.

Yesterday I showed her the empty space and said, 'The miser's stinginess makes the thief steal. Hence, it's only fair that the thief and the miser share the blame for the theft. What do you say?'

The Bee smiled a little and said, 'That picture wasn't a good one.'

I said, 'Can't be helped. A picture cannot improve upon itself. I'll have to be happy with whatever it is.'

The Bee opened a book and began leafing through it. I said, 'If you're upset, I'll fill that empty space somehow.'

Today I've done it. This photo of mine was taken when I was younger; my face was more innocent then, as was my heart. I still believed in life beyond the here and now. Although such beliefs often cheat you, they have one good feature—they cast a soft glow on your soul.

My photo is placed beside Nikhil's—the two friends.

Nikhilesh

I never used to think of myself before. Nowadays I try to see myself from the outside quite often. I wonder how I look through Bimal's eyes. Too stern, perhaps; I have the bad habit of taking everything too seriously.

It's just that it is better to laugh away your troubles than drown them in buckets of tears. That's what I am trying to do. Only because we brush aside all the sorrows that lie scattered at home and in the world, like a shadow or some illusion, that we can continue to eat and sleep; if we held on to them even for an instant as a reality, could we have swallowed a morsel or slept a wink? But I can't see myself as a part of that brushing aside or flowing away. It feels as though the earth is laden with my sorrows which are accumulating like an eternal burden. Hence the grimness, and hence a close look at myself makes me want to burst into tears.

Well, wretched one, why don't you stand in the world's marketplace and compare yourself with the crores of people collected over centuries and beyond and then decide what Bimal is to you? She is your wife! Whom do you call a wife? You have puffed up that word with your own breath and go around carefully protecting it; do you know that one pinprick from outside and it'll all deflate in a trice?

My wife, and hence she is all mine! If she wants to say, 'No, I am myself', immediately I'd say, 'Impossible; you are *my* wife!' Wife! Is that a reason! Is that a truth! Can you actually bind a person into that one word and lock her into it?

Wife! I have nurtured that word within my heart, lavished all that is gratifying, all that is pure upon it and never set it down upon the dusty earth. So many sacred incense sticks, musical flutes, spring blossoms and autumnal shefalis have gone into that name! If it suddenly drowns into the murky waters of the drain like the paper boats we played with, then along with it all my—

There I go, the same old seriousness! What are you calling the drain and which the murky waters? That was just spoken in anger. Something won't change into something else just because it'd upset me, would it? If Bimal is not mine then she simply isn't mine and all the persuasion and outbursts will only serve to make that clearer. My heart is bursting! Let it. It won't make either the world or me a poor man. Man is far greater than all that he loses in one lifetime; salvation awaits him even at the end of all the oceans of tears; that's why he weeps, otherwise he wouldn't.

But in the eyes of society—oh, let society bother with all that and do what they please. I weep for myself and not for society. If Bimal says she is not my wife, then whether society considers her my wife or not, I must abdicate.

Of course I am sad. But one particular misery will be quite untrue and I'll stop myself from feeling it at all cost. Like a coward, I refuse to feel that rejection has reduced the value of my life. My life is valuable; I wasn't born to use up that worth to merely buy up the inner chambers of my home. A time has come for me to realize that a business venture the size of mine will never run short of funds.

Today, as I look at myself, I should also look at Bimal as an outsider. Until now, I had adorned her with some ideals of my own imagination. My ideal woman didn't quite match with the Bimal of real life at all points; but still I have worshipped her through my fantasy.

It's not my greatness, it's my biggest drawback. I am greedy; I wanted to romance my perfect fantasy image in my mind and the actual Bimal only became an excuse. Bimal has always been what she is. She never really had to turn into the image of perfection for my sake. Obviously, the Maker does not work to meet my demands.

In that case, today I need to take clear stock of several things; I must firmly erase all the colourful doodles I have splattered with the colours of illusion. Until today, I have willingly turned a blind eye towards many things. Today it is obvious to me, that in Bimal's life I am incidental; the person whom Bimal's entire being can truly complement, is Sandip. Knowing this alone is enough for me.

This is not a day when I can be modest even to my own self. Sandip has many great qualities, which are attractive and they used to attract me too until recently; but, even on a modest scale, I'll have to admit that on the whole he is in no way greater than me. If a swayamvara is held and the garland goes to Sandip and not to me, then through this rejection the gods would've judged the one who made the choice and not me. I say this today, not out of pride. Now, if I do not realize my own worth truly within myself, if I think this injury is the ultimate humiliation, then I'll end up in the world's garbage-dump like a piece of trash; I'll be truly fit for nothing else.

Let the joy of freedom raise its head within me in spite of all the unbearable misery of this day. It's good that I understood; I got to know the inner and the outer. After all the debit and credit, whatever remains is all of me. It's not a physically handicapped me or an indigent me or even a feeble me raised on a convalescent's diet in the inner chambers of the home; it is the I who has been fashioned by the strong hand of Fate. Whatever had to happen has happened and nothing worse could be in the offing.

Just now my teacher came up to me, placed his hand on my shoulder and said, 'Nikhil, go to sleep, it is one o'clock.'

It's rather difficult for me to go to bed until Bimal is fast asleep, very late in the night. During the day I see her and even speak to her, but alone in the stillness of night in our bed, what can I say to her? My entire being shrinks in discomfiture.

I asked my teacher, 'Why haven't you gone to bed yet?'

He laughed ever so slightly and said, 'My days of sleep are over, now it's time to stay awake.'

I'd written thus far and was about to retire to bed when suddenly the thick clouds seen through my window parted a little and a lone star glimmered brightly through them. I felt it was saying to me, 'So many relationships sever and tear, but I still remain; I am the eternal flame of the wedding night's lamp, the everlasting kiss of a lovers' night.'

At that moment my heart was full and I felt that behind the curtain of this worldly life, my perpetual lover sat still. In so many lives, in so many mirrors I have seen her face—so many broken, distorted, dusty mirrors. The moment I say, 'Let me possess the mirror and put it inside a box,' the face disappears. Let it be— how does my mirror or that reflection matter! Dear heart, your faith stays intact, your smile will never fade; the sindoor with which you've covered your hairline, glows bright every day with the sun's rays.

A devil stood in a corner in the dark and said, 'Your imagination is fooling the child in you!' So be it, a child needs to be fooled—one lakh children, one crore children, one child after another—children cry so hard! Is it possible to fool so many children with anything but the truth? My love will not betray me—she's Truth, the Truth—that's why I see her again and again and will continue to see her always; I've seen her through my mistakes and through the mist of tears. In the midst of the marketplace of life I've seen her, lost her and found her again and when I slip through death's jaws, I'll see her again. Oh heartless one, don't mock me any more. If I have lost the way to the path on which you have walked, the breeze with the scent of your hair, please don't punish me forever for that single blunder. That star whose veil has slipped, is telling me, 'No, oh no, don't be afraid. Whatever is eternal will always be there.'

Now let me go and take a look at my Bimal; she's sprawled on the bed, in deep slumber. Let me place a kiss on her forehead without waking her. That kiss is my offering of devotion. I believe after death I'll forget everything—all mistakes, all tears—but the evocative resonance of this kiss will stay somewhere, because through life after life these kisses are being strung into a garland to be thrown around my lover's neck.

At this time my second sister-in-law entered my room. The clock in our hall chimed two o'clock in strident tones.

'Thakurpo, what are you up to? Please, dear brother, go to sleep—don't torment yourself like this. I cannot bear to look at the state you are in.'

As she spoke, tears trickled down her cheeks.

Silently, I bent down, touched her feet and proceeded to my room.

Bimala

Initially, I didn't suspect anything or feel any apprehension; I thought I was surrendering myself to the work of the country. There's such terrible exultation in total surrender! That day I discovered for the first time that the greatest pleasure lay in wrecking one's own self.

I don't know if this obsession would have evaporated amidst some vague emotions. But Sandipbabu couldn't wait, he made himself very clear. His tone of voice seemed to caress me like a touch, his glances seemed to fall at my feet, pleading. Yet, it held such furious desire, as if it wanted to drag me by my hair and tear me away like a heartless brigand.

I'll be honest: the destructive image of this rampant desire attracted me day and night. I began to feel there'd be a strange thrill in ruining myself totally. It'd bring such shame, such fear and yet, it was a bittersweet treat.

There was also unbridled curiosity—the mystery of his livid lust, of a person whom I don't know very well, a person whom I wasn't sure of having, a person whose powers were immense, whose youth burned in a thousand flames—it was great, it was immense! I had never ever dreamed of this. The ocean, which was far away and of which I'd only read in books, suddenly swelled up in a ravenous flood, overcame all barriers and laid itself down in all its timelessness, foaming at my feet in the backyard pond where I wash utensils and draw water.

To start with, I'd begun to revere Sandipbabu. But that reverence soon washed away. I don't even respect him—in fact I disrespect him. I have understood very clearly that he cannot compare with my husband. And gradually, if not at the very outset, I have even come to believe that the quality which one tends to mistake for manliness in Sandip is nothing but flightiness.

Yet, this veena of mine made of flesh and blood, thoughts and ideas, began to play in Sandip's hands alone. I'd like to hate those hands and this veena—but yet, it has sung for him! And when those tunes filled my days and nights, I didn't have any mercy any more. Each throb of my veins and each surge in my blood repeated to me, 'You and all that you possess should now sink to the nadir of that tune and revel in it.'

There is no denying it any more: I have something that— what should I say? Something for which, it's best for me to die.

Whenever the teacher has some time to spare, he comes and sits by me. He has a strength: in an instant he can take your mind to such a great height that you can clearly see the entire range of your life spread out before your eyes—what I've always considered to be the limit suddenly doesn't appear to be the limit any longer.

But what's the use! I don't want to see things that way. I can't even say that I want to be free of the seduction that has me in its grip. Let the home suffer, let the Truth within me grow darker by the minute and die, but I can't stop myself from wishing that my addiction should continue forever. When my cousin Munu's husband got drunk, he beat her and later repented for it and wailed and vowed never to touch that stuff again; he'd reach for the liquor the very next day and I used to seethe with rage. Today I find that my liquor is far more dangerous than his—this alcohol doesn't need to be bought from the store or poured into a glass—it spawns by itself in my blood. What should I do! Is this how I'll spend my whole life?

At times, startled, I look at myself and feel that all of this is a nightmare; this me isn't the real one. This is a terrible contradiction; there is no connection between the beginning and the end; this is dark disgrace painted in the shades of a rainbow by an illusory magician. I can't understand what happened and how it all happened.

One day my second sister-in-law came in, laughed and said, 'Our Chhotorani is very hospitable. She takes such good care of her guest that he doesn't want to budge from the house. In our times too, there were guests coming and going, but they never got so much care. In those times there were some customs, husbands needed some care as well. Just because Thakurpo was born in these times, he's been swindled. He should have come to this house as a guest—then perhaps he'd have stayed awhile—now, one wonders. Little brute, don't you even have the heart to glance at his face once and see what he's become?'

There was a time when these accusations didn't bother me in the least. I used to think they didn't have the capacity to understand the vow that I'd taken. There was a shield of emotion around me then; I'd thought that since I was giving up my life for my country, I had no room for shame and dishonour.

For some days now, there's been no talk of the country. Now the discussion revolves around the relationship between men and women in the modern times and other varied subjects. Under that pretext, there's also an exchange of English and Vaishnav poetry. The tenor of those poems is a very coarse one. I'd never had a taste of this tune in my home; I began to feel, this was the strain of manliness, of the powerful.

But today there are no shields any more. I have no answer for queries like why Sandipbabu is staying on thus for days on end and why I hold forth with him for no reason whatsoever. So, that day, I was very angry with myself, my second sister-in-law and the entire establishment and I said, 'No, I'll not go into the sitting room again; not even if I die.'

For two days I didn't step out. In those two days it became clear to me just how far I'd gone. I felt all the joy had gone from my life. I felt like throwing away everything that came my way, within my reach. My entire being seemed to wait for someone; the blood in my veins seemed to be waiting for a response from out there.

I tried working very hard. The floor of my room was clean enough; yet, I personally supervised it and had it scrubbed clean with pots and pots of water. Everything was arranged in one way in the almirah; I took it all out, needlessly, dusted it and rearranged everything. That day it was nearly two in the afternoon when I had my bath. That evening I didn't tie my hair. I just put it up in a bun and managed to hassle everyone into reorganizing the pantry. I found that a lot has been stolen from there in this time. But I didn't dare scold anyone for it, in case someone, even in their mind, retorted, 'Where were your eyes all these days?'

I went through the hustle-bustle of the day like one possessed. The next day I tried reading. I don't remember what I read, but suddenly I found myself, absent-minded and book in hand, standing in the corridor leading outside and silently peering through the blinds. Through it, a row of rooms outside on the north side of our yard was visible. Of those, I felt one room had slipped far away from the ocean of my life and ships couldn't ply there any more. I looked and looked! I felt I was a ghost of the day before yesterday, there in all the places and yet not there.

At one point Sandip stepped out into the balcony, newspaper in hand. I could clearly see the impatience stamped on his face. It felt as though he was getting angry at the yard, at the railings of the balcony. He hurled the newspaper away. If he could, he'd perhaps have torn away a bit of the sky. My vow almost broke down. Just as I was about to turn towards the sitting room, I found my second sister-in-law standing behind me.

'Well, well, quite a show!' She threw the comment in the air and walked away. I didn't go outside.

The next day Gobinda's mother came and said, 'Chhotoranima, it's time you handed out the food that'll be cooked today.'

I said, 'Ask Harimati to do it.' I threw down the bunch of keys and continued with the needlework that I was doing. At this time, the bearer came and handed me a letter and said, 'Sandipbabu gave it.' Look at his nerve: just imagine what the bearer must have thought! My heart was fluttering. I opened the note and found there was no greeting; just these words: 'Urgent need. Country's work. Sandip.'

Forget sewing! Hurriedly I checked my hair before the mirror. I changed my jacket and not the sari. I knew that in his eyes this jacket of mine had a special identity.

My second sister-in-law was sitting and cracking betel nuts on the balcony, which I had to cross on my way out. Today I didn't hesitate in the least. She asked, 'Where to?'

I said, 'To the sitting room.'

'So early? Morning games, is it?'

I went my way without replying. She started singing,

'My Radha keels over as she walks,
Like the crab of the deep sea,
And oh, she doesn't know of the sticky sugar.'

When I walked into the sitting room, I found Sandip lost in a book listing the paintings exhibited at the British Academy, his back to the door. Sandip considered himself quite a connoisseur of art. One day my husband said to him, 'If artists are in need of a tutor, they won't have a problem finding a suitable one as long as you are alive.'

It was unlike my husband to speak so derisively; but these days his temperament had changed. He never missed a chance to hurt Sandip's ego.

Sandip said, 'Are you of the opinion that artists don't need any further instruction?'

'People like us will always have to learn new lessons from the artists themselves because there are no fixed rules in art.'

Sandip scoffed at my husband's humility and laughed heartily; he said, 'Nikhil, you believe that indigence is the biggest wealth and the more you invest it, the richer you grow. I claim that if someone doesn't have an ego, he's like moss in the rapids, floating about aimlessly.'

My state of mind was a strange one. On the one hand I wished that my husband would win the argument and Sandip's ego would get a jolt, yet it was this same aggressive ego in him that attracted me—like the sparkle of an expensive diamond which nothing could put to shame. Even the sun couldn't outshine it—instead, it seemed to gain a surge of defiance from every challenge.

I entered the room. I knew Sandip had heard my footsteps but he pretended he hadn't heard it and continued reading. I was afraid he'd broach the topic of art. I still felt shy about the kinds of pictures and the kinds of things Sandip liked to discuss with me on the pretext of art. To overcome that shyness I had to pretend that there was nothing to be shy about.

So, for an instant I was tempted to just go back when suddenly Sandip heaved a great sigh, looked up and seemed startled to see me. He said, 'Oh, there you are!'

There was a covert censure in his words, both in his eyes and his tone of voice. I was in such a state that I even accepted this censure. Thanks to the claims that Sandip had acquired over me, it was as if my absence of two or three days was also a crime. I knew that Sandip's resentment was an insult to me; but I was too weak to be incensed.

I didn't respond and just stood there silently. Although my eyes were elsewhere, I was aware that Sandip's accusing eyes laid siege to my face and refused to budge. What was this all about! If he spoke something, I could at least hide behind those words and gain some respite. When my embarrassment became unbearable I said, 'Why did you send for me?'

Startled, Sandip said, 'Does there have to be a purpose? Is it wrong to be friends? Why this disregard for that which is the greatest in this world? Queen Bee, must you drive away the heart's adulation from the door, like a stray dog?'

My heart was fluttering. Dark clouds seemed to gather around me and there was no way to stop them. Fear and excitement struggled equally for mastery. Will I be able to bear the weight of this catastrophe or will it break my back? Perhaps I'd fall flat on my face on the dusty wayside.

My hands and legs were trembling. I stood very firmly and said to him, 'Sandipbabu, you sent for me saying there's some urgent work of the country and hence I dropped my household chores and came here.'

He smiled a little and said, 'My point exactly. Do you know that I have come here to worship? Haven't I told you that I clearly perceive the power of my country in you? Geography is not a Truth. One can't lay down one's life for a map. Only when

I see you before me I realize how beautiful the country is, how dear, how full of power and life. I will know that I've received my country's command only when you anoint my brow yourself and wish me luck. When I'll fall to the ground, mortally wounded as I fight bravely, I'll remember this and never think I've fallen on a piece of land in geographical terms, but instead on an anchal—do you know which kind? It's the anchal of the sari you wore the other day, red as the earth and its border as red as a stream of blood. Can I ever forget it! This is what makes life dynamic and death attractive.'

As he spoke, Sandip's eyes burnt bright. I couldn't figure out if it was the fire of reverence or hunger that burnt in his eyes. I remembered the day when I first heard his speech. That day, I'd forgotten if he was a live flame or a human being. It's possible to behave humanly with ordinary humans—there are rules and codes in place for that. But fire belongs to a different genre altogether. In an instant it can dazzle your eyes, turn destruction into an object of beauty. You begin to feel that the truth that lay hidden among the neglected driftwood of everyday life, has taken up its radiant form, rushing to scorch the reserves stashed away by the misers everywhere.

After this, I didn't have the power to speak. I was afraid that at any moment Sandip would run to me and grab my hand, because his hands were shaking just like the trembling flames and his gaze rested on me like sparks of fire.

'Are you determined to privilege the trivial domestic rules and codes?' Sandip spoke up. 'You women have so much energy, the very whiff of which can make life or death a trifling matter to us; is that to be wrapped in a veil and kept indoors? Today, please don't hesitate, don't listen to the wagging tongues around you; today you must snap your fingers at mores and margins and come rushing into freedom.'

When the adulation for the country mingled thus with the adulation for me in Sandipbabu's words and the cords of reticence were sorely strained, then did my blood throb and dance! The discussions of art and Vaishnav poetry, of the relations between man and woman and various other real and intangible subjects, clouded my heart with guilt. But today the gloom of the embers caught fire again and the blaze of light from it veiled my shame. I felt that it was a wondrous, divine marvel to be a woman.

Alas, why didn't that marvel in all its visible brilliance flash through my mass of hair at that very instant! Why didn't a word come forth from my lips, which could, like a chant, instantly take the nation through a fiery initiation!

At that moment, the maid Khemadasi appeared, wailing and screaming loudly. She said, 'Please settle my accounts and let me go. Never in my entire life have I been—' The rest of her words was drowned in sobs.

'What is it? What's the matter?'

Apparently my second sister-in-law's maid, Thako, had unnecessarily quarrelled with Khema and called her unmentionable names.

I tried to pacify her saying that I would look into it and she would get justice but it was impossible to get her to stop wailing.

It was as if someone had poured a bucket of dirty water on the musical piece that was moving towards a crescendo that morning. The muck that was inherent in woman, beneath the budding lotus, was dredged up. In order to cover that up in front of Sandip, I had to rush indoors immediately. I found my second sister-in-law sitting in the balcony, as before, cracking betel nuts with her head lowered; a small smile lingered on her lips and she hummed, 'My Radha keels over as she walks'—nothing about her indicated that anything had gone wrong anywhere.

I said, 'Mejorani, why does your Thako abuse Khema for no reason thus?'

She raised her brows and said, 'Oh really, is that true? I'll take the broom to that vixen's back and throw her out. Just look at that: so early in the day she has gone and spoilt your session in the sitting room. And I'd say, Khema is also quite a fool—can't she see that her mistress is chatting with a babu outside? She just landed up there with her tales—I see she's lost all sense of shame and decorum! But, Chhotorani, you don't have to trouble yourself over these domestic issues. Why don't you go on outside and I'll resolve the matter as best I can.'

The human mind is a strange thing; how suddenly the wind changes and the sail turns around. I felt it was so out of place in my usual domestic routine for me to go and converse with Sandip in the morning, leaving all my domestic duties undone, that I just walked back to my room without a word.

I knew for a fact that at the right time my second sister-in-law must have urged Thako to pick a fight with Khema. But I stood on such unstable grounds myself that I couldn't say anything on these matters. Just the other day, in the heat of the moment I'd fought so defiantly with my husband to sack Nanku, the guard, but I couldn't sustain it till the end. Gradually my own agitation made me feel embarrassed. To add to that, my sister-in-law came and said to my husband, 'Thakurpo, I am to blame. Look here, we are traditional women and your Sandipbabu's ways don't really seem very proper to us—so, I thought it was for the best and I instructed the guard—but I didn't ever think that this would be an insult to Chhotorani; in fact I thought the opposite—alas for my Fate, more fool I!'

Thus, whenever I tried to look at something in glorious terms, from the perspective of the country or worship, and it curdled from the bottom in this way, my initial reaction would be anger, followed by guilt.

Today I came into my room, shut the door, sat by the window and began to think, if only one stayed within the bounds of the preordained rules, life could be so simple. Looking at my sister-in-law sitting cheerfully on the balcony, cracking betel nuts, made me realize how inaccessible the task of sitting on a simple seat and doing everyday chores had become to me. Every day I asked myself, where will it all end! Shall I die, will Sandip leave, will I recover one day and forget all this like a febrile delirium— or will I break my neck and sink into such a disaster that I'll never be able to recoup from it in my lifetime? If I couldn't effortlessly accept the good fortune that Fate had sent my way, how could I tear it to shreds thus?

The walls, ceiling, floor of this room, which I'd stepped into as a new bride nine years ago, were all gazing at me in amazement on this day. When my husband passed his MA and returned from Calcutta, he had bought a vine of some island in the Indian Ocean for me. It had just a few leaves, but the long bunch of flowers that bloomed in it were so beautiful, as if a rainbow was born in the lap of those few leaves and swung in its cradle. The two of us took that vine and hung it up by the window here, in our bedroom. The flowers bloomed just that once and never again; I have the hope that it'll bloom again. It is amazing that I still water the plant routinely; it is strange that the thick twine binding the vine hasn't loosened one bit—the leaves are still as green.

About four years ago, I framed a photo of my husband in an ivory frame and put it up on the mantlepiece. Occasionally when my gaze rests upon it, I can't look away. Till six days ago I used to bow before that picture, place flowers around it after my morning bath. So many days my husband had argued with me about this.

One day he said, 'In worshipping me you make me bigger than I am and this embarrasses me.'

I said, 'Why should you feel embarrassed?'

He said, 'I'm not just embarrassed, I'm also envious.'

I said, 'Listen to you! Who are you jealous of?'

He said, 'That fake me. This makes me feel that you aren't satisfied with the ordinary me and you want an extraordinary someone who'll overwhelm your senses. That's why your imagination has created an ideal me and you're playing a game of make-believe.'

I said, 'I feel so angry when you say such things.'

He said, 'No point getting angry with me, instead you should be mad at your destiny. You didn't really pick me out in a swayamvara; you had to take whatever you got with your eyes shut. Hence you're trying to rectify as much of me as you can, with spirituality. Since Damayanti had a swayamvara she could pick out the man over the god and since all of you haven't had a swayamvara, every day you ignore the man and garland the god.'

That day I was so angry with what he said, tears sprang to my eyes. The memory of it stops me from raising my eyes and looking at the picture on the mantlepiece.

There's another picture inside my jewel box. The other day I pretended to dust and clean the sitting room and picked up the photo-stand in which Sandip's photo is right beside my husband's, and brought it inside. I don't worship that photo and there's no question of bowing before it either; it stays covered up amidst my precious stones and jewellery and it brings such a thrill only because it is a secret. I shut all the doors of the room before I open the box and look at it. At night, I slowly enhance the light of the kerosene lamp and hold the photo before it and look at it silently. Every day I think that I should just consign him to that flame, turn him to ashes and finish it off for all times; and again, every day, I heave a sigh, slowly cover him up with my precious stones and jewellery and keep the photo under lock and key. But wretched, hapless soul: who was it that gave you these precious gems and jewels? So many caresses are intertwined with these. Where will they hide their face now? I'd be happy to just die.

Once Sandip said to me, 'It's not the inherent nature of women to vacillate. They don't have a left or right, they can only go ahead.' He always says, 'When the women of the country will rise, they'll speak much more lucidly than its men: "I want"—on the face of that want, no good or bad, no possible or impossible will be able to stand its ground. They'll just have that one claim: "We want", "I want". These words are the core chant of creation. This chant burns tempestuously in the fire of the sun and the stars. Its predilection of love is extreme; since it has desired man, for ages untold it has been sacrificing thousands of living things to that desire. That terrible chant of "I want", of the devastation of creation, is alive only in the women today. That's why the cowardly men are trying to raise dams on the way of that primitive flood of creation, so that it doesn't wash away their frail-as-pumpkin-creeper-frames as it roars with laughter and dances on its way. Men think they have raised these dams for all times to come. It's collecting, the water is collecting—today the body of water in the lake is quiet and sombre; today it neither moves nor speaks; silently it fills the pots and pans in man's kitchen. But the pressure will mount and the dam will burst; then the dumbstruck powers of all this time will roar "I want, I want" and rush forth.'

These words of Sandip strike up a drumming in my head. So, whenever there's a conflict with my self within me, when shame swears at me, I think of his words. Then I realize that this shame I feel stems from the fear of social repercussions, which takes the form of my second sister-in-law who sits on the balcony cracking betel nuts looking at me mockingly. Do I even care about her!

My complete fulfilment is in being able to say 'I want' promptly, unwavering, with all the strength I possess. Failure lies in not being able to say it. What's with that vine or the mantle—do they have the power to insult or mock the radiant 'I'?

I had a strong desire to throw the vine out the window and bring the photo down from the mantle: let the shameless nudity of the destructive forces unfold. My hand did go up, but my heart ached and tears came to my eyes—I threw myself on the floor and began to weep. What, oh what will become of me? What is in store for me!

Sandip

When I read my own words I find myself asking, is this Sandip? Am I made of words? Am I a book with covers of flesh and blood?

The earth is not a dead creature like the moon; it breathes and its rivers and oceans send up vapours—it's enveloped by that vapour and dust rises all around it. It is covered by this film of dust. If someone looked at this earth from the outside, he'd only see the reflection of this vapour and dust; would he catch a clear glimpse of the countries and continents?

The same way, when a person is alive the sighs of Idea rise from within him and so he becomes misty through that haze. The spots where he is clear, with land and water, where he is peculiar, cannot be seen: it feels as though he is a sphere of light and shade.

I have begun to feel that like the living planet, I too am tracing that sphere of Ideas in me. But I am not entirely just what I desire, what I think or what I decide. I am also that which I *don't* like, which I *don't* desire. I was created even before I was born; I haven't been able to select myself. I have to make do with whatever fell into my hands.

169

I know this very well that the mightier one is also the cruel one. The law is for the commoners and the extraordinary ones are above it. The earth is a level ground and the volcanic mountain prods through it with its horns of fire and rises up above it. It doesn't mete out justice to others around; it only looks to its own self. It's only by successful malevolence and unfeigned brutality that anyone has ever become rich or powerful, be it a man or a race. Only by blithely swallowing one, will 'two' be able to come into its own or the unbroken line drawn by 'one' would have continued unscathed.

Hence, I preach the practice of the unlawful. I tell everyone, crime is moksha, crime is the burning flame; when it doesn't burn it turns to ashes. Whether race or man, crimes must be committed to get somewhere in this world.

But still, this is only my Idea and not the entire me. However much I extol crime, there're some holes, some gaps in the cloak of Ideas and some things slip out through it, which are indeed naive and gentle. It is because most of me was already created even before I became myself.

Sometimes I put my followers to the test of heartlessness. Once we went to a garden for a picnic. A goat was grazing there and I asked who'd be able to cut off its hind leg with a machete. When everyone faltered, I went and did it myself. The man who was the most merciless in the entire group, fainted when he saw this sight. My calm, serene face made everyone bow down and pay homage to me as a great man, above mortal feelings. That day everyone glimpsed only the vaporous sphere of my Idea. But it was best to hide those spots where I was weak and merciful— whether this was my own doing or that of Fate—and where my heart was weeping within me.

Many things have also been covered up regarding this chapter in my life that has evolved around Bimala-Nikhil.

It wouldn't have been hidden if I didn't have anything to do with Ideas. My Idea is moulding my life in its own fashion, but there's a lot of my life that is outside of it. My desires and those other bits of my life don't coincide entirely; hence I like to keep them stashed away, hidden in a corner, or else they would end up spoiling everything.

This thing called 'life' is abstract; it is made up of such diversity. We, men with Ideas, wish to pour it into distinct moulds and view it clearly in perceptible forms; the success of life depends on that clarity. From the famous conqueror Alexander the Great to the contemporary billionaire of America, Rockefeller, each has poured himself into a precise mould, be it of the sword or of money, and only then has he been able to call himself a success.

This is the point on which Nikhil and I start arguing. Both he and I claim that one should know oneself. But from what he says, all that becomes apparent is that not knowing oneself is all that's there to knowing oneself. He said, 'What you call "getting the results" is actually a result that excludes one's own self. The soul is greater than results.'

I said, 'That is an ambiguous one.'

Nikhil said, 'I have no choice. Life is more obscure than a machine; if you take life to be a machine, that won't help you to know life. Similarly, the soul is more nebulous than results; but I wouldn't say you are really seeing the soul for what it is, if you see it realized fully in results.'

I asked, 'So, where do you see the soul? Under which nose or between which brow?'

He replied, 'At the point where the soul knows itself to be eternal, where it leaves results far behind and goes beyond it.'

'So what would you say of your country?'

'The same thing. When the country says, "I'll only look to myself", it may well get results, but it loses its soul; but when it can see Truth as greater than itself, it can perhaps lose all results and yet achieve its own self.'

'Where in history have you seen that happen?'

'Man is so great that he can dispense with examples as much as he can overlook results. Perhaps there are no instances, just like there are no traces of a flower inside the seed; but still the seed does contain the flower. Yet, are there no instances at all? Was it a desire for results that made Buddha inspire India for so many centuries with his aspirations?'

It's not that I can't make any sense of what Nikhil says. That perhaps, is precisely my problem. I have been born in India; the toxin of religiosity permeates my blood. I may loudly assert that the path of denunciation is a crazy one. But I'm not able to brush it aside absolutely. That's why, today, such strange things are happening in our country. The chant of religion and patriotism, both are being sung heartily—we want the Bhagavad Gita as well as Vande Mataram—not recognizing that this makes both equally obscure, the result being like a clash between the ill-matched drums and the shehnai. The task of my life is to put an end to this discordant cacophony. I'll keep the drums intact, but the shehnai has been our ruin. We will uphold the flags of want and desire, which has been handed to us by Mother Nature, Mother Shakti and Mother Mahamaya when they sent us into the battlefield. Desire is beautiful and as pure as the fresh blossom, which doesn't run to the powder-room at the drop of a hat to scrub itself with Vinoliya soap.

One question has been bothering me for a few days: why am I letting my life get entangled with Bimala's? My life isn't just a banana-boat drifting around hitting the shore where it wishes. This is what I meant when I said that I wish I could mould my life on the lines of one Idea, but it spills over. From time to time, people slip and slide. This time I've slipped away a bit too far.

I am not ashamed of the fact that Bimala has become the object of my desires. I can see quite clearly that she desires me: she is my very own. The fruit hangs on the tree by its stem, but does that mean we'll have to accept that stem's rights on it as eternal! All the thirst, all the sweetness that she has was meant to fall into my hands alone; her triumph lies in submitting herself to that. That is her religion and that is her integrity. I will pluck her and bring her there, I won't let her life go in vain.

However, I am worried that I'm getting entangled and I feel that Bimal may become a huge burden on my life. I have come into this world to be a leader; I shall lead people with my words and in their work. Those masses are the horse for my crusade. My seat is on its back, its reins in my hands; it doesn't know its destination—only I know it. I will not let it pause and think when thorns will make its feet bleed or mud will splatter it all over, I'll only make it gallop.

That horse of mine is at the door today, impatiently pawing the earth with its hooves; the skies tremble with its neighing and what am I doing? What am I doing with my time? My auspicious moments are almost slipping away.

I had the impression I could run like the storm; I could pluck a flower, throw it away and it wouldn't slow down my pace one bit. But now I seem to be hovering around the flower like the honeybee and not like the storm.

Obviously when I colour myself with my own Ideas, the colour isn't as fast at all the spots and suddenly I can glimpse that ordinary mortal. If some omniscient God were to pen down the story of my life, I'm sure it'd be seen that there isn't much difference between me and that Harry there—or even Nikhilesh for that matter. Last night I was leafing through my diary written at the time when I'd just passed my BA and my head was fairly bursting with philosophy. Ever since then I'd vowed that I wouldn't allow any illusions, other people's or mine, into my life, and I'd make my life entirely real. But from then until now, what do I see in the story of my life? Where is that tightly woven fabric? This is more like a net; the threads are all there, but there are as many gaps. I have tried to fight those weaknesses, but failed to conquer them. For a while now I was surely moving at a good pace; today again I find a large gap in myself.

It hurts. 'I want it, it's near my fingers and I'll pluck it'— this is a clear declaration, the shortest route. I have always said that those who can walk this path vehemently are the ones who succeed. But Lord Indra didn't allow this penance to be a simple one; from somewhere, he sent the angel to cause suffering and blur the ascetic's vision with the vaporous mesh.

I see Bimala thrashing about like a trapped deer; such fear, so much pathos in those large eyes, her body lacerated by her attempts to free herself—the hunter should be happy at this sight. I do feel joy, but I also feel pain. That's why I'm not able to tighten the noose properly while time flies past.

There have been moments when, had I rushed up to Bimala, pressed her hand and drawn her into my bosom, she wouldn't have been able to protest; she too felt that any moment now something was about to happen, which will change the significance of her entire world—standing before that elemental ambiguity, her face was pale, her eyes filled with fear as well as excitement as if the heavens and the world were holding their breath and standing still, waiting for a decision to be made. But I let those moments pass; I didn't allow the imminent to become definitive, with unabashed strength. From this I can tell that those constraints that were innate to my nature have now come out and stand there blocking my way.

Ravana, whom I respect as the primary protagonist of the *Ramayana,* also died in this fashion. Instead of bringing Sita into his chamber, he kept her in Ashokavana. Thanks to that tiny bit of naive quandary that persisted in that great hero, the burning of Lanka was in vain. If he didn't have the dilemma, Sita would have given up her chaste airs and worshipped Ravana! In the same way, this hesitation always made him pity and disregard Vibhishana whom he should have killed; instead he himself lost his life.

This is the tragedy of life. It hides in a corner of the heart, curled up into a little ball and then in an instant it overcomes the giant. Man is not what he knows himself to be and that is why so many unpleasant things happen.

Although Nikhil is so weird and I laugh at him so often, deep down I can't squash the knowledge that he's my friend. In the beginning I didn't think of him at all. But as the days go by, I feel shame before him, and pain too. Some days, as always, I venture into an argument with him in the course of our conversation, but the enthusiasm flags suddenly—so much so, that I even do what I've never done before, that is, pretend to agree with him on some things. But this hypocrisy doesn't go down well with me and it doesn't suit Nikhil either—here too, we have something in common.

So, these days I try to avoid Nikhil and my day is made if I don't bump into him. These are signs of weakness. The moment one acknowledges the spectre of culpability, it turns into something very real; then, even if you do not believe in it, it catches hold of you. I simply want to let Nikhil know this very frankly, that we must look at these things in larger, more realistic perspectives. A genuine friendship shouldn't get messed up when faced with the Truth.

But I can't deny the fact that this time I have been weak. This weakness hasn't impressed Bimala one bit; she is the moth that singed her wings in the flame of my unreserved masculinity.

When the haze of emotions sways me, Bimala is also swayed by it, but she feels revulsion; at that moment, although she cannot take back the garland she has thrown around my neck, the sight of it makes her feel like closing her eyes.

For both of us there is no turning back. I don't have the strength to leave Bimala now. But neither will I let go of my own path. My way is that of throngs of people, not this back door to the inner chambers. I'll not be able to abandon my own country now, especially not in these times; at present I'll merge Bimala with my country. The same westward storm that has snatched away the veil of right and wrong from the face of the motherland, will raise the bridal veil off Bimala's face—there is no disregard for her in that nakedness. The ship will sway on the waves of the ocean of people, the victory flag of Vande Mataram will flutter at its helm, roars and foaming waters all around—that ship will be our vessel of strength as well as that of love. There, Bimala will perceive such immense freedom that on its face, all her inhibitions will drop away without shame, unknown to her. Fascinated by this visage of destruction she won't hesitate to turn cruel. In Bimala I have seen the face of that gorgeous ruthless, which is the natural strength of Nature. If women could free themselves of the phony binds placed on them by men, I'd have truly witnessed Kali on this earth—she is the brazen goddess, she is heartless. I am a devotee of the same Kali; one day I'll drag Bimala amidst that devastation and invoke Kali. Let me make preparations for that.

Nikhilesh

Every corner is flooded by the monsoon torrents; the glow off the young rice stalks is like that from the body of a child. There was water all the way up till the gardens in our house. The morning sun poured down on this earth unimpeded, matching the passion of the blue sky.

If only I had music in my voice! The water in the streams shimmered, the leaves on the trees glistened and ever so often, the paddy fields trembled and sparkled—in the morning music struck up on this July day, I alone was dumb! The tunes are locked within me; all the brightness of this world coming at me gets imprisoned within and cannot go back. When I look at this lacklustre, gloomy self I can understand why I am deprived. No one can endure my company day and night.

Bimal is so full of life. That's why, in all of these nine years, she has never ever seemed boring to me. But if there's anything in me, it is just mute profundity and not rippling surges. I am only capable of receiving but I cannot stir. My company is like starvation; when I see Bimal today I can understand what a famine she has survived all these years. Who is to blame?

Alas—

Monsoon floods, July and August,
My temple lies vacant!

My temple is built to stay empty; its doors are closed. I failed to understand all these years, that my idol was waiting outside the door. I'd thought he had accepted the prayers and also granted the boons—but, my temple lies vacant, my temple lies vacant.

Every year in the month of July when the earth was in all its glory, we toured the lake in Shyamaldaha in our barge. When the moonlight of the Krishnapanchami waned and hit rock bottom, we returned home. I used to tell Bimal that a song always had to return to its refrain; the refrain of union in life lay here amidst open nature; on these swelling waters where the wind blew gently, where the dusky earth drew the veil of shadows over her head and eavesdropped all night from one bank to another in the silent moonlight—this was where man and woman first united, and not within four walls. So, we returned here to the refrain of that first primal union, the union between Shiva and Parvati in the lotus gardens of Manasarovar in Kailash. After my marriage, two years were wasted in the hassle of examinations in Calcutta; since then for seven years now, every July, the moon has played its silent conch in our watery haven beside the blooming lotus garden. The first seven years of that life went thus; now the second phase begins.

I cannot possibly forget the fact that the full moon of July is here. The first three days have passed; I don't know if Bimal remembers, but she hasn't reminded me. Everything is quiet and the song has stopped.

Monsoon floods, July and August,
My temple lies vacant!

When a temple falls vacant from absence, the flute plays even in that vacuum. But the temple that falls vacant from parting lies very still and even the sound of weeping is discordant there.

Today my sobs are out of tune. I have got to stop this weeping. I shouldn't be cowardly enough to restrain Bimal with these tears. Where love has turned into a lie, tears shouldn't try and bind it. As long as my pain expresses itself, Bimal will not be totally free.

But I have to free her completely or I will not be free of the lie. Today, keeping her tied to my side is the same as shrouding myself in illusions. It doesn't help anyone, let alone bring any joy. Let me go, let me go—grief will be a jewel in the heart if only you can free yourself from lies.

I feel I have come close to grasping something. People have exaggerated the love between a man and a woman to such an extent that now I'm unable to bring it under control even for the sake of humanity. We've turned the lamp of the room into the fire on the hearth. Now the day has come when it should no longer be pampered but instead, disregarded. Having received the invocations of desire, it has taken the form of a goddess; but we won't accept the kind of prayers that require that a man sacrifice his manliness and have her drink his blood. We must rip apart the mesh of illusions that she has woven through looks and adornment, songs and tales, laughter and tears.

I have always felt a sort of revulsion for Kalidasa's poem *Ritusamhar*. How can man bring himself to thus belittle the joyous rhythm of Nature? All the flowers and fruits of this world simply lie at his lover's feet as objects of the veneration of desire. What was this intoxicant that clouded the poet's vision? The one that I was drunk on for all these years may not be so red in colour, but its effect was just as strong. It was this intoxication that made me hum that strain all day today—

> Monsoon floods, July and August,
> My temple lies vacant!

Vacant temple! I should be ashamed of myself. What has made this colossal temple of yours so empty all of a sudden? I have known a lie for what it is and that has taken all the meaning out of every truth I've ever known?

This morning I'd gone in to pick up a book from the shelf in the bedroom. It's been so long since I entered my room in the day. Seeing the room in daylight, I felt very strange. Bimal's sari lay crinkled up on that same rack and her discarded blouse and jacket lay in a corner waiting to be washed. Her hair pin, hair oil, brush, perfume bottles and even the sindoor box lay on the dressing table. Her tiny, zari embroidered slippers stood under the table—in the days when Bimal firmly refused to wear shoes, I'd had this made with the help of a Muslim friend of mine from Lucknow. She nearly died of shame just walking from the bedroom to that corridor there, in these slippers. Since then Bimal has gone through several slippers but she has kept this aside with special care. I'd joked with her and said, 'Every day you worship me by touching my feet when I sleep and today I have come to revere my living goddess by keeping the dust off her feet.' Bimal had said, 'Please don't say such things or I'll never wear those shoes.' This was my familiar bedroom. This room has a fragrance, which my heart knows intrinsically and which is perhaps not known to anyone else. My lovelorn heart has spread so many fine roots into these little and insignificant things: I have perceived this today in a way in which I never did before. The heart isn't free if the core root alone is destroyed. Even those slippers tend to draw him back. Even if Lakshmi deserts you, the mind hovers around the strewn petals of her lotus-seat. Suddenly my glance rested on the mantle. I saw that my picture stood on it as before and some dried, blackened flowers lay before it. The face in the photo was unchanged although the veneration was distorted. Today, from this room, these dry, black flowers were all I deserved. The reason they were still here was that even the need to discard them was gone. Anyway, I have accepted Truth in this stark and dreary form of it—when will I be able to achieve the indifference of that picture on the mantle?

At this point suddenly, Bimal entered the room from behind me. Quickly I looked away and walked towards the shelf, saying, 'I've come to take *Amiel's Journal.*' I don't know why this explanation was necessary. But I felt as if I was an offender here, as if I had no rights and had come in here to steal a look at something that was hidden, something that should stay hidden. I couldn't look her in the eye and quickly left the room.

When it became impossible to sit and read the book in the sitting room, everything in life began to seem difficult—I didn't have the slightest wish to see or hear anything, to say or do anything—exactly when all the days of my future had congealed into that one single moment and weighed down on my heart like a colossal weight, Panchu brought some ripe coconuts in a basket, kept them before me and touched my feet.

I asked, 'What's this, Panchu? Why this?'

Panchu was a subject of my neighbouring landlord, Harish Kundu; I knew him through my teacher. Firstly, I wasn't his landlord and then he was extremely poor—I had no right to accept any gifts from him. I thought, the poor fellow must be desperate and has thought of this novel manner to gain a few rupees' tip to take him through the day.

I dipped into the moneybag in my pocket, took out two rupees and was about to give it to him when he folded his hands and said, 'No sire, I can't take that.'

'Why, Panchu?'

'No sire, let me come clean. At a time when I was very hard up, I'd stolen some coconuts from your private gardens. I don't know when I'll die, and so I've come to repay the debt.'

Today, *Amiel's Journal* wouldn't have served me in any way, but these words from Panchu cleared up my mind in a trice. This world extended far beyond the sorrows and pleasures of unity and separation with one woman. Human life was substantial; I should take stock of my own mirth and tears only as I stand amidst that immensity.

Panchu was a devotee of my teacher. I know how his home runs itself. Every morning he wakes at dawn and takes a basket filled with paan, tobacco, coloured strings, mirrors, combs etc. which appeal to the farmer women, wades through the knee-deep pond and goes to the area where the lower castes live. Over there, he trades his wares for paddy, which fetches him a little more than a purely monetary exchange. On the days he can return early, he finishes his meal quickly and goes to make sweetmeats at the sweet shop. When he returns from there, it's late at night. Even after working so very hard, he and his family get two square meals a day only a few months of the year. His manner of eating is thus: at the very outset he'll fill his stomach with a jug of water and a large portion of his meal consists of the cheap variety of banana. At least four months in a year, he only gets to have one meal a day.

There was a time when I wanted to give him some financial aid. My teacher said, 'You may spoil people with your charity, but you can't end their misery. In Bengal, Panchu is not alone. The breasts of the entire land are dry. You will never be able to pour in money from the outside and make up for the milk which isn't there.'

It was food for thought. I'd decided to sacrifice my life to this kind of thinking. The other day I'd gone to Bimala and said, 'Bimal, let's devote our lives to banishing misery from our land.'

Bimal laughed and said, 'You seem to be my prince Siddhartha. See that you don't walk away one day and leave me stranded.'

I said, 'Siddhartha's penance didn't include his wife. I need my wife's presence.'

Thus the conversation ended in jokes and banter. Actually, by nature Bimal is what they mean by a 'gentlewoman'. Although she comes from a poor family, she's a princess. She believes that the standard of measuring the joys and sorrows in the lives of the people from the lower classes is also lower. They will obviously be needy but it is of no consequence. They are protected by the confines of their inferiority just as the waters in a tiny pond are contained within its shores. If one were to dig and extend those bounds, the water would run out and the muck below would rise up. Bimal had more than her fair share of that pride in her class, which is present in small sections circling independent seats of pride, within which resides, in spite of one's inferiority, a sense of pedigree and class befitting one's individual status. She is indeed a descendant of Manu. I suppose the blood of Guhak and Eklavya flows stronger in my veins. I'm not able to push away those who are below me as someone who is beneath me. My India doesn't belong to gentlemen alone. I'm fully aware that the further the lower classes slide down, it's India that is deteriorating and the more they die, it's India that is dying.

Bimal hasn't joined me in my struggle. In my life, I have given her such a large place that my cause has become smaller in comparison. I have pushed aside the goals of my life in order to make room for Bimal. The consequence of that is that I have only decked her up and adorned her day and night; my life is revolving only around her. I failed to keep in mind just how vast is man and how noble is life.

Yet, amidst all this, my teacher has protected me; as far as possible, he is the one who has guided me towards all that is great. Without him, I'd be sunk in the depths of despair on this day. He is an amazing human being. I call him amazing because there is a great difference between him and the age and times in which we live. He has been able to perceive God within him, and so nothing can distract him any more. Today when I sit down to balance the books of my life, I can see a gross error, a great loss on one side; but I should always be able to add that there is also a reward that outweighs all losses.

I had already lost my father and come into my own by the time my master finished educating me. I said to him, 'Please stay here with me and don't seek work elsewhere.'

He said, 'Look here, I have already received my wages for what I have given you. If I charge you for the extra that I gave you, it'll be like cheating my God.'

Rain or shine, Chandranathbabu has come to teach me from his house. I've never been able to make him use our cars or vehicles. He said, 'My father always walked to work from Bot tulla to Lal dighi and he never even rode a shared car. Walking to work runs in our family.'

I said, 'Fine, then take up a job with us handling our business or something.'

He said, 'Oh no, my boy, don't trap me in these rich folks' business. Let me remain free.'

His son has now completed his MA and is looking for a job. I said that there's a possibility of working for me. His son too wants the same. At first he'd mentioned this to his father. But when he received no response there, he dropped some hints to me in his father's absence. That's when I mentioned it to Chandranathbabu. He said, 'No, he will not work here.' His son was very angry that his father deprived him of such an opportunity. In response, he left his widower father alone and took a job and left for Rangoon.

My master always said to me, 'Look Nikhil, you are not indebted to me and I am not obligated to you—that is our relationship. If a beneficial relation is bound in terms of money, it is an insult to greater powers.'

Now he is the headmaster of the Entrance School here. Until now, he wasn't even staying at my place. For a while now, I would go over to his house in the evenings and spend time there until late at night. Perhaps he thought that his tiny, damp room was not good for me in the heat of summer and so he has taken up residence at my home. It is amazing how he feels as compassionately for the rich as for the poor—he doesn't ignore the troubles and sorrows of the rich man or those of the poor.

Why is it that the closer you look at reality, the more it affects you? When we see Truth as formless, we can be free. Today Bimal has made the reality of my life so glaring that the Truth seems obscure. Hence, I am not able to hide my misery in this entire world. And so I have spread my tiny bit of despair amidst the people of this earth and sat down to hum:

Monsoon floods, July and August,
My temple lies vacant!

When I can glimpse the Truth from the window of Chandranathbabu's life, the meaning of the song is transformed into:

Vidyapati says how will you spend
Your days and nights without Hari?

All misery, all mistakes come from eluding that Truth. If I don't fill my life with the Truth, how will my days and nights pass? I can't take this any more; Truth, fill my vacant temple now.

Bimala

I can't explain what happened suddenly to the hearts and minds of the people of Bengal in those days. It was as if the waters of the Bhagirathi came and instantly initiated the sixty thousand sons of Sagar. The ashes of many centuries lay hidden beneath; no spark would light them up, no feelings could stir them and then, on this day, they suddenly woke up and said: 'Here I am.'

I've read in books that in Greece a sculptor brought his sculpture to life by the grace of some gods. There was a gradual evolution from beauty into life there, a quest. But in the ashes of this crematorium of a country, where was that exquisite harmony? I'd have understood it if the ashes were a hard, stone-like object—the petrified Ahalya had also turned into a human being one day. But this was all scattered, they constantly slipped through the fist of the Maker, fluttered around in the wind, sat in a pile but never became one. Yet, all of a sudden, that thing came into our yard and growled in a thunderous voice: 'Ayamaham Bhoh!'

On that day we felt all this was magical. The present moment fell into our palms like a solitaire from the crown of an inebriated god; there was no logical connection between our past and this present. This day was like being on medication which we didn't seek out, didn't buy, didn't receive from a doctor but instead brought on through a dream.

That is why we felt all our sorrows and problems would dissolve by themselves in this mantra. The boundaries of the possible and impossible vanished. We kept feeling that at any moment now, it's about to happen.

That day we felt history has no conduit, it arrives on its own heavenly chariot. At least its mahout didn't have to be paid, there were no costs for its upkeep; its champagne glass needed to be topped up from time to time and then, it was straight to heaven with this mortal body.

It wasn't as if my husband was indifferent. But it seemed like an anguish burned within him through all the excitement, as if he could see something beyond all that lay before him. I remember, one day while arguing with Sandip he'd said, 'Good fortune arrives suddenly and yells out before our door only to show us that we don't have the strength to welcome him and we haven't made any arrangements to invite him in.'

Sandip said, 'Look Nikhil, you don't believe in God and so you speak like an atheist. We can clearly see that the goddess has come to grant us a boon and you are doubting it?'

My husband said, 'I believe in God and that's why I know deep in my heart that we haven't been able to arrange for His puja. God has the power to grant us a boon, but we must have the strength to receive it.'

Such words from my husband always made me angry. I said to him, 'You think this fervour in the land is only an intoxication. But isn't there a power in inebriety?'

He said, 'There's power, but no weapons.'

I said, 'God grants power and that is hard to come by. Weapons—even an ordinary blacksmith can provide those.'

My husband laughed and said, 'The blacksmith won't give it for free, he'll charge you.'

Sandip proudly thrust out his chest and said, 'We'll pay, my dear, we'll pay him.'

My husband said, 'When you do, I'll call in the musicians for the festivity.'

Sandip said, 'We're not waiting for you to call them. There's no need to buy our priceless festivity for a price.' He started singing in his hoarse, intense voice:

'My penniless admirer wanders in the garden
And plays the penniless flute most melodiously.'

He looked at me, laughed and said, 'Queen Bee, this was just to prove that when a tune throbs in your throat, you sing even if you are totally out of tune. If you sing heartily, it doesn't matter if the song is perfect or not. Now a tune has taken our country by storm. Let Nikhil sit and practise the notes. Meanwhile, we will sing ourselves hoarse and set everything on fire.

'My home says where will you go,
You'll lose everything when you venture out.
My heart says, let all that you have,
Burn and perish quite merrily.

'What is the worst that can happen to us—we'll be destroyed, right? Fine, I'm ready for it.

'If it has to go, do let it go,
I'll lose everything with a smile,
I'm on my way to drink
From the fountain of death.

'The truth, Nikhil, is that we are energized. We can no longer stay within the bounds of all that is right and smooth. We have to set off on the path that is difficult and impossible.

'The dear ones who draw us close
Know naught of this nectar.
The friend of the wild path
Has called out to me.
Now let the straight bend to the wild
And fall apart in pieces.'

I felt that my husband had something to say. But instead he just walked away.

This tumultuous emotion that was crashing on the shores of the country, came into my life on a different note. The juggernaut of my Fate was approaching and the distant sound of its wheels was making my heart beat louder and faster. Every second I felt a strange and sublime phenomenon was almost upon me, and I wasn't at all responsible for it. Sin? The path that moved away from the spaces of sin and chastity, fair and legitimate, pity and sympathy had already opened up on its own. I had never desired this, never waited expectantly for this; if you look at my entire life, I was in no way answerable for this. All my life I had devoutly prayed and when it was time to grant the boon, a different God had come and stood in front of me! Just as the nation suddenly woke up, looked ahead and said 'Vande Mataram', my heart and soul and every nerve in my body today woke up to say 'Vande' to some unknown, exotic—something that defied explanation!

This was the peculiar similarity between the song in the heart of the country and in my own heart! Many a days I crept out of my bed silently, and went and stood on the terrace. Just beyond the boundary of our house lay the half-ripe paddy fields.

To the north, the glistening river could be seen through the thick cover of trees in the village. Beyond that lay the forest. It was formless like the foetus of impending creation, sleeping nestled in the womb of the immense night. I looked ahead and saw my country standing there—a girl just like me. She used to be content in her own corner of the house. But suddenly she heard the call of the wild. She didn't have time to think. She just walked blindly into the dark. She didn't wait to light a little lamp. I knew, on that slumberous night, just how her breast heaved and fell. I knew that the distant flute called her thus, that she felt she was there already, she had found it and now she could even walk with her eyes closed and not be afraid any more. This wasn't the mother who would remember that the house had to be swept, the lamps lit and the child fed. Today she was the lover. This was our nation in the days of the *Vaishnava Padabalis*. She had left her home and forgotten her duties. All she had was endless passion; fired by that passion she walked on, heedless of the road. I too was a traveller on the same tryst. I too had lost my home and my way. The goal and the means were both misty before me—all I knew was the passion and the journey. Oh nocturnal one, when the night would melt into the crimson dawn, you wouldn't even see a sign of the road back home. But why should I return—I'd rather die. If the darkness that summoned me with its flute destroyed me totally and left me with nothing, all my worries would be over. Everything would be destroyed; not a trace of me would remain. All my sins would mingle in the darkness; after that—what mattered laughter or sorrow, good or bad?

In those days, the time machine was in full steam in Bengal. Hence, even the impossible was becoming a reality in the blink of an eye. It began to feel as if even in that corner of Bengal where we lived, nothing could be stopped any more. Until then, in

those parts, the speed of events was a little slower than in the
rest of Bengal. The main reason for that was that my husband
didn't like to put any pressure on anyone. He used to say, 'Those
who sacrificed for the country, are the great souls. But those who
troubled others in the name of the nation, are the enemies. They
want to hack away at the roots of freedom and nourish its trunk
and leaves.'

But when Sandipbabu came and settled here, his followers
began to move around and sometimes there were speeches in
the marketplace and in public. The waves began to sway these
parts too. A group of local youths joined up with Sandip. Many
of them were notorious in the village for deeds best untold. But
the flame of enthusiasm ignited from within and without and
they glowed. It became clear that when there was elation in the
nation's air, people's foibles disappeared on their own. If there
was no joy in the country it was difficult for people to be healthy,
straight and strong.

At this time, everyone noticed that imported salt, sugar and
cloth were not yet banned from my husband's land. So much
so, that even my husband's employees began to grow restless
and mortified on this account. But, a few months ago when
my husband had brought in the home-grown goods into this
area, everyone here had laughed at him, either to themselves or
openly. We had scoffed at them when the indigenous goods had
no link with our heroism. Till date, my husband sharpened his
home-grown pencil with the indigenous knife, wrote with the
quill pen, drank from the brass pot and in the evening he read by
lamplight. But this colourless brand of swadeshi didn't inspire us.
On the contrary, I always felt ashamed of the lacklustre furniture
in his living room, especially when the magistrate or any other
foreigner came to visit. He always laughed and said, 'Why do you
let such little things get to you?'

I said, 'But, they'll go away thinking we are uncouth and uncultured.'

He said, 'If they think that, I am free to think that their culture extends only till the polish of the fair skin and doesn't reach the red bloodstream of the world's humanity.'

There was a common brass pot on his desk which he used as a vase. Often, when a British visitor was expected, I hid that pot and replaced it with a colourful ceramic vase and placed flowers in it.

My husband would say, 'Bimal, my brass pot is as un-selfconscious as these flowers. But your foreign flower vase doggedly lets you know that it is a vase. I'd rather keep artificial flowers in it than real ones.'

My second sister-in-law gave my husband a lot of encouragement on this matter. Once she came up to him in a real rush and said, 'Thakurpo, I've heard that they've come out with an indigenous soap—of course, our days of using soap are over. But if it doesn't have animal fat, I'd like to use it. This is one bad habit I have picked up after coming to this house—I gave it up long ago, but still a bath doesn't feel complete without soap.'

That was enough to cheer up my husband. Crates of home-made soap began to arrive. Was that soap or lumps of clay? It was obvious that the foreign soaps that Mejorani used earlier, were still in use. These home-made soaps were just for washing her clothes.

Another day she came and said, 'Thakurpo, I believe they've come out with locally made pens. I really must have some. Please, I beg of you, get me a bunch of those—'

Thakurpo was thrilled to bits. All the sticks that were being passed off as pens in those days began to gather themselves in Mejorani's room. But that didn't matter to her because she was hardly into any form of writing. The daily accounts could have been written with a breadstick for all she cared. I noticed that the ancient ivory pen was still in her writing box and on the rare occasion when she wanted to write something, that was what she reached for. As a matter of fact, she used to enjoy these antics only to highlight the fact that I did not encourage my husband's whims. But there was no way I could explain this to my husband. If I tried, his face became so sullen and thunderous that I realized it was having the opposite effect. Trying to protect such people from being fooled only resulted in getting cheated yourself.

Mejorani loved sewing; one day when she was sewing, I spoke my mind to her, 'What is this! On one hand you drool when your Thakurpo mentions some locally made scissors; but when you sew, you have to have the foreign ones?'

Mejorani said, 'What's wrong with that? See how happy it makes him! I have grown up with him and I cannot hurt him as cheerfully as you can. He's a man and he doesn't have any other passion—one of them is playing around with all these indigenous things and the other deadly passion is you—that'll be the end of him!'

I said, 'All said and done, I don't think it's a good thing to say one thing and believe in something else.'

Mejorani laughed and said, 'Oh my simpleton, you seem to be as straight as a headmaster's cane. Women can't be that straight—simply because they are soft, they bend a little and there is no harm in that.'

I will never forget what she said—one of his deadly passions is you and that'll be the end of him.

Now I firmly believe that a man needs a passion, but it's best if it isn't a woman.

The market in Sukhsayar was the largest in our district. Every day there was a market on this side of the river and on the other side a big marketplace was set up every Saturday.

This marketplace began to grow really busy only after the rains. The waters of the pond merged with the river and made the crossing easy. At that time the import of thread and warm clothes stepped up.

In those days there was a wave of revolt against foreign clothes, salt and sugar in the markets of Bengal. All of us were up in arms. Sandip came to me and said, 'Since we have this huge marketplace within our jurisdiction, we should turn it into a totally home-grown one. We must exorcise the foreign evil from this region.'

I agreed vehemently and said, 'Yes, we must.'

Sandip said, 'I have had many arguments with Nikhil on this score—I simply couldn't convince him. He says speeches are fine, but there should be no coercion.'

With a trace of self-importance, I said, 'Fine, leave that to me.'

I knew just how deep my husband's love was for me. If I had the least bit of sense, I'd have died of shame rather than go to him on that day and make demands on that love. But I had to prove to Sandip how powerful I was. In his eyes I was Shakti— the goddess of power! With his powers of articulation, he had explained to me time and again that the supreme Shakti revealed itself to different people in the form of a special person. He said, 'We are all wandering fervently in search of the "Radha" of the Vaishnava Idea. Only when we truly find her do we understand clearly the meaning of the flute that plays in our heart.' As he spoke, sometimes he began to sing,

'When you didn't show yourself, Radha, the flute
    did play.
Now that I have looked into your eyes, my tune has
    washed away.

Then, in many beats and tunes
I had cried for you all over the place.
Now, all my tears have taken Radha's form and turned
    into smiles.'

As I heard all this constantly, I forgot that I was Bimala. I was Shakti, I was rasa, I had no ties and all was possible for me; whatever I touched was recreated by me—my whole world was created anew by me. The autumn sky was not so golden before my heart touched it. Every single moment I rejuvenated that brave, that mystic—my devotee—that remarkable genius enlightened by knowledge, fired by courage and blessed with passion. I could palpably feel that I was infusing new life into him every moment; he was my creation. One day Sandip brought one of his favourite followers, Amulyacharan, to me after much persuasion. Within a second I saw his eyes lit by a different light; I realized he had glimpsed Mother Shakti and I knew that my creation had begun its process in his bloodstream. The next day Sandip came to me and said, 'What kind of a mantra is this—that boy is not the same any more. Within minutes the flame within him has lit up. No one will be able to keep this fire of yours under a bushel. One by one they will come and light their lamps until the country will be ablaze in a festival of lights.'

I was intoxicated by this sense of my own glory and I decided to grant my disciple a boon. I also knew very well that no one could stop me from doing what I wanted to do.

That day I loosened my hair, combed it afresh and tied it again. My British teacher had taught me to draw the hair from around my neck and pile it high up into a knot, which was a favourite with my husband. He would say, 'God has chosen to reveal to me, a non-poet, instead of to Kalidasa, just how beautiful are a woman's neck and shoulders. Perhaps the poet would have likened it to the lotus stem. But I feel it is a burning torch with your dark knot raising its black flame upwards.' And he would reach for my naked shoulder—but alas, why bring that up now.

Then I sent for him. Long ago I used to send for him thus on many pretexts, true or false. Lately all such excuses had come to a stop and I had run out of fresh ideas.

Nikhilesh

Panchu's wife was stricken by tuberculosis and she died. Panchu would have to atone for it. The society did its calculations and came up with a cost of twenty-three and a half rupees.

I was angry and I said, 'So what if you don't atone for it—what are you afraid of?'

He raised his patience-laden eyes, tired as a cow's, and said, 'I have a daughter; she has to be married off. Besides, my wife's last rites will also have to be done.'

I said, 'If there has been a sin, there has also been enough atonement in the last few months.'

He said, 'Well sir, that there has been! Some of my land had to be sold and some mortgaged to pay the doctor's bills. But if I don't give the necessary alms, and feed the Brahmins, there is no release.'

There was no point in arguing. I said to myself, 'When will those Brahmins, who are being fed, atone for their sins?'

Panchu had always lived on the edge of starvation. But his wife's illness and the subsequent expenses for the rituals threw him in at the deep end. He became a follower of a local hermit perhaps for some consolation. This offered him a new drug to dull the pain of his children being unfed and starving. He realized that life was nothing. Just as there was no joy, the sorrows were also mere dreams. Eventually, one night, he left his four children in the hovel and renounced his material aspirations.

I had no knowledge of any of this. My mind was fraught with the combat between accord and discord. My teacher didn't even tell me that he had taken in Panchu's children and was raising them alone. At the time his own son and daughter-in-law were in Rangoon. He was alone at home and all day he had to be at the school.

When a month had passed thus, one morning suddenly Panchu appeared. His 'renunciation' was a thing of the past. When his two elder children squatted at his lap, on the floor, and asked, 'Father, where did you go?', his youngest took over his lap and the third child, a girl, hugged him from behind and rested her cheeks on his back, he broke down. They just wouldn't stop. He said, 'Master-babu, I don't have the strength to feed them two square meals a day, and I don't have the strength to leave them and walk away. Why do I get beaten like this? What have I done to deserve this?'

Meanwhile his trade, the faint thread on which his survival depended, had gone to pieces. The first few days that he took refuge in the professor's home, turned into a permanent arrangement. He began to while away his time there and never mentioned going back to his own home. Finally Chandranathbabu said to him one day, 'Panchu, why don't you go on home? Your house will soon fall apart. Let me lend you some money. You can start a clothing business and pay me back gradually over a period of time.'

At first Panchu was a little upset. He felt the world was a place devoid of human sympathy, and when the professor made him sign a handnote before giving the money, he felt, 'What's the point of such help when I have to return the money in the end?'

The professor hated the idea of giving alms to someone and making them feel encumbered. He always said, 'Loss of dignity is equal to a loss of pedigree.'

After taking the money thus, Panchu couldn't really bring himself to really bow down low at the professor's feet. The professor smiled to himself. He always wanted a short greeting anyway. He says, 'I would like to respect and be respected in turn. That is my ideal relationship with others. I do not deserve any veneration.'

Panchu bought some clothes and winter-wear and began to sell it to the farmers. He got his payment in instalments. But similarly, the rice, jute or other crops that he got when he made the exchange, were a bonus. Within two months he was able to pay back the professor one instalment of the interest and also a part of the principal. This payback obviously also affected the length of the greeting once again. Panchu began to feel that it was a mistake to take the teacher for a great soul. He actually had his eye on the good old silver.

Thus Panchu's days passed. At this point, the wave of swadeshi swept through the countryside. The young boys from our village or the neighbouring ones, who went to school or college in Calcutta, came back for the holidays, some of them already having abandoned their studies. They appointed Sandip as their chief and wholeheartedly lent themselves to the task of spreading the swadeshi-message. Many of these boys had passed out of the free school run by me; a lot of them had scholarships borne by me. One day they came up to me in one big group and said, 'You'll have to ban foreign threads and clothes from the Sukhsayar market.'

I said, 'That is impossible.'

They said, 'Why? Will it affect your profits?'

I realized the barb was meant to hit home. I was about to retort, 'Not mine, but certainly the poor people's.'

My teacher was present. He exclaimed, 'Of course it will; that will never be your loss.'

They said, 'For the sake of the country—'

Chandranathbabu overrode what they were saying by exclaiming, 'The country is not just this land and soil, it is also the people. Have you ever bothered to spare these people a second glance? Today, suddenly you have woken up to the fact that you must decide what they'd eat and what they'd wear. Why should they tolerate that and why should we let them tolerate that?'

They replied, 'But we ourselves have also taken to indigenous salt, sugar and cloth.'

He said, 'You are all angry on a whim and that has given you the strength to do all this happily. You have the money and if you use a few paise more to buy homespun goods, they don't come and stop you. But what you want them to do is sheer abuse of power. They are caught in the fray of life every single day of their lives, struggling to just stay afloat—you cannot even imagine the value of a few paise to them—you have nothing in common with them. You spend your days in a different section of the palace of life; today you want to transfer your burden on to their shoulders, you want to use them to take the edge off your anger? I believe this is cowardice. You are free to take it as far as you wish, as far as you can go, even till death. I am an old man. I am ready to salute you as the leaders and follow in your footsteps. But if you trample on these poor people's freedom and sing songs in praise of liberty, I will personally stand in your way, even if it kills me.'

They were, nearly all of them, ex-students of the professor and so they couldn't retort to his face. But their blood was on the boil. They looked at me and said, 'Look, are you going to be the only one resisting the vow that the entire nation has taken today?'

I said, 'It is not my place to resist. On the contrary, I'll do my best to encourage it.'

An MA student smiled slyly and asked, 'How are you encouraging it?'

I said, 'I have stocked the homespun cloth and threads in our markets; we also send these out to other markets in the area—'

The student shouted, 'But we went to your market and saw that no one is buying these.'

I replied, 'For that, neither I nor the market is to blame. The only reason for that is that the whole country has not yet taken the same vow as you.'

Chandranathbabu said, 'Moreover, even those who have taken the vow seem more intent on causing havoc. You would like to force the uninitiated to buy the thread, weave the cloth and also buy the fabric. By what means? By force and the use of the zamindar's henchmen and their lathis. In other words, the vow is yours, but the ordinary people are the ones who'll fast and you will celebrate that fasting.'

A student of science asked, 'Fine, then go ahead and explain which part of the fasting have you yourselves undertaken?'

My teacher said, 'Do you want to know? Fine then, hear this: it is Nikhil who has to buy that thread from the indigenous mills. He sponsors the weavers who weave the cloth and conducts classes to train them. Given his business sense, by the time a towel is woven from those threads, it'll be worth the same as a piece of expensive silk. So he will buy that towel himself and hang it up as drapes in his drawing room; it wouldn't even cover the half of it. By that time if you are through with your vow, you'd be the first to laugh at the rustic designs on his curtains. If at all that coloured fabric is appreciated anywhere, it is by the British.'

I had been with him for so long, but never had I seen my teacher quite so upset. I realized that the grievance had been collecting in his soul over the past months, simply because he loved me so much. It was that pain that had chipped away at the dam of his patience, and finally given way.

A student of medicine spoke up, 'You are all elders and so we shan't argue with you. So, in a word you are saying that you will not ban the foreign goods from your markets?'

I said, 'No, I will not do that, because it is not mine to ban.'

The MA student smiled derisively and said, 'You won't because that'll cut into your profits.'

My teacher confirmed, 'Yes it will, and so it is entirely his business.'

Thereafter all the students shouted 'Vande Mataram' and walked out.

A few days later, Chandranathbabu brought Panchu to me. What was up?

'His landlord, zamindar Harish Kundu had fined Panchu a hundred rupees.'

'Why, what did he do?'

'He sold foreign cloth. He went to the zamindar and fell at his feet saying that he had bought this cloth with money taken on loan and once these were sold off, he would never do such a thing again. The zamindar said, "Impossible. Burn the cloth in front of me and only then will I let you go." Panchu couldn't take it. He shouted, "I cannot afford it, I am poor; you have enough. Why don't you buy the cloth and then burn it?" At this the zamindar flared up and said, "You bastard, your tongue wags too much— give him the shoe." One round of humiliation followed and then he was fined a hundred rupees. These are the kind that follow

Sandip around, shouting Vande Mataram. These are the so-called servants of the land.'

'What happened to the cloth?'

'Burnt.'

'Who else was there?'

'Hordes of people. They began to shout Vande Mataram. Sandip was also there. He picked up a handful of ash and said, "Brothers, this is the first time the pyre of foreign commerce has been lit in your village. These ashes are sacred. You will have to smear these ashes on yourselves in order to work towards ripping away the shroud of Manchester and turning into naked saints."'

I said to Panchu, 'Panchu, you'll have to go to court.'

Panchu said, 'No one will bear witness.'

'No one—Sandip, Sandip, come here.'

Sandip came out of his room and said, 'What is the matter?'

'This man's bag of cloth was burnt by his zamindar in front of your eyes. Won't you bear witness?'

'Of course I will,' Sandip laughed. 'But I am a witness for his zamindar.'

I said, 'How can you be a witness *for* someone? You'll be a witness for the Truth.'

Sandip said, 'And the Truth is merely what has taken place, is it?'

I asked, 'What is the other Truth?'

Sandip said, 'That which *should* take place. The Truth that we need to formulate. Many lies are needed to make the Truth just as many illusions are needed to make the world. Those who have come into this world solely to create, they do not accept Truth, they formulate it.'

'Hence—'

'Hence, I will be a witness for that which you call a lie. Such false witness has been proudly presented at the courtroom of your Truth by those that have colonized, built empires, formed societies and framed religions. Those who will rule need not fear lies. The iron shackles of Truth are meant for those who will be ruled. Haven't you read history? Don't you know that in the largest kitchens of the world where the mishmash of politics and civics is cooked up, the ingredients are all lies?'

'That may be true of history, but—'

'Oh no, why should you cook that mishmash, instead you'll be forced to gobble it, right? They'll split up Bengal and claim it is for you; they'll close down the doors of education and claim that it is with every good intention towards you; you will be saintly and shed tears and we shall be evil and build fortresses out of lies. Your tears won't stay, but our forts will.'

Chandranathbabu said to me, 'Don't argue over this, Nikhil. If a man is incapable of comprehending that the great Truth within us all is the root of everything, he cannot ever comprehend that man is finally meant to unveil that Truth from all its shrouds and not to create a debris outside oneself.'

Sandip laughed and said, 'You have spoken like a true teacher. These words are fit for the pages of a book. But my eyes tell me that it is man's aim to make a huge pile of things outside oneself. And the people who have achieved that aim successfully are telling lies in bold letters on commercial advertisements every day. They fill in fake figures in the ledgers of civic management, their newspapers are full of lies and just as flies are carriers of the dengue fever, these people's followers spread the message of deception. I am their disciple. When I was with the Congress, I didn't hesitate to to add ninety per cent water to the ten per cent Truth, in accordance with the market conditions. Today I have left the party and I still believe in the principle that it is success and not Truth that is the goal of mankind.'

Chandranathbabu said, 'The fruit of Truth.'

Sandip said, 'Yes, it takes many a lie to grow that fruit. The ground beneath one's feet has to be mashed into a pulp before that fruit can grow. And the Truth, that which grows by itself, is the weed, the wild flower. Those who expect fruits from that plant are the biggest fools of all.'

Sandip finished speaking and stormed out of the room. Chandranathbabu smiled a little, looked at me and said, 'Do you know something, Nikhil? Sandip is not a-religious, he is anti-religion. He is the new moon; no doubt, he is the moon, but circumstances have forced him to rise opposite the full moon.'

I said, 'That is why he and I have never agreed on anything. He has harmed me a lot and will do more harm to me. But I cannot bring myself to disrespect him.'

He said, 'I am beginning to understand that. I have often wondered how you have tolerated Sandip for so long. In fact, at times I have suspected that you are weak in doing so. But now I can see that the two of you may not speak the same words, but you have the same rhythm.'

I spoke in jest, 'Friends in amity have caused enmity. Perhaps Fate has in store another epic in blank verse for our lives.'

Chandranathbabu said, 'Now what should we do about Panchu?'

I said, 'You had once told me that the land on which Panchu's house stands, is ancestral property and has come to belong to him. His zamindar has been trying to get him off that land for a while. Why don't I buy that land and make him my subject?'

'And the hundred rupees' fine?'

'How can they realize that? The land belongs to me now.'

'And the bag of cloth?'

'I will send for more. As my subject he will be allowed to sell whatever he wants, wherever he wants.'

Panchu folded his hands and said, 'Sire, in the battle of kings there'll be a crowd of policemen, lawyers and many such vultures, watching the fun. But I'll be the only one to die.'

'Why, what will they do to you?'

'They'll set my house on fire and I'll die, along with the children.'

Chandranathbabu said, 'All right, let your children stay with me for the next few weeks. Don't be afraid. You are free to do business from your own home, no one will lay a finger on you. I will not allow you to run away, defeated by a wrong done to you. The more you bear, the more the burden grows.'

That same day I bought Panchu's land, registered it and laid my claims on it. Then the squabble started.

Panchu's property belonged to his maternal grandfather. Everyone knew that Panchu was his sole heir. But suddenly a maternal uncle's wife materialized, laying claims to the inheritance, and settled down in his house with her bags, bundles, sacred books and a young widowed daughter. Surprised, Panchu said, 'But my aunt died long ago.'

Her reply was, 'Your uncle's first wife may have died, but the second one came soon enough.'

'But my aunt died long after my uncle's death and so there really wouldn't have been time for a second wife.'

The woman admitted that the second marriage had taken place before and not after death. She didn't want to share space with her co-wife and so she'd stayed in her father's house. When her husband died, she renounced the material world and went to Vrindavan. Some of the officers of the zamindar, Kundu, were aware of all this and perhaps some of the subjects knew about it too; if the zamindar hollered loud enough, then even some of the people who had eaten the wedding feast would surely crawl out of the woodwork.

That afternoon, when I was thoroughly preoccupied with this new hassle in Panchu's life, suddenly Bimala sent for me from her chambers.

I was startled. I asked, 'Who has called?'

The bearer said, 'Ranima.'

'The eldest one?'

'No, the youngest.'

The youngest one—I felt as if a hundred years had passed since she had last sent for me.

I left everyone sitting in the drawing room and went into the inner chambers. In the bedroom I was even more surprised to see Bimala had cared to dress up a little. For a while now this room had begun to look quite untidy; everything was so cluttered up that it felt like the room was also preoccupied. Today, I noticed that the room looked a little like its old self.

I stood silently looking at Bimala. She blushed a little, twisted the bangles on her left wrist with her right hand and said, 'Listen, in all of Bengal our market is the only one stocking foreign cloth; does it look good?'

I asked, 'What will be the best thing to do?'

'Why don't you tell them to throw those things away?'

'But those things do not belong to me.'

'But the market is yours.'

'It belongs much more to those people who come there to buy and sell.'

'Why can't they buy indigenous goods?'

'I'd be happy if they do buy it, but if they don't?'

'What? How can they dare to? You are after all—'

'I don't have much time; what is the point of arguing over this? I cannot bring myself to exploit people.'

'The exploitation is not for your gain, it is for the sake of the country—'

'I suppose you won't understand that torturing for the sake of the country is the same as torturing the country itself.' I left. Suddenly, I felt the whole world was alight in front of my eyes. The weight of the earthly world lifted from my shoulders. Suddenly I perceived how, for an eternity, the earth hurtled through the skies by a strange force, turning night and day like a sacred chant in spite of nurturing the life forms placed on her and maintaining a balance between all the changes and evolution that she undergoes. Responsibilities were endless, but so was freedom. No one, but no one, will ever tie me down. Suddenly, a deep fount of joy sprang from my mind like a swollen wave from the ocean's breast, and reached for the clouds.

I asked myself again and again, what was the matter with me? At first there was no clear answer. And then it became quite clear: the impasse that had tortured me all these days had suddenly ended. As clearly as the glass on a photograph, I could see all of Bimala's actions in my mind's eye. It became obvious that Bimala had dressed herself up to get something from me. Until this day, I had never learnt to see Bimala's dressing up as separate from her. But today her western-styled chignon seemed a mere pile of hair; moreover, there was a time when this chignon was priceless to me and today I realized it was ready to be sold for a lot less.

Sandip and I argued about patriotism every step of the way. Those were real differences. But the words that Bimala spoke in the name of the country, were coming from Sandip's mouth and not from a greater Idea. If Sandip changed his words, so would Bimala. I could see all this very clearly—all traces of the fog had lifted.

As I left the broken nest of my bedroom and emerged into the open air of the autumn noon, I saw a bunch of mynahs chattering in great excitement in my garden. To the south of the garden lay the cobbled path, lined by rows of kanchan trees that overwhelmed the skies with the scent of their pink blossoms which were in abundance. In the distance, by the winding village road the empty bullock cart lay upturned and the two cows, no longer yoked, were roaming free. One was chewing grass and the other basked in the sun while a crow sat on its back, pecking away at its hide as the cow closed its eyes in sheer bliss. At this moment I felt I had suddenly come very close to the soul of this universe which was very simple and yet so profound; its warm breath fanned my heart as the fragrance of those kanchan flowers. I felt that I did exist, and so did everything else; this created a feeling— deep, munificent and indescribably beautiful within me.

The next moment I remembered Panchu, stuck in the mire of poverty and cunning. I thought I saw Panchu amidst that pensive grassland in the autumn noon, lying with his eyes closed, just like the cow—not from bliss but from sheer exhaustion, weariness and starvation. He seemed to personify all the poor farmers of Bengal. I caught a glimpse of the severely religious Harish Kundu, forehead marked with sacred sandal paste. He was no mean feat. He was huge too. He was like a layer of oily green floating on the ancient, rotting pond beneath the bamboo clump, covering it entirely and giving out toxic vapours by the second.

Eventually I would have to fight with those shadows that lay emaciated, tired and blinded by ignorance on the one hand, and on the other hand those that had thrived on the blood of the poor and was crushing the earth under its own immovable weight. This task had been kept aside for many hundred years. Let my trance break, my daze disappear and my manhood be freed from the ineffective mesh of the inner chambers. We are men, freedom is our goal, we shall hark the call of the Ideal and rush forth, we must scale the walls of the demon king and rescue the goddess trapped within. The girl who makes the victory badge for us with her deft fingers is our true partner. We must see through the masquerade of the girl who sits by the door and weaves her spells on us, we must see her true form without illusions—we shouldn't dress her up in the colours of our own dreams and desires and send her out to distract us. Today I felt I shall be a winner. I stand on the straight road; I can see everything clearly. I have been freed and I have also freed—my salvation lies where my work is.

I know there will come a day when my heart will be wracked by pain again. But now I am familiar with that pain. I can no longer respect it. I know it is mine and mine alone—does it really have any value? The pain of the world will grace my brow. Oh Truth, save me, help me. Don't let me go back to that fake world of illusion and artifice. If you must make me a lone traveller on a solitary journey, let the road lead to you. Today I have heard your drums within my soul.

Sandip

That day the dam of tears was on the verge of giving way. Bimala sent for me, but she was silent for a while, her eyes glistening with unshed tears. I knew she had failed with Nikhil. She had been certain that she would somehow get the results, though I had no such hopes. Women know the weak spots of men, but sometimes find it hard to fathom their strengths. In reality, men are a mystery to women and vice versa. If that wasn't the case, the difference between the two sexes would have been a superfluous creation of Nature.

Indignation! It was not about the important task not being fulfilled. The indignation was all about not being granted what she asked for so plainly. There is no end to the shades of gestures, tears, games over this demand of the 'I' that women have. That is what makes them so sweet. They are much greater egoists than we are. When the Maker made us, He was the schoolteacher, His tools were theories and notes. But when their time came, He had resigned from his job and become an artist; His tools were a brush and paints.

Hence, when Bimala stood there on the edge of the setting sun like a tearful, fiery red cloud coloured by that melancholy distress, I found her very sweet. I went close to her and took her hand. She trembled but didn't take her hand away. I said, 'Bee, we are co-workers, we have the same goals. Now sit down.'

I sat her down on a stool. Wonderful. All that emotion and it took just this to clamp it shut. The monsoon-floods of the Padma that were rushing forth, seemingly not prepared to stop for anything or anyone, suddenly appeared to change its course and began to flow smoothly between its banks again. I took her hand in mine and pressed them, every nerve end in my body playing like the strings of a bow; but why did it have to stop at the first two notes, why couldn't it complete the aria? I realized that the bottomless depths of the flow of life are formed by many years of conduct. When the flood of desire gushed briskly enough, in places it was strong enough to erode that course and in places it met its match. There was a deep-rooted restraint within me, what *was* it? It was not just one thing, but many things tangled together. So I could never figure it out, but I knew it was an impediment. What I really was would never stand a court inquisition and be a writ of law. I was a mystery to myself and that's why I loved myself so much; if I knew that 'I' completely, it would be so easy to root it out, discard it and reach a state of nirvana.

As Bimala sat on the stool watching me, her face paled. She knew in her heart that one of her problems no longer existed. The comet had zoomed past her, but the whiplash of its tail left her feeling enervated for a while. In order to get her out of the stupor, I said, 'There are obstacles, but we shouldn't regret them. We will fight, won't we, Queen?'

Bimala coughed a little to clear her throat and then just said, 'Yes.'

I said, 'Let us work out the details of the plan for our actions in the future.'

I took out a pencil and paper from my pocket and began to discuss how I would delegate work amongst the boys who had come to join us from Calcutta. Suddenly Bimala said, 'Not now, Sandipbabu, I'll come again at five o'clock; we can talk then.' She got up and quickly left the room.

I realized that she simply couldn't bring herself to concentrate on what I was saying; she needed to be alone with herself for a while. Perhaps she'd have to throw herself on the bed and weep for some time.

When Bimala left, the atmosphere in the room became headier. My mood seemed to get tipsier just as the sky is tinged with more pink after the sun actually sets. I began to feel I had let the moment pass. What kind of weakness was this? Perhaps Bimala went away disgusted with my inexplicable hesitation. Possible.

At this time, when my blood was throbbing with the effects of this inebriation, a bearer came and informed me that Amulya wanted to see me. For a moment I wanted to send him on his way, but before I could make up my mind, he came into the room.

Then it was back to news of the battle of salt-sugar-cloth. The heady feeling evaporated. I felt like the dream had snapped. I got ready for battle and off to the battlefield it was.

The news was this: Kundu's subjects who used to bring stuff to the market had finally come around. The officers in Nikhil's employ were all secretly on our side. They were supplying the inside information. The Marwaris were begging to be allowed to sell the foreign cloth in exchange for a fine, or they'd go bankrupt. The Muslims were refusing to give in.

A farmer had bought some cheap German shawls for his children. Some of our boys from the local villages had grabbed the shawls from him and burnt them. That had caused a furore. We offered to buy him some desi warm clothes. But there were

no cheap desi warm clothes to be found. Obviously we couldn't
buy him Kashmiri shawls. He came and put his case before
Nikhil. He ordered him to lodge a complaint against the boys.
The local officers had taken the responsibility of seeing to it that
the complaint didn't go through smoothly; their chief was also
on our side.

The point was, if we had to buy desi cloth for those whose
things we burnt, and then also pay for the court case, where
were we supposed to get that kind of funds from? And all this
burning would hot up the market for foreign fabrics. When the
nawab was so taken with the sound of breaking glass that he went
around smashing all his chandeliers, the glass-blowers had the
time of their lives.

The second question was: there weren't any cheap desi warm
clothes to be had. Now in winter, should we allow the foreign
shawls, wrappers and merino to stay or not?

I said, 'We will not gift desi clothes to the man who wants
to buy foreign clothes. He is the one to be punished, not us. If
they went to court, we would set their crops on fire; the gentle
approach wouldn't work. Hey Amulya, don't look so shocked.
I don't get my kicks out of setting the farmer's crops on fire. But
this is war. If you are afraid to hurt, go and have fun, be genteel
and keel over with love.'

And the foreign warm clothes? Whatever the inconvenience,
those will not be allowed to stay. We cannot have a compromise
with the foreign stuff under any circumstances, in any condition.
When there were no foreign wrappers to be had, the farmer's
children double-wrapped their cloth and kept themselves warm.
That's what they'd have to do again. I know that wouldn't satisfy
them, but this wasn't the time for satisfaction.

We had somehow, by hook or by crook, managed to bring
around some of those who brought the shipments to the markets

by boat. Mirjan, the most powerful of them all, refused to give an inch. We asked Kulada, the chief-clerk here, if Mirjan's boat could be sunk. He said, of course it could, but the blame would eventually come to rest at his door. I said the blame shouldn't be kept so loose that it could come to rest anywhere; but if at all it came to that, I'd come forward and take it.

At the end of the market-day, Mirjan's empty boat was docked at the pier. There were no boatmen in it. The chief-clerk had cleverly invited them to a show nearby. That night the boat was set adrift with a hole in it and bags of rubbish piled into it.

Mirjan understood. He came to me, weeping and with folded hands, 'Sire, I was wrong. Now—'

I said, 'How did you come to figure it out so clearly just now?'

He didn't answer that, but said, 'Sire, that boat was worth two thousand rupees, if not more. Now I have come to my senses, if you please forgive me this one time—'

He fell at my feet. I told him to come again in another ten days or so. I could buy his loyalty for two thousand rupees. We needed to have people like this on our side. I needed to get hold of some money quickly.

That evening when Bimala came into the room, I stood up and said, 'Queen, the work is almost done; now we need money.'

Bimala said, 'Money? How much?'

I said, 'Not much, but I need the money somehow.'

Bimala asked, 'Tell me how much money you need.'

I said, 'Right now, about fifty thousand would do.'

Bimala was shaken to hear the amount, but she hid it well. How could she say she wasn't up to it, again and again?

I said, 'Queen, you can make the impossible happen. You have done it too. If I could show you what you have achieved, you'd have seen it too. But this is not the time for it; perhaps another day. Now we need the money.'

Bimala said, 'I'll get it.'

I knew that she had decided to sell her ornaments. I said, 'Don't touch your ornaments now. You never know what might come up in future.'

Bimala stood there staring at me.

'You'll have to get this money from your husband's funds.'

Bimala was struck speechless. A little later she said, 'How can I take his money?'

'But isn't his money yours too?'

With anguished emotion she said, 'No.'

I said, 'In that case it isn't his either; it belongs to the country. When the country is in need of it, Nikhil has kept it away from her, stolen it from her.'

Bimala asked, 'How will I get that money?'

'By hook or by crook; you can do it. You will bring the money back to its rightful owner. Vande Mataram. Today this chant of "Vande Mataram" will break open the iron chest, bring down the walls of the store room and it would pierce the hearts of those who, in the name of faith, refuse to bow down to its power. Bee, say it with me: Vande Mataram.'

'Vande Mataram.'

We are men, we are kings, we have the right to collect tax. Ever since we have stepped on to this earth, we have been looting it. The more we have demanded from her, the more homage she has paid us. We are men: since the beginning of time we have plucked and plundered, chopped down trees, dug up the soil, killed animals, birds and fish. From the depths of the ocean, the womb of the earth and from the jaws of death, we have only ever seized. We are the male species. We have not spared a single iron chest ordained by God; we have pillaged and seized.

The earth takes pleasure in satisfying the male of the species. Day in and day out, the earth has met our demands and thus grown greener, more beautiful and more fulfilled; or else, she would have stayed shrouded in woods and forests and never found her true self. All the doors to her heart would have been locked, her diamonds would have stayed buried in mines and the pearls of the oyster would never have seen the light of day.

By the sheer force of our demands, we the men, have discovered the women today. In the process of giving themselves to us constantly, they have found themselves more fully, more completely. Only when they come to submit the solitaires of their joy and the pearls of their sorrow to our treasury do they get a true sense of those jewels. Thus, for men to take is the best charity and for women to give is most profitable.

I have placed a tall order before Bimala. At first I had a doubt: was this in my nature or was it just a petty squabble with my own self? I felt this was a bit harsh. Just once I thought of calling her back and saying forget it, don't go into all this. Why should I stir up your life like this? For that moment I forgot that this was the reason why the male species was an active one: we are meant to stir up the lives of the passive ones and make it a life worth living. If we hadn't made the women weep for so many years, the door to the vast treasury of their grief would have stayed shut forever. The male was meant to make the universe weep and gratify it thus. Why else would his hands be so strong, his fist so powerful?

Bimala's very self desired that I, Sandip, should make a heavy demand on her, call upon her to stake her life. She wouldn't be fulfilled otherwise. She had been waiting for me only because she hadn't been able to express her emotions through tears all these years. She had been so happy for so long that the moment she looked at me, the blue clouds of grief moved over her horizon. If I took pity on her and tried to dry her tears, then I would not be doing my duty.

Actually the reason for my slight hesitation was that this was a demand for money. Money belonged to men. Asking for it brought an element of beggary into it all. Hence I had to make the amount a hefty one. If it were a few thousand, there'd be a strong stench of pilfering. But fifty thousand was a veritable raid.

Moreover, I should really have been very rich. All these years I have had to stifle many desires for the sheer lack of money. This was something that didn't sit well on me of all people. If this was a fault of my Fate, I'd have let it pass; but this was indecent, tasteless. If I have to scrounge to pay my rent and dip into my moneybag only to come up with the fare for an intermediate class when I travel by train, it was not just pathetic but ludicrous. It was clear to me that for someone like Nikhil the ancestral property was quite superfluous. Poverty would have suited him just as well. He would have, quite easily, kept his Chandranathbabu company in a decrepit old buggy.

Just once, I want to have fifty thousand rupees in my hands and blow it in two days, on my own comforts and a few deeds for the country. I want to shed this poor man's disguise and look at the real me, the rich me, in the mirror just once.

But I don't think Bimala would be able to procure the money easily. Perhaps eventually it'll come down to the few thousand after all. Well, so be it. 'It is wise to forego half'—so they say. But since the sacrifice is not by my choice, the wisdom lies in foregoing eighty or even ninety nine per cent.

All that I have written so far are vital matters; I will go back to it in detail again later when I have the time. Now there is none. The chief-clerk of this place has asked me to meet him immediately; I've heard something has gone wrong.

~

The chief-clerk said that the police suspect the man who drowned the boat. The man was a veteran and he was now in custody. It would be difficult getting him to talk. But it was a matter of time and since Nikhil was upset, the clerk couldn't do anything too obvious. He said, 'Look, if I get into trouble, I'll drag you with me.'

I asked him, 'Where are the ropes by which you'll hang me?'

The clerk said, 'I have one letter written by you and three written by Amulyababu.'

Now I understood why the clerk had written to me and got me to send a reply; it served no other purpose. These wiles were new to me. The clerk had enough respect for me to know that I could drown my friend as easily as I did my foe. The respect would have increased if I had answered the letter verbally rather than given a written reply.

Now the point was, the police had to be bribed. If the matter worsened, then we'd have to settle out of court and offer compensation to the man whose boat we drowned. It was also clear to me that in this vile mesh being woven, the clerk would come by his fair share of the profits. But I couldn't say any of this. On the face of it, I was saying 'Vande Mataram' and he was also saying 'Vande Mataram'.

The fixtures that one has to deal with to do this work are often below par. I suppose a conscience is so ingrained within us, that at first I felt very angry with the chief-clerk. I was about to write some very harsh words in this diary regarding the fraudulence of our countrymen. But if there is a God, I owe him this debt of gratitude: he has given me a clear mind. Nothing, both within and without, ever remains unclear to me. I may fool others but never could I fool myself. And that's why I couldn't stay angry for too long. The truth is never good or bad, it is merely the truth and that is empirical. Water bodies are formed only by the water that remains after the earth has sucked up as much water as it wants to. The layer of soil below our 'Vande Mataram' was bound to absorb some water and both the clerk and I were a part of that process. What will remain after that absorption, will be the true Vande Mataram. We may curse it and call it deceit, but this is the Truth and it has to be accepted. At the bottom of every noble deed in this world, there is a layer of pure filth, even at the bottom of the ocean. Hence, in doing noble deeds, one must take into account this filth and its demands. So, the clerk would grab some and so would I: it was all a part of the greater need. Feeding the horse some grains wasn't enough, the wheels also have to be oiled.

Anyway, money was sorely needed. I couldn't wait for the fifty thousand. I'd have to collect whatever I could, right now. I know that on the face of such pressing needs one has to let go of the larger goals of the future. A bird in hand is worth two in the bush after all. That's why I tell Nikhil that those who walk the road of surrender never have to curb their greed; but those who choose the path of greed have to surrender it every step of the way. I had to forego my fifty thousand—this was something Nikhil's Chandranathbabu never had to do. Of the seven deadly sins, the first three and the last two are common to man and the two in the middle are for cowards. Lust is fine, but there should be no greed and no envy. Otherwise lust turns to dust. Envy clings to the past and the future. It can waylay the present with ease. Those who cannot concentrate on the immediate present, those who dance to a different drummer's beat, they are like the sad lover, Shakuntala: they fail to attend to the guest at hand and the curse makes them lose the distant one for whom they yearn.

Today I had held Bimala's hand and she was still under that spell. I too was bound by that spell. This echo had to be kept alive. If I were to repeat it often and bring it down to the level of the mundane, then today's symphony would turn into a cacophony tomorrow. Now Bimala was incapable of questioning any of my demands. Some people need illusions to survive—why cut down on it? Right now I have a lot of work; so for now, let this cup of love skim the mere surface. Drinking the last dregs now would only stir up trouble. When the right time comes, I shall not gainsay it either. Oh lustful one, forfeit your greed and master the instrument of envy, playing it like the maestro.

Meanwhile, our work was on a roll. Our group had infiltrated deep inside and set up a stronghold. A lot of cajoling and sweet talk made me realize one thing: the Muslims were not going to come round by coaxing. They'd have to be subdued and shown who was the boss in no uncertain terms. Today they bare their fangs at us; but one day we'll make them dance to our tune.

Nikhil says, 'If India is a true entity, then Muslims are a part of it.'

I say, 'That may be so. But we need to know which part of it they are and then squash them right there, or they'd be bound to revolt.'

Nikhil says, 'Do you think you can quell the revolt by stepping it up?'

I say, 'What is your plan?'

Nikhil says, 'There is only one way to resolve the difference.'

I know that every one of Nikhil's arguments is bound to end in a moral, just like the didactic writings of a philosopher. The strange thing is that even after fiddling around with these maxims for so many years, he still actually believes in them. No wonder I say that Nikhil is a born pupil. Fortunately, he is made of genuine stuff. Like Chand-saudagar of the *Manasamangal*, he has initiated himself into the mantra of fantasy; the bite of reality may kill him but he won't accept it. The problem is that for people like this, death is no final proof. They have closed their eyes and decided that there is something beyond it.

For a while now, I have formulated a plan. If I can bring it to fruition, the entire country will be ablaze. The people of our land won't wake up to her unless they can actually see her. They need a goddess with a form to denote the country. My friends liked the idea. They said, 'Fine, let us build an idol.' I said, 'Our building it won't work. We'll have to use the idol that has always been in worship and make her the symbol of the country. The channels of devotion run deep in our land and we'll have to use the same to channelize the devotion towards the country.'

Nikhil and I had an argument over this a while back. He said, 'If I consider a task to be true and genuine, I cannot use illusions as a means.'

I said, 'Yes, but sweetmeats do win you friends; the common man has to have his illusions and three-fourths of this world is made up of common men. It is to keep these illusions alive that every country has formulated its own gods. Man knows himself.'

Nikhil said, 'Gods are for breaking illusions; only demons keep them in place.'

Fair enough, let them be demons, but they are essential to get the work done. The problem is, in our land, all the illusions are in their place. We pay homage to them and yet, do not put them to good use. Take the Brahmins for example: we bow to them, give them alms and yet we never utilize them. If we used their superiority to the fullest, we could take the world by storm because there is a bunch of people in this world who are doormats and they are the largest in number.

They cannot accomplish much in life unless they get trod upon. Illusion is a means to make these people work. All this while we have sharpened these people as weapons and now the time has come to put them to use—I can't put them away now.

But it was impossible to get Nikhil to see this point. Truth was lodged in his mind as firmly as a prejudice, as though Truth was an absolute, empirical given. I have told him many a time, in situations where falsehood was the Truth, it *was* the Truth. It was because our country knew this for a fact that it was said in olden days that for the ignorant the lie was the Truth. If he moved away from it, he would be deflecting the Truth. The man who could accept an idol as the symbol of the country would actually be working on that as the Truth. Given our nature and culture, it wasn't easy for us to accept the nation in its abstraction, but we could easily accept the symbol. Since this was a fact, the ones who wanted results would work on this premise and work effectively.

Nikhil got very agitated and exclaimed, 'Just because you have lost the capacity to strive for the Truth, you want an instant reward to fall into your lap. That's why for hundreds of years, when all the work is left undone, you have turned the nation into a goddess and sat in front of her praying for a boon.'

I said, 'The impossible must be achieved and that's why the nation has to be a goddess.'

Nikhil said, 'In other words, you are not interested in achieving that which is attainable but must be striven for. Everything should stay as it is and the consequences alone should be miraculous.'

I said, 'Nikhil, your words are mere advice. It may be a good thing at a certain age, but not when a man's teeth are itching to bite. I can see it right before my eyes: the harvest that I have never sown is flourishing and growing. On what basis? It is because I can see my nation as a goddess. Turning this into an eternal symbol is the need of the day. A genius doesn't argue, he creates. I will give shape to what the nation thinks today. I will go from one house to another saying the goddess has appeared in my dreams and she wants homage. We will go to the Brahmins and say you are the true priests of the goddess and since you're not giving her her dues, you have lost your status. You'd say I am lying. No, this is the truth. Millions of people all over the country are waiting to hear these words from my lips and that is why it is the truth. If I can successfully spread my own message, you'd see the miraculous results for yourself.'

Nikhil said, 'But how long would I live? Even after the results you would hand to the nation now there may be other far-reaching consequences, which may not be so apparent now.'

I said, 'I want the consequences of here and now, only those are mine.'

Nikhil said, 'I want the consequences of tomorrow, only those belong to everybody.'

Fact of the matter is, perhaps Nikhil had his fair share of that gift so common to Bengalis: imagination. But a parasite of a plant called morality grew around and over it and nearly crushed the life out of it. The worship of Durga or Jagatdhatri that the Bengali had initiated in India was an amazing display of his true nature. I am very certain that this goddess is a political being. These two goddesses are different forms of that spirit of the nation to whom people prayed at the time of the Mughal rule, asking for strength to overthrow the enemy. No other people of India have been able to come up with such external manifestations of their enterprise. It was apparent that Nikhil's imagination had died entirely when he said to me, 'At least when the Muslims took up arms against the Marathas or the Sikhs, they held their own weapons and wanted victory. Bengalis placed the weapons in the hands of the goddess, mumbled some mantras and hoped for victory; but the nation is not a goddess and the only victory was the sacrifice of some goats and of bulls. The day we will work for the welfare of the nation, is the day we will get our reward from the true deity.'

The problem is that on paper Nikhil's words sound very nice. But my words are not meant for paper; they are to be engraved on the nation's heart with a branding iron. It is not the kind of farming the pundit theorizes about in books but the kind of dreams the farmer etches out on the earth's bosom with his plough.

When I met Bimala I said, 'Is it possible to realize that deity, the one for whose homage we have come into this world after a thousand births, until She appears before me in tangible form? How many times have I told you that if I hadn't seen you, I would never have visualized my nation as one entity? I don't know if you understand me. It is very difficult to explain that gods may stay hidden in the heavens, but they are visible on this earth.'

Bimala looked at me strangely and said, 'I have understood you very well.' For the first time, she addressed me with the informal 'you' as opposed to the formal equivalent.

I said, 'Krishna was not just Arjun's charioteer; he had a more colossal form and when Arjun perceived that, he realized the whole Truth. In this entire land I have perceived that colossal form of yours. Ganga-Brahmaputra are the strands of pearls gracing your neck; in the line of forest on the distant banks of the blue river I have glimpsed the lashes of your kohl-black eyes; the young rice fields undulate with the shadow of your striped sari rippling through them; I have glimpsed your cruelty in that raging summer sky, panting like a desert lion with its red tongue lolling. When the goddess has deigned to grant her devotee such a miraculous vision, I have decided to spread the word of her homage in the entire land and only then will my countrymen come alive. "It is your form that I build in every temple." But everyone hasn't quite understood it yet. So I have decided to create the statue of my deity with my own hands, before all the people of this land and worship her in a way that will help everybody believe in her. Grant me that boon, give me that strength.'

Bimala's eyes were half closed. She sat still like a statue, almost one with her seat. Had I spoken some more, she would have fainted. A little later she opened her eyes and said, 'Oh voyager of destruction, you have set out on the road and there is no one who can stop you. I can see that no one can come in the way of your desires. The king would come to lay down his sceptre before you, the rich would come to donate all his wealth to you and even those who do not have anything, would be gratified to lay down their lives at your feet. Ethics and principles, morals and values would all fly away. Oh my Lord, my God, I do not know what you have seen in me, but I have just glimpsed your colossal form in the midst of my heart. It reduces me to nothing. Lord, oh Lord, what a tremendous force it is. It will not rest until it has destroyed me completely; I cannot take it any more, I cannot bear this pain.' She fell to the ground, reached for my feet and lay there sobbing, sobbing and sobbing.

This *was* hypnotism! This was the way to win the world. This magic spell was better than any other method. Who said Truth wins the day? Victory to illusion! Bengalis have realized that and hence they started worshipping the goddess with ten hands and placed her astride a lion. The same Bengali will build another goddess today and win the world with mesmerism. Vande Mataram!

I picked her up gently and made her sit on the stool. Before the weariness hit her after all this excitement, I quickly said, 'The goddess has assigned me to reinstate her in this land, but I am a poor man.'

Bimala's face was still red, her eyes misted with tears. She spoke in an emotion-laden voice, 'You and poor. Everything that anyone has belongs to you. Why do I have a box full of jewellery? Please seize all my jewels and gems for your work—I don't need any of them.'

Once before too, Bimala had offered me her jewellery. I baulk at nothing but this was my limit. It bothered me because traditionally it was the man who decked the woman with jewellery and hence, taking it from a woman would feel like a blow to my manhood.

But I had to get beyond myself. I wasn't the one taking it. It was for the worship of the Mother and all of it would go for that. The puja would be so glamorous that no one ever would have seen anything like it. In the history of the new Bengal, this would be enshrined for all times to come. It would be my greatest gift to the country. The fools of the land worship the deity; Sandip *creates* the deity.

So much for the big talk. The small talk was also required. As of now I had to have at least three thousand, five thousand would be even better. But could I possibly broach the topic of money at an emotional time like this? Time was running out. I trampled upon my hesitations and spoke up, 'Queen, the treasury is almost empty and the work is grinding to a halt.'

Immediately Bimala's face crumpled in pain. I realized that she thought I was demanding the fifty thousand. It was probably weighing on her mind; perhaps she had worried about it all night and yet had found no solution. After all, she had no other way to show her love—she couldn't possibly give her heart to me overtly and so she wanted to bring this money to me as a mark of all her covert caresses and desires. But the lack of a way to do so was stifling her. Her pain struck me to the quick. She was now all mine. There was no need to worry about uprooting her; now I needed to tend to her and keep her alive.

I said, 'Queen, that fifty thousand won't be needed right now. I have worked it out and just five thousand, or even three will do for now.'

Bimala was overwhelmed by the pressure lifting so suddenly. Like a song she sang, 'I will bring you five thousand.'

This was the tune to which Krishna's lover Radha had sung,

For my love I'll don flowers in my hair,
The likes of which has never been seen in all the world,
The notes of the flute played in the wind,
Not for every ear is it meant,
Oh look at that, Yamuna has overflowed her banks.

It was the same tune, the same song and the same words: 'I will bring you five thousand.' 'For my love I'll don flowers in my hair.' The flute played so sweetly *because* the wind had a narrow passage, there were so many restrictions in its way. If my greed had forced me to break the flute and flatten it, I would have heard, 'Why? What do you need this money for? I am a woman, where shall I get so much money, etc. etc.' It wouldn't have a single syllable in common with Radha's song. That's why I say, illusion is the king, it is the flute and without illusion, it is the flute cracked open—I think Nikhil has got a taste of that pure emptiness these days. I feel sorry for him. But Nikhil boasts that he wants the Truth and I boast that I'd never let illusion slip through my fingers. 'Jadrishi bhabana jasya siddhirbhabati tadrishi.' One must act on one's own desires. So there was no point regretting it.

In order to keep Bimala soaring in those lofty heights, I finished the matter of the five thousand quickly and got back to the adulation of that fierce goddess. When and where would we have the puja? The fair in Hosaingaji that was held in September at Ruimari under Nikhil's jurisdiction, had thousands attending it and that would serve as a good locale. Bimala was excited. She felt this wasn't about burning foreign cloth or burning down homes; Nikhil would surely not object to this. I laughed to myself—how little did they know each other, even after nine years spent together. Their knowledge was limited to the bounds of the home. The moment the world came into it, they were all at sea. For nine years they sat and believed that the home and the world matched in spirit. Today they are beginning to feel that some things that have never been coordinated could not suddenly complement harmoniously.

Anyway, let the ones who do not understand one another gradually stumble and find their way around; I don't have to waste too much time on it. But I couldn't leave Bimala in this heightened state, like a flying kite for too long and so I had to get my work done as quickly as possible. When she rose and walked towards the door, I asked, quite nonchalantly, 'Queen, about the money—'

Bimala turned around and said, 'At the end of this month, when the monthly revenue comes in—'

I said, 'No, that would be too late.'

'When do you want it?'

'Tomorrow.'

'Tomorrow you'll have it.'

Nikhilesh

The dailies have started running a column about me and letters are pouring in; I believe a limerick and cartoons are also in the pipeline. The channels of mockery have opened up, as have the floodgates of lies and everyone is delighted. They know that in this game of mud-slinging, the slings are all in their hands. I am just a gentleman walking by the road, my clothes will be mud-stained.

They write, in my area every single individual is eager to participate in swadeshi and all that holds them back is the fear of retribution from me. The handful who dare to sell desi goods are harassed by me in true zamindari style. I am in cahoots with the police, I correspond with the magistrate regularly and the daily had been informed by reliable sources that all this was aimed at earning myself some titles in addition to the ones inherited by me. They have written: 'A man should earn his own name, but we also know that his own fellowmen have demanded that he be dethroned.' Although my name isn't mentioned, it is quite obvious from all they have said. On the other hand, the paper is also flooded by letters in praise of the patriotic Harish Kundu. They write that if there were more such diehard patriots in this land, then by now the factory chimneys of Manchester would also have taken to singing Vande Mataram in tuneful submission.

Meanwhile, I have received a letter written in red ink detailing the number of zamindars whose offices have been burnt down because their loyalties lay with Liverpool. It says that the fire of God has now embarked on this mission of cleansing; steps will be taken to evict those from the mother's lap, who were never her children in the first place.

It is signed, 'A humble claimant to the mother's love, Ambikacharan Gupta.'

I knew that all this was the handiwork of local students. I called a few of them and showed them the letter. Solemnly, the BA said, 'We have also come to know that there is a group of desperados in the land who would do anything to rid the land of the enemies of swadeshi.'

I said, 'If even a single person buckles down under their unfair pressure tactics, it is a shame for the entire nation.'

The MA in history said, 'I don't understand.'

I said, 'Our country quakes under every gaze, be it God's or the constable's. Now, in the name of freedom, if you bring back that terror with a new name to it, if you want to plant your victory flag through oppression, then the ones who love the country would never bow down to that rule of terror.'

The history MA said, 'Is there a country where the law of the land is not one of terror?'

I said, 'The limit of that terror determines how free the people of that land are. If it is used solely to curb violence on others then it's obviously there to protect every individual from the cruelty of another individual. But if the reign of terror determines what one should wear, where he should buy his goods, what he should eat, with whom he should have his meal, then it denies the basics of individual freedom. And that is tantamount to denying man his human rights.'

The history MA asked, 'Isn't there such a system of denying the individual's freedom from the roots in other countries as well?'

I said, 'Of course there is. The existence of slavery in any country is proof of that.'

He said, 'In that case slavery is also a part of man's objective and that is also humanism.'

The BA said, 'We have really appreciated the example raised by Sandipbabu the other day: if you were to sweep up the entire estate of Harish Kundu or the Chakravartys of Sankibhanga, you wouldn't find an ounce of foreign salt. Why? Because they have always ruled with an iron hand. For the masses, who are meek by nature, the greatest danger is in not having a ruler.'

The young man who had failed his FA piped up, 'I've heard this from someone: the Chakravartys had a Kayasth tenant. He refused to obey them over an issue and it went to the courts. The situation came to this that he had hardly enough to eat. After two days of starvation, he set off to sell his wife's jewellery. It was his last resort. But no one bought them from him, fearing retribution from the zamindar. The chief-clerk offered to buy them for five rupees. They must have been worth nearly thirty. Desperate, he agreed to five rupees. The clerk took the bundle of ornaments from him and informed him that the five rupees would go towards paying off his tax arrears. When we heard this, we told Sandipbabu that we should boycott Chakravarty. But he said, if you boycott such vibrant people, who would you work with—the dead ones? They are the masters because they desire with a passion. Those who cannot crave so passionately, would either go along with others' wishes, or die for others. He drew a comparison with you and said, today there isn't a single person in Chakravarty's area who would dare to oppose swadeshi. But Nikhilesh wouldn't be able to do that, however hard he tried.'

I said, 'Of course I wouldn't, because I want greater things than swadeshi. I do not want a lifeless post, I want a live tree. My work will take time.'

The historian laughed and said, 'You'll get neither, because, I agree with Sandipbabu: to have is to seize. It took us a while to learn this lesson, because these are the antithesis of textbook wisdom. I have seen with my own eyes: Gurucharan Bhaduri, the Kundu family's clerk, went out to collect taxes. A Muslim subject had nothing to sell or give. He only had his young wife. Bhaduri said you'll have to marry off your wife and raise the money. A candidate for this nikaah soon turned up and the debt was paid off. I can tell you, that husband's tears almost robbed me of my sleep; but whatever the misery, I have learnt this, that when it comes to collecting money, the man who can make the debtor marry off his wife and raise the debt is a greater human being than I am. I cannot do it, tears come to my eyes and so all is lost. If anyone can save my country, it'll be people like this clerk, this Kundu and this Chakravarty.'

I was dumbfounded. I said, 'If that is so, then it is my job to save the land from these clerks, these Kundus and Chakravartys. Look here, when the poison of slavery that runs in the blood begins to come out, it takes horrible shapes. The one who is tortured as the daughter-in-law turns into the greatest tormentor when she is the mother-in-law. A man may walk with his eyes lowered but when he goes as the groom's party, the bride's household is hard pressed to meet his random demands. You have unequivocally accepted the rule of fear, known that as the right path, and so now you choose to terrorize everyone and bend them to your will. My battle is with this brutality inherent in weakness.'

My thoughts are very simple and any common man would understand them in a minute. But for these MAs who were flexing their historians' brains in this land, the point was to trounce out Truth.

Meanwhile, I was bothered about Panchu's fake aunt. It would be difficult to prove. It was difficult, and almost next to impossible, getting witnesses for the truth. But for something that hasn't happened, one could easily rally forth a whole host of witnesses. This was a ploy to spoil my purchase of the original deeds from Panchu. I was cornered and I even considered giving Panchu some land in my own area and setting him up. But Chandranathbabu said he wasn't keen on letting evil defeat him so easily. He wanted to try himself.

'You will try?'

'Yes, I.'

I couldn't understand what a teacher hoped to achieve in these matters of legal twists and turns. That evening he failed to keep our daily appointment. I went looking and found that he had left with his clothes and things; he had left a message with the servants that he'd be back in a few days. I figured he may have gone to Panchu's uncle's home in the hope of rounding up some witnesses. If that was the case, I knew nothing would come of it. His school was closed for a few days on account of Jagatdhatri Puja and Muharram. So there was no news of him there either.

When the autumn evenings draw to a close, turning the light into a muted yellow, the shades in one's mind also turn colour. Many people live their mental lives indoors—they can totally ignore the 'outside'. My mind seems to reside under a tree, exposed to every nuance, every gust of wind from the outside, resonating every single aria of the sunlight. When the sun was high in the sky and a host of chores jostled for space all around me,

I felt I needed nothing more from life. But when the sky grew dimmer, my heart seemed to feel that dusk came upon this world only to draw a curtain over life; at this time solitude would fill up the endless darkness. The life that blossomed amidst others in the day was supposed to withdraw within itself at dusk and that was the true essence of light and shade. I could scarcely turn my back on this profound truth. Hence, when dusk began to glow on this earth, like the glittering dark eyes of a lover, my heart kept repeating, 'It's untrue, the true meaning, the true purpose of a man's life is not work; man is not merely a labourer, be it the labour of Truth, or the labour of life. Nikhilesh, have you lost sight of that man, who lives and rests in the starlight, away from all his work? The man who is completely alone in that space where all the world's multitude cannot give him company, must be so truly alone.'

That day, when the evening had just reached the crossroads of dusk, I had no work; neither did I feel like working. Chandranathbabu wasn't there either. When my empty heart yearned to cling to something, I went to the garden indoors. I love chrysanthemums. I had planted many of them in clay pots and when they all bloomed together, it looked like waves of colour in a sea of green. It was a while since I'd visited the garden. So I smiled to myself, 'Let me lighten up the mood of my bereaved chrysanthemums today.'

When I stepped into the garden the sickle moon just peeped over the walls of our house. Dark shadows lay pooled at the base of the wall and the moonlight arched over it to cast its radiance on the western side of the garden. I suddenly felt the moon had tiptoed up from behind, covered the eyes of darkness and was smiling mischievously.

When I approached the gallery-like steps on which rows and rows of chrysanthemum plants rested, I spotted someone lying quietly beneath the steps, on the grass. My heart missed a beat. She also stood up, startled.

I was in a quandary. I wondered if I should go back; perhaps Bimala also considered leaving. But staying and leaving, both were equally difficult. Before I could come to a decision, Bimala stood up, covered her head with her sari and started walking back to the house. In that one instant, Bimala's unbearable grief stood before me, personified. My own grief and grievances vanished in a second. I called out, 'Bimala.'

She stopped, startled. But she didn't turn towards me. I came and stood in front of her. She stood in the shadow, the moonlight fell on my face. She stood there, hands bunched in fists, eyes shut tight. I said, 'Bimala, my cage here is walled from all sides—how can I keep you here? You cannot live like this.'

Bimala kept her eyes closed and didn't say a word.

I said, 'If I keep you here like this, my life will turn into iron shackles. That's hardly likely to bring me any joy.'

She was silent.

I said, 'I speak the truth, here and now—I release you. If I can be nothing else to you, at least I won't be the handcuffs on your wrists.'

I walked away towards the house. No, this wasn't my magnanimity and hardly my indifference. It's just that if I didn't let go, I wouldn't be free myself. The garland of my heart could not be a burden on it forever. I only pray to the Omnipotent One, that if He doesn't give me any joy, or only saddle me with grief, I would take it all, but never should he keep me shackled, bound and tied. Trying to hold on to the lie as a Truth was like strangling your own self. Please, spare me from killing myself thus.

I came into the living room and found Chandranathbabu sitting there. My heart was swelling with emotion at that point.

The moment I spotted him, I burst out saying, 'Professor, freedom is man's greatest possession. Nothing else can compare, nothing at all.'

He was surprised at this excited outburst. He just stared at me.

I said, 'Books don't tell you anything. I have read in the shastras that desires bind you; it binds itself and also others. But they were empty words. The day I truly let the bird fly from the cage, I felt that the bird has really left me and not the other way round. When I keep something chained, I am actually chained by my own desires, stronger than iron shackles. I tell you, this is the Truth people fail to understand. Everyone thinks the cure lies elsewhere; nowhere, nowhere else—just set your desires free.'

Chandranathbabu said, 'We think that freedom lies in getting in your hands whatever you have wished for. But in reality, freedom comes from giving up within yourself whatever you have desired.'

I said, 'Professor, if you put it in mere words it sounds so bald, like a moral. But when I get even a glimpse of it, I feel this is the elixir of life. This is what the gods drink, and conquer death forever. We fail to perceive beauty until we set it free. If I claim that it was Buddha who conquered the world and not Alexander, it sounds like a lie. When will I be able to sing these words? When will these truths of the universe leap out of printed textbooks and flow like the eternal spring of Truth?'

Suddenly, I remembered that the professor had been gone some days and I didn't know where he had been. A trifle embarrassed, I asked, 'Where did you go?'

He said, 'To Panchu's house.'

'Panchu's house? You were there all these days?'

'Yes. I figured I would talk to the woman who is posing as his aunt. She was surprised to see me at first. This was unexpected behaviour from a gentleman. But then I stayed on. So finally, she began to feel a little ashamed. I told her, "Ma, you won't be able to insult me and send me away. And if I stay, so does Panchu. I won't allow him and his motherless children to be thrown out into the streets." For two days she heard me quietly, neither concurring nor disagreeing. Eventually, today I found her packing her bags. She said, "We will go to Vrindavan; give us some money." I know she won't go to Vrindavan, but she'll have to be given a big amount as a send-off. So I have come to you.'

'Certainly, I'll give whatever is needed.'

'The old lady isn't all bad. Panchu wouldn't let her touch the water jug and always kicked up a ruckus if she so much as walked into the room; but when she heard that I don't mind eating food cooked by her, she took very good care of me. She's a good cook. The little respect that Panchu had for me, vanished altogether. Earlier he thought I was at least a simple man. But now he believes the reason I ate food cooked by this woman was simply to manipulate her. Manipulation may have its place in life—but to compromise your caste over it? If I could have outwitted her as a false witness, he may have understood. Anyway, I'll have to stand guard over Panchu's house for a while even after the old woman leaves, or Harish Kundu may cook up more mischief. I believe he has said to his subjects, "I got him a fake aunt and he has gone one up on me and got himself a fake father. Let's see how his father saves his skin."'

I said, 'His skin may or may not be saved. But if we even lose our lives fighting these various traps these people are designing for our countrymen, in the shape of religion, society, business, etc., I would be a happy man.'

Bimala

It's hard to believe so much can happen in one lifetime. I feel I have lived seven times over, as if a thousand years have lapsed in these few months. Time was galloping so fast that I scarcely felt it moving. That day I got a jolt and came to my senses.

When I went to speak to my husband about abolishing foreign goods from our markets, I knew we'd have an argument. But I somehow believed that I would have no need of dissembling dissent. There was magic in the very air around me. The fact that an immense ocean of maleness like Sandip came and crashed at my feet like waves, when I had not called out to him, was proof of the fact that this magic existed. And the other day I saw Amulya—young and simple as the tender bamboo reed—come and stand before me, gradually a colour emerging from within him like the river at dawn. That day, a glance at Amulya's face told me just how impressed the goddess could be when she looked upon her devotee. Thus, I had already seen how my magic wand worked.

So, that day, I went to my husband like a bolt of lightning, heading an army of clouds with immense faith in my powers. But what happened? In all of these nine years, I had never seen such indifference in his eyes. It was like the desert sky without a drop of moisture, draining all colour from the object it chanced to look upon. I'd have been happier if he had at least shown some anger. I couldn't touch him anywhere. I felt I was a lie, a dream: and when the dream ended, I was just the dark night.

All these years I had envied my beautiful sisters-in-law their beauty. I knew in my heart that Fate had deprived me of powers and all my power lay in my husband's love for me. Today, I had drained the cup of power to the dregs and I was inebriated. Suddenly, the cup fell to the ground and shattered. How was I to live?

Quickly, I sat down to tie up my hair. Shame. Oh the shame. As I walked passed Mejorani's room, she called out, 'Hey there, little princess, the topknot is leaping out over your head; is your head still in the right place?'

The other day, my husband told me so easily in the garden: I release you. Is it so simple: giving release or being released? Is freedom tangible? It's empty. Like the fish, I had always swum in the waters of love. All of a sudden if I am held up to the sky and told, here is your freedom, I cannot survive.

Today, when I came into my bedroom, I found mere furniture—racks, mirrors, bed. The heart was missing. There was only release, freedom, emptiness. The water had dried up, exposing the rocks and pebbles. No love, just furniture.

When I was so badly hit by doubts about where exactly Truth resided in this world for me, I ran into Sandip again. As the heart slammed into another heart, the fires burned the same as before. Where was the lie? This was Truth brimming over. These people walking around, talking, laughing, Bororani counting her beads, Mejorani laughing with her maids, singing songs—the awakening within me was a far greater Truth than all of this.

Sandip said, 'I need fifty thousand.'

My drunken soul sang out, 'That's nothing. I'll get it for you.' It didn't matter how, and from where. Here I was, rising above everything from the depths of nothing in a matter of seconds. Just like that, things would happen with just one gesture. I can, I can, I can. No doubts about it.

So I walked away. But then I looked around me—where was the money? Where was that magic tree showering currency? Why did the world shame the heart so? But I had to have the money. By hook or by crook—there was no shame in it. Crime stalked guilt. True power was exempt from all fault. The thief steals, but the victorious king loots. I began to look into where the treasury was, who guarded the money and whose hands it came into. At night I stood on the veranda gazing fixedly at the office room. How was I to snatch away fifty thousand from within these iron bars? I had no mercy. If a spell could make the guards of the room drop dead in that instant, I would have rushed in like a crazed soul. Within the heart of this family's queen, a gang of robbers, rapiers in hand, began to dance before their goddess, begging for a boon. But the world remained silent, the guards changed every few hours and the clock chimed every hour—the huge mansion slept on, fearless and undaunted.

Finally, one day, I called Amulya. I said, 'The country needs money. Won't you be able to get it from the treasurer somehow?'

His chest swelled with pride and he said, 'Why not?'

Alas, I too had spoken thus to Sandip, 'Why not?' Amulya's confidence didn't give me the slightest hope.

I asked, 'Tell me what you'll do?'

He began to lay out such outlandish plans that they were only fit for the monthly magazines and nothing else.

I said, 'No Amulya, don't be so naive.'

He said, 'Fine, I'll bribe the guards.'

'Where is the money for that?'

He replied nonchalantly, 'I'll loot the market.'

I said, 'There's no need for that, I have my jewels and that will do.'

Amulya said, 'But the treasurer can't be bribed. There's a simpler plan.'

I asked, 'What?'

'You don't have to hear that. It's very simple.'

'Tell me still.'

First he fished out a small edition of the Gita from his shirt pocket, kept it on the table and then placed a pistol on it; he didn't say anything.

Oh my God—he didn't blink twice before contemplating the murder of our old treasurer. His face was so cherubic that it was hard to imagine him even harming a fly; but appearances are so deceptive. The fact of the matter was, that the old treasurer wasn't real to him—in his place there was a blankness: it held no life, no pain, just a sloka, 'Na hanyatey hanyamane sharirey'. The soul does not die, only the body does.

I exclaimed, 'No, Amulya. Our treasurer has a wife, children, he is—'

'Where in this country would you find a man who doesn't have a wife and children? Look here, what we call mercy is only a kind of self-indulgence: so that our weak minds are not hurt, we refrain from hurting others. This is the depth of cowardice.'

Sandip's words coming from the lips of this child sent a chill down my spine. He is a so raw, so young, he should still believe that goodness exists. Poor thing, this was his time to live, time to grow. The mother in me awakened. For me, there was neither good nor evil—there was only death in alluring shapes; but when this eighteen-year-old could so easily decide that killing an innocent old man was the right thing, I shuddered in terror. When I realized that he had no sense of sin, the sin hidden in his words took a fierce shape before my eyes, as if the sins of the 'father' were visiting the child.

As I looked at those large, ingenuous eyes, brimming with faith and fervour, my heart wept. He was on his way to hell—who could save him? Why wasn't my country taking the form of a true mother and drawing this boy to her bosom? Why didn't she tell him, 'Do not lose yourself in the process of saving me'?

I know that the greatest powers on earth have reached their summit only by selling their soul to the devil; but the mother stands alone, only to lock horns with this very devil. The mother doesn't want results, however glorious; she only wants to save. Today my heart cried out to reach out and draw this boy into safety.

Just a few minutes ago I had asked him to steal. Now whatever I said to the contrary, he was bound to laugh it off as female weakness. That is something they give in to only when it entertains or ruins the world.

I said to Amulya, 'Go on, you don't have to do anything. It's my job to get the money.'

When he was at the door, I called him back and said, 'Amulya, I am your elder sister. I bless you and pray that God keeps you safe and sound.' He was taken aback at these words of mine. But then he bent low and touched my feet. When he stood up, his eyes were moist.

'Dear brother, I am headed for disaster; let me take on all your troubles—let me never plant fresh thorns on your path.' I said to him, 'You'll have to gift your pistol to me.'

'What will you do with it, Didi?'

'I'll practise death.'

'That's what is needed—women too have to die and kill.' Amulya handed me the pistol.

Amulya's youthful face and the glow on it left a trail in my heart like the first streak of light at dawn. I held the pistol to my heart and said, 'This here is my last resort to salvation, a gift from a brother to his sister.'

The window in the heart that guarded the tender spot of maternal feelings flew open just this once. I thought it would stay open from now on. But good always loses out. The lover-woman came and obstructed the mother's way to liberation. The next day I ran into Sandip again. A crazy madness gripped my heart and began its wild dance all over again. But what was all this—was this my true self? Never. Never before had I set my eyes upon this brazen, this audacious self. The snake charmer came suddenly and unwrapped this snake within me. But this snake had never been within me—it was brought by the snake charmer himself. The devil seemed to have me in his thrall. Whatever I did now, was not my doing, but all his.

That same devil came to me one day, blazing torch in hand, and said, 'I am your country, I am your Sandip, you have nothing that matters more than me, Vande Mataram.' I folded my hands and said, 'You are my religion, you are my heaven, I will sacrifice my all for the love of you, Vande Mataram.'

You want five thousand? Fine, you shall have it. Tomorrow? I'll bring it tomorrow. The scandalous insolence of the act will make that five thousand froth and foam, like heady liquor. Then there would be the inebriated dance. The motionless earth would sway beneath the feet, the eyes would burn with hidden fire, a fiery wind would blow past the ears and everything before my eyes would seem blurred; tottering, I shall stumble to my death; in a moment, the fire would extinguish, ashes would fly in the wind—nothing would be left.

I was totally at a loss as to where the money could come from. Then, the other day, in the throes of extreme excitement, I saw the money right before my eyes.

Every year, for the Durga Puja, my husband gifted his sisters-in-law three thousand rupees each. That money lay in the bank, gathering interest. This year too, the money had been gifted. But I knew that it hadn't gone into the bank yet. I also knew where the money was. There was an iron chest in the ante-room adjoining my bedroom where I changed my clothes. The money was in that chest.

Every year my husband went to Calcutta to deposit this money in the bank there. But this year he couldn't make the trip. This is why I believe in Fate. The country needed this money and that's why it was still there. Who would dare to take this money to the bank? And would I dare *not* take this money? The death-goddess has reached out her begging bowl, she says I am hungry, feed me. I would bleed myself to death, for that five thousand rupees—oh Mother, the one who has lost this money hasn't lost much. But you have drained me of all virtues.

So many times have I called Bororani and Mejorani thieves in my heart; they were looting my trusting husband, only taking money from him—this was my grievance. Many times have I told my husband that after their husbands' death they had stolen many things that didn't belong to them. He always held his peace and never answered me back. This irked me; I would say, 'If you wish to donate, do so openly. Why would you allow them to steal?' The Fates must have heard my allegations and smiled to themselves; today I was about to steal money belonging to my sisters-in-law.

At night my husband changed his clothes in that same ante-room. The keys to the chest were in his pocket. I took them and opened the chest. The slightest sound seemed loud enough to wake the whole world. A sudden chill stole over me, petrified me from head to toe, giving me the shivers.

Inside the chest, there was a drawer. I pulled it open and found that there were no notes, only guineas wrapped in paper.

There was no time to count how many there were in each wrapping, how much I needed, etc. There were twenty in all and I piled them all into my anchal and tied the knot. It was no mean weight. The burden of guilt dragged me down to the earth. If they'd been wads of notes instead, I may have felt less guilty. This was all gold.

That night, when I had to enter my own room feeling like a thief, the room no longer seemed my own. I had the strongest claim on this room. But my fraud had made me forfeit it.

I muttered to myself, 'Vande Mataram, Vande Mataram. Country, my motherland, my golden land—all this gold belongs to her and to nobody else.'

But in the dark of night the heart is weak. My husband slept in the next room. I closed my eyes and passed through his room. I went straight to the open terrace in the inner courtyard, placed that bundle of guilt under my heart and lay on the floor—the packets of coins hurt my soul. The silent night sat near my head, pointing fingers at me. I had failed to separate my home from the world. Today I have robbed my home, and therefore robbed the land; for this sin, my home was lost to me in the same instant that my land slipped away from me. Had I gone begging in order to serve the country, and even lost my life before completing my service, that incomplete service would have been accepted by God as obeisance. But theft was no worship—how would I hand this to my country? The boat would sink with the weight of this burden. Just because I was headed for death, I didn't have to drag my motherland into the muck, did I?

There was no way of returning this money into the chest. I did not have the strength to go back into that room, open the chest and put the money back this very night. If I tried, I would surely faint at the threshold of my husband's room. Now there was only the road ahead and no other.

I was too ashamed to even sit and count how much money there was. Let it stay hidden, the way it was. I could not possibly calculate the value of theft.

In that dark winter night, the sky didn't hold a single drop of moisture. The stars glittered blindingly. I lay on the terrace thinking: if I had to steal those stars, one by one, in the name of the country, pluck them from the heart of the sky, then the following night the sky would be a widow; the dark sky would go blind and the theft would be from the entire universe. This theft of mine, today, was not merely about money: it was also like stealing the light from the sky, stealing Truth and faith from the entire universe.

The night crept away as I lay on the terrace. In the morning, when I realized my husband must have left the room by then, I got up slowly, wrapped myself in a shawl and walked towards my room. At that time, Mejorani was watering her plants in the corridor. The moment she spotted me, she said, 'Hey there, little one, have you heard?'

I stopped short; my heart quaked within me. I felt the guineas tied in my anchal were sticking out a mile. I felt any moment now that my sari would give way and the gold coins would clatter to the floor all around me; today, the thief who has stolen her own wealth would stand exposed before all and sundry in this house.

Mejorani said, 'That gang of robbers has written to Thakurpo, warning him that they'd raid his treasury.'

I stood there silent as a thief.

'I told Thakurpo he should go to you; goddess, smile upon us and save us from your vengeful followers. We will dutifully chant your mishmash Vande Mataram. So much has been happening lately; now for God's sake, don't let them break into the house.'

I walked to my room quickly without another word. Once you step on to the quicksand there is no way out—the more you struggle, the deeper you drown. I would be so glad to take this money from my anchal and drop it into Sandip's hands. I cannot bear this weight any more, it's breaking my back.

Early in the day I got the message that Sandip was waiting for me. Today I didn't bother decking up; just wrapped the shawl tight around me and walked out quickly.

I stepped into the room and found Amulya sitting there with Sandip. The little self-respect I had remaining seemed to shudder through my entire frame like a lightning bolt and drained out through my feet, straight into the earth. Today, in front of that youth, I would have to unmask the woman in her ugliest form. My crime was being discussed in the group today—they didn't spare me the thinnest of veils.

We will never understand men. When they decide to pave the way to their goals, they never hesitate to break the heart of the whole universe and scatter it as pebbles all along the way. When they are drunk on the pleasure of creating with their own hands, they take great joy in shattering His creations. They wouldn't spare my terrible shame a second glance, their hearts know no mercy, they only have eyes for the Ideal. Alas, who am I to them? I am a mere wildflower in the path of a turbulent deluge.

But what did Sandip gain by snuffing me out thus? Just the five thousand rupees? Did I have no greater value than that? Surely I did. I had heard all about it from Sandip himself and that is what made me ride roughshod over everything in my world. I would give light, I would give life, I would give strength and elixir—the sheer exultation made me overflow my own shores. If someone had fulfilled those promises, I would have been happy even in death; I'd have felt it was worth losing everything.

But did they mean to tell me today that all of it was a lie? The goddess in me didn't have the power to set her devotees' fears at rest? The eulogy I heard, the one that brought me from heaven unto this dust: wasn't it meant to turn this dust to heaven? Was it meant just to turn heaven into earth and soil?

Sandip cast a sharp glance at me and said, 'We need the money, Queen.'

Amulya stared at my face, that boy who wasn't born from my mother's womb, but came forth from his mother's womb— that mother, oh it was the same mother. What a youthful face, such serene eyes, oh the sheer youth of the boy. I am a woman, the same as his mother. If he says to me, hand me some poison, would I do it?

'We need money, Queen.'

Anger and shame made me feel like hurling that bundle of gold coins straight at Sandip's head. I simply couldn't untie the knot of my anchal. My fingers trembled. And when the paper wrapped bundles rolled on to the table, Sandip's face grew dark. He must have thought those wrappers held copper coins. What hatred. His face reflected such crude disdain for failure. He looked as if he would hit me. Sandip thought I was here to bargain with him, that I would try to palm off a few hundred rupees against his demand for five thousand. For a moment he looked as if he'd throw those bundles out of the window. He was no beggar—he was the king.

Amulya asked, 'Is that all, Ranididi?'

His voice dripped sympathy. I felt like bursting into tears. I gripped my heart and slowly nodded. Sandip was silent; he didn't touch the bundles or say a single word.

I wanted to leave, but my feet wouldn't move. If only the earth had split into two and sucked me in, this lump of clay would have been so happy to return to dust. The young boy felt my terrible mortification. He pretended to be greatly thrilled and said, 'Well, this is a lot too. This would be enough. You have really saved us, Ranididi.'

He unwrapped one of the bundles and the gold coins sparkled!

In an instant Sandip's face came out of the shadow. He glowed with joy. Scarcely able to control this sudden emotional turnaround of his heart, he jumped off the seat and leapt towards me. I do not know what his intentions were. I shot a lightning glance at Amulya's face and saw that it had turned pallid, as if struck quite suddenly. I gathered all my strength and pushed hard at Sandip. He fell and his head hit the corner of the marble table; he didn't stir for a while. After this mammoth effort, I had no strength left in me. I collapsed on the chair. Amulya's face was bright with elation. He didn't spare a second glance for Sandip, but touched my feet and sat on the floor at my feet. Oh dear brother, dear child, this veneration of yours is the last drop in my empty cup today. I could no longer hold back my tears. I buried my face in my anchal and sobbed my heart out. The occasional, sympathetic touch of Amulya's fingers on my feet from time to time only brought forth fresh bouts of tears.

A little later I composed myself, opened my eyes and found Sandip sitting by the table, tying up the guineas in his handkerchief, looking as if nothing had happened! Amulya stood up from his place at my feet; his eyes were bright with unshed tears.

Sandip looked up at our faces without the slightest trace of embarrassment and declared, 'Six thousand.'

Amulya said, 'Sandipbabu, we don't need so much. I have done some calculations and I think three and a half thousand would be enough for us right now.'

Sandip said, 'Our work is not just the here and now. There is no limit to how much we need.'

Amulya said, 'Whatever. In future, I take responsibility for gathering funds. For now, please return the two and a half thousand to Ranididi.'

Sandip looked at me. I said, 'No, no, I don't even want to touch that money. Go and use it as you please.'

Sandip looked at Amulya and said, 'Men can never give the way women can.'

Amulya was enchanted, 'Woman is the goddess herself.'

Sandip said, 'We, men, can at the most give our strength, but women give themselves. They nurture a child in their body, give birth, and raise him, all from within. This is the true gift.' He now looked at me and said, 'Queen, if your gift today had been mere money, I wouldn't have touched it—but you have given me something greater than life itself.'

Perhaps we have two minds. One of my minds told me I was being fooled, but the other one was happy to be fooled. Sandip lacked integrity, but he had power. Hence, he nourished life and destroyed it at the same instant. He had the divine scabbard, but the weapon in it was the devil's. Sandip's handkerchief was too small to hold all the guineas; he asked, 'Queen, could I borrow one of your handkerchiefs?'

I handed it to him and he immediately raised it to his brow in a salute. Then he dropped down at my feet and touched my feet devoutly, 'Goddess, I had rushed towards you to offer you this very salute. But you pushed me away; I shall take that as my blessing—I have anointed my brow with it.' He pointed to the scar on his temple.

Was I wrong then? Did he really rush towards me, arms outstretched, just to touch my feet? But I thought even Amulya had winced at the sudden inebriated lust that had glistened on his face. But Sandip had fine-tuned the art of eulogizing so well that I could never argue; the eyes seeking Truth always drifted shut, as if drugged. Sandip returned the wound inflicted by me twice over and my heart wept. When I received his obeisance, my act of theft was raised to glorified heights. The guineas lying on the table could then overlook all the shame, the ethical violation, the pain, and sparkle in their laughter.

Just like me, Amulya was also waylaid. The slight loss of respect that he had felt for Sandip in that one instant, seemed to have been replaced by renewed veneration and his eyes glowed with respect for both Sandip and me. It filled the room with a sense of innocent trust as pure as the lone star at dawn. I paid homage, I received homage and my sins glowed bright as embers. Amulya gazed at me, folded his hands and said, 'Vande Mataram.'

But the strains of eulogy fade as time passes. I had no ways and means to salvage some self-respect from within myself. I couldn't enter my bedroom. That iron chest frowned upon me, our bed seemed to raise an accusing finger. I wanted to run away from this deep humiliation that rose from within. All I wanted to do was rush to Sandip and listen to him sing my praise. From the nadir of guilt that ran deep inside, that was the one shrine that was alive. Beyond that, wherever I turned there was only oblivion. So I wanted to cling to that shrine day and night. Applause, applause, my soul thirsts for applause. If the level in that wine glass went down by a notch, I gasped for breath. And so, all day long I yearned to go to Sandip and talk to him; I needed Sandip so desperately today, if only to perceive my own worth on this earth.

When my husband came home for lunch, I couldn't go and stand before him; but not to go would be so much more shameful, that I couldn't do that either. So I sat at an angle from him, such that I wouldn't have to meet his eyes. The other day, I sat in that same fashion as he was eating, when Mejorani came and sat down. She said, 'Thakurpo, you are always laughing off all those dares and anonymous letters about a raid, but I feel very scared. Have you sent our gift-money to the bank yet?'

My husband said, 'No, I haven't had the time.'

Mejorani said, 'Be careful, you are so callous sometimes; that money—'

My husband smiled and said, 'But it is safe in the iron chest in the ante-room next to my bedroom.'

'If they get their hands on it? You never know.'

'If burglars can get all the way into my room, then they can even steal you away one day.'

'Oh dear, no one would take me, don't worry. Whatever is worth taking is in your room, not mine. But seriously, don't keep cash in the house.'

'In about five days or so the estate-taxes would be sent to the bank and I will send that money along with it to the bank in Calcutta.'

'Make sure it doesn't slip your mind—you can be so absent-minded sometimes . . .'

'If the money gets stolen from my room, it will be my loss, Bourani; your money will be safe.'

'Thakurpo, when you talk like this, I feel so angry. Am I making a distinction between mine and yours? Would your loss be any less painful for me? Vicious Fate may have taken everything from me and left me with just a devout brother—but I do know his value. Look here, I cannot stay lost in all those prayers like the eldest queen. I value what God has given me more than God himself. What is it, little princess, you look stiff as a board. Know something, Thakurpo, the little one thinks I curry favour with you. I guess if it came to that, I *would* have too.

But you aren't that kind of brother, whose ego one has to pander to. If you were like Madhav Chakravarty, even the eldest queen would have forgotten her gods and hung on to him like a leech, begging for the odd half penny. But I do believe that would have been for the good, because then she wouldn't have had so much time to go making up stories about you.'

Mejorani babbled on, interspersed with her attempts to draw her Thakurpo's attention to the curry or the fish. My head was spinning. There was no time. Something had to be done, and soon. As I was frantically trying to figure out what could be done, Mejorani's incessant babble seemed intolerable to me. Especially when I knew that her eyes missed nothing. Her glance was flicking at me from time to time—I didn't know what she saw, but I felt the whole truth was writ large on my face for all to read.

Audacity can be unbounded. I forced a seemingly amused laugh to my lips and said, 'The fact of the matter is that Mejorani doesn't trust *me*—all that prattle about thieves and burglars is an eyewash.'

Mejorani gave a snide smile and said, 'You've got it right there—a woman burglar is deadly. But of course, I will catch you out—I am not a man. How would you fool me?'

I said, 'If you are so afraid, then let me keep all my belongings in your care as a deposit; if I ever cause you to lose anything, you can deduct it from there.'

Mejorani laughed and said, 'Just listen to the little one talk. There are losses that can't be retrieved through deposits in this life or another.'

My husband didn't say a single word in this whole exchange. He went out as soon as he finished his lunch; these days he never went into the room to rest.

Most of my expensive jewellery was entrusted to the treasurer. Still, the price of whatever little I had with me would be no less than thirty to thirty-five thousand rupees. I took the box of jewellery and opened it up in front of Mejorani and said, 'Here's my jewellery; let it be with you. From now on you can breathe easy.'

Mejorani's brows rose in surprise, 'Oh dear, you really amaze me sometimes. Do you think I can't sleep at night worrying about you stealing my jewellery?'

I said, 'There's no stopping the worries. Besides, what do we ever know about our fellow beings?'

She said, 'And so you have come to teach me a lesson by trusting me so much? Please, I can barely keep track of my own jewellery, what with all this hired help swarming the place. Keep your own jewels with you.'

I left Mejorani's room, went into the living room and sent for Amulya. But Sandip came in along with Amulya. I had little time to lose; so I said to Sandip, 'I need to speak to Amulya about something, could you please—'

Sandip gave a crooked smile and said, 'Do you see Amulya as different from me? If you want to take him away from me, I guess I won't be able to stop it.'

I just stood there silently. Sandip said, 'Okay fine, once you have finished your special discussion with Amulya, do spare some time for a talk with me too, or I would stand defeated. I can take anything except defeat. I have to have the lion's share. I have always fought with Fate over this—I'll conquer Fate and never be defeated.'

Hurling Amulya a fierce glance, he walked out of the room. I said to Amulya, 'Dear child, you'll have to do something for me.'

He said, 'Didi, I will do your every bidding with all my heart.'

I drew out the jewellery box from the folds of my shawl and placed it before him, 'Either by pawning or selling these jewels, you have to bring me six thousand rupees as quickly as you can.'

Amulya was pained, 'No Didi, no, not pawn or sell your jewellery—I will get you six thousand rupees.'

Exasperated, I said, 'Oh, forget all that—I have no time. Take this box and leave for Calcutta by the train tonight; by day after tomorrow you must get me the six thousand rupees.'

Amulya took out the diamond necklace from the box, held it up to the light and put it back with a pained expression. I said, 'All these diamond pieces won't sell easily. That's why I have given you jewellery worth nearly thirty-five thousand rupees; I don't mind if all of it goes, but I have to have the six thousand rupees.'

Amulya said, 'Look here, Didi, I have fought bitterly with Sandipbabu for taking the six thousand rupees from you. Oh, the unbearable shame of it. Sandipbabu says for the motherland you have to sacrifice all sense of shame. Perhaps that is so. But this is a little different. I am not afraid to die for my country and I have the strength to show no mercy while killing; but I cannot get over the shame of taking this money from you. In this, Sandipbabu is far stronger—he suffers no such shame. He says one has to transcend the illusion that money belonged to the person whose purse it was in, or the mantra of Vande Mataram is in vain.' Amulya was inspired as he spoke. With me as an audience, his fervour always doubled. He continued to speak, 'According to the Gita, Lord Krishna has said that the soul cannot be killed. Killing someone is a mere phrase. Stealing money is the same. Whose money is it? No one creates money, no one carries it in death, it is not linked to anyone's souls. It belongs to me today, to my son tomorrow and to the money-lender the day after. If this whimsical money theoretically belongs to nobody, then if it goes towards serving the country instead of falling in the hands of my worthless son, what is the harm in it?'

Every time I heard Sandip's words from the mouth of this innocent boy, my heart quaked. Let the snake charmer play his tune and fiddle with snakes; he is aware of the dangers. But for pity's sake, these are the youth—all the world's blessings should go in keeping them safe; when they, in all ignorance of the snake's venom, reach for it with a smile, I realize just how poisonous a curse this snake is. Sandip was right in thinking that—I may be killed by him but I must snatch this boy away from his grip and save his soul.

I laughed and said, 'So, the money is also needed to serve those who are serving the country, right?'

Amulya raised his head proudly and said, 'Of course. They are our kings, and poverty would only take away their strength. Do you know, we never let Sandipbabu travel in anything less than first class. He never feels embarrassed to have lavish meals. He has to maintain his status, not for his sake, but for ours. Sandipbabu says, that the greatest weapon in the hands of the rulers of this world is the lure of lucre. If they welcome poverty, it won't just be a sacrifice, it'll be suicidal.'

At this point, Sandip slipped into the room silently. Hurriedly I dropped my shawl on the jewellery box. Sandip's voice dripped sarcasm as he asked, 'You still haven't finished your special business with Amulya?'

A trifle embarrassed, Amulya said, 'Oh, we have finished talking. It's not much, really.'

I interrupted, 'No Amulya, we aren't done yet.'

Sandip said, 'So it's exit Sandip once again?'

I said, 'Yes.'

'But what about the re-entry of Sandipkumar?'

'Not today, I don't have the time.'

Sandip's eyes flashed; he said, 'So you only have time for special work and no time to waste, eh?'

Jealousy. Where the mighty have exposed themselves, the weak can hardly resist a jaunty swagger. So, in a firm voice I said, 'No, I don't have the time.'

Sandip went away with a glum face. Amulya was a little disturbed, 'Ranididi, I think Sandipbabu is upset.'

I spoke vehemently, 'He has no reason, or the right, to be upset. Let me tell you one thing Amulya, you are not to mention the job I have trusted you with, to Sandipbabu, even if it costs you your life.'

Amulya said, 'I won't tell him.'

'Then why wait? Leave by the night train.' I left the room along with him. But outside, on the veranda, I found Sandip waiting. I knew he would catch hold of Amulya. In order to stop him doing that, I had to intervene, 'Sandipbabu, what did you want to talk about?'

'Oh, my chatter is not important, it's mere idle talk, and since you don't have any time to spare—'

I said, 'I have the time.'

Amulya left. Sandip stepped into the room and said, 'I saw a box in Amulya's hand, what was it?'

So it hadn't escaped his eyes. I spoke a trifle harshly, 'If I wanted to tell you about it, I'd have given it to him in front of you.'

'Do you think Amulya won't tell me?'

'No, he won't.'

Sandip's anger was palpable now. He burst out saying, 'You think you will score over me. You can't. That Amulya—If I crushed him underfoot and killed him he'd think it was heaven. And you think you can take him away from me? Over my dead body.'

The anger of weakness—at last Sandip had understood that his power failed when compared to me. Hence the untrammelled outburst. He knew that his force wouldn't work against my strength and one condemning glance from me could shatter the walls of his citadel. Hence this show of power today. I smiled silently. At long last I was in the rung above him; I hope to God I never lose it or come down from it. I hope that even amidst my greatest misfortune, I am left with a modicum of self-respect.

Sandip said, 'I know that was your jewellery box.'

I said, 'You may guess as you like, but I won't tell you.'

'You trust Amulya more than me? Do you know that he is the shadow of my shadow, the echo of my echo, and without me at his side, he is nothing?'

'In that space where he is not your echo, he is Amulya and there I trust him more than I trust you.'

'Don't forget that you have promised me all your jewellery for the initiation of the Mother's puja. You have already donated your jewels.'

'If the gods spare me any jewellery I will give it to them willingly. But how can I promise to give the jewellery that has been stolen?'

'Look here, don't think you can give me the slip. Right now I am busy; let me finish the work first and then there'll be time for all your elaborate feminine wiles and games. I may even join in them myself.'

The moment I had stolen my husband's money and handed it to Sandip, the last bit of melody had gone out of our relationship. I had certainly cheapened myself and reduced my worth but Sandip too had lost his powers over me. You can't shoot arrows at something that is already within your fist. So, today Sandip lacked his brave warrior charm. His words held the despicable, harsh echoes of squabbling.

Sandip went on staring at me with his bright eyes and gradually they grew as dark and thirsty as the afternoon sky.

His feet moved restlessly. I realized he was about to rise and any moment now he would rush forward and take me in his arms. My heart lurched, my nerves jangled and ears buzzed—I knew that if I continued to sit a moment longer, I would never be able to get up. I called on my entire reserve of strength, tore myself from the seat and ran towards the door. Sandip's choked voice vibrated dully, 'Queen, where do you run?'

The next moment he jumped up after me but the sound of footsteps outside made him return to his seat. I turned towards the bookshelf and stared at the names of books.

As soon as my husband entered the room, Sandip said, 'Hey Nikhil, don't you have Browning in your collection? I was telling Queen Bee about our college-club—you do remember the row amongst the four of us over translating that poem by Browning? What, you don't remember? You know, it went—

She should never have looked at me
If she meant I should not love her!
There are plenty . . . men you call such.
I suppose . . . she may discover
All her soul to, if she pleases,
And yet leave much as she found them:
But I'm not so, and she knew it
When she fixed me, glancing round them.

'I had somehow managed a Bengali translation, but it was quite unreadable. There was a time when I'd thought of being a poet—any moment the inspiration would grip me. But God was kind enough to let that whim pass. But our Dakhinacharan, if only he wasn't an inspector with the British today, would surely have made an excellent poet; he did a brilliant translation—it read like it was written originally in

Bengali, and not in the language of a country that doesn't exist geographically:

> If she had known that she would never love me
> Was it right that she'd cast her eyes upon me?
> Many are the men that walk this earth
> (Though I don't know what they are worth)
> To whom if she had laid her soul bare
> They'd still have stood straight and bare.
> But she knew that I am not of that class
> So why did she pierce me with her glance?

'Oh no, Queen Bee, you search in vain; Nikhil gave up reading poetry when he got married. Perhaps he had no need of it any more. I had also given it up from too much work, but I do feel that crazy fever is about to grip me once again.'

My husband said, 'Sandip, I have come to give you a warning.'

Sandip said, 'About the crazy fever of poetry?'

My husband didn't join in the joke and continued, 'For some time now, maulavis from Dacca have started visiting regularly, trying to provoke the Muslims in this area. They are not too happy with you and something may happen if you don't watch out.'

'Are you advising me to escape?'

'I have come to inform you, not to advise you.'

'If I was the zamindar here, the Muslims would have to worry, not I. It would be better for both you and me if you put some pressure on them instead of coming and getting me apprehensive. Do you know that your weakness has even robbed the neighbouring zamindars of their true powers?'

'Sandip, I didn't offer you advice and it would be nice if you returned the favour. It's pointless. There's one more thing:

for some time now your followers have been ganging up and terrorizing my subjects. This has to stop; you'll have to leave my territory.'

'For fear of the Muslims or are there other threats too?'

'Sandip, there are such threats that it'd be cowardly *not* to be scared, and being aware of those threats I am asking you to leave. I am headed for Calcutta in another five days or so. I want you to leave with me. You could stay in our house in Calcutta, that's not a problem.'

'Good, at least I get five days to think. Meanwhile, Queen Bee, let me start humming songs about having to leave your beehive. Oh poet of this day, unlock your doors, let me loot your songs—actually you are the thief, you stole my words and made them yours—the name may be yours but the songs are mine,' he started singing in his slightly off-tune, baritone voice a song set in Bhairavi:

'The sweet season is here to stay in your land of honey,
The smiles and tears of coming and going drift in the air.
The one who leaves is all that goes, the flowers still
      bloom and thrive,
The ones meant to go, droop at the day's end.
When I was close, so many songs I gave:
Now I go away, is there a reward to have?
In the shade of the flowery grove I leave behind this
      hope—
That the rains would drench in tears this fiery spring of
      yours.'

His unbounded audacity had no veils, naked as the flames. It didn't wait to be stopped; trying to do so was like denying the thunder, which the lightning laughed and brushed aside. I left the room. As I was heading towards the inner sanctum, suddenly Amulya appeared before me, 'Ranididi, don't worry at all. I'm leaving now. I won't come back empty-handed. '

I looked upon his sincere, young face and said, 'Amulya, I don't worry about myself—but let me always worry for you all.'

As he was leaving, I called him back and asked, 'Amulya, is your mother alive?'

'Yes.'

'Sisters?'

'No. I am my mother's only son. My father died when I was very young.'

'Go Amulya, go back to your mother.'

'Didi, here I see my mother as well as my sister in the same person.'

I said, 'Amulya, before you leave tonight, have your dinner over here.'

He said, 'No time, Ranididi. Give me your blessing to carry with me.'

'What do you like to eat, Amulya?'

'If I was with my mother, I'd have gorged myself on sweetmeats this time of the year. When I come back, Ranididi, I'll have sweets made by you.'

Nikhilesh

I woke up suddenly at three in the night and felt that my long-familiar world had died and was sitting like a spectre, guarding my bed, my room, all my things. I understood now why people were afraid of ghosts, even those of their close ones. When the eternally familiar turned unfamiliar in an instant, it was a nightmare. When your entire life was running along a certain track and you had to change tracks and make it run a course that wasn't even marked, the task was a difficult one. Even being yourself became a challenge; one felt that he himself was also perhaps a changed being.

For a while now it was clear that Sandip and his gang were terrorizing people. If I'd been my normal self, I would have firmly told him to leave the area. But all this trouble had made me lose my footing; my path was no longer straight and narrow. I felt ashamed to ask Sandip to leave—something else cropped up between us. And that made me feel very small.

Marriage was private and personal; it wasn't merely a duty or about a structured family life. It was the expression of my life. And that was why I couldn't put any pressure on it from without. If I did, I would be insulting the God within. I cannot explain this to anyone. Perhaps I am different and that's why I've been cheated. But how could I cheat everything within me to stop being cheated from without?

I am initiated into the mantra of Truth—that which creates the world outside through the heart. That is why today I had to rip apart all the mesh of the world like this. My inner deity would release me from the slavery, the bondage of the world. I would gain that freedom by bruising my heart. But when I gained it, the kingdom of the heart would be all mine.

I could already taste that freedom. Every now and then, the sound of the birds chirping at dawn burst through the all-permeating darkness of my heart. The man within me reiterated from time to time: there is no harm in letting go of the dream that was Bimala, the illusion.

Chandranathbabu informed me that Sandip had joined up with Harish Kundu and they were preparing to host a puja of Mahishamardini Durga, with great pomp and grandeur. Harish Kundu had already begun to raise the cost for this puja from his subjects. Our court poet and pundit were employed to write an eulogy that could be read in two ways. Sandip and Chandranathbabu had also had a debate over this. Sandip claimed that God has an evolution: if we do not modify the God constructed by our forefathers to suit our needs, it would be an act of atheism. It was Sandip's mission to give the old gods new colours, release them from the shackles of the past: he was the salvation for the gods.

I have seen this from our childhood days—Sandip was the magician of Ideas; he was never interested in discovering the Truth, because juggling with it gave him greater pleasure. If he had been born in central Africa, he would have taken great pleasure in proving that human sacrifice and feeding on human flesh was the best way to bring human beings close to one another.

The one who truly thrived on illusion, could scarcely escape being deluded himself. I believe that every time Sandip created a novel web of illusion with his words, he himself believed 'I have found Truth', however disparate his one Truth was from another.

Anyway, I was loath to offer any assistance in building up this tavern of illusion over my motherland. I would rather not have a hand in getting the young lads, who wanted to serve the country, into the addictive habit right from the beginning. To those who want to cast a spell on young minds and get some results, it is the end that justifies all and those spellbound minds have no intrinsic value. If I could not save the country from frenzied intoxication, then her puja would lay the foundation of her downfall and every action meant to serve her would return back to her bosom to wound her.

I ordered Sandip to leave my house in front of Bimala. I suppose both Sandip and Bimala would read my intentions wrong. But I need to be free of this fear of being misunderstood. Let Bimala misunderstand me too.

The maulavis from Dacca were swarming the place. The Muslims in our area bore as much hatred for cow-slaughter as the Hindus did. But now there had been a few instances of cow-slaughter here and there. I heard about it first from a Muslim subject and he too, voiced his dissent. I realized that it'd be difficult holding them back. There was a false sense of obduracy at the root of the matter. Resistance would only give it credence. That was precisely what the opposition wanted to achieve.

I sent for some of my influential Hindu subjects and tried to talk to them. I said, 'We are free to practise our own religion but others' religion is out of bounds. Just because I am a Vaishnav doesn't mean the Kali worshipper should give up bloodshed. There is no choice. The Muslims should be allowed to practise their religion in their way. Don't create a problem over this.'

They said, 'Raja, all these demonstrations were not there before.'

I said, 'They weren't, but that was their wish. Try to find ways to desist them of their own free will. That is not the violent way.'

They said, 'No Raja, those days are gone. Now you have to snub them or you cannot control them.'

I said, 'Snubbing will not put an end to cow-slaughter, but only increase a desire to kill humans as well.'

One of them had studied English and learnt to chant the language of modern times. He said, 'Look here, this is not only about a tradition; our country is primarily agricultural and for us the cow—'

I said, 'In this country, buffalo-milk is also drunk and that animal also ploughs the land. But when we all slaughter it and dance about with its head, it looks strange if we fight the Muslims over this, using religion as our excuse. Religion ridicules us and violence increases. If it's only the cow that shouldn't be killed and not the buffalo, then it isn't about religion, it's about superstition.'

The British-educated said, 'Can't you see who is behind this? The Muslims now know that they won't be taken to task. Have you heard what they have done in Pachurey?'

I said, 'That a day has come when the Muslims can become weapons against us, is a result of what we have fashioned with our hands. This is how Fate brings justice. What we have heaped over the ages, is now going to be wreaked on us.'

The British-educated said, 'Fine, then let it be wreaked. But there's a joy in it for us—we have won a victory. The law that they held so dear to themselves has been razed to the ground by us: so long, they have ruled but now we will make them robbers. This will not be recorded in history, but we will remember this forever.'

Meanwhile, I became notorious through the many mentions in newspapers. I came to know that 'patriots' had made my effigy and burnt it with great pomp in a cremation ground by the river, in Chakravarty's area. There were plans for more humiliation. They had come to me, to get me to buy shares into a joint enterprise in opening a cloth-mill. I said, 'If it was just my money that would go, I wouldn't hesitate. But along with it several poor people would lose money and so I won't buy the shares.'

'Why, pray? Don't you want the country to progress?'

'A business may eventually benefit the country, but setting off to serve the country doesn't make for good business sense. When we were all calm and peaceful, no business took off and now that we are excited, do you think business would suddenly boom?'

'Why don't you simply say that you won't buy the shares?'

'I'll invest when I truly feel your business is worth its salt. The fires in your heart may or may not light up your hearths—I don't know that yet.'

They think I am a calculating miser. Sometimes I feel like showing them my books with the accounts of my work for the country. I suppose they are ignorant of the fact that I once tried to improve the quality of crops harvested in our motherland. I tried to get the farmers to grow sugar cane by importing seeds from Java and Mauritius; I left no stone unturned, as per the advice of the agriculture department of the government. But finally, what was the result? Just the sneaky snigger of the farmers in my area. To this day it has remained sneaky and covert. Later when I tried to translate the governmental agro-journals and went to speak to them about growing Japanese beans or foreign cotton, I realized that the covert snigger was in danger of becoming overt. At the time there was no support from the 'patriots' and the Vande

Mataram mantra was silent. And my shipping business—oh, what's the point of harking back to all that? The fires they have lit in order to serve the country, should hopefully be banked by burning my effigy and spread no further.

What is this I hear? Our treasury in Chakua has been looted. Last night the estate taxes worth seven and a half thousand rupees were deposited there and it was supposed to leave for this office by boat at dawn today. The clerk, in order to facilitate sending it, had changed the money into tens and twenties and kept them in bundles. Late in the night a gang of robbers looted it with guns and pistols. Quasim Sardar had taken a bullet and was wounded. The strange thing was that the robbers only took six thousand rupees and left the remainder strewn on the floor. They could easily have taken all the money. Anyway, the robbers have left and now the police processes would start. The money has already gone, but there won't be any peace either.

I went indoors and found they had all heard the news. Mejorani came and said, 'Thakurpo, how terrible.'

I tried to make light of it, 'Terrible is still a long way off. There's still enough to clothe and feed us for a few more years.'

'Oh no, don't joke about this: why are you their sole target always? Thakurpo, why don't you try to appease them a little? How can you fight all the people—'

'For the sake of the people, I cannot let the country go to hell.'

'Just the other day I heard they've done something by the river— it's an insult to you. Shame on them. I am so scared. The little princess has studied with a British woman—she is quite fearless. I can only rest if you let me call the priest and do some pujas to ward off the evil. For God's sake, Thakurpo, go away to Calcutta; if you stay here, they may do something any day now—'

Mejorani's fears and concern were like a balm on my soul. Fair mother, your kindness will always be upon us.

'Thakurpo, keeping that money next to your bedroom is not a good idea. Lord knows, they may hear of it somehow and eventually—I am not worried about the money, but who knows—'

I tried to calm her fears, 'Okay, I'll take out that money right now and send it away to our treasury. Day after tomorrow I'll go and deposit it in the bank in Calcutta.'

I went into the bedroom and found the ante-room locked from within. When I knocked on it, Bimala answered from within, 'I am changing.'

Mejorani said, 'Early in the morning the little one has started her toilette—strange, that one. I guess today there'll be one of those Vande Mataram meetings of theirs. Ahoy there, Devi Choudhurani, are you busy gathering the loot?'

'I'll come back later and straighten it all out,' I came outside and found the police inspector waiting for me. I asked him, 'Did you find anything?'

'We have our suspicions.'

'On?'

'Quasim Sardar.'

'What? But he has been wounded?'

'No real wound that one: just a grazed foot, slight bleeding, he could have done it himself.'

'I cannot suspect Quasim, he is trustworthy.'

'Perhaps, but that doesn't mean he cannot steal. I have seen such things like an employee of twenty-five years, totally faithful, has suddenly one day—'

'If that is the case, I cannot send him to prison.'

'Why should you send? It'll be done by those in charge of the job.'

'Why would Quasim take six thousand and leave the rest behind?'

'Just so that you don't suspect him. Whatever you may say, that man is shrewd. He guards your treasury, but I'm sure he's behind all the looting and raids on the treasuries in this area.' The inspector quoted many instances of how robbers can loot treasuries twenty to thirty miles away and come back the same night to report to the master's office.

I asked him, 'Have you brought Quasim here?'

He said, 'No, he is at the police station; the deputy would be here any moment to investigate.'

I said, 'I want to see him.'

The moment he saw me, Quasim fell at my feet, weeping, 'I swear on my God, sir, I haven't done this.'

I said, 'Quasim, I do not suspect you. Don't be afraid, I won't let them punish you if you are innocent.'

Quasim couldn't describe the robbers very well; he simply muttered away, 'Four-five hundred people, such huge guns, swords, etc.' I realized this was all rubbish. Either fear lent wings to his imagination, or the shame of defeat made him exaggerate. He was of the opinion that since there was bad blood between Harish Kundu and me, this was done by him. In fact, he believed that he had clearly heard the voice of Ikram Sardar, one of Kundu's men.

I said, 'Look Quasim, don't you dare drag someone else's name into this just on the basis of conjecture. You are not responsible for fabricating proofs of whether Harish Kundu is involved or not.'

At home, I sent for Chandranathbabu. He shook his head and said, 'Now there is no peaceful way. We have moved aside ethics and placed the country on that pedestal; now all that is bad in the land would shamelessly raise its ugly head and reveal itself.'

'Do you think this was done by—'

'I don't know. But crime is on the rise. Go ahead, send them all away from your area.'

'I have given them another day's time. Day after tomorrow they will all leave.'

'Listen, let me tell you just one thing: you take Bimala with you to Calcutta. From here, she is getting a narrow vision of the world, she cannot place every person, every object in their right perspectives. Let her truly see the world; let her, for once, see man and his space of work in its true magnitude.'

'I was thinking the same thing myself.'

'But don't wait any longer. Look Nikhil, human history has evolved along with all the races and all the countries and that's why even politics shouldn't sell out on ethics to establish itself or the country. I know that Europe doesn't truly believe this, but neither can I accept that we have to look to Europe for our guidelines. Man dies for Truth and gains immortal fame and if the same is done by a country or a race, it will have the same results. We must strive to let that perception of Truth become all-important and the ultimate in this India of ours, amidst the roaring laughter of the devil himself. What is this foreign failing that has taken the whole nation by storm?'

The whole day passed in taking care of all these problems. Exhausted, I went to bed at night. I decided to take out that money from the iron chest the next day.

At some point in the night I woke up. The room was pitch dark. I could hear a noise, like someone weeping. Every now and then, a tearful sigh floated in the room, like gusts of wind on a cloudy night. I felt the room was sobbing its heart out. There was no one else in my room. For some time now, Bimala slept in another room. I left the bed. Outside, on the veranda, I found Bimala lying on the floor.

These things are difficult to write. It is known and felt only by Him, who sits amidst the kernel of the universe and absorbs all the pain of the earth. The sky was mute, the stars silent, the night was still—and in the midst of it all, this sleepless weeping.

I could perhaps take all my joys and sorrows, compare and contrast them to the world at large, to the written word, and give it a fancy name, thereby ending the matter. But could I give a name to this source of pain welling up and flooding the bosom of this darkness? That solitary night, when I stood in the midst of those millions of silent stars and gazed upon her, a voice fearfully asked me, 'Who am I to stand judgement?' Oh life, oh death, endless creation and the Lord of it all—I salute the mystery contained within you.

For a moment I thought I should go back. But I couldn't. Silently I sat near her and gently stroked her hair. At first her entire body stiffened up and the next instant it began to break apart and disintegrate into sobs. I could scarcely comprehend how the human heart could hold so many tears.

I stroked her head gently for a while. And then, at some point she groped around and took my feet in her hands. She pressed it so hard to her heart that I felt it would break from the burden of my feet.

Bimala

Amulya was expected back in the morning. I instructed the bearer to inform me the minute he arrived. But I couldn't sit still. Finally I went and waited in the living room.

When I sent Amulya to Calcutta to sell my jewellery, I had no thought for anyone but myself. It never occurred to me that he was so young and if he went to sell such expensive jewellery anywhere, he'd be under suspicion. Women are so helpless that we seem to have no other option than to pass our problems on to someone else. When we die, we drag five other people with us.

I had said with great pride, 'I shall save Amulya.' But how could one drowning person save another? Oh Lord, perhaps I have already pushed him into hell—little brother of mine, I am such an unfortunate sister that the day I prayed for you in my heart must have been the day Yama smiled to himself. Today, I was a burden of ill omens.

I feel sometimes a plague of crime grips people and its sudden arrival brings death that much closer. At these times isn't it possible to keep it far, far away from the world? I could clearly see how damaging its claws were. It was like the torch of danger, burning away merrily only to set the world alight.

The clock struck nine. I began to feel Amulya was in trouble, he was in police custody: my jewellery box was raising a storm of questions, whose was it, how did he get it, questions which eventually I alone could answer. What would I say in front of the whole world?

Mejorani, I had really held you in very low esteem all these years. Now it's your turn. Today, you'll take the form of the whole wide world, and have your revenge. Dear God, please help me now, I'll quit all my pride and lay it willingly at Mejorani's feet.

I couldn't be still. I rushed indoors and went towards Mejorani's room. She was fixing herself some betel leaves, sitting in the veranda with Thako beside her. At the sight of the maid, I hesitated for a moment; but I brushed it aside and bent down to touch Mejorani's feet. She exclaimed, 'Hey there, little one, what's the matter with you? Why the sudden surfeit of respect?'

I said, 'Didi, it's my birthday today. I may have done you many wrongs—please bless me, that I may never hurt you again. I am so mean-minded.'

I quickly touched her feet again and left. She started saying, 'Listen, little one, if it's your birthday why didn't you tell us earlier? You're invited to lunch in my room. Sweet sister, don't forget.'

God, please do something so that it really becomes my birthday today. Can I not be born anew? Wipe the slate clean and test me afresh, oh Lord.

As I was about to enter the living room again, Sandip appeared. Hatred burned acrid in my soul. The face that I saw in the bright light of day today, didn't hold an ounce of genius. I said, 'Please go away from here.'

Sandip laughed and said, 'Amulya is not here. Now it's my turn to talk business.'

Hell and damnation. How could I refute the very rights that I once granted him? I said, 'I need to be alone.'

'Queen, the presence of another person doesn't get in the way of being alone. Don't push me into the throngs of other people. I am Sandip, alone even in a crowd.'

'Please come another day; today I am—'

'Waiting for Amulya?'

Irritated, I was about to leave the room when Sandip fished out my jewellery box from the folds of his shawl and placed it on the table.

I was startled, 'So Amulya didn't go?'

'Go where?'

'To Calcutta?'

Sandip smiled a little, 'No.'

Thank God for small mercies. I am a thief and the punishment should stop at me—let it not harm Amulya.

Sandip saw my expression and mocked it, 'So thrilled, Queen? Is the jewellery box worth that much? Then how did you promise all of this to the goddess? You have already given it away—are you going to take it back from the deity's feet?'

Pride doesn't quit, even when you're gasping for breath. I felt like showing him how little those jewels were worth to me. I said, 'If you have your eyes on these jewels, you're welcome to take them.'

Sandip said, 'I have my eyes on all the wealth in the whole of Bengal. There is no greater virtue than greed. For the lords of this earth, greed is the vehicle. So then, all this jewellery is mine?'

Sandip picked up the box and covered it with his shawl. At this point Amulya rushed into the room: his eyes were bloodshot, face pallid and hair dishevelled. He seemed to have shed his youthful innocence in a single day. My heart was stricken at the sight of him. Amulya didn't spare me a second glance, walked up to Sandip and said, 'You have taken that jewellery box from my valise?'

'Does the jewellery box belong to you?'

'No, but the valise does.'

Sandip laughed out loud. He said, 'I can see you have a strong sense of possession where your valise is concerned, Amulya. I guess you will also turn a moralist before you die.'

Amulya dropped down on the chair, covered his face and rested his head on the table. I went up to him, stroked his hair gently and asked, 'Amulya, what's the matter?'

He shot up on his feet and said, 'Didi, I wanted to bring this jewellery box to you myself and Sandipbabu knew that; so he quickly—'

I said, 'What use is that box of jewellery to me? Let it go, who cares?'

Stunned, Amulya said, 'Why should it go?'

Sandip said, 'These jewels are mine—it's a gift from the Queen.'

Amulya went crazy, 'No, no, never. Didi, I have brought it back for you—you cannot give it away to anyone.'

I said, 'Dear child, your generosity will stay in my heart forever, but let the jewels go to those who lust after it.'

Amulya looked at Sandip as a wild animal surveys its prey, 'Look here Sandipbabu, you know that I'm not afraid of capital punishment. If you take this box of jewellery—'

Sandip tried to give a mocking smile, 'Amulya, you should also know by now that your threats do not scare me. Queen Bee, I have not come here today to take these jewels. I came to give them to you. But I couldn't tolerate the injustice of your accepting something that belonged to me, from Amulya's hands and hence I made sure you accepted they were mine first. Now I am gifting my possession to you—here it is. You may sort things out with that child, I am going. For some days now you two have been discussing special matters and I want no part in it. If something "special" happens, do not blame me. Amulya, I have sent your valise, books and all other belongings to your rooms in the market. You may no longer keep your things in my room.'

Sandip rushed out.

I said, 'Amulya, ever since I gave my jewellery to you for selling, I have lost my peace of mind.'

'Why, Didi?'

'I was scared you may be in trouble because of this, they may suspect you of stealing it and take you away. I do not need the six thousand rupees. Now, you must obey this one instruction: go home, go back to your mother.'

Amulya brought out a bundle from under his shawl and said, 'Didi, I have brought the six thousand rupees.'

I said, 'Where did you get it?'

He didn't answer me. Instead he said, 'I tried and tried to get guineas but I couldn't. So I brought notes instead.'

'Amulya, for pity's sake, tell me where you got the money.'

'I cannot tell you.'

I felt the world was drained of all light. I said, 'What have you done, Amulya? Is this money—'

Quickly Amulya broke in, 'I know you will say I have got this money by crime—all right, I'll accept that. But you pay the price of your crime and I have paid that price. Now this money belongs to me.'

I had no wish to hear all the details about getting the money. My nerves were cringing and my entire body felt as if it was wilting under pressure. I said, 'Take it back, Amulya, put it back wherever you got this money from.'

'That is very difficult.'

'No, child, it's not difficult. Cursed is that moment when you came to me. I have done you more harm than even Sandip did you.'

Sandip's name seemed to set something off in him. He said, 'Sandip. It's because I came to you that I could recognize him for what he is. Do you know, he hasn't spent a single paise of the six thousand rupees that he took from you the other day? He went from here, locked his room, poured out all the guineas on to the floor and stared at them in bemused wonder. He said, "This isn't money, it is heavenly wealth, notes from the eternal flute that hardened as they fell to earth—these cannot be changed into banknotes. They desire to adorn the throat of a nymph—oh, Amulya, don't you boys cast your visceral eyes on these—the smile of the goddess, the grace of the deity; no, oh no, these weren't meant to fall into the uncouth hands of that head-clerk. Look Amulya, he has been lying, the police have no news of any boats being stolen and he wants to use it to his own purposes. We must get hold of those three letters from that man." I asked him, "How?" Sandip said, "By force, by threats." I said, "I'm game. But these guineas must be returned." Sandip said, "We'll see about that." How I threatened the clerk and got those letters from him and burnt them is a long story. That same night I came to Sandip and said, "The danger is past. Now give me the guineas, I'll return them to Didi tomorrow." Sandip said, "What is this foolishness that has gripped you? I suppose now your motherland is shrouded under Didi's anchal. Say Vande Mataram, let your illusions go." You know Didi, how Sandip works his magic. The guineas stayed with him. I spent the dark night sitting by the pond and chanting Vande Mataram. Yesterday, when you gave me the jewellery to sell, I went to him again in the evening. I could tell he was furious with me. But he didn't show it. He said, "Look, if I have those guineas anywhere in my belongings, you are free to take them." He hurled his bunch of keys at me. They weren't there. I asked, "Tell me where you have kept them?" Sandip said, "I'll tell you only when you are free of your trance. Not now." I realized he wouldn't give in and so I had to take another way. Even so, I tried to give him these six thousand rupees in banknotes and get back the guineas. He said he's getting them, kept me waiting, went to his room, broke into my valise and brought the jewellery box to you. He didn't let me bring this box to you. And he claims these jewels are his gift to you? How can I say how much he has cheated me? I will never forgive him. Didi, I am totally free of the hold he had over me. You have done it.'

I said, 'Child, that gives me great joy. But there's more. Freeing yourself isn't enough, you have to wash your guilt away. Don't wait Amulya, go now—put this money back where it came from. Can you do that, dear brother?'

'With your blessings I can, Didi.'

'This is not only your success; it is mine too. I am a woman and the way to the world is closed to me, or I would never let you go—I'd go myself. This is the greatest punishment for me, that you are having to pay for my sins.'

'Don't say that, Didi. The path that I took was not your way. It was challenging and so it seemed alluring. Now you have called me to your path—even if this is a thousand times more difficult, I shall win with your blessings; I'm not afraid. So you would like me to return this money where it came from, right?'

'It's not what I'd like, child, but what *He'd* like.'

'I don't know all that: it's enough for me that His wishes have come from your mouth. But Didi, you owe me a meal. I'll go only after you have fed me. Then I'll try and finish the work by tonight.'

I tried to smile and my eyes brimmed over; I said, 'All right.'

The moment Amulya left, my heart sank. I felt I had pushed him into murky waters. Dear God, why do my sins have to be expiated so elaborately, with others' blood? Wasn't my own enough? Must you lay the burden on so many shoulders? Oh, why should that poor soul suffer for it? I called him back, 'Amulya.' But he had left, 'Bearer, bearer,' I called.

'Yes, Ranima?'

'Send Amulyababu in.'

Perhaps the bearer wasn't familiar with Amulya's name; so a little later he brought in Sandip. He stepped into the room and said, 'When you sent me away, I knew you'd call me back. The high and the low tide are both caused by the same moon. I was so certain you'd call me that I was waiting right by the door. The minute I saw your bearer I spoke before he could say anything, "Fine, fine, I'm coming right now." The rustic fool stood open-mouthed, certain that I knew magic. Queen Bee, the greatest power in this world is of this mantra. Hypnosis can conquer anything. It works by sound alone, and often even soundlessly. At long last Sandip has met his match in this duel. Your quiver holds many arrows, my dear. In this whole wide world, you are the only one who has been able to turn Sandip away at your will and call him back the same way. So now your prey is here. Now what would you like to do to it—finish it off or keep it caged? But let me warn you, Queen, killing this being is as difficult as holding it captive. So don't hesitate to use whatever celestial weapons that are within your powers to use.'

Sandip rambled away in this manner only because today he was plagued by a fear of defeat. I believe he was well aware that I had sent for Amulya; the bearer must have given his name. But he cheated and came over himself instead. He didn't even give me the time to set him right. But now I had glimpsed the weak and the swagger was in vain. Now I wasn't ready to give up even an inch of my hard-won ground.

I said, 'Sandipbabu, how can you jabber so much so fast? Do you come prepared?'

Sandip's face turned crimson with rage. I said, 'I have heard that raconteurs have a ready stock of long, descriptive paragraphs that they use whenever the occasion arises. Do you also have a notebook full of these?'

Sandip chewed over each word as he spat it out, 'The Fates have blessed you women with enough graces and then the tailor, the jeweller, are all in league with you; why should we, men, be without our own weapons—'

I said, 'Sandipbabu, go and look up your notebook—these are not the right words. I have noticed that you get mixed up sometimes. That is the problem of learning by rote.'

Sandip lost his temper and roared in outrage, 'You! How dare you insult me? Just think how much I know about you. You are—' He was lost for words. Sandip was a seller of spells and the minute his spells failed, he was left with nothing—from a king he turned into a beggar in an instant. Weak, oh so weak. The more he turned nasty and spoke rudely, my heart danced with joy. He was done with tying me up in his spells; I was free. Oh thank God, thank God. Insult me, abuse me, that is your true form. Don't raise me on a pedestal—that's a lie.

At this moment my husband came into the room. Today Sandip didn't have the strength to control himself, as he did on other days. My husband saw his expression and looked a little surprised. Earlier this would have caused me embarrassment. But today I was glad. I wanted to take a good look at this weakling.

Since we were both silent, my husband sat on the stool after some hesitation. He said, 'Sandip, I was looking for you and heard that you are here.'

Sandip spoke with extra vigour, 'Yes, the Queen Bee sent for me early in the day and since I am a mere working bee in the hive, I had to drop everything and rush at her command.'

My husband said, 'I am leaving for Calcutta tomorrow, you'll have to come with me.'

Sandip said, 'But why? Am I your valet?'

'All right then, you go to Calcutta and I'll come along as your valet.'

'I have no work in Calcutta.'

'Which is why you have to go there—you have too much work here.'

'I am not budging.'

'Then you'll be made to budge.'

'By force?'

'Yes, by force.'

'Fine, I'll budge. But the world doesn't consist of two poles—Calcutta and your area. There are other places on the map.'

'Looking at you one would think there is no other place in the world besides my area.'

Sandip stood up and said, 'There comes a time for every man when the whole world shrinks into a tiny space. I have perceived my world amidst this living room of yours and that's why I wasn't moving. Queen Bee, these people won't understand what I say and perhaps you wouldn't either. I worship you and I will continue to do so. Ever since I have seen you, my mantra has changed; no longer Vande Mataram, it's now Vande Priyam, Vande Mohinim. The mother protects us, the lover destroys—and there is beauty in this destruction. You have raised a storm of tinkling anklets—the death-dance—in my heart. The image of this land of mine used to be 'komala sujala malayajashitala'; you have changed this in the eyes of your devotee. You have no mercy; you have come, oh temptress, with the cup of poison in your hands; I shall drink that poison, be ripped apart by it and either die or conquer death. The days of the mother are gone. Lover, oh lover—gods, heavens, ethics, Truth: you have turned them to dust. All else are mere shadows, all bonds of control, order all torn away. Lover, oh lover—I can set fire to the rest of the world and dance exultantly on the ashes at the very spot where you have laid your feet. These are good men, they are very good, they want what is good for all—as if it is the Truth. Never, there is no other Truth in the whole world; this is my only Truth. I worship you. My loyalty for you has made me ruthless. My devotion for you has lit the fires of hell within me. I am not good, I am not devout, I do not accept anything in this world—all I accept is the one whom I have perceived tangibly.'

Strange, surprising. A short while ago I had hated him with all my being. What seemed like ashes suddenly blazed into life. This was true fire. Why does God make us such mixed beings? Was it just to show off his magical prowess? A half hour ago I was quite certain that the man I had once taken for a king was nothing but a mere actor in a play. But no—sometimes a true king may lurk in the guise of an actor. He has much lust, much greed and much that is fake, that he hides within layers of flesh; but yet—it's best to accept that we do not know, we never know the whole truth, not even our own selves. Man is a strange being; only the omnipotent one knew the sublime mysteries that are woven around man. In the process, I am scalded, scarred. Storm. Shiva is the Lord of storms, He is the Lord of joy and he'll set me free of my ties.

I have been feeling for quite some time now, that I have two minds. One is fully aware of the destructive powers of Sandip; the other finds it ever so sweet. When a ship sinks, it drags with it all those who were swimming close to it; Sandip was like that deadly ship. Even before fear gripped me, his magic pulled at me—in the blink of an eye it wanted to swallow me whole, drag me away from all light, everything good, the freedom of the sky, the waft of breath, away from a lifetime's reserves, every day's little thoughts. He was like the spirit of the dreaded piper, walking the streets with his unholy chants, pulling all the youths of the land to him like a magnet. The mother at the heart of the land wailed aloud. Desecrating her stash of nectar, they drink on sinful liquor. I understand it all, but magic can't be kept at bay. This was the test of Truth—drunken brazenness danced before the ascetic and said: 'You are a fool; penance wouldn't set you free, it's a long and hard road to travel. The heavens have sent me, I am the temptress, I am the madness, in my embrace you will achieve moksha in an instant.'

After a moment's pause, Sandip spoke to me again, 'Goddess, the time has come for me to say goodbye. This is for the best. My purpose for coming to you has been fulfilled. If I overstay, all the good will be undone gradually. If you are greedy and cheapen the greatest thing in this world, it can be disastrous. That which is endless in the space of an instant should not be dragged over time or it will be constrained. We were about to destroy that eternal, and at that point you raised your warning hand, saved your own worship as well as that of your devotee. Today, this parting is the greatest proof of my devotion for you. Goddess, on this day, I too set you free. In my earthen temple your formless form was hardly contained; it threatened to fall apart every moment; I take your leave to worship you in your greater form in the midst of greatness—I shall truly perceive you when I am away from you. Here I got your indulgence, but there I shall have your boon.'

My jewellery box was on the table. I held it out to him and said, 'I have given these jewels to the country. Please reach these to the feet of the goddess where they belong.'

My husband stood there silently. Sandip left the room.

I was making some sweets for Amulya, when suddenly Mejorani came in: 'Well hello, little one, are you cooking up a feast for yourself on your own birthday?'

I said, 'Can't I be cooking for someone else?'

Mejorani said, 'Today we will cook for you. I was all set to enter the kitchen when the news all but threw me; apparently some five or six hundred burglars raided one of our treasuries and looted six thousand rupees. Rumours are that they are now headed this way, towards the estate.'

This piece of news set my mind at ease. So it was our money then. I wanted to call Amulya immediately and tell him to return the money to my husband right here and now. Later I would give him my explanations.

Mejorani saw the play of emotions on my face and exclaimed, 'You surprise me—aren't you even the least bit scared?'

I said, 'I can't believe they'd actually come to loot our home.'

'And why not? Who could ever imagine they'd actually loot a treasury?'

I didn't answer her. Instead I bent my head and continued to fill the stuffing into the sweetmeats. She gazed at my face a little longer and finally said, 'Let me send for Thakurpo—our six thousand rupees must be sent off to Calcutta immediately, without further ado.'

The minute she left, I dropped my shawl on the floor and rushed into the ante-room which had the iron chest. My husband was so absent-minded that his shirt with the keys to the chest still hung on the rack in that room. I took the bunch from the pocket, extracted the keys to the chest and hid it in my clothes.

At this point there were knocks on the door. I said that I was changing. I heard Mejorani say, 'Just now she was making sweets and now suddenly she's getting dressed. The things I have to see. I guess they'll be having one of those Vande Mataram meetings today. Ahoy there, Devi Choudhurani, are you busy gathering the loot?'

Something made me open the iron chest slowly. Perhaps I was wishing the whole thing would be a dream and I'd open the tiny drawer and find the paper wrapped bundles right there. But alas, it was as empty as the trust betrayed by the traitor.

Without any reason, I had to change my clothes. I tied my hair anew. When I ran into Mejorani and she asked why I was so dolled up, I said, 'Birthday.'

She laughed and said, 'You need the smallest excuse to go and dress up. I've never seen another creature as whimsical as you.'

I was looking for the bearer to go and fetch Amulya, when he came and handed me a piece of paper with a note scribbled in pencil. Amulya had written, 'Didi, you'd invited me, but I couldn't wait. I am off to do your bidding first and then I'll have the meal. I'll be back by dusk.'

Where had Amulya gone, to what new traps? I could only always shoot him like an arrow, but if I missed my mark, I couldn't ever bring him back. This was the right moment for me to go and own up my own part in this whole fiasco. But in this world, women survived on trust—it was their whole world. It would be very difficult for me to live in this world after revealing how I had cheated that same trust. I'd have to keep standing on the very thing I'd broken—the jagged pieces would poke and stab me every now and then. It wasn't difficult to err. But nothing was more difficult than to atone for one's sins, especially for women.

For a while now, the channels of normal conversation with my husband were closed to me. Hence, I simply couldn't figure out when and how to suddenly broach such a big issue to him. Today he was late for lunch; it was nearly two o'clock. He was so preoccupied that he hardly ate anything. I had lost my right to plead with him to eat some more. I turned away and brushed away the tears.

For a moment I wanted to overcome my hesitation and say to him, 'Go and rest in the room—you are looking very tired.' I cleared my throat and was about to say it when the bearer came with the news that the police inspector was here with Quasim Sardar. My husband looked worried as he got up and left.

Soon after he left, Mejorani came and said, 'Why didn't you let me know when Thakurpo came to eat? Today he was late and so I went for my bath. But in the meantime—'

'Why, what's the matter?'

'I heard you are all leaving for Calcutta tomorrow? In that case I cannot stay on here. The elder queen won't leave her idols and deities. But what with all these burglaries I refuse to guard this empty house of yours and keep jumping out of my skin at the slightest sound. Is it fixed for tomorrow?'

I said, 'Yes.' I thought to myself: Lord knows what events and intrigues will transpire in this short while between now and then. After all that, whether I go to Calcutta or stay here, it won't matter to me. Who knows after that what the world would look like, how life would seem. It was all bleary, a dream.

Couldn't someone drag out, by the day, these few hours that were left before my Fate became a reality? I could use the time to tie up the loose ends. At least I could prepare myself and my world for the forthcoming pain. As long as the seeds of destruction stayed underground, they took so much time that one's fears can be lulled. But the moment the tiny shoot shot up above the ground, it grew rapidly and it was impossible to cover it with your heart, your life or your soul. I wanted to blank out, lie in a stupor and wait for whatever tumbled on my head. It would all be over before the day after tomorrow—the knowing, the mockery, the tears, questions and answers—all of it.

But Amulya's face, that innocence that glowed with the light of sacrifice, would not let me rest. He didn't wait around for his Fate—he rushed into the thick of things. I, unworthy even of womanhood, saluted him. For me he was God in the form of a child; he'd come to take my burden of sins quite playfully on to his own shoulders. How could I possibly tolerate this terrible mercy of God, that Amulya would take the punishment for my sins? Oh my child, I salute you. Oh brother dear, I salute you. You are pure, beautiful, brave, fearless and I salute you. I pray with all my heart that in the next life I have you on my lap as my son.

In the meantime, rumour was rife, policemen swarmed the place and the maids and servants were anxious. Khema, the maid, came to me and said, 'Chhotoranima, please put my gold chain and armlet away in your iron chest.' How could I tell her that it was I who had kicked up this storm of anxiety in the entire household and was now stuck in its eye? Like a good little mistress I had to take Khema's jewellery, Thako's savings. Our milkman's wife left a Benarasi sari and some other precious valuables with me in a tin box. She said, 'Ranima, this sari was given to me on your wedding.'

Tomorrow, when the iron chest will be opened, this Khema, Thako, milkman's wife—anyway, what's the point of dwelling on that? Instead let me think that a year has passed after tomorrow, another 3 January was here—would the sores and wounds of my family still be as raw?

Amulya had written that he'd be back by tonight. Meanwhile, I could hardly sit alone in my room, doing nothing. So I went to make sweets again. What I had made earlier was actually enough, but I made some more. Who would eat all this? I'll feed all the maids and servants in the house. I must do that tonight. My days were numbered. Tomorrow was no longer in my hands.

One after another I made the sweets, tirelessly. Every now and then I felt there was some commotion in the general direction of my rooms. Perhaps my husband had come to open the iron chest and found the keys missing. So Mejorani was summoning all the maids and raising hell over it. No, I wouldn't hear it, I'd keep the door firmly closed. I was about to shut the door when I saw Thako rushing towards me. Out of breath, she panted, 'Chhotoranima—'

I said, 'Go away, don't disturb me now.'

Thako said, 'Mejoranima's nephew Nanda has brought a weird machine from Calcutta—it sings like a person. So Mejoranima sent me to fetch you.'

I didn't know whether to laugh or to cry. A gramophone in the middle of all this. Every time it was wound up, it emitted the nasal tones of theatrical songs. It had no worries. When machine imitated life, it resulted in this terrible irony.

The sun set and dusk crept in. I knew whenever Amulya arrived he'd send for me. But I couldn't be at peace. I called the bearer and said, 'Send word to Amulyababu.'

The bearer came back a little later and said, 'Amulyababu is not there.'

It was just a few words, but my heart heaved with fear. Amulyababu is not there—in the melancholy dusk the words rang out like a wail. Not there—he's not there. He appeared like the golden ray of the sunset and then he's not there. I began to imagine many scenarios, both possible and impossible. It was I who pushed him to his death. That he didn't think twice was his greatness, but how would I live with this?

I didn't have a single memento of his; all I had was his loving gift to his sister—the pistol. It seemed like a divine intervention. My own personal God, in the shape of a child, had placed the tool to wipe out the blot that soiled the roots of my life and then vanished into thin air. What a loving gift—what an overtly pure signal.

I opened the box, took the pistol out and touched it to my forehead reverently. At that very moment, the bells and cymbals from our temple courtyard rang out to signal the evening arati. I bowed low on the ground and prayed.

That night I fed the sweets to everyone. Mejorani came and said, 'You went to all this trouble for your own birthday—why didn't you leave something for us to do?' She began to play a host of stage artistes on her gramophone, raising high voices in stretched decibels. To me it sounded like the neighing of the horses from the stables.

The meal took a while. I wanted to touch my husband's feet tonight. I went into the bedroom and found him fast asleep. The whole day he had been roaming around, plagued by endless troubles. I moved aside the mosquito net very carefully and softly lay my face on his feet. As my hair touched his feet, unconsciously he pushed my head away with his feet.

I went and sat in the veranda. In the distance a silk-cotton tree stood in the dark like a skeleton; it had shed all its leaves and the sickle moon gradually sank out of sight behind it. Suddenly I felt all the stars in the sky were afraid of me and the huge nocturnal world looked at me askance, because I was all alone. A lonely human is perhaps the biggest anomaly of Nature. Even the person who has lost every relation to death is not truly alone—he has company from beyond the grave. But when a person has everyone near and yet far away, who has simply fallen away from the daily rhythm of life, a glance at her face in the depth of night would send a chill down the spine of the universe. I am not present at the spot where I stand, I am far away from the people in whose company I stand. I walk, talk and live right on the face of a fissure, like the dewdrops on a lotus leaf.

But, when a person changes, why doesn't everything about her change? When I look to my heart I find everything there as before, only the positions altered. What was once neatly kept is now a muddle, what was once strung on a thread now lies scattered in the dust. That's why my heart was breaking and I wanted to die. But all of it still lived in my heart and so death didn't seem to be an end. I felt death would bring a more terrible sorrow. I would have to clear the accounts by living—there was no other way.

Oh my Lord, please forgive me this once. All that you had once handed to me as the fortune of my life, I have now turned into a burden. Today I can neither bear it nor relinquish it. Just once more, play the tune on the flute that you once played by the pink sky of my dawn and all this will be resolved; only that tune from your flute can possibly join all that is broken, turn the sullied into pure again. Play the flute and recreate my life all over again. I do not see any other way open to me.

I lay face down on the floor and wept my heart out; some pity was needed, some refuge, a hint of mercy, some consolation that all this may yet be resolved. I said to myself, 'I'll lie like this night and day, oh Lord, I'll fast, I won't drink water until your blessings reach me.'

At this point I heard footsteps. My heart swayed. Who says gods never show themselves? I did not look up, in case he found my gaze repulsive. Come, come, come—let your feet touch my head, come, stand on my swaying heart, oh Lord—let me die this very instant.

He came and sat near my head. Who? My husband. In my husband's heart that Lord of mine was touched, who could no longer bear my pain. I felt I'd faint. And then the floodgates of tears opened, my nerve ends burst and let loose a storm of sorrow. I pressed his feet to my heart—wouldn't they get imprinted there for all eternity?

Now I could have easily confessed everything. But after this, could there be any words? Let my confessions be.

Gently, he stroked my head. I was blessed. I would be able to take my cup of hemlock and humbly touch my Lord's feet on the face of the humiliation that lay before me the next day.

But it broke my heart when I realized that the shehnai that had played nine years ago will never be played again, in my entire life. I came into this room, a new bride. Which gods do I have to pray to, so that the bride could come back, dressed in red and stand on that ceremonial threshold once again? How much longer, how many aeons, before I could go back to that day nine years ago? The gods may be able to create anew, but did they have the power to recreate a broken piece of creation?

Nikhilesh

Today we are leaving for Calcutta. A meaningless accumulation of joys and sorrows only increases one's burdens. Sitting idle is pointless and accumulation is a futile activity. It is a mere construction that I am the lord of this house; my true identity is of a traveller on the journey of life. Therefore, the lord of the house would be repeatedly injured until the final injury—death. My union with you was along the way—as far as we could go together, it was for the good; beyond that, stretching and pulling would only make a noose of it. Let that noose be, I am setting off today. As we walk along, the little shared glances, the brush of the hand is all very well. And then? Then there is the way of the eternal, the unbounded force of life—how much can you cheat me of, my beloved? If I pay heed to the tune playing ahead of me, I can hear the sweetness dripping through every crevice of our parting. The goddess's infinite cup would never run dry and so she sometimes shatters our cup, makes us cry and laughs at our misery. I shall not go about picking up the broken pieces. I shall carry my regrets in my heart and carry on.

Mejorani came and said, 'Thakurpo, your books have all been packed into cases, loaded on to bullock carts and sent off. What does that mean?'

'It means that I still haven't been able to give them up.'

'It's good to be attached to some things. But are you planning not to return?'

'There will be visits and trips, but no dwelling here any more.'

'Is that so? In that case come with me once and take a look at all the things I am unable to give up.'

I went to her room and found bundles and bags of all sizes. She opened one box and said, 'Look here, Thakurpo, the things I need to make my paan. I have powdered the dry lime and stored it in a bottle. These jars here each contain a masala. Here are the cards, I haven't forgotten those—even if you don't play with me, I'll find people. This comb here is the home-grown one that you gave me, and this—'

'What is all this, Mejorani? Why have you packed your things into boxes?'

'Because I am coming to Calcutta with you two.'

'What?'

'Don't worry, dear brother—I shan't try to be friends with you or squabble with the little princess. Death is inevitable and so the sooner one reaches the Ganges the better. When I think of the barren banyan tree under which you'll cremate me here, I shudder to even die—why do you think I'm troubling you all for so long?'

It was as if this house of mine had spoken up at long last. Mejorani came to this house when she was nine and I was six years old. I have sat in the shade of the high walls of the terrace and played with her. I have climbed mango trees, plucked the raw fruit and hurled them down as she gathered them from below, chopped them up, mixed them with salt and chilly and made tasty tidbits. I was entrusted with the grave duty of stealing all those things from the pantry that were necessary for the wedding of the dolls, because in Grandma's eyes I could do no wrong. Later, when she wanted my brother to indulge her fancies, I was the messenger boy; I always badgered Dada until he gave in and she got her way. I also remember: in those days the local doctor had strict orders for a fever—three days on a diet of lukewarm water and cardamom seeds. Mejorani couldn't bear my predicament and she often smuggled food into my room; many a times she was caught and severely reprimanded. As we grew older, our joys and sorrows plumbed deeper shades; so often we fought. The issues of property and finance also caused some rifts, jealousy and bitterness. Then Bimal came into it all, and sometimes it felt like the rifts would never heal. But then it was always obvious that the bonds of childhood surpassed the superficial wounds. Thus, a genuine relationship had been nurtured from those early days into the present times. This relationship spread out its branches into this huge mansion, into the rooms, courtyards, verandas, gardens and its shadows lurked all over. When I found Mejorani had packed all her belongings and was ready to leave the house with us, this eternal relationship in my heart was shaken down to its very roots. It became apparent to me why Mejorani, who had never stepped out of this house since the day she was nine, was actually prepared to let go of her familiar world and surrender to the unfamiliar. But she simply couldn't utter those words, and made so many other trivial excuses. This woman, betrayed by Fate, without a husband or a child, had nurtured just this one relationship with her heart and soul. As I stood that day, amidst all her possessions strewn around the room in various stages of packing, I felt her pain in a way I had never felt it before. I realized that the many petty squabbles that Bimal and I had with her, together or individually, were not really about materialism. It was because she had never been able to establish her claim over this one relationship. Bimal appeared from nowhere and she paled into insignificance—it pained her ever so often but she had no grounds for complaint. Bimal had also understood that Mejorani's claims over me went beyond mere social norms, and that's why she was so resentful of this childhood bond of mine. Today, my heart stood shocked with a realization; I sat down on a trunk. I said, 'Mejoranididi, I feel like going back to those days when you and I first met in this house.'

Mejorani sighed heavily and said, 'Oh no, this time not as a woman, not again. All that I have borne is enough for one lifetime, never to be repeated.'

I said, 'The liberation that comes through sorrow is greater than the sorrow itself.'

She said, 'That's possible, Thakurpo. Liberation is for you men. We women want to bind, we want bondage—you won't get your liberation from us so easily. If you want to spread your wings, you'll have to take us with you; you can't throw us away. Why do you think I have set out this medley of baggage? You men shouldn't be left light and airy.'

I laughed, 'That is obvious. It's easy to see what a burden it is. But since you tip us generously for carrying this burden, we don't complain half as much.'

Mejorani said, 'Our burdens are of trivia; whatever you want to leave out will protest "I am trivial, I don't really weigh much"—and thus with trivial weights we load your back. What time are we leaving, Thakurpo?'

'Eleven thirty at night—there's still a lot of time.'

'Thakurpo, please promise me one thing—you'll have an early lunch and take a nap this afternoon. You won't get much sleep in the train at night. Your health is in such bad shape that you look just about ready to collapse any time. Come now, go and have your bath.'

At this point Khema came forth and murmured, 'The inspector has brought someone with him and he wants to see his majesty.'

Mejorani flared up, 'His majesty is not a thief or burglar that the inspector is always after him. Tell him he has gone to have his bath.'

I said, 'Let me go and have a look—it may be something urgent.'

Mejorani said, 'Not on your life. I will send some of the sweets that the little one made yesterday and that ought to keep him busy for a while.' She dragged me by the hand, pushed me into the bathroom and bolted the door from outside.

From inside I said, 'But my clean clothes—'

She said, 'I'll see to that. You finish your bath.'

I did not have the strength to go against such indulgent torture. It was one of the precious things of life. Let the inspector have sweets, let there be a slight neglect of my duties. In the last few days, the inspector had been routinely rounding up suspects in connection with the robbery. Every so often he'd drag an innocent man to the estate and have a circus. Today was probably a repeat performance. But would the inspector have all the sweets himself? No! I banged loudly on the door from inside.

Mejorani spoke up, 'Pour some water on your head, quick, your temper is shooting up.'

I said, 'Send enough sweets for two people. The man whom the inspector has dragged in as a suspect deserves them more—tell the bearer to give him the bigger share.'

I finished my bath as quickly as possible and came out. At the door I found Bimal sitting on the floor. Was this the same Bimal, my Bimal—proud, arrogant, stubborn? With what prayer in mind could she have come to *my* door? As I stalled in surprise, she stood up, bent her head down and spoke softly, 'I need to speak to you.'

I said, 'Come into our room.'

'Are you going somewhere for some urgent work?'

'Yes, but let that be. First let's talk—'

'Oh no, you finish your work. We can have our talk after you've had your meal.'

Out in the living room, I found the inspector's plate was empty and the suspect whom he had brought in was still eating the sweets.

I was amazed, 'What's this—Amulya?'

He looked up with a mouth full of sweets and said, 'Yes, sir. I have eaten my fill and if you don't mind, I'll take the rest with me.' He bundled the remaining sweets into his handkerchief.

I looked at the inspector, 'What is going on?'

The inspector laughed and said, 'Your majesty, the mystery of the thief still remains unsolved and now I am puzzling my head about the mystery of the stolen loot.' He spread out a torn bundle that held a bunch of notes, 'Here is your majesty's six thousand rupees.'

'Where did it come from?'

'Right now, from Amulyababu's hands. Last night he went to the head clerk of your treasury in Chakua and said to him that the stolen loot had been recovered. The clerk was more frightened at this development than when the actual robbery took place. He was afraid that everyone would suspect him of hiding the money and now when the noose was tightening, he'd cooked up this improbable story to return it. He made an excuse of bringing something for Amulyababu to eat and rushed to the police station. I went there on horseback and since dawn I have been with him. He says he won't tell me where he got the money. I said then he wouldn't be allowed to go. He said he'd lie. I said, fine, give it to me. He said he found it hidden in the bushes. I said lying is not so easy—you have to give me all the details of where the bush is and what you were doing there. He said he'd have plenty of time to make up all those stories.'

I said, 'Haricharanbabu, what's the point of dragging this gentleman's name in the mud?'

He said, 'Not just any gentleman, he's the son of Nibaran Ghoshal who was my class-friend. Sire, let me tell you the real story. Amulya came to know who has stolen the money. He knows him well through this Vande Mataram nonsense. He wants to take the blame on himself and spare this other person. Herein lies his bravado. Son, we too were once eighteen years old, just like you; I was studying in Ripon College. Once, on the Strand, I wanted to save a bullock-cart driver from the wrath of a policeman and nearly landed up in jail myself. It was a narrow escape. Sire, now it's almost impossible to catch the thief, but I can tell you who it is.'

I asked, 'Who is it?'

'Your head-clerk Tinkori Dutta and that Quasim Sardar.'

The inspector left, after giving many justifications to support his conclusion. I asked Amulya, 'If you tell me who had taken this money, no harm will come to anyone.'

He said, 'I took it.'

'But—they said a gang of robbers—'

'I was alone.'

Amulya's tale was a strange one. After finishing his dinner, the head-clerk was rinsing his mouth outside, where it was dark. Amulya had a pistol in each pocket. One was loaded with bullets and the other with blanks. Half his face was covered by a black mask. He held up a lantern to the clerk's face and fired a shot from the pistol with blanks. The clerk screamed in terror and fainted. A few of the guards came running and he fired shots over their heads. They ran into rooms and slammed shut the doors. Quasim Sardar came forward with his lathi. Amulya shot him in the leg and he fell down. He then got the clerk to open the iron chest, grabbed six thousand rupees and borrowed a horse from our estate. He rode all night long, left the horse somewhere in the night and was back here at dawn.

I asked, 'Amulya, why did you do this?'

He said, 'I had a great need.'

'Then why are you giving it back?'

'If you send for the person who has ordered me to return it, I'll confess everything.'

'Who is that person?'

'Chhotoranididi.'

I sent for Bimala. She had draped a white shawl around her head and she walked into the room slowly. Her feet were bare. I felt I had never seen her quite like this before. Like the moon at dawn, she seemed to have hidden herself in the morning light.

Amulya bent down low at Bimala's feet and took her blessings. He stood up and said, 'I have obeyed you, Didi. I've returned the money.'

Bimala said, 'Thank you, my child.'

Amulya said, 'I had you in mind and so I didn't tell a single lie. My Vande Mataram chants lie here at your feet. The minute I entered this house, I have also received food blessed by you.'

Bimala didn't quite get the last part. Amulya took the handkerchief from his pocket, untied the knot and showed her the sweets, 'I didn't eat them all—I wanted you to put them on my plate with your own hands and so I saved these.'

I realized I was no longer needed here; I left the room silently. I said to myself, I could only talk and make speeches and they in turn made my effigy and burnt it by the river. But could I really pull someone back from the clutches of death? The one who *can*, did it without words. My words did not hold that flawless signal. We are not flames, we are embers, dying ones. We would never be able to light a lamp. The story of my life is living proof of that—I failed to light the lamp I wanted to light.

Slowly, I walked back to the inner chambers. Perhaps my heart raced towards Mejorani's rooms once again, because I needed to feel that my life too has been able to strike a true and pure note in another life. The quest for one's identity seldom led inwards—it lay somewhere out in the world.

The moment I came before Mejorani's room, she came out and said, 'There you are, Thakurpo, I wondered how much longer you will be. Your lunch will soon be here, so hurry up.'

I said, 'Let me just go and take that money out.'

As I walked towards my room, Mejorani asked, 'So what happened about the inspector—has that matter been resolved?'

I somehow didn't feel like talking to Mejorani about the recovery of the six thousand rupees. So I said, 'Still going on.'

I went into the ante-room, took out the bunch of keys from my pocket and found the one to the iron chest missing. I am so careless—all day long I've been opening so many boxes and doors with the same bunch of keys and I never noticed that one is missing.

Mejorani asked, 'Where's the key?'

Without answering her, I groped around in each pocket, looked high and low and gradually it became obvious that the key wasn't lost, but someone had slipped it off the ring. Who could it be? In this room—

Mejorani said, 'Relax and have your lunch first. I believe Chhotorani must have put it away safely since you are so careless.'

The whole thing confused me. It wasn't like Bimala to take a key from my key ring without telling me first. Today Bimala wasn't present when I ate. At the time she had sent for rice from the kitchen and supervised Amulya's lunch as he ate it. Mejorani was about to send for her, but I stopped her.

I was almost done when Bimala came there. I hadn't wanted to discuss the matter of the missing key in front of Mejorani. But that was a lost cause. As soon as she saw her, Mejorani asked, 'Do you know where the key to Thakurpo's iron chest is?'

Bimala said, 'It's with me.'

Mejorani said, 'That's what I said. In these troubled times, Chhotorani wears a brave face but she is careful nonetheless.'

Something in Bimala's face made me doubt that remark. I said, 'Fine, let the key be with you for now. I'll take the money out in the evening.'

Mejorani exclaimed, 'Why wait till evening, Thakurpo, take that money now and hand it to the treasurer.'

Bimala said, 'I have taken that money.'

I was startled.

Mejorani asked, 'And where did you keep it?'

Bimala said, 'I spent it.'

Mejorani said, 'Oh lord, listen to her talk. Where did you spend so much money?'

Bimala didn't answer her. I did not ask her anything either. I just stood at the door quietly. Mejorani was about to say something to her, but she stopped. She looked at my face and said, 'Fair enough; whenever I could, I too stole all of my husband's money that I could lay my hands on. I knew it'd be wasted in the wrong places. Thakurpo, you are in the same boat. So many whims and fancies. Your money will be safe only when we steal it away. Now go and rest a little.'

Mejorani dragged me towards my room. I wasn't conscious of where I was or of anything around me. She perched on the side of my bed and said, 'Hey there, little one, can you give me a paan? You youngsters are so lazy these days—don't you have any here? Why don't you send someone to get me some from my room?'

I said, 'Mejorani, you haven't even eaten yet.'

She said, 'Of course I have.'

This was a blatant lie. She sat beside me and began to prattle about this and that. The maid came and spoke from the door. She said Bimala's lunch was getting cold. Bimala was silent. Mejorani said, 'Oh dear, haven't you had lunch yet? It's way past time.' She pulled her by the hand and dragged her away.

I understood that there was a link between the six thousand rupees that was robbed from the treasury and this money that was in the iron chest. I didn't even feel like delving into it. Never, ever would I ask that question.

The Almighty sketched the lines of our Fate with a blurred pen—He wanted us to make some changes here and there, draw some afresh and realize it in our own ways. I have always felt the ache to take His signal and make my way myself, to pour all of me into expressing one larger Idea.

I have spent my life attempting that. Only the God within me knows how much I have curbed natural impulses, suppressed my baser instincts. The difficult part was that one's life wasn't entirely one's own. If the creator does not include all that is around him, his creation is in vain. Hence, my innermost desires were to draw Bimala into this creative process. I strongly held that since I loved her with all my heart, it was more than possible.

At this point it became apparent to me that I was not the kind of person who could recreate oneself and others around him with ease. I had initiated myself, but I couldn't initiate another person. The ones to whom I laid my soul bare had taken everything from me except this one cherished detail. My test had been hard. Where I had really needed the most support I was most alone. But I vowed to succeed even in this test. Until the last breath I draw, my way would be mine alone.

Today I began to feel that there was coercion deeply ingrained in me. I was hell-bent on moulding my relationship with Bimala in one set, perfect mould. But life is not to be poured into moulds. And goodness, if mistaken for an inanimate object, dies on you and takes a cruel revenge. I never knew it, but this oppression gradually took us away from one another. Bimala could have been someone else, but my pressure suppressed her effervescence and forced her to remain at the bottom—the harsh cement of life tore away at her person. Today she had to steal this six thousand rupees. She could not be frank with me because she sensed that somewhere I stood apart from her. The ones who matched with stubborn idealists like us, harmonized with us, and the ones who didn't cheated us. We corrupt the innocent. In creating a partner we destroy the woman.

Was it possible to go back and begin at the beginning? Then I could walk the simple way. This time I wouldn't want to bind my fellow traveller in the chains of idealism. I would merely play the flute of my love and say, 'Just love me. In the light of that love, may you blossom in your truest form, let my demands disappear, may the Almighty's desires in you win the day—let my desires be shamed into oblivion.'

But would it be possible for Nature to work its healing balm on the wound that has manifested itself today, festering in our severance from one another? The veil that shields the workings of healing Nature has been ripped to shreds. Wounds need salves and I shall soothe this one with my love. I shall wrap the pain with all my heart and shield it from the eyes of the world. A day will come when there won't be a sign of this wound. But is there time? It took me so long to learn my mistake, today I have understood it, how much longer will it take until I can correct it? And then? The wound may heal, but will there be any recompense?

There was a sound at the door. I turned and found Bimala leaving. Perhaps she had stood at the door all this while wondering whether to come in or not, and now she was going. I got up quickly and called, 'Bimal.'

She stopped, her back towards me. I held her hand and pulled her into the room.

In the room she fell to the floor, pressed a pillow to her face and wept. Without a word, I held on to her hand and sat by her side. When her tears dried and she tried to sit up, I tried to pull her into my arms. She forced my hands away, knelt before me and repeatedly touched her forehead to my feet. As I made to move my feet, she pulled them back with both hands and spoke with emotion, 'No, no, no, don't take your feet away, let me offer homage.'

I was silent. Who was I to stop this reverence? If the puja was true, so was the deity—why should I be hesitant when I was not that deity?

Bimala

Come now, let's leave for that holy shrine where universal love joins the ocean of devotion. In the depths of that untainted blue, all murky patches will disappear. I am no longer afraid, of myself or anyone else. I have walked through fire; whatever had to burn has burnt to ashes and what remains is eternal. I have bestowed myself at his feet—of he who has absorbed all my crimes deep within his own sorrow.

Tonight we leave for Calcutta. So long I was absorbed with such turmoil, within and without, that I could hardly concentrate on packing our things. Now I pulled out the boxes and began to pack. A little later I found my husband had joined me. I said, 'No, no, that won't do. You promised you'd take a little nap.'

He said, 'I may have promised, but sleep did not. There is no sign of it yet.'

I said, 'Oh no, you go and rest.'

He said, 'How will you manage all alone?'

'I'll manage very well.'

'You may want to show off how well you can do without me, but I can't do without you and so sleep eluded me in that room all by myself.' He began to sort through things with me. At this time, the bearer came and said, 'Sandipbabu is here. He sent me to inform you.' Neither of us could ask who the information was for. In an instant the light went out of the sky for me and I turned into a shrivelled vine.

My husband said, 'Come Bimal, let's go and hear what Sandip has to say. He had bid goodbye and left. If he has come back, it must be something urgent.'

Since it would be more embarrassing not to go, I went with him. In the living room Sandip stood gazing at a portrait. The minute we entered he said, 'You must be wondering why this man has come back. Until the last rites are duly completed the spirit cannot leave in peace.' He fished out a bundle from under his shawl and placed it on the table—it held those guineas. He said, 'Nikhil, don't get me wrong; I haven't turned ethical in your company. Sandip is not such a wimp that he'd weep tears of regret as he returns these guineas worth six thousand rupees. But—'

Sandip didn't finish the sentence. After a brief pause he looked at me and said, 'Queen Bee, after all these years a "but" has entered Sandip's immaculate life. Every night I have woken up at three and tussled with it; finally I realize that it isn't an empty sound; Sandip isn't free until his debt has been paid off. So, in the hands of my terminator "but" I lay these guineas as a final mark of respect. I thought long and hard and realized that this "but" is the only being in this world from whom I cannot accept wealth—I can only bid you goodbye if I am penniless before you, oh goddess. Here, take it.'

He took out the jewellery box as well and placed it on the table and tried to rush out of the room. My husband called out to him, 'Come here, Sandip.'

Sandip spoke from the door, 'I don't have time, Nikhil. I've come to know that the Muslims want to loot me like the

Kohinoor and bury me deep in their burial grounds. But I must live. The train bound northwards leaves in twenty-five minutes and so, for the time being, I say goodbye. Later, if I have a chance, I'll finish the rest of our conversation. If you take my advice, you'll not waste any time either. Queen Bee, hail the queen of hearts, the harbinger of storms.'

Sandip almost ran out of the room. I stood there, turned to stone. Never before had I felt just how meaningless the guineas and the jewellery were. Just a little while ago I had been thinking how much I'd take with me, how to fit it all in and now I felt nothing was important, except just walking out.

My husband rose from the chair, came up to me, held my hands and said, 'There isn't much time left; we should get the work done now.'

At that moment Chandranathbabu walked in. My presence threw him in a bit of a quandary. He said, 'Ma, forgive me, I didn't give notice before coming in. Nikhil, the Muslims are enraged. They have looted Harish Kundu's treasury. That is not so fearful by itself. But the way they are treating the women—it is unbearable.'

My husband said, 'I'll be off then.'

I grasped his hands and said, 'What can you do there? Professor, please stop him.'

Chandranathbabu said, 'My dear, this isn't the time to stop him.'

My husband said, 'Don't worry, Bimal.'

I rushed to the window and saw him galloping away on horseback. He wasn't carrying a single weapon.

Mejorani ran into the room and said, 'What have you done, little one, what crazy calamity have you brought on? Why did you let Thakurpo go?' She ordered the bearer, 'Go, quickly, call the estate manager.'

Mejorani had never appeared before the estate manager. But today she had no shame. She said, 'Quick, send out forces to bring back his majesty.'

The manager said, 'We have all tried to stop him; he wouldn't listen.'

Mejorani said, 'Go and tell him Mejorani has collapsed, she is dying.'

Once the manager left, Mejorani began to curse me, 'You witch, you siren. You sent Thakurpo to his death.'

The daylight waned. Standing at the window I saw the sun set behind the flowering tree in the west, near the milkmen's colony. Till this day, every line of that setting sun is engraved on my heart. With the setting sun in the centre, a rush of clouds had spread their wings to the north and south like the wings of a huge bird. Its flame-coloured feathers unfurled in layers. I felt the day was flying swiftly to cross the ocean of the night. Gradually darkness crept in. Intermittent sounds of hubbub rent the air, just as the occasional flames would lick the dark sky if there was a fire in a distant village. The temple bells sounded for the evening arati. I knew Mejorani was there with folded hands, praying. I couldn't take a step away from the window by the street. My eyes blurred over the road ahead, the village, the distant field empty of crops and the line of trees further afield. The huge lake of the estate stared at the sky like a sightless eye. The ballroom to the left stood on its toes as if peering at something.

There was no end to the masquerades that night-time sounds indulged in. If a twig swayed close by, it felt like someone running away in the distance. The sudden noise of a door banging shut felt like the entire sky missing a heartbeat. Sometimes I spotted lights beneath the row of trees by the roadside. Then there was nothing. I heard the sound of horses' hooves, only to find the rider galloping out of the estate gates and vanishing in the distance.

All the time I felt if I died, all troubles would cease. As long as I lived, the world would be plagued by my sins. I remembered the pistol that lay nestled in the box. But my feet wouldn't budge from this window, even to go and fetch the pistol—you see, I awaited my Fate.

The clock tower of the estate gonged away—ten o'clock.

A little later, there were many lights on the streets, a big crowd had gathered. In the darkness, the throng of people seemed like a huge black snake slithering in through the estate gates.

The manager heard the noise and rushed towards the gate. At that moment, a rider came up and the manager asked him nervously, 'Jatadhar, what's the news?'

He said, 'Not too good.'

I could hear every syllable clearly from up here.

Then there were some whispers, which I couldn't hear very well. A palanquin and a doolie drew into the gates. Doctor Mathur walked beside the palanquin. The estate manager asked, 'Doctor, what do you think?'

The doctor said, 'Can't say for sure. Serious head injury.'

'And Amulyababu?'

'He took a bullet in the chest. He is no more.'